ELEGY FOR SAM EMERSON

BOOKS BY HILARY MASTERS

Novels

Elegy for Sam Emerson
Home Is the Exile
Strickland
Cooper
Clemmons
Palace of Strangers
An American Marriage
The Common Pasture
Manuscript for Murder
(under the pseudonym P. J. Coyne)

Short Fiction

Success: New & Selected Stories
Hammertown Tales

Memoir

Last Stands: Notes from Memory

Essays

Shadows on a Wall: Juan O'Gorman and the Mural in Pátzcuaro
(a book-length single essay)
In Montaigne's Tower (an essay collection)

ELEGY FOR SAM EMERSON

A Novel

HILARY MASTERS

Southern Methodist University Press

Dallas

Copyright © 2006 by Hilary Masters
First edition, 2006

Jacket and text design by David Timmons

Library of Congress Cataloging-in-Publication Data

Masters, Hilary.
    Elegy for Sam Emerson : a novel / by Hilary Masters.—1st ed.
        p. cm.
    ISBN 0-87074-507-7 (acid-free paper)
        1. Restaurateurs—Pennsylvania—Pittsburgh—Fiction. 2. Middle-aged
men—Pennsylvania—Pittsburgh—Fiction. I. Title.

PS3563.A82E64 2006
813'.54—dc22

                                                            2006042286

Printed in the United States of America on acid-free paper

                10   9   8   7   6   5   4   3   2   1

For Kathleen

ACKNOWLEDGMENTS

The information on Atlanta's Neighborhood Union was derived from *To 'Joy My Freedom: Southern Black Women's Lives and Labors after the Civil War,* by my colleague Tera Hunter. My thanks to her for this historical anecdote.

Also, and again, my gratitude to Yaddo, where much of this novel was put together.

I'll not forget you when I'm gone,
I shall not see you any more.

—Andrei Voznesensky
(Translated by William Jay Smith and Vera Dunham)

ONE

A LITTLE MORE than halfway in his life's journey and scarcely out of the woods around Mansfield, Pennsylvania, Sam Emerson eased the rattling Ford station wagon into the intersection with Route 220, going south toward Pittsburgh. Someday, he promised himself once again, he would get that loose muffler fixed. The faintly antiseptic odor of the mustard greens he had picked up before daylight at market rinsed the car's interior, not completely cleansing the mustiness generated by the worn upholstery and the debris collected on the floor beneath the seats. Yesterday afternoon, he and his chef, Sterling Wicks, both sipping from mugs of coffee, had gone over the week's menus as they stood in the restaurant's kitchen. The two men had been friends since their time at the Hotel School at Penn State, when they had casually pushed awry the racial bars of that time by rooming together.

"I thought the greens were a little sharp the last time you made them," Emerson told Wicks. "Maybe more feta would smooth them out. Mind you, I'm not being critical. The little grape tomatoes are a nice touch. Colorful. It's your *contorni.*"

His partner's long, elegant face seemed to pull down even more, into something resembling a sneer, though the expression was only playacting. "That's right, it is my *contorni.* Listen, Boy, just go get the groceries, but any time you want to do the cooking—Rita," he gestured toward a line cook prepping a mound of mushrooms, "step to one side, please, so that *Numero Uno* can take his rightful place." The kitchen crew laughed and hooted, and Emerson retreated through the doors into the dining room waving his arms to signal his surrender.

A western sun splattered the windshield with a dazzle of flashes and flickers gaily inappropriate to the somber Chopin prelude that played from the car's speakers. Emerson had taken this tape with him to play on his return trip as a kind of farewell performance. Not many possessions left from his mother's life in her room at Crestview Meadows—photographs and old theatre programs, some with her picture on the cover. A strand of amber beads. A few clothes hung in the closet, including her scarves and the down overcoat she had bundled about herself eight years ago as if in a last defense against the elements of time when she had walked into the nursing home on her own. Edith Olson had already given her papers and books to the Mansfield College Library, not so much a gift as a kind of dumping exercise performed upon the good-natured if not hapless academics. Whatever had happened to the two steamer trunks, Sam Emerson could not remember—portable vaults that had been moved and set down in the different rooms of his childhood.

Last night when the nursing home had called him, Phoebe had been dressing, preparing to get home to her house in the Mexican War Streets. Her neighborhood had been designated a historic area, several streets of brick row houses built right after the Civil War and named from battles in the previous conflict. It was Monday night, the restaurant on the floor below his penthouse closed on Mondays, and they had had the place to themselves.

"They say she's not responding," he told her inquisitive glance. "Edie Olson not responding—sounds serious." His effort was half-hearted. "I guess I better get up there tomorrow."

"I'll go with you," Phoebe replied quickly. "I have no appointments tomorrow." She put some folders into her briefcase and snapped the clasps. Earlier she had reviewed some of her clients' profiles while he made their supper.

"That's swell of you to offer. Thanks, but this is a solo job."

Phoebe had held his gaze for a moment; then shrugged and gathered her things together. "So, we'll see you Wednesday. Nick is looking forward to the game. I think you may have wooed him from lacrosse."

"Maybe before then," Emerson said. "I may pick up some basil at that old nursery on the way back. I could come over to put it in the planters when I get back."

"I should be home near six. We'll be happy to see you." Phoebe embraced him, and her heavy perfume, Opium, rose around him. "Be careful on the road."

Sam Emerson always wanted to delay these moments; the lovemaking that had preceded them of course, but just as delicious were the intimacies that accompanied Phoebe putting herself back together after his joyous destruction of the professional woman's image she carried off so well. The different snaps and fastenings, the slipping on and adjusting, the arrangements and critical appraisals made of those arrangements—all composed a particular erotic litany, one that sounded profoundly in Emerson's sensibility. It was a ritual that somehow enriched the ceremony of flesh and rushing blood that had preceded it, made it even more endearing, but sometimes, like last night, her very efficient way of putting things back in order nudged him again, a reverent witness, with the thought that he might be only a convenient, but no less appealing, fuck for this vital woman on her way home from work.

The several years they had been together had caught Sam Emerson up in a sweet addiction, a fragrance of joyful routines, that attended him through day and night, which he could almost inhale even as he slipped the Rubenstein Chopin into the car's tape deck this morning. The crystal notes of the prelude cheered him, and he decided the music celebrated this time with Phoebe, however it might end. He had brought his mother this particular version along with some other piano works, some arias of Puccini and several Beethoven sonatas, also pieces by Ravel, but whether she had ever played them for herself he could only wonder. Sometimes, on a visit, he would carefully arrange them in the drawer of the stand by her bed, but by the next time he went up to Mansfield, he would have forgotten that sequence and could not tell if they had been touched. But the music gave them something to share—pleasant sounds to fill the silence between them.

"Let's have a little music," Emerson would suggest in the early years of her residency in the nursing home.

"Oh, yes, let's do have music," his mother would say, clapping her hands, her eyes becoming brilliant, as if footlights had suddenly come on at the end of her bed. She had given the line like something from an old drama, a comedy with French doors that opened onto a terrace of sculpted shrubbery.

"What shall it be—Chopin? Beethoven? Ravel?"

"Not Ravel. He's too wishy-washy. Chopin—always Chopin."

"Chopin it is," Emerson would say and slip the tape cartridge into the player on her nightstand. This scene was played out, with minor variations, year upon year, mother and son with little to say to each other, conversation worn down and suspended in the recorded harmony. It had been a kind of intimacy, one of those attempts to make the best of an awkward destiny neither of them could explain. An affordable connection, Emerson often thought, but if he had expected the music playing on the car's tape deck now to stroke some sentimental chords within himself, the idea was shredded by the raucous shrapnel of illumination that burst from the woods on either side of the road. It was May, fresh and luminous, and the incorrigible sunlight revealed his folly and the truth. He could not be sad altogether.

"Let it go, Edie," he had spoken softly into the ear of the shrunken figure in the bed on this last visit. She resembled an exhibit in the corner of an out-of-the-way museum. So, it had all come down to this final interview—all the gaudy gaiety, the sturdy optimism—the whole adventure. "Let it go." The rapid breathing did not hesitate. There was no sign she had heard him, that she was even aware of his presence. He couldn't wait any longer; he had to get back to the restaurant, and she could float in this odd suspension for hours, for days maybe.

The young leaves of birch and scrub maple seemed to mint the afternoon as he approached the Y-shaped junction the county road made with Route 220, the state highway. Earlier this morning as he had neared the intersection from the south, Sam Emerson had considered, and not for the first time, how this meeting of byways disappearing into the grove of young trees resembled a mons veneris. On his many trips to Mansfield, he amused himself by deftly bearing left to enter the turnoff onto the county road, smoothly without braking, all in one gliding advance. Not to halt or even slow down for oncoming traffic became a good omen for the day, for the time with his mother.

"I feel like I'm slipping into a giantess," he told Phoebe on another evening, laughing at his own silliness and expecting her to gather up the dumb joke and weave it into one of her own high-spirited inspirations. But the imagery had irritated her, for she had put on her professional manner, an invisible smock, to regard him somewhat primly in the candlelight.

"So, Sam, are you more comfortable entering this intersection or leaving it? Which do you prefer?"

"Oh, spare me the analysis, Dr. Konopski. Save that for your clients downtown." He poured more Pauillac and directed her to the view, the bejeweled skyscrapers of Pittsburgh that rose just across the Monongahela River. The skyline seemed to rise directly from beneath his penthouse. It was a splendor that diners in the restaurant below paid handsomely for. "I understand what you're saying. I really get it."

Coming up to this intersection at the end of what some have called the American Century, the end of the millennium, and more than halfway in his own journey—does Sam Emerson get the whole picture? He had just left the village of Mansfield, on another leg of a round trip—three hours each way—that had been eight years in the making. For nearly two hours he had sat by his mother's bed to monitor her shallow breathing, the rapid intake of breath like that of a girl on the edge of discovery, but the gaunt lines of the face on the pillow were both sad and frightening in their antiquity.

"How's she doing?" The practical cheerfulness of a nurse had bustled into his reverie. The woman had swept into the room, officially straightened the bed sheets, and felt for his mother's pulse.

"She's doing."

"Your mom was an actress, wasn't she?"

"Oh yes, Broadway and elsewhere," Emerson heard himself say. "A lot of television roles. *One Heart's Journey.*" The program's name did not distract the nurse's professional attention, and he felt a little chagrinned by his spurt of press agentry. "She also started the famous theatre festival you have here every summer."

"I've heard of that," the nurse replied, carefully settling the withered arm and its hand down on the coverlet. "We never got to it."

And Emerson had to admit, he himself had trouble with the identity of the figure in the bed; she bore little resemblance to the woman on the theatre programs. He didn't recognize her. In her contest with the century, if not to beat it, at least meet it at the finish line, she had left him far behind, as she seemed about to do this morning. She was the original good-bye girl, which may have been her best role. "Let it go, Edie. You have done well," he told the figure in the bed.

Nor did the withered countenance bear much of a resemblance to the woman in his mind, not even to the haughty visage of just a few years ago. Yet the relentless pulse of the temples was familiar, sending out signals from the wreck. He had understood long ago that her competition had been not just with him, and this insight—its ameliorative quality—had gratified him. Something had compelled her to challenge even the century.

Though these trips to Mansfield took him away from the restaurant and often inconveniently, he had sometimes enjoyed the break from his usual routines. The village of Mansfield was a picture book community; in fact, its history records that it was constructed from an actual picture book carried in the toolbox of a journeyman carpenter in the mid-nineteenth century. With the support of the town's leading citizens, the carpenter had replicated a typical New England village green surrounded by white clapboard houses—all on this plateau of the Allegheny Mountains of western Pennsylvania. The campus of Mansfield College stretched from one end of this commons, and its Palladian correctness offered the rare traveler passing through unexpected visual refreshment. The isolated perfection of the place had impressed Emerson, and in the early days of his mother's residency, he had briefly toyed with the idea of opening a restaurant in Mansfield—Sam's North. It would have catered to the audiences of the Shakespeare Festival that Edith Olson had begun, but his business sense vetoed the sentimental urge—the restaurant would not be able to sustain itself year round, and he had already experienced that kind of seasonal venture.

"Sure, I know what you're thinking," he said to Phoebe. He had been telling her some of this history. "Why go to all that trouble just to link up? We always needed some sort of subterfuge, a cover for what others considered a normal relationship. Ours had to be a demonstration of some wacko idea from one of those books on child rearing she was always reading. I used to think it was like a show business tradition—the kid abandoned in the dressing room while mother stepped into the spotlight. You see it in all the tabloids. But, of course, she wasn't a star."

"She wanted to be."

"Yes, she wanted to be. It was kind of fun in a way, but often I felt like baggage left on the station platform. The few times she showed up here—when we pretended to be normal—it was awkward. I sometimes felt we were performing a scene from a play we weren't meant to be in."

"I've always had luck in Pennsylvania," his mother had said during her first appearance at the restaurant, as if that had been her excuse—enough of an excuse—to suddenly come back into his life. She nodded, a gesture that usually seconded an opinion to make it an overwhelming majority. "You remember that time in Bucks County?"

They were sitting on the balcony of Sam's Place with the splendid vista of Pittsburgh before them, the ceviche on her plate barely touched.

His version of the dish garnished the scallops with braised apricots. She had been explaining why she had accepted the position at Mansfield College—not to be near him, of course, she was careful to say—but to put herself in the way of good fortune. No, not in his way. Earlier, he had looked up to see her standing in the foyer of the restaurant. It was early, and they had been setting up the dining room for the evening, and she had appeared like a customer without a reservation, a tourist too early but still hoping to be seated. Surely she wouldn't be turned away, her pose suggested. She was not only the owner's mother, but also someone who must certainly be recognized from all those moments on *One Heart's Journey*—just to mention that one program. Surely, this endearing failure at anonymity must be seen through? She flickered her eyelashes at Cynthia, his front, and held one hand to her bosom, fingering the strand of amber beads as if prepared to be turned away—turned back into the blizzard outside, though it was one of those rare days in Pittsburgh, a paragon of balmy weather that makes the residents sometimes wonder at the depth of cruelty that ordered the rest of their climate. It had been a capsule performance worthy of an award. He had a vague recollection of the time in Bucks County—something to do with a summer theatre, but why it had been lucky for her he could not remember.

"I've just a small place upstairs," he had told her. "But I have friends who run a pleasant bed-and-breakfast over on the Northside." He pointed to the urban landscape beneath them, as if she might see the place from the restaurant's balcony.

"Not at all, not at all," she answered quickly. "I must get back this evening. I just wanted to see what you are up to, old Sam." Yes and by seeing, he added to himself, absorb something of him, assume some of the credit. "They are having a sort of function in my honor this evening. To welcome me to the campus." She seemed on the verge of inviting him to attend but didn't. "I will hold the Gwendolyn Brown Stafford Chair of Theatre at Mansfield College," she continued, deftly pushing the food on her plate this way and that. She held the knife and fork in an exaggerated manner of the European style, as if she were performing a delicate operation on the scallop. When she had started to use the implements that way, he couldn't remember. Probably in some play that required this fashion. It certainly wasn't something she learned in East Liverpool, Ohio.

Beyond the central sward of Mansfield with its nineteenth-century clapboard houses, other houses were built later, at the turn of the twentieth century; these were of brick with enormous porches around three sides and large windows on the second floors that would always be open in summer. Emerson imagined the voices of brothers and sisters in every house could be heard teasing and primping for dates with the other siblings next door or down the street. The fantasy stirred a sweet longing within him, a daydream by Thornton Wilder that lulled his heart.

Immediate to the college campus was the town's business district: several restaurants, one Chinese gone Vietnamese; two drugstores; a JC Penney; several bars, one offering pool tables for ladies; a corner bank; a state liquor store; a video rental; a small supermarket; and an assortment of specialty shops whose proprietors and clerks seemed to have grown gray with their merchandise. Offices on the second floors of these buildings completed the package. Emerson enjoyed the thought that the rest of Pennsylvania, the whole world, could fall into chaos and despair, but self-contained Mansfield would be undisturbed.

He also credited his mother with contributing to this archival atmosphere. She had left her mark upon the cultural setting. She had harangued and coaxed and finally persuaded the college trustees to take over the old movie house and turn it into the Mansfield Theatre Festival. Her productions of Shaw and Shakespeare, using seasoned actors from New York in the major roles, gave the remote community a fresh, exuberant identity. Some of the college administrators who had been initially put off by the dimensions of Edith Olson's proposal, by the fierce stride of her argument, quickly adjusted to the fame it brought the college, not to mention the jump in enrollments. Even so, one or two emeriti still complained that the college's prized collection of stuffed birds of western Pennsylvania, immaculately mounted and codified, had been minimized by the glitter of the theatre festival.

When Emerson visited his mother in the early years of her tenure, she would take him on a tour of Mansfield. He could never decide whether these excursions were meant to impress him with her celebrity among the shopkeepers or to embarrass him with the paucity of the place where, it was implied, she had chosen to live just to be near him— but not be in his way, to use her language. Here, he imagined this performance was meant to convey, is the meager dimension of the self-administered exile they both must endure—one more melodrama they made up good-humoredly as they acted it out. And he would have ready reasons to return to Pittsburgh. "I have to go over the restaurant's books with the accountant," he'd say. Or, "The guys who pick up the garbage are giving us trouble. I have to meet with them." Often, his mother talked him into lunch at the Tavern on the Green, an establishment run by a pair of Greek brothers on the edge of the campus.

"Let's have something nice," Edith Olson would say eagerly, her large gray eyes wide with anticipation. She knew the menu. It listed omelets, corned beef, meat loaf with gravy and mashed potatoes. Swiss steak. "Have what you wish," she always invited. "I'm just going to have a hamburger. Yes, the hamburger."

Emerson had discovered there was another menu, different from the printed card the waitress put down before them, which the owners seemed hesitant to advertise. Salad, stuffed grape leaves, pita bread, and yogurt with honey and walnuts for dessert. The brothers must have made their own yogurt; maybe they had brought from the Old Country a strain of hardworking bacteria that turned ordinary milk into solid blocks of deliciousness. The honey and nuts made a gorgeous combination of flavors and textures, and he thought about putting the concoction on the menu of his restaurant—with a few extra touches, of course. But could yogurt like that be found in Pittsburgh? They might have to make it themselves.

The window next to their usual booth looked out on the town's green and the facades of Mansfield College. The view resembled one of the faded postcards on sale at the drugstore. "Here we are," his mother would say after they had ordered, but Emerson was fairly certain that she really meant, here *she* was—she—Edith Olson—who had appeared with Noel Coward, toured with the Lunts, and had played the self-sacrificing mother to a young Paul Newman in a live *Studio One* TV play. Here was this somewhat famous actress, three hours north of Pittsburgh in Mansfield, Pennsylvania, and not in New York.

"He is so very busy with his restaurant, you know," she would tell a woman in a gift shop. "Sam's Place, you've heard of it, I'm sure. Written up in *Gourmet* magazine and the *New York Times*. In Pittsburgh. And what a view! I thought I should wear a parachute just to have lunch there." The humor was wrapped in a curious modesty that discouraged questions as to how many times she had been to this famous restaurant. Sam's

Place. By the slight turn of her head, the shift sidewise of the large eyes, and a faint curl of the mouth—sometimes a toss of fingers for good measure—she conveyed the sense that this arrangement suited them both—just right. Both independent, yet somehow a team. It was Paul Newman's mother all over again, standing in the dusty aisle of the Bon-Ton Gifts. Emerson admired these performances for their stylish, face-saving technique, though he knew they were meant for him as much as the shopkeeper. They were meant to reach out and pinch his conscience just a little, but she had also taught him how to absorb guilty feelings and move on. How to get on.

But, in truth, she had never had a place to get on to since she left East Liverpool, Ohio, no landing where she could permanently set down the steamer trunks and the portfolios of his father's photographs. When she retired from Mansfield College, she went to Greece to run theatre festivals in Sparta, only to return to Mansfield to live out the century—first in a small apartment near the campus and then finally in Crestview Meadows. "I used to think she was playing Hecuba or one of those queens in a play she might have produced in Greece," he told Phoebe. "Standing on the ridge of the Nittany Range to expose herself to all who passed by on Route 220 just to shame me."

"But maybe she actually liked being alone. To be near you, but on her own too."

"That's the story of my life," Emerson replied with half a laugh.

"Why do you do it? Why do you go at all?" Amanda had asked him one night on the telephone. They were still talking on the phone, though she had long since returned to Vermont. That particular day, he had only just made it back to Pittsburgh and had been late to take up his stand in the dining room. He had apologized to Sterling, who had had to deal with the linen service people while setting up the evening's menu. That drive had been particularly harrowing due to a February storm that had iced the mountain roads. Two semis had gone off into ditches. "Why do you do this?"

"Sometimes, I think I'm trying to catch up to the past and redo it before it happens again. Silly, I guess."

Amanda had said nothing, then, "No."

For the first few years after their divorce, he and Amanda still talked. At times, she sounded angry, and he could find no language in himself that would either satisfy or alleviate that anger. And after all, he often told himself, it was she who had decided to leave him, to go back to Vermont and her family. He would have been uncomfortable mentioning the idea of duty, though that would have been true. Aunt Rho in Ohio had shown him how to make do. Along with her flapjacks and the biscuits with white sausage gravy, she had also served him examples of how to get a grip on a given chore, finish the job, make the best of what each day brought. Every morning as she cooked his breakfast, she had demonstrated the word. *Duty.* She had, in her own simple manner, educated him in its satisfactions.

Emerson felt the sad drama at play whenever he entered Mansfield, this domain of young voices and energies. Year after year the students' laughter and shouts rising around his mother, as her mind and body degenerated, became a false elixir to her age, a prescription cruel in its impotency. Her mind and body, so resolute for most of the century, were finally submitting to the uneven contest.

As her grasp on time slowly loosened, and it became clear that intervals of a week or a month or a day measured the same length in the shortening vista of her dementia, these journeys to Mansfield and back became even more onerous. Phoebe had convinced him once a month was enough, but Emerson worried that the nurses and staff at Crestview Meadows might notice. Maybe they kept track, talked among themselves about relatives who abandoned their own to the paid maintenance of others. Yes, abandoned—he knew about that, but at this point Phoebe would become impatient, pull on her thick reading glasses, and turn her attention to a patient's dossier. She had no time for vanity, for false pride. She had clients with real problems. Emerson imagined she might have a folder in her file with his name on it stamped "Unresolved Mother Issues."

"That's a lovely dish," his mother had told him that afternoon on the balcony of the restaurant. She had barely tasted it. "Sweet for a ceviche—maybe a little more salt would help."

"More salt?" Emerson had countered, trying a spoonful of the sauce. "No, I don't think so."

"No matter," she said standing and flicking breadcrumbs from her dress. She surveyed the view of the rivers below, the magnificent city skyline. "Yes," she said nodding, but he could not tell what met her approval—Pittsburgh or the restaurant's view of it, his place. He was happy to accept either. "You remember, I played Pittsburgh," she said.

Gradually, Edith Olson had slipped from one level of alertness down to the next and then into a predawn from which she would never fully wake. She who had always been on the move, always on tour with her steamer trunks—running her fingers through the heavy auburn hair as she introduced bits of business to carry a scene—had stuck herself in this nursing home only to plead with him to get her out or at least to find another place where the residents were on her intellectual level, people who might recognize her. She could quickly fill them in. "The old television—*Studio One, Philco Playhouse*—that was live television. Live television," she would repeat, drilling the phrase into her listener's attention. "You really had to know your lines, know how to move. It couldn't be redone. It had to be right the first time."

Crestview Meadows became the last stage of the melodrama. Emerson suspected that beneath the hard-boiled manner of the ingenue's pal or in her later roles as a stoic mother, Edie was a waif who hoped to be taken up, longed to be cared for and brought to a safe and cozy hearth, but on her own terms. She would never have let him do that; she would skip away from that role.

"What if I bring her here to Pittsburgh?" he asked Phoebe. "Say, I could find a house for her. I could put her in the corner of the restaurant where she could shell peas and chat with the customers like the star mama. Tell old gossip and show biz stories. The newspaper would do a feature piece. Former soap queen preps in son's restaurant."

"How picturesque," Phoebe said and rose from the bed to dress. His joke amused her. It was late-ish afternoon, and she had to get home. Nick got home from school at five. "You could get her one of those large bandanas to tie around her head like the ladies up on Polish Hill."

Emerson laughed. "She would love it. Her signature role. No, she's already found her role. The Gwendolyn Brown Stafford Chair."

But she found her best part, Emerson thought, in her bed at Crestview Meadows—underplayed and milking her audience of one as some old script filtered through her senility to direct a roll of the magnificent eyes, turn a gesture, or pull up a piece of business half-remembered from a potboiler that had nearly made her famous. "Maurice Evans begged me to do Ophelia, but I couldn't do the tour. I had you to worry about. Your father was off taking pictures of some war." Emerson never took the blame for her second billing; he had learned from his father's blithe handling of her ambition. It had nothing to do with him—her success and failures were hers alone. She wanted it that way. In fact, he had seen her in too many melodramas to be moved by the poor copy of those performances she reproduced for his benefit in the hospital bed in the nursing home—the pathos worn down to the gums, the motivation trembling. She wasn't supposed to play this part, but she couldn't turn it down. It wasn't fair. "How did I get here?" her expression sometimes seemed to ask.

"If you could only break through this wall you've put up around yourself," Phoebe would say. "It must be damn heavy to carry around. I know I can feel it. You sometimes shift the weight onto me, and I'm not too happy about that. Good grief, I think of the strained backs of all those other women you've entertained in this place. You should have a chiropractor in residence."

Emerson laughed, though slightly offended too. "There were not that many of them."

"What was the name of that girl on television who did the weather?"

"Wendy," Emerson answered grudgingly.

"Oh yes, 'Wendy Does the Weather,'" and Phoebe was taken by deep laughter that shook out her blond ringlets. It was unseemly to Emerson that Phoebe should ridicule the young woman who had never been her rival, who had passed through his life long before Phoebe had entered it.

"She went to a station in Chicago. She's become a news anchor," he said with a little pride.

"Well, all I'm saying is that some of us have shared the burden, and it has not been very nice of you."

"I'm sorry," he replied and he meant it.

Sam Emerson lingered at the intersection of Route 220 and looked both ways. He must have put thousands of miles on the Ford, making these trips. Duty, yes, that. For an hour and a little more, he would sit bedside and look down at the atrophied visage that a strong breeze might blow off the pillow. He could not place the boisterous Swedish heartiness of the old showbills nor trace the weary lines of later roles—those worldly women of early television and the later soap operas. Some afternoons in Ohio, home from school with a cold, he had warmed himself before her image, as she appeared on the small black and white set in Aunt's Rho's parlor. So close to him, he could touch the face on the cool glass screen, yet these shadows came from a great distance—as a boy he knew that—and later he would understand that the tenderness and wisdom of that image had been scripted. Now the shrunken residue of those images was lying in the hospital bed; her great age exaggerated the overbite that had made for a teasing coquetry in earlier days. The few teeth left in her head now projected straight out like the seashells from the withered fiber mask of a crude icon. He wished he could view her through some sort of lens, special glasses he could put on that would blur the picture, when he entered her room and sat down beside her bed.

People who observed him at Crestview Meadows, nurses and staff, would note his patient pose at her bedside. More than observing her, he had been also listening for any scrap of sound from behind the high forehead, higher now and splashed with purple stains. Emerson was convinced a kind of newsreel was continuously running inside there, like a movie theatre on Times Square he remembered that showed newsreels around the clock. He had spent hours in the darkness of that theatre, catching up on the events of the day, on the awful events of the century, before he sought out where he would be staying on a school break, where he would lie down on the sofa or bed she had borrowed in some part of the city for his use that night.

He wondered if something like that endless program was being played in the darkening theatre of her mind—the old scenes revisited, the opening nights, the auditions. How Dennis King had greeted her one time during Ladies' Day at the Players. The century's personalities— she had known some of them—the raw, unedited footage of the era's horrors and its few triumphs all unwinding spool after spool. She would also appear. The vivacious Edith Olson would turn in the flickering light to take her place in the panorama, a supporting player to assist a scene, lend her energy to a turning point in the cavalcade. She was never bored with the program. After all, it was her story.

Those of us who believe in the sequential narrative of history sometimes confuse the casual with the causal and forget how promiscuous memory can be as it hops from one version of the past to the next with no allegiance to accuracy. The only requirement is to offer a decent order to events that will satisfy some version of the present. Such visions and revisions took place, Emerson was convinced, behind her arched forehead. As he sat beside her bed, plots were redone to give her the stardom she had never been given, her name above the title. For example, what Hemingway had said to her one night at 21, leaning over the table, with O'Hara sitting there, too. "Your husband is the real McCoy." That remark, whether actually made or not, was repeated from one situation to another, to unloose a ream of justifications for her name to appear in the program.

Or what about that afternoon, earlier in the century, when Steichen had brought her into focus at his new studio? Pictures for *Vanity Fair.* He was taking pictures for Condé Nast then. "Sunny, I have a nice young man you should meet. He's helping me out here." The musical of that name had just opened and people called her that for a time, as if they understood she had some right to the title. Because Jerome Kern had asked her to audition—that was the truth—but she had been busy with something else. "Dear little Marilyn Miller got the part. She was very lovely."

The shadows of these scenes and others seemed to flit across her forehead; he knew all of them by heart. He had heard the scenarios often enough at different supper tables, in conversations with strangers, and eventually in the stores around the Mansfield Green. At the last, any audience would do, and then she became her own best audience, which had been the case all along.

"Let it go, Edie," Emerson whispered.

Route 220 had begun to descend toward the town of Tyrone, and, as the Ford lost altitude, the landscape began to lose its unspoiled grandeur. Odd settlements came into view, and billboards corrupted the prospect. He could drive the road in his sleep and had done so in his dreams more than once. At the moment, Emerson still did not completely believe that he might be reaching the end of this particular circle, this stitching back and forth that never seemed to sew up anything. Until now. That he could anticipate the end, to be no longer in its seam, no longer in the repetitive pattern, was not so much a cause for celebration as it was a mark put down on the endless roll of time. Spontaneously, he pulled off the highway and into the graveled parking lot of a roadside tavern. THE TABLETOP—*This is the Place*. He would buy a round.

It was dark inside and empty and smelled sourly of beer. The tidy interior was illuminated by lights behind the bar and the plastic signs advertising different beers. Abruptly a man appeared in the doorway that led to the rear, as if Emerson's entrance had interrupted him in some illegal activity. His nose was large and purplish and had lost the usual definition of a nose as it spread across the cheekbones like a three dimensional stain. His eyes were small and belonged to another animal. "The kitchen's closed," he said quickly.

"That's okay," Emerson replied. "I'll just have a Coke." He could hear faint talk in the back room—a radio.

"The radio's in the kitchen," the man explained amiably. He filled a glass with ice cubes from the bar tap. "The wife listened to programs when she cooked." He carefully set the glass of soda down on a square coaster, which he had rather gracefully produced from beneath the bar top.

"She's off today," Emerson said.

"Actually, she took off last week," the owner said and shrugged. Close up, his small eyes had a gleam that could be merry or ominous, depending on what was being told him, Emerson figured. "I don't know where she is. There's a story in it."

"I see," Emerson said and sipped the Coke. "Good cooks are hard to find these days. I'm in the business myself, so I know."

"You have a place?"

"In Pittsburgh—a restaurant."

"Oh, yeah. What's it called?"

"Sam's Place."

"Hey, I know about it. My son and his wife went there for their anniversary. Looks over the city. Fancy."

"Has a great view," Sam said.

"And that's your place?"

"My place."

"You're Sam?"

"That's me," Emerson replied and put out his hand. The other man hesitated just a little then took it. His eyes glistened, and Emerson thought he might start a long story. But he only splashed a bit of plain soda into a glass and returned to raise it as if in a toast. Emerson tapped his glass against the other's and both men drank.

"What brings you up this way?"

"Visiting my mother in Mansfield. She's not well. In fact, she's dying, but she's over ninety."

The fellow ran one hand over his face and sipped at his soda. "So, you do the cooking in your place? I can fry up a hamburger, and we got the machine for the hotdogs, but anything more intense is beyond me. We were known for our wedding soup," he said, looking intently at Emerson. "She made the bread too. So, I had to close the kitchen when she left."

"My partner runs the kitchen. Sometimes I help out on the heavy nights."

"You know it's a helluva thing." The fellow had clearly changed the subject. "I was just listening to the radio, and some woman is saying President Clinton tried to sex her up in a hotel room. This was years ago. When he was governor. Some woman named Jones." He laughed shortly, as if the name and the accusation were incongruous.

"Something to do with Whitewater?" Emerson asked and finished the Coke.

The question obviously was turned over several times as the fellow rotated his glass of soda water on the coaster. "I don't remember," he said finally. "But she's suing him. She said he had a state cop bring her to his hotel room for the sex. She's suing the president. It's a helluva thing. Another?"

"Better not; I'm driving."

The owner nodded soberly and briskly took Emerson's empty glass and washed and rinsed it.

"I hope it gets better," Emerson said and went toward the door.

The guy shrugged.

He came to the hamlet of Port Matilda, which he always thought should be somewhere in the Caribbean, with banana boats instead of scrub fields and a wetland running to sumac and stunted cedars. Where's the port? Emerson always wanted to ask if he stopped for gas at the one station on the corner. A funky nursery stretched out beside the road, a dilapidated greenhouse parallel to the highway. He had sometimes found some interesting plants there, more for Phoebe's garden. It was a little early to plant anything big—May fifteenth, when a frost could still be waiting in the Ohio Valley—but the old lady who ran the place often had odd perennials. And he had mentioned basil to Phoebe—those plants could be covered if need be. Right at the entrance, a large stand of bee balm attracted him. He remembered the giddy blossoms like clown wigs in Aunt Rho's garden when he was a boy, and he could imagine the plants taking well to a spot along Phoebe's back fence, where the sun hit in the afternoon. But he withstood the temptation. It would be wrong to transplant them this early, and he could come back when the weather settled for sure. He would certainly be coming back this way.

The screen door of the house that was set back in some high rhododendrons slapped shut, and the proprietor appeared wearing her usual costume, corduroy men's pants, high rubber boots, a turtleneck sweater, and a Pittsburgh Steelers wool cap. He'd never known her to wear anything different, even in winter. She walked steadily in a line athwart him toward the foundation of the small greenhouse and immediately took up a spade and began to turn over a patch of earth. He knew she had seen him, had appeared because of him, but her manner would seem otherwise, as if to afford him a sort of privacy. She worked the soil with vigorous and knowing thrusts of the spade. The soil was so rich, it looked like chocolate pudding.

"I envy you that humus," Emerson said. She continued her work. She was a frail-looking woman, but on closer look she seemed to be all tendons and tough stringiness. "I bet you could grow almost anything in it."

"Well, I guess all that garbage of some thirty years has done something. Are you looking for anything particular?"

"No, just looking. It's too early, I guess. But I always get pangs to do something this time of year. I get eager."

"It does happen," she said and put one foot on the spade's hilt to drive it deep into the ground. Her spare physique worked smoothly, as if she meant to demonstrate a rudimentary garden chore. "I see you looking at the monarda. They need a good amount of sun."

"Yes, I know," Emerson said. "I grew up on an old farm my great aunt had in Ohio. She had a bunch of them growing against an old barn. The wood of the siding had become gray, silvery."

"Must have been nice." Then, as if the spadework had fulfilled some obligatory amenity between them, she laid the tool against the foundation and looked at Emerson expectantly. "I could save some of them for you if you want—I guess you live near. You come back this way. I remember you from before."

"That would be swell of you," he said. "My name is Sam Emerson."

He had almost repeated the information he had given to the owner of The Tabletop but caught himself and only smiled.

"That's all right, I'll remember. You buy my basil."

"That's right. If you have any, I'll take some now. I could cover it with newspaper if we get a frost."

"Flats in the greenhouse," she said.

Inside the greenhouse the air was sultry and moist. A couple of sparrows chirped and played overhead, then darted through a broken pane. Emerson selected a couple of trays marked by the small, fresh leaves of the herb, and he could feel the woman's silent questioning as he made his choice. "I run a restaurant, and we use a lot of basil in summer season." She accepted the information with the same composure with which she took his money. She helped him carry the square trays to the station wagon, where they lifted them into the back. "I grow them in a friend's backyard, in large boxes on her back deck." He answered what he thought was a query in her silent regard.

Phoebe would have questions for him, too—this friend he had referred to in the silent exchange with the nursery owner. Well, it was a shorthand cut to eliminate a lot of verbiage that would describe their relationship. He could have talked on into the afternoon, all the while the old lady standing beside the open end of the station wagon, holding a tray of basil plants as he tried to describe Phoebe Konopski, Ph.D., licensed counselor. Specialist in addictions—who had become his addiction. No, that wasn't fair—just a smartass quip. Didn't come close to how he felt about her. "I'm in love with your history," he'd told Phoebe more than once. She had laughed and looked a little embarrassed. For him probably, for using such language. Rarely was Phoebe Konopski discomfited.

She had brought that history to him one night at the restaurant as she dined with several executives from the Mellon Bank five years ago. Some of the narrative was complicated, made even more challenging by an ex-husband who had not yet realized she was no longer his property. No longer his personal punching bag, though he had hit her only once and that had been enough, but the verbal assaults had been pretty bad too. One time he had broken her glasses, just plucked them from her face and snapped them in two as if to blind her. At least until she found her contacts. And he was still a nuisance, phoning at awkward times ostensibly to speak to Nick, their son, or to engage her in laborious and gratuitous discussions about the financial terms of their divorce or the mortgage on the house on the Northside, though it was no longer his concern.

"Listen, I have some pals downtown—they're regular customers—who could lean on him a little," Emerson had said one time.

"Oh, please don't do that," Phoebe implored. She had been blowing off steam about the ex's latest intrusion. It was late, Nick was asleep on the third floor, and she had fixed them coffee in her kitchen. "That would only make him crazier."

"How did you ever end up with this guy?"

"You mean, how did an intelligent, educated, spirited woman like me become trapped by a man who wants to control her and punish her when she doesn't do what he wants?" She had settled in his lap as he sat at the kitchen table and pulled at his hair. "Is that the question you're asking me, Sam? Is that the question? Are you really asking me that question?" The mild amusement in her voice was lightly seasoned by sarcasm. She had said nothing more, and her abrupt silence suggested he knew the answer, or he should know the answer and that it might be within him.

"Dear Sam, I'm not sure this protection you offer isn't more of the same—however sweet you are. I'm just a little shell-shocked. Don't rush me. Give me a little breathing time."

So, there was hope, Emerson thought, as he sometimes remembered this talk. He had passed a semi and turned on the car radio. There might be some more news about this woman suing the president. Who said hope was a thing with feathers? Like a turkey, maybe? A boring bird, Emerson had decided, both to cook and to eat. He had just entered a sort of null point where local Christian evangelical stations overwhelmed the signals from Pittsburgh radio stations. Only hymns and pleas for money. They were always asking for money and forgiveness.

He was about an hour from the city, and the territory had become staked out by junkyards and auto repair shops, home beauty parlors, and a few nondescript stores around a fast food drive-through. A couple of diners were next—one of them, he knew, served a classic meatloaf sandwich—and then a church with a needle-nosed steeple of burnished aluminum and a lawn so green it must have been dyed. A mile farther were a veterinarian and a used bookstore in an old farmhouse and a place that boasted curtains and drapes made to order but also offered—maybe for those customers who waited for their curtains to be made—imported chocolates. Emerson called up the pleasurable flavor of the thick, peppery gravy ladled over the meatloaf and the mashed potatoes at the Two-20 Diner. It was the genuine article; not something poured from a can but stirred slowly from drippings and flour. He had introduced Phoebe and Nick to its ordinary wholesomeness. They had had Sunday dinner there more than once, and she had been very happy during these outings, probably amused that he would set them down to such common fare. Those afternoons had been completely satisfying, and to see Nick mop up the gravy with a piece of bread made Emerson as happy as if he had cooked the dish himself.

The landmarks on both sides of Route 220 had become for Emerson the settlements that lay outside the walls of his domain—Sam's Place set high above the Monongahela River like a medieval battlement. As he had traveled back and forth to Mansfield, these sites marked the distances from Pittsburgh as reliably as the numbers on the Ford's odometer. The Two-20 Diner was about an hour from the Squirrel Hill Tunnel, the eastern entrance to the city. The church with the aluminum spike of a steeple was less than forty-five minutes. Then came Fancy Duds, a place that rented tuxedos and formal wear—but why way out here? The Happy Daze Grill on the left was a few minutes less, and the Texaco station with the sour-faced woman behind bulletproof glass spotted the thirty-five minute mark. It was a little like turning the pages of a travel guide.

Now he had come to a point thirty minutes from his restaurant on Mt. Washington. The Highway Paradise would be coming up on the right. The red flash of the neon arrow pointed toward the cement block building set back from the highway. It was windowless and resembled a defense outpost designed for a war that had bypassed the position, gone around its feckless defense. The scraped-down parking lot made it appear even more desolate, despite the several cars and pickups nosed into the front wall. The zealous red neon raised a silent alarm in the afternoon, impaling the weakening light with a repetitious urgency: TOPLESS AND BOTTOMLESS DANCERS.

Emerson understood the nature of the performances inside, and in all the years he had passed the Highway Paradise, the sign had provided him entertainment, something for conjecture while toiling along the pavement. From the automobiles in the parking lot, a mix of pickups and SUV's, Emerson often put together a profile of the audience inside.

Some may have even rented tuxedos from Fancy Duds for the occasion. Opening nights. Bottomless and topless. It sounded like one of those arcane jokes physicists tell each other, and which, for some reason, were minutely detailed in the *New York Times*. Space undefined, and only speculation at the center of it. What would a bottom without end be? Perhaps the dancers had discovered a direction of movement yet to be named or described. Not sideways or up and down, but into a void that had been there all along—say, parallel to the conventional spaces but yet unknown. Until now. Over the years of his travels on this road, he had witnessed the Highway Paradise prosper. A second block building had been erected to one side of the original with a high, wooden fence installed between them. In fair weather, a large banner hung on this fence: THE POOL IS OPEN—NUDE SWIMMERS. Just kids down by the river. Tom and Huck and Becky, but mostly Becky, he figured.

Recently, an item on one of the Pittsburgh news programs reported that the Highway Paradise had added a drive-in facility. It couldn't be seen from the road, but apparently around back of the block house was a setup where the horny traveler, behind in his schedule and eager to get back to hearth and home, could simply drive up to a window and attend a performance just for him. "The guy could keep the motor running and his pants open," he told Phoebe. She had been reviewing a client's folder and merely let her eyes slide to one side within the heavy rims of her glasses.

"It wasn't so much a face that launched a thousand ships," he had continued, knowing it was probably a mistake to do so. Phoebe had kept reading as if to ignore him. She was spending the night; Nick was on a school tour to Washington. "Well, I'm not alone in this idea, for Christ's sake. The fascination has been around from the very beginning." He had been cleaning up their supper dishes in the penthouse. The city's skyline sparkled, and Three Rivers Stadium glowed as if some enormous ritual were being observed within. And that was the case: the Pirates were in town. He was about to go downstairs to help Cynthia close up the restaurant. "It's what makes the world go around, as someone said."

"Yes, it is a fascination, but that's a nasty version," Phoebe said. "How the woman is observed is important."

"You mean that voyeur business—controlling someone by spying on her. You told me all bout that."

He had tried to remember all the points of a lecture Phoebe had given him in her back garden one evening. And what about now? He continued this silent discussion with her as he tried to get a Pittsburgh station on the car radio. Here's the president of the USA doing something naughty in a hotel room. Or trying to. But to be fair to Clinton, he wasn't president then—only a governor—but doesn't that prove the point that places like the strip club were making? Not only change some poor guy's route on the way home but change his history too. Everybody's history. The more he thought about it, the less he liked his argument. He turned off the radio.

But the imagined debate with Phoebe had kept him diverted for the rest of the journey. He made good time through the tunnel and up the parkway, the traffic leaving the city going against him. Rising to the top of Mt. Washington, the Monongahela River and the city on his right, Sam Emerson imagined he was riding a magic carpet that lifted him high above the grind and halting advance below. A solitary tugboat moved placidly upriver.

He turned down into the deep well behind the restaurant, where he parked, and quickly went into the building's basement and the wine vault. He was just looking in to see if all was right, so he left the flats of basil in the back of the station wagon. He could run them over to Phoebe's house and then come back for the evening, which promised to be busy. Almost twenty reservations had been on the book when he left this morning. Upstairs, he found Cynthia chatting with Constance Ho, the bartender, and he became quickly aware that the kitchen sounded different. Not silent, but different. Neither of the line cooks was whistling in the kitchen, and one of them was always whistling. Cynthia turned and came toward him, a strange look on her face. "Bad news," she said.

"About Clinton? I heard."

"No, it's Sterling. His nephew was killed. Some cops beat him up." A fury within the young woman suddenly bloomed in her face. "He was just out driving, and they killed him. Just beat him to death, the fuckers." She started to cry and held a napkin to her face. "Sterling's not here."

PROGRAM NOTES

Getting On

"Stand aside for people who know where they're going." The command comes from the sidewalk where they wait to board a bus. "Another holdup," young Sam's mother complains, ostensibly to him, though he knows she means to be heard by others, maybe some god who will clear the way for her. An obstacle has been put in her path.

Meanwhile, the offending hindrance has continued to mull over change at the fare box, trying to tell a quarter from a nickel. Say it's someone not familiar with the shape of a nickel, with the profile of a Sioux chief—someone like a new citizen. Or it could be an older resident with failing eyesight. It makes no difference to Edith Olson. She has one foot on the first step of the city bus and is ready to get on. "Now what?" she asks with a wearied levity. She has been ready to get on with her destiny, her career, but the fates apparently want to test her stamina, her will. Young Sam is pretty sure who would win.

Sometimes he wonders if he were a little slow getting on the bus behind her, and if the doors would close and the bus pull away, would she say anything? Would his mother leave him behind on the sidewalk as some kind of lesson to him to be alert, to keep up the pace, and to teach him that he had deserved to be left behind? It would have been his fault.

In his memory, these visits to his mother in New York always commenced at the Greyhound bus station across Eighth Avenue from the main post office. The station was the gateway for these brief reunions. The square-nosed buses creaked like old ships as their heavy gears downshifted and sobbed when they edged into the diagonal stalls. Then, after a quick march to a nearby corner, he and his mother would board a city bus to take them to another part of town—usually a couple of transfers away—where she happens to live. Cross-town to East End Avenue. Up Broadway to the West Side near Columbia University. Downtown to the Village. She hates subways. "They go underground," she explains. Mostly the apartments are borrowed and temporary. "She's on tour with Cornell," she tells him when they enter a darkened foyer smelling of sandalwood and musty drapes. It is never the same place twice, and the variety of places is sort of glamorous. At least, Sam tries to make it so, for he never knows what to expect. It's like starting over all the time.

Say it is early summer and she has no place large enough to put him up this time, no bed for him to sleep on, but they would manage, she says. "I have a surprise for you." She hugs herself, the tip of her tongue between her large, perfect teeth. "Roller skates." For a moment, he wonders if she plans for him to stay on the streets the whole time, skating up and down and around, all day and night. Then she explains that the person in the next apartment has agreed to let him use the sofa. "But don't use his bathroom. We don't want to make a mess for him. Just hold it until you come next door to my bathroom."

At last, they have eased past the obstacle at the coin box. His mother leads the way to seats at the rear. Then, comfortably seated, she leans over him and in a soft voice that projects throughout the interior, says, "It takes them longer to figure things out." Her tone conveys a majestic understanding of the person's plight—everyone should observe her tolerance, but at the same time, everyone should have the opportunity to learn how to put bus fare into the slot. In the meantime, they should not block the progress of those with this expertise. She packs all that into the one sentence—it's what she does for a living, after all. Sam tries to shrink within the stiff, all-purpose tweed suit she got him at Macy's last year. It's become too small and it is hot and the pants stick to his legs.

There are other settings. The Automat where they eat most of their meals. The dim destitution of a theatre lobby at midmorning, where he waits as she reads for a part inside. Also, the miles and miles of sidewalk they foot to save a nickel. There's also a cramped studio apartment in Hell's Kitchen—he thinks that was the best place. There had been other kids to play with. These are hard times and money is a problem, and he never could understand why. His father is always away mysteriously, taking pictures. She can no longer play the ingenue; her time has come and gone. She's outgrown the brassy flapper whom Bob Benchley took to the Algonquin for lunch, and she is no longer the amusing young woman the van Dorens and the Benet brothers invited to fill out their soirees. "They were full of conventions," she used to say, "and lacking in disorder."

Say it is a warm spring day, and they are standing at the Nedick's on Times Square, sharing a hot dog. Lunch. Around the corner is the Plymouth, where she had appeared with Pauline Lord and Rex O'Malley another time. Farther up the street is the Algonquin. She's high on the audition she's just done. She gives Sam the last bite and the details. The bare stage light. The vast darkness of the theatre before her. Then a voice from that black emptiness: "Oh, Edie, you look splendid. Truly splendid." That was George Abbott. Then, another voice: "Yes, read anything you like, Edie. The phone book will do." That was dear Gilbert Miller. And they enjoyed her reading, but she doesn't get the part. Soon after this morning, she sends Sam to live with her aunt in East Liverpool, Ohio.

These occasions are before television and before *Playhouse 90* and *Studio One* and others begin to call her for roles for which her post at the Elizabeth Arden counter in Macy's seems to have given her special preparation. Like an older sister or a sisterly aunt, she has given advice on pancake makeup, on scents for day and evening, and these intimate exchanges with other women are like rehearsals for roles William Inge and Horton Foote seem to have written with her in mind. "It's an Edie Olson character" became a familiar description in early television. Then came the soap operas, and her specialty became the sadder but wiser woman of a certain age, comfortably widowed and still up for a dalliance with a young composer or a troubled park ranger. Young Sam watches her materialize in the gray rippling of Aunt Rho's small TV next to the fireplace. But this history happens long after that lunch at Nedick's.

Christmas at the Automat

Chrome art deco counters and light panels with block lettering. Walls of small rectangular glass doors, behind which plates of food magically appear. Young Sam guesses that cooks stand inside, like navy gunners in the newsreels, ready to supply the empty chambers as they swing around. They display plates of pies, baked beans, and potato salad. He likes the macaroni and cheese best.

In the center of the room within a glass booth a woman dispenses nickels, dimes, and quarters like one of the mechanical gypsy fortune-tellers in the penny arcade on Forty-second Street. But this is a real woman, and she spills out real coins with fantastic speed, and the change is always correct. His mother always counts it carefully. Christmas decorations hang against the polished marble walls, and celluloid Santas lean between the salt and pepper shakers on every table. Say the two of them have just come from the bus station, and Sam's suitcase is underfoot. He's just arrived from the school up in Connecticut, and he's joining her for the Christmas break. "It's not Exeter," she had told him, "but it's good enough." Aunt Rho is unable to keep him any longer in Ohio.

The cheesy aroma of the macaroni rises from the dark green ramekin and his mouth waters. He knows it's going to burn his tongue, that it's too hot to eat, but he can't help himself. "You burned your mouth the last time," she warns him, and delicately cuts up her cucumber salad. A hard roll with butter completes her supper. "And don't tap your spoon like that. You're off tempo."

Sam notices a woman a few tables over staring at them. His stomach tightens, because he knows what is about to happen. Sure enough, after a little hesitation, the woman stands up and walks toward them, holding her purse before her with a look of pleased discovery on her face. "Excuse me, but you're Edith Olson, aren't you? I saw you in *Save Me This Dance*. You were wonderful. I'll never forget . . ."

"I'm sorry but you are mistaken." His mother cuts the woman off. Her scarlet lips turn into a lovely smile, forgiving and lenient but firm all the same. She breaks the crusty roll and dusts the cucumbers with the crumbs. "People often make that mistake. We're just traveling through from Toledo. I guess there must be a resemblance."

The woman doesn't move. Her confusion cements her to the floor. She looks embarrassed, as if she's forgotten her lines, her way out of this bumbled scene. His mother continues to slice the cucumbers in some sort of demonstration of the process as well as a gesture of dismissal. "But thank you anyway," she says and lifts a forkful to her lips. It's a good-hearted rejection.

"She wasn't begging or anything," Sam finally says. The macaroni is still too hot.

"Oh, but she is, Sam. People like that want to become part of your life. Interfering. Clearly you and I are sharing a moment of closeness, a family moment. Just the two of us, and she comes barging in like Paddy Flynn." She tears another roll into pieces. "Anyway, *Save Me This Dance* was a godawful play. Who wants to be remembered for that turkey? Eight performances, though Max was a dear. I couldn't wait to get out of it."

"What part did you play?" The pungent cheese sauce sticks to the top of his mouth, and the chocolate milk combines wonderfully with the wad of pasta stored in his cheek. He has a nickel left, enough for another glass of milk, but mostly he wants to watch the chocolate stream from the mouth of the lion head. He just has to pull down the handle and the stuff pours out, magically stopping just at the rim of the glass. Nothing like that in East Liverpool, Ohio. "Were you a princess?"

"Just another brainless upper-crust dolly."

"Why Olson anyway?" He's wanted to ask why she doesn't use his father's name, like other women. It's seems a good moment, but he's a little afraid she will become impatient. So he's surprised when she puts down her silverware and leans forward. She looks pleased and serious, as if she might have been waiting for him to ask the question all along.

"I was in the theatre before your father and I met. Before we married. It would have been too complicated to change. And nobody else did. Ethel Barrymore, Laurette Taylor. Others." It's becoming a lecture, remarks for some women's club. "In private life, of course, I am proud to bear your father's name. He's a man of the century. By the way, have you heard from him? I think he's in Africa with the English."

The green cellophane streamers on the wall with large red bows give the Automat an odd funereal look. The glass doors of the food wall open and snap shut. He's had nightmares about eating in a funeral parlor with glass doors like that, only larger, that spin around to throw out corpses, and one of them is his father. He doesn't finish the macaroni, though he knows there will be no dessert. It's close to curtain time.

"You're done. Here, I'll finish that," she says. "I have to check in to the theatre. Fat chance Tallulah won't go on. That woman is a truck. Just the other day, Wilder took me aside and said he longed to see me do the part. But what can he do? She'd go sky-high. But darling Sam, after I check in, we're free as birds. We'll go over to Schiavis for some biscuit tortoni. You like tortoni," she reminds him.

"And I have a surprise for you. O'Hara gave me tickets for his new play. It's opening Christmas Day. It's a musical and has pretty girls in it." She is already standing, the small purse in hand as if it were a baton she has just grabbed up to run her part of the relay. The pink tip of her tongue sticks out from between her teeth, an expression of a glee so intense that it has to be held back.

Pal Joey is not the only gift that year. On Christmas Eve he receives a travel kit in leather from Macy's. She unwraps the flannel nightgown he has bought in the small town general store near his school. "Perfect and just right," she says, holding the shapeless mass of it up. He thinks she means it; the reading of the line had been just right, too.

On the Road

"You'll be better off with Aunt Rho," she tells him one spring afternoon when he is six. "You have to go to school, and you need chums your own age. The school in East Liverpool is excellent. I went there, so did Aunt Rho, and so did your grandparents. They met in the fourth grade, in fact." She notes his sidelong glance at the curtain that screens the tiny pantry of her one-room studio. Within on shelves are teacups and several plates and an assortment of saucepans that fit perfectly within each other. A two-burner gas grate. The silver pepper grinder and salt cellar Burton Roscoe had given his parents as a wedding gift. The silver glints like pirate treasure next to the sugar bowl.

"We'll be together on holidays. And what fun we'll have then." She gives a throaty reading of the line, as if she's already looking forward to their first reunion. "Ah, Sam, it's not what it should be, but it's the best for you. Your father's in Spain, and God knows when we'll see him again. I don't mean that," she says quickly. "But we have to be practical. He's always in the thick of things. That's his way—he's famous for it. And this is a nasty war. A civil war. Always the worst."

As she talks, even as she chooses this new life for him, she's been folding up and putting away lingerie into the top drawer of a large steamer trunk that stands open in the corner of the room. The place this time is in the West Thirties. The trunk's sides are plastered with the names of all the theatres she has played, the hotels she has passed through on different tours. The bottom drawer holds his underwear, socks, and some shirts, and it is so tightly packed he always has trouble opening and closing it. The scent of her clothing drifts down into his drawer, to perfume his garments with her smell, and that bothers him a little.

If they only had a proper bureau, he reasons, even this move to Ohio might not happen. Not have to happen. He's seen bureaus displayed on the sidewalk, outside furniture stores on West Twenty-third Street; he's skated all over that neighborhood, and if she got one of those, he could stay with her. He wouldn't have to go to Ohio. And the furniture seemed cheap, and some dressers even had mirrors attached. But what would she do with the trunk then? Somehow, it is part of what she does. Day after day, he skates around the area, as she is in rehearsal or sells cosmetics at Macy's. She also spends time at the library at Forty-second Street, and he skates all the way up Fifth Avenue, thinking he might meet her. She could watch him skate on the way back to the apartment. She says she is doing research.

"We have to pull together, Old Sam." She sits down next to him on the bed. The soft fragrance of her, the warmth of her side through the red silk kimono brings a sob from his throat. There's a picture of her holding him just born, that appeared in a Sunday photogravure, and she is wearing this same kimono. His father had not taken the picture. Of course in the picture, the kimono is not red. "This is not a proper life for you. You're getting too big for playing gypsy with me. You need some buddies of your own. And you'll love Aunt Rho's place." Her arm has gone around him. "She has chickens."

"I hate chickens."

"What's this? You the great finagler of chicken fricassee. The dean of dumplings?" She's slipped into her W. C. Fields imitation; something his father does also. Despite himself, he is giggling, snot nosed and still a little mad at her. "Sweetheart, we'll have fun times. We'll have seminars, and when Daddy gets back, we'll get a little place in Putnam County."

"What's Putnam County?

"That's where everyone is going," she says. "Remember that little house we looked at last summer?"

He remembers. The roof in the back room had caved in, and the steps up to the front porch were missing. Hornets from a nest under the eaves patrolled the kitchen so you had to run through them. Inside, he and his father watched her make different exits and entrances through the several doorways. She had been wonderful to watch in the different parts she played. The bored sophisticate. The desolate mother in a WPA melodrama. The mindless slut from a Southern documentary. His father had been the important audience, and he clapped his hands, speechless in his laughter. Strangely high laughter. "Oh stop, Edie. I can't—I can't—I can't take any more." The flat black hair fell over his face, and he looked boyish.

This happened the summer before she tells Sam he has to live in Ohio. Things are looking good for her. She is up for a part with the Group Theatre. The new Odets play. She's taken Sam to Romany Marie's for dinner to splurge. It's run by a Romanian gypsy who sometimes comes to your table to tell your fortune. Just the two of them, and his mother feels good about the audition. His father is somewhere—maybe China. The Japanese are in Nanking.

"The part's as good as mine," she tells him with a wide-mouthed, toothy assurance. She looks fierce in the candlelight. "Harold told me I had the character cold. If I can just get in with that bunch. Of course, they are a little on the red side, and mostly Jewish, but that's the world these days. It doesn't matter."

If he has any objections, she waves them away with one hand, but Sam doesn't quite understand what she's talking about, or who this Harold is, and the stew is too spicy. But it's like getting on a bus, and he doesn't want to be one of those people who get in her way, who may get left behind. So, he nods, and in the next several years he attempts to keep up with her stride. He gets on a peculiar shuttle between Ohio and New York and then between Connecticut and New York. The nudge of his suitcase against the back of his knees becomes a curious pedometer marking off the distance of his travels.

Some Snapshots of the Photographer

One day his mother opens an issue of *Life* magazine and shows him the photograph. It depicts a Spanish peasant boy, about his age, being garroted by two of Franco's Moors. The boy's face is childishly round, and his popped eyes look straight into his father's camera. The mote of death takes shape in the eyes, and the kid looks as if he's trying to ask a question. But he can't get the words out, and his tongue sticks out straight as if the air in his lungs is trapped in the middle of a cough. Like the whooping cough Sam had in Ohio last winter. The soldier twisting the garrote is standing to one side, as if he is showing off the technique but is only mildly interested in the result. The second one is lighting a cigarette.

The picture wins Owen Emerson much acclaim. Everyone says that if the Pulitzer had been given for photography then, he would have won the prize with this picture. It is part of the permanent collection of the Modern Museum of Art. The young boy's breathless agony has been reproduced many times to sustain the moment of his death. The youth's murder goes on and on, as he holds his breath forever. Sam's mother has shown him the picture proudly, but he wonders why his father didn't do something, untie the knot and rescue the boy. Why did he only take his picture?

"He's in Spain," she reports. Sometimes, his father's field of vision would be Finland or Germany or Mexico or China. She names these locations as if they were just across the river, just beyond Hoboken. Some afternoon, young Sam thinks, he might take the ferry across the river and look for his father, find him there, but he eventually understands, those times the three of them are together, how far apart they live from each other. It becomes obvious. Painful. And his father always acts anxious, nervous, and ready to rush off with his bag of cameras.

A Family Outing

Bleak's—sometimes called Artists' and Writers'—is one of his father's favorite spots. Even in wartime, the roast beef is thick and tender. "Au jus," his father would say and laugh. Some kind of a joke, Sam thinks, so he says it, too, "Oh, juice," and giggles. They all laugh. Heavy chairs and tables. Dark paneling. A convivial bar carries over the raffish disorder of the restaurant's days as a speakeasy. You expected the feds to come crashing through the door at any moment, but that would not happen; everyone knew Harry Bleak had "taken care of things." Young Sam absorbs this special information, the insider stuff, to become knowing without knowing the context. "Those goddamn pilgrims damn near ruined us, made us gangsters."

"Not pilgrims, darling," his mother corrects his father. "Puritans."

"Oh, yeah?" His father's eyes fasten on his mother. It must be the way he looks before he takes a picture. Clicks the shutter.

Harry Bleak always stands at the far end of the bar. He is a formal man with a quiet voice, and he calls everyone by name. His manner is in contrast to the good-natured, loud crowd always at the bar. Most are from the *Herald Tribune,* just around the corner, and theatre people and writers. A lot of arms are placed around shoulders, like the statues in the Metropolitan, Sam thinks. Men shove their hats onto the back of their heads. Wives and girlfriends turn and talk to each other in the glow of this exuberance.

"There's Geraldine Fitzgerald," his mother says. She wags several fingers toward a table at the rear. "I must speak with her." The other actress waves back and smiles. She is wearing a large round straw hat.

"Good eats at Bleak's, old timer," his father says to Sam. "Pull your socks up and tie on the feed bag."

"Oh, juice," Sam says, and his parents laugh. His father hugs him. There's a happy feeling in Sam's belly that's almost like getting sick. As usual, they are sitting at a table near the front door, and Sam gets the idea it's a special place. Like for royalty maybe. He's only just realized his father is famous, and he's also figured out that his frequent absences have something to do with that fame. So, it is a hard choice to make. He likes people coming up and talking to his father, clapping him on his thin shoulders, but he misses him too. Their table always gets a lot of attention. Those absences make evenings like this one at Bleak's all the more wonderful—redolent with success, a delicious flavor of being special poured over everything like a tasty sundae. There are balls of butter the size of golf balls, and the bread tastes swell. Oh, juice.

"Here's Victor," his father says. He's pulled the dark knit tie loose from his unbuttoned shirt collar.

"Good to have you back, Mr. Emerson." The waiter wears a tuxedo, like in the movies Sam has seen in Ohio, but a long white apron is tied around his waist underneath the jacket. His father pulls his tie looser. "Miss Olson, always an honor to see you. You look splendid," Victor says and bows toward his mother. She's lighting a cigarette fixed in an amber holder, and she does look splendid. Young Sam is happy to be ignored and studies the handles of the heavy cutlery.

"Has Harry got any of that George Dickel around? With a splash, please Victor, of the best from the Croton Reservoir. And what will you have Miss Olson?" The thin sharp face Sam Emerson will remember mostly in profile, always turning away, has swiveled toward his mother. A wan smile creeps over his father's generous mouth.

"Whatever you think I should have, sir." She bats her eyes. Her auburn hair is rolled thick to her shoulder and held in a net she calls a snood. The large gray eyes lower but not demurely. They humorously keep a joke. "Mother says I must be home by twelve o'clock," she says. His parents giggle; even Victor laughs. Sam laughs too, though he doesn't know what's so funny. It's the way she said it, he thinks.

"Well, Victor, that sounds like a daiquiri to me," his father says still smiling. "And bring Master Sam here that vintage ginger ale Harry saves for the Prince of Wales."

Young Sam doesn't know how to handle the situation, how to contain his joy. He's never learned how to manage the exquisite happiness of these occasions, the exciting blur of places like Bleak's and the clubby atmosphere where important notes are written on the backs of envelopes and stuffed into coat pockets. So, he becomes busy. His knees rub together, and he tries to fill himself out to match the adults around him. People barge through the doors and jam up at the bar. Others lean back in their chairs to talk sideways with diners at the next table. "Stop rattling the silverware," his mother says. "You're going to spill the water."

"The boy is just happy to see his old man," his father says. He breaks a crusty roll in two and offers his mother half.

"A lot of us are happy to see his old man," she says. "How long are you in town for, Scoop?" Just then, Sam understands he is only visiting, too. He and his father, the two of them, coming into town to be with his mother, and he is all at once sad for her, since it means she's been by herself all that time and will be by herself when they leave. In East Liverpool, at least, he has Aunt Rho.

Victor has returned with their drinks, and his father takes a long sip of the whiskey. "That's the real stuff," he says and smacks his heavy lips together. "Can't say for sure. Something is up. Everyone guesses Africa, including the Nazis probably. The Brits are being whipped, and Joe Stalin wants a second front. So, Africa."

"I read the papers too," his mother says and lifts the cocktail glass. She sights him over the rim. "What I want is your version. Do I change the sheets or what?"

"I know a guy on Ike's staff. He's been telling me that—"

Just then a very large man wearing a very large slouch hat pushes through the door and propels himself toward the bar. Then, he stops midway and swings back toward them. "Owen, you old cocksucker— oops. *Excusez-moi,* Edie." He swipes off his hat and bows deeply.

"Oh, is that what you boys call it," his mother says, fluttering her eyelashes. Everyone laughs, including Sam.

"Well I was afraid I wouldn't be seeing this old dog for a long time," the guy has continued. "Are you happy with that wire service? I might have a better deal for you."

"Oh, yeah." Sam admires his father's poise. The photographer has leaned back in his chair and squints at the man standing over them, calmly measuring him and his offer through the smoke of the cigarette he holds with two fingers and a thumb. Like Humphrey Bogart. His mother holds the amber holder with her cigarette high and to one side of her face. She looks like the ad on the back cover of a magazine.

"Step into my office, and I'll tell all," the man is saying. He turns to Sam's mother. "Sorry, Edie. Business you know." Then he strolls over to the bar, where several men make room for him after pounding him on the back.

"I'll just be a minute," Owen Emerson says and stands up with a shrug, so he has left them once again, even at Bleak's and to be sure only at the distance from the bar, but it could be North Africa just as well. His mother asks Victor for the lemon sole and questions Sam's choice of chicken Marengo. "I thought you didn't like chicken anymore."

"I like chicken. I just don't like chickens." He makes the distinction carefully. Also, he likes the sound of it—chicken Marengo.

"Then bring Mr. Emerson the roast beef," she tells the waiter, "rare as possible, with a baked potato. And he likes that horseradish sauce, so please give him a lot of that, Victor. And when you bring the food, kick him in the butt on your way."

Several people stop on the way to their tables to chat with her. Exchange gossip and news. One woman sits down abruptly like a conspirator. She and his mother have a close, quiet talk sprinkled with gleeful laughter and language that makes Sam uncomfortable. He doesn't like to hear his mother use such words. Another woman cries out as she passes, "I hear you're replacing Cornell."

"Not true," his mother cries back almost merrily. Her smile is all teeth. Then a lull falls over their table—just the two of them. The excitement of their presence seems to have worn off; people in the restaurant have got used to them sitting there. She tries to amuse him by doing different voices from radio shows. She's been doing some of these lately. "Grand Central Station, where a million dramas are acted out daily . . . Good evening, Mr. First Nighter."

Age is not all that important on these radio serials. She's forty-two now, but on radio she can be a weary waitress or a young debutante. In Kansas City or Oak Bluffs or East Liverpool, no one knows the difference. One time, during a school holiday, he recognized her voice on a program, and he listened hard in Aunt Rho's parlor, where the radio stood, thinking she might send him a coded message while she was acting, like at the end of the *Orphan Annie* show. But you needed a special ring to decode the message, and it usually had something to do with drinking Ovaltine.

As his mother chats with others, young Sam studies the men at the bar, how they stand and talk to each other. His father turns easily among them in a kind of affectionate basting. He's the center of attention. Owen Emerson shakes hands, clinks glasses. He's thumped between his sloped shoulders. The camaraderie makes Sam impatient with his boyhood. His father's suit hangs rumpled on his wiry frame, and the tie has been further loosened and pushed askew on the dark blue shirt. Heavy brogues are on his feet, and he shifts his feet like a boxer as he talks. He is restless and eager, and the animation that works the thin face gives him an odd handsomeness. He resembles the scout of a ragged outfit that has just liberated Forty-first Street, and he might have unshouldered his rifle just outside the place—actually he's pulled off the two or three cameras that hang around his neck in some pictures, like that one in *Collier's*. And without the cameras, even in the amnesty of this old saloon, his father looks unprotected, which is probably the reason everyone at the bar seems to be touching him, taking care of him.

War has discovered Owen Emerson and his cameras; the favorite enterprise of the century has become his subject. His eye has seen through the romantic claptrap novelists and journalists have dumped on war. Through different lenses, he has looked at it straight on with the cold appraisal he keeps from wife and child, regarding them from the side, mostly out of the corner of his eyes, as if he would harm them if he looked at them directly.

"I don't make pictures anymore." His father's voice is calm, without emphasis. It is late at night, and Sam has wakened from his sleep on the daybed in the living room. "I'm an undertaker. I can't do that impressionistic crap. I'm a straight shooter."

"You and Tom Mix." His mother's voice is easy, sleepy and happy. How long they have been talking, he doesn't know. Their voices have pulled him from sleep. She has sublet this apartment on East Twenty-sixth Street, across from the Armory. The radio shows are doing well, and she has a small part in a show that is enjoying a long run. The ground-floor flat opens onto a small garden, and Sam hopes they can live there forever, though he knows he must go back to East Liverpool for school. Around the corner on Lexington Avenue are restaurants with Arabic lettering on their front windows and wonderful smells wafting through their screen doors, like the smell of cinnamon in Aunt Rho's cupcakes, and, for a moment, he's sad, thinking of her alone back in Ohio. Tomorrow, he can roller-skate down to Gramercy Park, where there are a couple of kids his age usually playing. Or he might spend the afternoon in the free science museum in the Chrysler Building, where there is a model of the Panama Canal and you push buttons to open and close the different locks. It's been the best summer ever.

As he drifts back to sleep, he wonders if his father knows Tom Mix. It wouldn't surprise him, and he tries to stave off sleep, to listen more, to find out. One of them has lit a cigarette; he hears the snap of a lighter and then smells the aroma of tobacco burning. The summer air is still in the open windows—no one has air conditioning. "I'm not a soft-focus guy. I make the picture that's out there, not in my head. You understand? Yes, you do."

In truth, Sam Emerson cannot remember all the details of this summer night on East Twenty-sixth Street, the voices in the bedroom and what they said. He often heard their voices in the dark as he fell asleep on the pullout bed. His mother reenacts the scene over the years, over and over, so the interlude assumes an archival quality. Sometimes, he will question her. Did he really say that about becoming an undertaker?

Of course he said that, she would snap back. She would brook no editing of the material, no checking of facts. Like all memoirists, she carefully reassembled the elements of the past so the final version of an event would possess a truth the original lacked but should have possessed.

"Edward," and she always meant Steichen, "said to me one day in his studio . . . this was after 291 had closed."

"What's 291?" Emerson would ask. They would be having lunch at the Tavern on the Green in Mansfield.

His mother would look at him as if he had suddenly become one of those foreigners who always offended her by their ignorance. Then after a moment to allow her astonishment to sink in, she would continue. "Why the gallery he and Stieglitz ran, of course. The studio on Fifth Avenue. 291 Fifth Avenue. Edward said your father never knew how good he was, yes." She nodded to second the opinion. "Yes, he was crushed when your father went his own way. 'It is like I have lost a son,' Edward told me." She would repeat the line, imitating the older photographer, his speech and gesture.

One of the best parts of his father's return was playing with the cameras in his bag. The soft leather satchel would be dropped in the middle of the floor of wherever they stayed. Once, at the Chelsea Hotel, in a couple of rooms borrowed from a playwright's widow. Next to the camera bag would be the small duffel, pungent and warm, as if it had been just removed from an oven.

"Be careful with those," his mother would warn.

"Oh, hell, Edie, they're just machines. They can be replaced, and he's not going to hurt them. Here's what you got to be careful of." He would point to his eyes. Young Sam looks away quickly as his mother leans forward to kiss the dark eyes of his father.

The leather bag usually contains three cameras and several extra lenses. Film cartridges, a small pair of pliers, a pocket of thin tissues, two note pads, and dog-eared cards with PRESS in red letters. A small soft brush in what looks like a lipstick tube of brass. Phrase books in Spanish and French and another in English syllables that when Sam pronounces them to himself sound like Chinese. The cameras are small and square and weigh compactly in his hands. They feel heavy with a mechanism so perfect inside their plain black bodies that he can only guess at it. They are like weapons in his hands, rectangular pistols, for he has already guessed that his father's work takes him into dangerous regions, and these ingenious devices are important to his survival. The metallic, slightly oily smell on them suggests adventure and foreign peril.

In the meantime, as he would play with the cameras, his parents might go on talking. "Sid Brown got his mother out of Germany," his father would say. "The Nazis are going crazy over the Jews."

"Well, they've brought it on themselves," his mother would say. "They are greedy and want to run everything. It's no different here. They run the theatre. The movies. Not Sid's mother, of course. She's not like that, she's different."

"Yeah, she's different," his father would say and then look away. "Everyone's different."

Some lenses have long barrels and are a little scary. Carefully, young Sam would take off the cap and peer into one barrel and quickly look away. Becoming bolder, he would stare into the polished glass surface, thinking it might yet hold the image of someplace his father has been, a face that has looked into it. But only the moon of his own face—the Ohio Swede in him, his father would joke—floated on the convex surface, just another passing reflection.

"You never take our pictures," his mother would sometimes complain. Half seriously.

"Get yourself a Kodak," his father would say back. But he did take some pictures of her; Sam is sure of it. One afternoon, he skates the whole way to the Empire State Building and back to the Chelsea. He even skates onto the clunky elevator and into the suite on the fourth floor. The hotel was casual about such behavior.

"Just a minute, Sam," his mother cries from the bedroom. Both his parents are laughing and sound funny. Bedsprings squeak. Then she appears, pulling and belting the red kimono around her, and his father's face is about the same color. His eyes have a strange, wild look young Sam has never seen before and just his pants have been pulled over his

BVD shirt. He holds the Leica in one hand and he's barefoot. If pictures were taken that afternoon, they never show up in Owen Emerson's files. Maybe they were never developed. Remembering this incident later, Emerson would amuse himself with the idea that there may not have been film in the camera that afternoon at the Chelsea.

Now the chicken Marengo has arrived with yellow rice that seems strange but tasty. He's only had the white rice that Aunt Rho cooked up for her chow mein, a popular item on the menu of the High Standard Café. Anyhow, he has hoped for mashed potatoes at Bleak's, but he does like the main dish, and the black olives in it are a happy surprise. And the tomato sauce is like spaghetti. His mother delicately pieces her fish and tells him about Napoleon's personal chef fixing this special dish after the battle of Marengo. The picture of the cook scrounging the countryside for the ingredients amuses him, and he laughs at the image of the man chasing down a chicken in someone's yard. Like Aunt Rho in her back-yard, grabbing up a chicken for supper. Then the guy had to find toma-toes and black olives. His mother makes the story interesting, describing how the ingredients were put together for the first time to make this combination that tastes good. His father's roast beef has not been touched; its juices have become dull and congeal in the cooling plate. Oh, juice.

Owen Emerson seems to be held captive at the bar. He can't escape the people who want to talk to him, hear where he's been. What he saw. They want to touch him. Both men and women; two of these women stand almost toe to toe with his father in the roiling talk. Their faces break into wide smiling mouths, and their eyes flash. They lean into his father, almost in tandem, and one stands with feet apart as if to brace herself against something. Her companion turns the toe of a spectator pump out and holds a burning cigarette at one hip. His father is smiling and looking down, face to one side—the way Will Rogers looks. His black hair is slicked back from the hatchet profile, and the hair is long for the time, jauntily unkempt.

"Hand me that potato, Sam," his mother says. "Yes, that one." She waggles her fingers impatiently, and the three large ivory bracelets clack and rattle.

"Do you want butter on it?"

"Oh, for Christ's sake, just hand me the goddamn potato." She takes it from him and rears back and throws a perfect pass, the baked potato spiraling like a Sid Luckman pitch to hit his father on the side of his head. "Game's over, Sport," she yells.

Bleak's goes up all at once. Two men at the next table stand to raise their glasses. Heads turn at the bar, many cheer. She responds with a maidenly reserve as his father, smiling and applauding her also, swaggers back to them. Young Sam is certain the whole world with all its problems turns on its axis just for them at this moment.

TWO

Sam's Place overlooks downtown Pittsburgh from Mt. Washington, about a thousand feet above the Monongahela River where it joins the Allegheny to become the Ohio. A protégé of Frank Lloyd Wright's designed the house while supervising the construction of Fallingwater, Wright's masterpiece, built south of the city by a wealthy department store owner. A steel baron, anxious to compete with the Jewish merchant who had commissioned Fallingwater, hired the apprentice to make him a similar house on this lip of topography and to use the same design of stressed concrete cantilevers. Viewed from across the river, the parallel lines of the structure's flat roof and two balconies distinguish it from the other houses that mark the palisade. From downtown Pittsburgh, the steeple of St. Mary's of the Mount and the circumflex roofs on either side of the church look surprised by these long hyphens of cement that compound their peaked silhouettes.

Sam Emerson took his morning coffee and a piece of sourdough bread on the top balcony of this house, just off the living room of his penthouse. His tree house as Phoebe called it, and the view was splendid, especially this morning. He breathed in the panorama of Pittsburgh. The bridges that crossed the rivers were thick with early morning traffic, an arterial movement flowing into the city to give it life. The gleaming grove of skyscrapers rose from the delta, the so-called Golden Triangle where the three rivers joined, and to complete the picture this morning, a tug pushed several empty barges up the Monongahela. A large jet had begun its descent toward the airport. How he loved this view, this skyline. Often, Emerson wondered what sort of life it would be to work and live on one of those tugboats, moving against or with the current, but with good coffee at hand and decent pals as shipmates—all on board and self-contained but making headway, too. It was a cool morning for late spring, and the whole street grid of downtown Pittsburgh tipped a little more toward the east, turning to the right—he imagined he could detect the motion—to reveal the sun that had been hiding behind the black slab of the US Steel Building. He felt its sudden heat. This was Sam Emerson's city, and he loved it.

He looked toward Three Rivers Stadium—in the direction of Phoebe's neighborhood. He imagined her over there reviewing folders in her briefcase and getting Nick ready for school, cleaning up their breakfast dishes, putting some final touches on her appearance—the look of a successful professional woman. She was a knock-out—brains and beauty and that take-no-shit manner. Would this reflection make him a voyeur? At this distance he couldn't even see her house. Not even her block.

"Now look here, Phoebe." He had put on his best Jimmy Stewart stutter one evening. She had been leaving him to get home, even though her son was spending the night with friends. "We're just going to have to quit this shilly-shallying and set up a single residence. All this back and forth business has got to stop. It's gone on long enough. It's just wasteful. We have to get legal."

"You mean move in with you?" The idea amused her. "You want me to give up my own space that I have only just won? My own closets? And where would you put us in this charming bachelor pad, dear man?" She looked around the apartment's living room, separated from the sleeping area only by the partition that also defined the efficient kitchen unit, where he prepared their intimate suppers. Where he had cooked for other women, she knew. Her look as she made the brief survey of the room suggested her familiarity with that history.

"I could add on to the place," he had replied, his voice level, serious. "I own the property adjacent. Sterling and I have been talking about expanding the restaurant. Closets? You want closets? I'll give you closets, grandma." But he just as quickly dropped the appeal; their banter had become less playful. Her mouth was closing down strictly on the subject, and he didn't want to sully the sweet time they had had that afternoon. Neither wanted to speak directly about their future; neither wanted to voice a conjecture that might become a certainty.

This morning the air was slightly chilly, but Emerson relished the fresh sharpness of it as he sat on the balcony. He hadn't been able to call Phoebe last night because of the emergency in the kitchen with Sterling out. It had got too late. He was going to his chef's house later, and he could run the trays of basil over to Phoebe's house at the same time. Last night he had put the small plants in the wine vault in the basement. He enjoyed these early mornings, a time of order and peace. He planned the day's marketing, went over accounts, thought about the restaurant's personnel. His maitre d' was having problems with her boyfriend. Suspended over the amazing urban complex, he felt like one of those early balloonists rising above Paris, breaking free of the ground for the first time, and to see—for the first time—the whole splendor of the design that had been put together street by street, piecemeal, and blindly on the ground. An example of human ingenuity that always amazed him. Emerson could watch the continuous play of the rivers and their commerce endlessly. Just now, a tug moved downriver, guiding several barges deep in the water with heaps of black coke from the mill above. It would pass into the Ohio River at the point and then, about three hours later, glide by the landing at East Liverpool, where he had watched similar near-silent processions as a boy.

"I've really only just moved upriver," he sometimes said to a table of diners. "I'm from East Liverpool, down the Ohio, and I've always been happy living on a river. Here in Pittsburgh, I have three of them." But that casual biography by the host of Sam's Place wasn't completely accurate.

"I'd be certified if it hadn't been for Aunt Rho." He had pointed out a woman in the picture that hung over the apartment's neat kitchen counter and bar. This was early in their affair on a Sunday afternoon, before they slipped into the large Jacuzzi installed in the downriver part of the penthouse. The wall of glass by the tub faced the skyline. Phoebe lowered her section of the Sunday paper to look at him as they relaxed in the bathwater. She wore the thick-lens horn rims that gave her a studious look. For a second, he saw her as a young girl, bending over her schoolwork in the family's kitchen. "You are saying that the mess you are now is to be overlooked because of the mess you might have been if it were not for her?" Her mouth turned down to signal a point made, her lips curling to suggest she was about to do or say something wicked. In fact, her small feet had slyly crept up his thighs underwater. It was what Emerson thought of as her "bad-girl" look, a cant of mouth she may have acquired growing up in the blue-collar mill town of Turtle Creek. Emerson had been reading the comics to her, taking the different voices in *Peanuts* as they lolled in the warm water. Phoebe had pinned up her hair with a couple of the long ebony pins that had belonged to Aunt Rho, which he kept in a black lacquer vase on the window ledge. Phoebe's use of them had prompted his acknowledgment of the woman in the photograph that afternoon.

Someone with a telescope on the top floor of the US Steel Building could possibly have made them out; maybe even one of her colleagues at the Mellon Bank could see them, Emerson conjectured—the corporation keeping track of its employee on her day off. But they idled in the oversize Jacuzzi, their privacy confirmed by the vapor that frosted the glass wall beside the tub. Even so, they bathed in an arena of daylight, in the open air, and this exposure—the chance of discovery—sometimes seasoned their play and delighted Phoebe. "My goodness," she would say with mock alarm when his erection poked above the water's surface. "What's happening here?"

But this one time, Emerson had folded up the comics and laid the paper aside. "You mean, dear doctor, that there's no hope for me? That I am fully formed, finished, and unalterable? Why, just the other day, I got a message—at the 7-Eleven of all places. The gods have a way of showing up in odd neighborhoods." Phoebe had leaned back to listen, recognizing an even better story was about to be told. Her plump arms stretched out along the edge of the tub, and her breasts sweetly bobbed in the water. "We had run out of orange juice for a marinade. The 7-Eleven is just down the hill; I was standing in line, waiting to check out and became aware of this woman ahead of me. Talking to the clerk. They knew each other."

Phoebe had fixed the tight curls of her hair into a topknot held by the ebony pins, but a twist of purple ribbon fell in a coil to imitate several strands of her own blondeness. It was a style she had adopted for bathing or making cookies in her kitchen—as Emerson had watched her do—and the tight purchase of the knot seemed to pull up the soft concentrics of her face. The pink shells of her ears were exposed. She looked childlike, though she had just had a birthday that clearly defined her maturity. He had made a cake for her and decorated the apartment with paper streamers and candles. "Here I am at forty," she said merrily and a little tipsy from the champagne. She had straddled him and pounded herself energetically on his cock, still wearing one of the silly paper hats Emerson had insisted they wear. At first, he could tell the hat had made her feel foolish, but she had worn it as a good sport to his plans and eventually forgot it as the ceremony progressed. "Yes, yes," Emerson replied, keeping up with her. "Here you are indeed." And just for a moment, the difference in their ages fleshed out his pleasure.

In the Jacuzzi, the oval of her face was washed clean of its usual flamboyant makeup, the vivid emphasis of eyes and high cheekbones and the generous lips—the whole image so unlike the subdued look of other women he had known. Next to Amanda's prudent use of cosmetics, Phoebe's application of eye shadow, rouge, and lip-gloss was almost outrageous, and Emerson adored her for it. It tickled him for reasons he never tried to explore. Her hands molded the bath water impatiently. Emerson had fallen into a silent reverie that included Amanda and large parts of his past, a jumbled review of his personal history passing in seconds that often could immobilize him. Phoebe slid lower to pull scoops of warm water over her chest and throat. "So, Sam, there you are standing in line holding your orange juice."

"I gradually began to listen to this woman talk. She had a beautiful little boy with her. Large brown eyes kept staring at me. 'It will all even out,' she said to the clerk. 'God willing, it will all even out.' And the woman behind the counter agreed. That's all there was to it. But I had a strange feeling then. It was like someone had opened all of the wall coolers, but the air that swept over us wasn't cool. A different atmosphere. It was a different kind of warmth."

Phoebe had continued to gently ladle bathwater over herself. Her eyes had lowered to an expression that was patient and knowing. She had heard the story before, just another variation. "That child Amanda and I lost could have been this young woman. About the same age, and the little boy too. The kid kept looking at me like he knew me. And for a moment, everything seemed to have come out right. Like she said. It all seemed right." He hadn't meant to talk about it, to mention his former wife—that whole past. It had just come up and caught him off guard, as the past always seemed to do.

Phoebe's mouth shaped a sad nuance, then she pulled herself straight up in the tub and half floated in the water toward him, her scarlet toenails momentarily surfacing, to put her arms around him. She kissed him. "Where does it come from?" she asked. "That hope inside you—it never gives up, and that's not what I bargained for. I had only expected something tasty, and look what you have done to me."

So on this morning as he sat on the balcony overlooking the city of Pittsburgh, Emerson was stung by a longing for this woman who so challenged and affected him, took his measure, and then loved him for it—or seemed to. Phoebe Konopski. She was only just down there, across the point from where the Allegheny meets the Monongahela, but this beautiful prospect before him only seemed to widen the distance between them. They never talked much about the age difference, and the times he made some reference to it—say, a probing jest—she would dismiss the subject with a sprightly endorsement of his lovemaking or make some other light-hearted comparison of him with other men, but Emerson wondered if the very nature of her indifference might suggest the issue wasn't important to her because she didn't plan to stay with him much longer.

Sterling Wicks's absence from the kitchen made for more complications—nothing Sam Emerson couldn't handle, but he hadn't really had time to tell Phoebe about yesterday's visit with his mother. How she might die any day now. He'd have to wait until this evening, if Phoebe would be home then. Sometimes he would dial her number knowing she wouldn't be home, just to hear her voice on her answering machine; that soft glottal sound of her Pittsburgh accent falling into his ear transported him.

"You have reached Dr. Phoebe Konopski. I am very sorry not to be here to receive your call, but please leave your name and number and I will return your message as soon as possible. If this is an emergency call my cell phone number . . ."

One time Nick answered the phone and he and Sam worked through an awkward five or ten minutes talking about the Pirates. The boy has been patient and respectful; after all, he was interested in lacrosse and soccer.

Occasionally, Emerson pretended he could make her out in the city below—one of the tiny figures that briskly followed a route in the downtown streets. He fancied he could see her miniscule form toting a microscopic briefcase as she disappeared down a street or turned a corner. A speck gone from his eye, but he imagined she was there and very likely would turn up later, breathless and flushed with news of her day. He remembered the times she had appeared, excited by a client's breakthrough, then sat down to calmly explain the importance of that success. Her quick smartness had initially drawn him. Emerson admired people who did their jobs well, whatever they might be, and Phoebe Konopski was clearly one of these. The night they met, she had been at a table of lawyers—corporate types. It was a table in one corner of the dining room, so the city skyline was behind her, a luminous diadem. He had returned to the table more times than usual in his role as host to look at her, observe her. Hear her fluency. The others listened and paid her attention. Her quips made them laugh, and her opinions made them nod and pass their agreements around with the olive oil. She wore her professionalism with confidence, casually reaffirming the points she made as she touched the heavy cuff links that fastened her long-sleeved blouse.

When they became lovers, a decision that both of them seemed to have made that first night, her appearances at the restaurant became casual and unexpected. When he invited her to supper in the penthouse above the dining room, she told him it would have to be an early supper because of her son. She had to get home. She was fiercely protective of Nick and fearful that she might be judged an unfit mother, so their times together were carefully notched into the boy's schedule of classes and athletic practice and stay-overs at a friend's house.

"It's almost like . . . ," Emerson started to say once.

"Like what?" Phoebe paused, applying her makeup. "Like what?"

"Well, like we're deceiving him—like he's being wronged somehow."

She had become quickly solemn, clearly turning the idea around. "I don't want to ever feel that way," she said at last.

Often Emerson would glance across the restaurant to find her sipping a cup of tea and chatting with Constance Ho, his bartender. The supple leather briefcase would be on the stool next to her. Phoebe had taken on a domestic rightness in Sam's Place. Soon she came and went as if she belonged there, and he told himself that the very variability of her coming and going suggested a curious permanence in their relationship, a stability that did not need to be verbalized or kept to a specific schedule. When she had no time for lovemaking, she made it clear to him she was denying herself as well as him. She had become an older sister to Constance, who was finishing her graduate work in economics at UPitt. Heads together, the two women talked about schoolwork with Phoebe listening and counseling, offering her experience in the academic thicket. Emerson was warmed witnessing these encounters.

Other times, Emerson would look around after chatting up some customers to find that Phoebe had gone home. With not even a wave of her hand, but the abruptness of her departure somehow told him she would return, and he would continue to describe a wine to a customer with a feeling of wholeness. No need to say good-bye if she was coming back—it was that simple. Still, he would be disappointed. "You left kind of early. Are you all right?" he would ask on the phone later. Her part of town was dark.

"I had some cases to review. I have to be in family court early tomorrow morning." She sounded all business and not too far away.

"If we got legal, we wouldn't have to do these smoke signals across the rivers." The minute he uttered the words, he was sorry.

"Oh, Sam, let's not go through this old wash again. I'm just not ready to even think about it. It puts me all lopsided."

"It's Nick, isn't it?"

"He adores you. And his mom likewise," she said quickly to forestall his question, which only shamed him. "Now good night, sweetheart. I will give you lots of kisses tomorrow."

Or, when she had more time—Nick might be spending the night at a friend's house—she would go upstairs to the penthouse to wait for him. If the boy was on a school trip, she might stay the night. Emerson would find her going over court documents and case histories when he climbed the private corkscrew stairway to the top floor. The contact lenses were replaced by thick glasses that became a visor making her look oddly vulnerable. She would smile hesitantly when he came to her, a little anxious maybe of what he thought of her like this, wearing these heavy glasses. Perhaps an uncertainty left over from girlhood that yet claimed her. Emerson would see her as the serious scholar she must have been, doing her homework at the kitchen table in Turtle Creek, always reading. It was this industry, the history of her industry, that had first attracted him. There was almost a sexual rush to it.

One time he emerged into the open floor of the penthouse to find her clacking a couple of tablespoons together like an old-time vaudeville act at the Nixon Theatre. Her grandfather had taught her the Morse code this way. He had been a telegraph operator for Westinghouse. "How about 'Bye-bye Blackbird,'" he joked.

"Just keeping in practice," she replied and put the spoons down quickly. "Never know when it might come in handy. An emergency."

Later, on an evening when the restaurant had many regulars dining, a happy murmur circulated among the tables. The view of Pittsburgh was marvelous from every seat, and a genial hum declared the evening's satisfactions. The muted scrape of china and silverware, corks pulled, and whisks of laughter colored the velvety aromas of Sterling Wicks's cooking. Phoebe had been testing a new Sancerre that Emerson had just ordered specially, when she asked Constance for a couple of spoons. Diners looked up at the strange noise to see Phoebe standing on the bar level slightly above the dining room, and as if onstage, twirling the two spoons in the fingers of one hand. The clatter they made was syncopated and oddly purposeful, and her look was concentrated. Focused. The clacking paused and started, paused again, and then continued for longer intervals, and it was clear to everyone they were attending an unusual recital. Then she stopped the spoons at her side. A cook whistled a tune in the kitchen; water ran in a sink. Several diners still held forks above their plates. Phoebe took a deep breath.

"That's the message in Morse code the steamship *California* received from the *Titanic* as it was sinking," she said proudly and gave a little laugh. She looked at Emerson for approval over the applause. One or two diners raised wineglasses to toast her. The moment struck a chord deep in Emerson, which he couldn't identify, but he knew Phoebe Konopski was one of a kind.

Some Sundays would find Emerson sitting in her kitchen across the river in the Mexican War Streets. Sam's Place was closed on Sundays and Mondays. Then she cooked for him. Few women had ever cooked for Sam Emerson except for Aunt Rho, but Phoebe went about it with a beguiling insouciance. Her hair in a topknot and barefoot if the weather was warm, she methodically worked up her mother's recipes for stuffed cabbage, pirogues, and cheese steak. She made excellent bread. As she padded happily about her kitchen, Emerson examined the two of them from outside himself. The scene was both typical and serene, completely satisfying in its commonplace goodness. Sometimes Nick would come in for a cookie and some milk and stand at the open door of the refrigerator to chugalug from the plastic bottle, the laces of his sneakers undone. Emerson would chat with him about the Pirates, about the latest trade meant to beef up the bullpen. The boy worked at being interested. These conversations were never very relaxed, and Emerson was aware of Nick's politeness and his dutiful responses. He was darker than his mother, and now and then a fleeting amusement crossed his face, as if he was a little entertained by the charade the two of them played before him, as if he didn't know what was going on with his mother and this guy who kept talking to him about baseball.

Emerson understood that he was enjoying a kind of ready-to-wear domesticity—complete with child—that could be slipped off as easily as it had been put on, accompanied by the same offhand but practical consideration with which Phoebe rearranged the pots of geraniums on her back porch. She put them wherever the sunlight fell. Nick's nonchalance suggested he wasn't taking them that seriously—his attitude drawn from his child's realistic eye. As he came and went in his mother's kitchen, the boy projected a security, an ease, that Sam Emerson enjoyed watching, for it brought him back to that kitchen in East Liverpool where he also had had free rein. Phoebe's tender management of their daily lives had fashioned this ease in her son, and Emerson promised himself he would never harm that relationship. As for Phoebe's cooking, it was made special by the exuberance that claimed her because she was doing it for him, the chef featured in *Gourmet* magazine. He knew that. Her stuffed cabbage was peppery and succulent, though he wasn't all that taken by the doughy pirogues.

Some of their best times happened in this made-up family setting. Or in her back garden, which had grown wild when he met her. She wasn't a gardener, not that she was lazy or uninterested, but the activity didn't seem to fit into her professional routine, her schedules and court appearances. So Emerson had taken it over, bringing the patch under control and finding plants that would flourish in the heavily shaded area. A huge ailanthus tree grew up from the center to cast an all-encompassing shadow, so he had put in daylilies and hostas and myrtle. He lined the brick walkways with impatiens. And petunias, whose heavy sweetness revived the memory of his aunt's garden in Ohio. Phoebe would sit on the back steps and watch him work, aware, without saying anything, of the other transplanting that was taking place, which occupied him in her backyard.

"What's that?" she asked one Sunday evening, pointing at a plant.

"Foxglove. *Digitalis purpurea.* It will have little pink bell-like blossoms. Bees like to play inside them. But the blossoms are poisonous."

"You're putting poisonous plants in my garden?"

"To be in the presence of beauty is always hazardous."

"Oh dear me, maybe I should write that one down." She laughed and patted the space beside her. "Take a break. Come sit a while."

He stuck the trowel into the ground and came to her, sat down on the step, dusting his hands. Phoebe put one arm around his shoulder and squeezed him a little. The two of them sat silently for a moment, letting the darkness of the garden envelop them, letting the night sounds of her neighborhood play over them. Up the alley, someone was dribbling a basketball. Someone was always dribbling a basketball it seemed to Emerson, and the rhythmic smack of the ball against the pavement became a pulse that registered his own.

"That must have been some garden," she said gently. "That one in Ohio."

"It really wasn't all that much. She had sun, so she could grow a lot of things. I remember cosmos and bee balm around the barn. Some sort of vine—morning glory, I think—climbing up the back porch."

"There were worse places to be abandoned."

"I never felt like that. No, don't get me wrong. My present exasperation doesn't reflect past history." He thought the word choice might amuse her, though he knew when he tried such language, it often sounded flat. Not right, and maybe not even true. "It was sort of fun in a way, those entrances she made. Edith Olson, the star. A regular life might have been too much for us." The siren of an emergency vehicle trailed through the evening's hush several blocks away. "But what am I to do with her, Phoebe? You know, when she dies. Or should I say, *if* she dies." He laughed shortly.

"You will bury her, Sam. That's the usual procedure."

One Sunday afternoon, he took Phoebe and Nick to the Two-20 diner for an early supper. Nick's enjoyment of the ordinary fare could augur more such occasions—maybe a whole lifetime of them, Emerson thought. He had already showed the kid how to cook an omelet. Phoebe had looked pleased with the food too, though she had scarcely touched the green beans, which, Emerson had to admit, were soggy and clearly came out of a can. But in the diner's booth, the highway outside busy with traffic, a tranquility had fallen over them, not to be rattled even by the clatter of a truck roaring down Route 220. For a moment, they were like the people in the other booths—families going out for their Sunday dinners. Emerson noted another couple eating with a little girl, but the parents sat together across from the child, as if to share the wonder of her table manner. Phoebe and Nick sat together, opposite him. Next time, he promised himself, he would sit beside Phoebe. But no one knew the difference; they looked to be a unit, and Emerson sat back against the leatherette and stretched his legs out. He knew he was only putting on an appearance, as if Fancy Duds down the road had also rented him this semblance of a relationship, and maybe that's all he could hope for, but his pulse drummed happily. The sign in the diner's parking lot read: IT'S YOUR FUTURE—BE THERE.

Emerson was fairly sure that a couple of his regular customers had mob connections, and, more than once, he had fantasized about dropping a few hints at their table about Phoebe's ex-husband. This was when her ex had continued to ignore court orders and made threatening, abusive phone calls in the middle of the night. He was a prick, simple as that. Emerson thought he'd say something like, *I know this woman who needs some protection. Her ex is giving her trouble.* The rat had hit her at this point. Then, he might offer another bottle of Pommeau Sainte Anne on the house. *Oh yeah?* they'd say. *Oh, yeah? Guys like that should be discouraged,* they'd say. *Good women ought to be protected from guys like that,* and then they would look at him with wide eyes, waiting for him to say something—to give them the go-ahead.

The sun had just splashed a golden varnish on the glass sides of the PPG towers, and Emerson was momentarily blinded. He could almost feel the light's reflected heat, even as freshness rose from the metropolis across the river to make the very air vibrate. The city's towers were miraculous. He had to get moving. He had a long list to fill at the Strip, the wholesale market area that lay along the south shore of the Allegheny River. Sterling was busy with his family, making arrangements for his nephew's funeral. There was talk of a suit against the police—it was in the morning *Post-Gazette* on his lap. How long Sterling would be out had to be decided between them. Emerson shrugged off the fantasy about the wise guys; get real, he told himself.

Some of the people in the bumper-to-bumper traffic on the bridges below probably had reservations for dinner at Sam's Place tonight. At this moment as they crawled into the city, some of them looked forward to an elegant evening at table. Already, some of them anticipated the magnificent view of their city from up here where he was sitting, looking down at them in traffic; already they anticipated that first crisp edge on their tongue of one of Constance's world-class martinis. What's for dinner? He better get off his ass.

"Sterling's not here," Cynthia had said yesterday, quickly puncturing that dreamy glide down from Mansfield and his mother's bedside. The large mirror behind the bar reflected the skyline and the bartender arranging the glassware of her domain. The announcement had landed him with a bump. The first reservation due just two hours away, and no one in the kitchen running things. Cynthia had told him about the nephew's death, the cops, the furor that already might be boiling up from the city's streets below—all this as he pushed through the swinging door into the kitchen, the basket of mustard greens in his arms. The two line cooks were prepping basic items; one tended a stockpot, and they looked nervously at him. A waiter was having a snack at a service table and seemed uncomfortable. Emerson took off his jacket, slipped on a freshly laundered smock, and went to the bulletin board to look at the master list. Sterling's meticulous script appeared normal, and that calmed him a little as he handed off the greens to one of the cooks. "Put these in the cooler for tomorrow," he said. "We're doing the A menu tonight. What's the special?"

"It was supposed to be the pork roast orange using the greens," Rita, the other line cook, replied. Of course, Emerson told himself. He knew that. He had to get a grip on himself. He could do most of their menus blind.

"We're scratching that." He paused to think, take a breath. "Let's do a gratin—what do we have for it?"

"We have that poached salmon from yesterday. Enough, I think," the second cook said.

"Good. Make me a roux and sauté a lot of celery. Second thought, chop up some of those greens there also and make a puree out of them, put some nutmeg in them."

"Ah, it's the old nutmeg trick," Rita said, and they all laughed as the tension eased.

"How about something for a *contorni*? Something chewy, crisp."

"How about sunchokes, Sam?"

"No, not sunchokes. How about the stalks from yesterday's swiss chard? We saved them, didn't we?"

"Sir, saved and blanched, sir," the junior line cook said with military correctness. The tension had disappeared. They were having fun now.

"Right, fill them with parmesan, butter, and a little parsley and run them under the broiler."

"How about some teensy bits of prosciutto scattered through the cheese?" Rita suggested.

"Perfecto," Emerson agreed, and the two cooks both curtseyed.

Emerson laughed and looked over three carrot cakes made earlier in the day by a pastry chef he shared with another restaurant. The recipe by Marcella Hazan substituted ground almonds for flour, and it was one of the restaurant's more popular desserts. Sterling always added a dollop of crème fraîche fortified with bourbon.

"What do we call tonight's special?" the waiter asked. He had brought in two stacks of ceramic ramekins from the storeroom. "And how much we asking?"

"How about Neptune's Surprise?" Emerson replied. "It's certainly been a surprise to me. Let's say twenty-two-fifty." Smiles made the rounds. They were going easy now; the kitchen had become normal, and familiar routines had clicked into place. The line cooks worked smoothly beside him; one of them even sang a line from a Willie Nelson song. Cynthia Barton, the maitre d', had arrived to have her supper; she had picked up a pen and was scripting the menus. She could reproduce that flourish of penmanship common to French bills of fare.

"You say twenty-two-fifty for the special?" she asked him. "How's Sterling?"

"I haven't had a chance to talk to him."

"Fucking cops."

"Yeah. What's this?" Emerson had taken up one of her wrists in his fingers. The flesh looked sore, a bracelet of bruised skin.

"It's okay, Sam. I'll drape a napkin over it."

"Listen, Cynthia, is everything okay with you?"

"Sure, I'm fine." She continued the careful lettering. "*Surprise* you spell with an *s* and not a *z*, right? Sure, I'm fine."

When Sterling Wicks laughed it was mostly without sound, so the expression that spread across his face could just as easily be a register of pain. At Penn State, when they were students at the Hotel School, Emerson sometimes wondered if the grimace was an affectation to keep Sterling's real feelings, amusement or not, to himself. It could be laughter, but then again, maybe not, and after all these years Emerson wasn't always sure which.

"Can you believe it?" Wicks was saying, "the Prez-E-Dent standing there with his pants open and his unit hanging out."

"Well, that's her story," Emerson said, laughing along with his partner. "But he wasn't president then," he added in some kind of justification. "He was only a governor." Strangely, the lesser office made it even funnier, and they laughed even more.

The two men sat in Wicks's back living room in Shadyside, a trendy neighborhood of the city. The room was in the rear of the house and looked out through a glass wall onto an enclosed garden in the Japanese style. Emerson had been following the play of a pair of cardinals, male and female. The bird's lilting cries sweetened the air. Beyond the garden in a parking space was Wicks's silver BMW. It was a brazen challenge in the back alley, a tempting attraction for urban mischief or even more, but it had never been touched.

"I'll be back in a couple of days," Wicks said after sipping some tea. "We've got Jesse Jackson coming in to keynote a gathering at the courthouse. It will be a historic affair." The irony in his friend's eyes hurt.

"Count me in for the legal stuff," Emerson said.

Wicks's attention slowly rolled over Emerson. "Thanks," he said finally. "But I'd just as soon you didn't come to the funeral. It is to be uniformly black. A family affair, you might say."

"I understand," Emerson said.

In their Spartan elegance, these rooms of his partner's house were quite different from his own penthouse above the restaurant, though both were clearly the domains of single men designed to entertain women if not to permanently house them. Sterling was something of a man about town. He had become a familiar personage to society pages, in the *Scene* weekly column of the morning paper—a suave coffee-colored figure in ornate waistcoats whose cooking at Sam's Place had made him a celebrity. The image seemed to amuse him, a game he was playing, though Emerson sometimes saw exasperation rise in his partner's composure.

The large room was partially marked off from a handsome kitchen-dining area by a double-sided hearth, which threw out little warmth, Emerson knew, but made an architectural point. A pristine crystal vase on the Danish sideboard held a cutting of lilac from the garden. Another time, Emerson remembered a single scarlet zinnia in the vase. He had never seen the upper floors.

"I should have known better," Wicks said quietly. "A kid driving a silver BMW. A black kid driving a silver BMW."

"You're not to blame."

"The old days have got wheels, dude. You think you've left them behind, but then something bumps at your heels and you look around and there they are—they've been rolling right along with you. Like a shopping cart. Sometimes they catch up. Maybe I ought to pack it in." The chef paused and then seemed to calculate something just over Emerson's head. "Hell, aren't you getting a little winded? I know how old I am, and you must be about the same—halfway to seven-oh.

"They were suburban cops," Emerson heard himself say.

Wicks looked at him for only a few seconds, but it was enough. Emerson felt stupid. Then his friend said, "It was a kind of hubris on my part, and Jimmy paid for it. That's what I have been thinking."

Jimmy Overstreet was the son of Sterling Wicks's sister. He had a full scholarship to the University of Pittsburgh and was a hands-down favorite for All-American honors as a defensive end. The Steelers and the New England Patriots had already been talking about offers. He was a big kid. The four cops who had stopped him testified he had put up a fight, and they said it had taken all four of them to restrain him, getting him out of the silver BMW and face down on the ground, where they could question him. That was their statement. In the struggle his windpipe was crushed and he died. Demonstrations had already taken place downtown this morning.

The cardinals in the garden had darted out of sight, and the murmur of street traffic sifted through from the front of the house. Someone in the back alley was trying out glissandos on a trombone. Obviously self-taught, Emerson guessed. "You saw your mom?" Wicks asked.

"She's about to die. She was pretty much out of it yesterday. I sat there for about an hour and listened to her breathe. That's all. "

"She's got some years on her," Wicks said gently.

"Oh, yes, she's very old." Emerson nodded, thinking unlike Jimmy

Overstreet, who was only nineteen. He was pretty sure Wicks was making the same comparison, and he was briefly saddened. "But as you know, it was not the usual mom-son deal."

"I remember," Wicks said and nodded. His voice was comforting.

"Part of me is going over odd pieces, trinkets, a scavenger hunt, and the rest of me feels nothing."

"You ought to bring it up with your in-house shrink." Sterling immediately looked sorry for his bad joke. "I mean Phoebe must have some advice. She's a sensible lady."

Emerson nodded. "I've had some good hugs."

"Hey, that's the best therapy."

"It's not that. It's not that. I don't know what to do with her—when the time comes. You know, burial and the rest. She deserves something, but what am I to do with her? You'd think dying would solve a lot of the problems. I mean, I never knew what to do with her when she was alive."

"How about the family plot downriver?"

"No, that wouldn't be right—she never had any feeling for the place. The family buried there would be pretty surprised to see her show up. Permanently, I mean. Anyway, she wanted to be cremated." Emerson took a gulp of the tea that had grown cool. "It has to be right."

"As I remember, your pad doesn't have a mantel, so you can't put her on display—even if you wanted to." Sterling Wicks slid deeper into the leather sling chair and crossed his arms. Between them, a black marble-topped table held a cobalt blue vase in which appeared an orange dahlia like a signal of some sort. The chef grew dahlias on an upper deck of the house. Emerson knew little about Wicks's personal life except what he might glean from a newspaper social note. Sterling was very discreet. Sometimes he was featured in a charity affair or some gala in the theatre district. Other times he would refer to "this woman I'm seeing," but the person was never identified further. Wicks gave an odd laugh.

"What?"

"It's just occurred to me we both got funeral arrangements to make."

"Yes, and I better get down to the Strip," Emerson said, standing up. A car with its radio full blast passed on the street in the front. The vibrations of the bass speakers seemed to wrinkle the illumination in the room. Then the sound was swallowed up. Suddenly gone.

"I expect you'll be reverting to some doo-dah from the Escoffier family cookbook tonight. One of those concoctions with jellies and cream," Wicks admonished Emerson.

"Actually, I'm checking out the veal shanks at Schribus Brothers." Emerson was sorry to sound so stiff, but his friend's jibe had riled him a little. He realized the talk about his mother had stripped him of what usually protected him in such banter. He felt vulnerable. In any event, they cooked pretty much alike, with Emerson leaning more toward the Italian menu. His osso bucco with polenta in a sauce made with ground pistachios had been featured in that issue of *Gourmet*.

"This lady of yours is a winner, I'm thinking," his partner said as they walked toward the front of the house.

"She's still shy about marrying."

"She has an agenda," Sterling nodded wisely.

"It's not just the sex."

"That's what Clinton is going to say."

At the front door, Sterling put his arm around Sam's shoulders, and the two men stood for a moment in the open doorway. Kids with book bags raced by. Late for school. The Pittsburgh weather had turned summery, and gobs of low cumulus clouds passed serenely across the morning's brilliance. They were like piles of whipped cream, Emerson thought and not for the first time.

The fall the two of them had met at State College, Sam Emerson's mother had just finished a twelve-week summer stock tour in a play called *Time Out for Ginger*. She played one of her wise, tolerant mothers, and she had sent him some money for his tuition. One day he found himself chopping vegetables beside this tall black guy. Sterling Wicks had done a little traveling after his tour in Korea and had decided to use his GI bill to enroll in Penn State. His family was from Pittsburgh. He had begun as an economics major but had changed his mind and signed up for the Hotel School. By the time the two of them had learned to whip egg whites, they had formed an alliance neither questioned. Sterling had an apartment off campus and had been looking for someone to share it, someone with no problem living with a black guy. Sam had wanted to get out of his single dorm room and the soggy fare from the cafeteria steam tables.

Their landlady never questioned their arrangement, white and black sharing rooms; in any event she spent most of her time in bed, watching quiz shows on TV. Their parties became famous for food and good times. Coeds were eager to join their small dinner parties, and some of them stayed overnight. One of these was Amanda Benson.

Because of Amanda's regular visits, the place got cleaned up. How the chores were divided contributed to their friendship, but sometimes Sterling would forget to take down what he called his "laundry." These were the two or three condoms he hung on a string across the shower on Monday mornings, as if to commemorate the weekend. When dry, they would be rolled up carefully to be used again; Amanda didn't seem to notice, or maybe she put the display into some category of male boasting. She used a diaphragm.

When the three of them graduated—she also had attended the Hotel School—Sterling Wicks was hired by a casino in Las Vegas, and Sam Emerson went to Benson Falls, Vermont, where Amanda's family owned an old hotel. The local Congregationalist minister, one of her uncles, married them, and another uncle, who ran the local bank, extended a mortgage to refurbish the hotel's kitchen.

The morning light in Shadyside seemed to polish the silvery cap of hair on Sterling Wicks's head, and Sam Emerson pleasured in the warmth of his partner's embrace. For a moment and in spite of the visual evidence, it seemed to him that some mysterious process—something in the sunlight maybe—had digested the years of their friendship, and that they were undergraduates still. Emerson had wanted to expand this moment even with all he had to do. But he had to find a new dishwasher before nightfall—the position seemed to attract a steady turnover of losers—and he wanted to get over to Phoebe's to put in the basil plants.

So, he moved purposefully through the streets and alleys and among the warehouses and markets of the Strip district. Here Pittsburgh restocked its larder, and this commerce always restored his confidence. He knew of other cooks, restaurant owners, who had grown tired, even impatient with this aspect of the profession—buying the food to be cooked. He felt he would never be bored by the aroma and appearance of fresh produce. The market district's energy tapped into him, charged him up. Moreover, he was known and knew his way around the crates of vegetables and fruits, the fish spread out on ice, and the carcasses of meat hanging in dim, cool caverns. He inhaled the odors of the place; the potatoes, onions, and turnips still smelling of the earth from which they had been pulled. Their history underground clung to them, and even on the coldest day of the year, the area gave off a peculiar heat. Some kind of friction, too slow to be seen by the naked eye, rubbed the fruits and vegetables to give off a warmth that seemed to be turned up on this spring morning. He had double-parked the station wagon, as usual ignoring signs and parking regulations. No one paid attention to these signs, and there seemed to be even more reason to disobey them this morning. Planning the night's menu, the specials he'd been thinking of, created an optimism in him that made him a little light-headed.

Moreover, he could quickly tell the difference between a perfect artichoke and one going to wood; and this mystical knowledge—irrelevant to many—made him sure of himself. He met the roguish stare of a sockeye salmon, and could discern its freshness by the thump of his thumb on its side. He was not about to be tricked. He moved through the area with the swing of a man who had just had good news from his doctor. And to make the morning complete, the tomatoes just in from Mexico didn't look half-bad. They had a heft and a tangy aroma, not as fine as those from Ohio that would show up later, but these would do for now.

"The best I've seen, Sam," Sol Weisberg said. The produce man held a tomato up to the light as if it were a rare wine. "I had one for breakfast."

"I'll take a box," Emerson said and drew a line through his list. The grocer's son carried the rest of his order to the station wagon.

"How's your mother?" Weisberg asked, totaling up the bill.

"Okay."

"My wife used to watch her on those programs," the man said and handed Emerson the bill. "Maybe I told you. She had a quality about her like—," the grocer searched for the right word, as he had for describing the tomatoes.

Emerson patted his shoulder. "Thanks, Sol."

Sam Emerson never expected perfection in a tomato or the sum of a day's events, but he did anticipate a moment to be savored with a cold beer or a glass of chilled Saint Veran. "Understand me," he had said to Phoebe during one of their first nights, "I don't expect perfection. But nearly perfect, how can we tell? Maybe we don't know better—don't know perfection when we see it, taste it. It could be served up and no one would recognize it because we've expected something better—something with more flavor."

"I read somewhere," Phoebe told him, "yes, it was Pascal who said the souls in Purgatory don't know they're in Purgatory. They don't know any better either."

"So stuff that in your tomato and eat it, is that it?" He laughed, happy with the way she had punctured his posing. He liked smart women even at his own expense.

Sam Emerson knew the tomatoes he had just bought would be nearly tasteless, but they were the best the season offered. He had come close to perfection one humid summer evening; all the dazzle of downtown Pittsburgh was enclosed and framed by the immense glass wall of Sam's Place. The bridges across the rivers were diamond bracelets. They had put up 150 plates and taken in close to fourteen thousand dollars by ten o'clock. He had made some tasty contributions to Sterling Wicks's saffron fish stew, and the *farcis a la Nicoise* had been richly stuffed and redolent of cilantro and toasted pine nuts. The vegetable shells couldn't have been better. Perfectly al dente.

Phoebe had been talking animatedly with Constance at the bar, and both were laughing like sisters. That afternoon, he had dutifully and happily followed Phoebe around her favorite discount stores as she went through rack after rack of dresses. She always shopped for the perfect ten-dollar dress and sometimes found it. Emerson amused himself in the role of the older man patiently watching his younger lover try on different clothes that, just as patiently, he would remove later. Though he didn't tell her of this fantasy—a decadent farce representing the male controlling ego, she would say—but how many pleasures are allotted a lifetime? And she did find a bargain—a designer's knockoff in lime green—that she wore that night, a dress only she could carry off with her own flamboyance.

He had planned a late supper for them on the balcony upstairs. Nick was on a school trip, so she was spending the night. Their supper would be light and elegant before they made love. A cone of light spewed from the stadium across the Allegheny, where the Pirates were methodically shutting down Philadelphia—a small radio in the restaurant kitchen had brought the good tidings—and that meant there would be fireworks about the time they had dessert and kisses. It was a perfect night, he remembered telling himself as he stood in the middle of the dining area, taking all of it in. He took mental inventory of that flawless evening as he stood before the cheese counter at the Macaroni Company. That one evening all the ingredients of perfection were under the roof of Sam's Place. And the aged crotonese cheese being offered him to sample tasted just fine.

In old chinos, a T-shirt, and misshapen moccasins, he might pass for an ordinary citizen, sniffing about the more exotic stalls, and he would be happy with the assigned role. The wares in the Asian and Middle Eastern storehouses always attracted him, though he cooked Chinese poorly; some trick with the spices always eluded him. He felt a special kinship for these merchants. The guys who run the forklifts, the butchers, and produce people carefully turning over mangoes or arranging lemons, the sausage and ham providers—they formed a special union, a fraternity that accepted him. People working at their jobs—he was in danger of being sentimental.

As a boy, Sam's first job was helping Mr. Wilkins deliver milk in East Liverpool. For a whole year, Aunt Rho would get him up at four in the morning, give him breakfast, and then drive him out to the Wilkins dairy farm in her Plymouth coupe. The cows would murmur sleepily, shift in their stanchions under the two or three bare bulbs that hung from the barn's low ceiling, seeming too bright, as if they used a different kind of electricity. The ammoniac odor of the animals' waste stung his nostrils. How that smell was kept out of the milk he never knew. Then for a little more than an hour, he would ride beside the dairyman in an old International truck with a round hood and no knob on the gear shift. He learned to jump to the street even before the truck came to rest at a curb, and then run up to a front porch with a wire basket of bottles. Each bottle had a band of thick yellow cream at its top, and sometimes he'd leave butter or a tub of cottage cheese. The clinking of the bottles he carried accompanied the waking bird songs. By seven-thirty they had made the rounds, and Mr. Wilkins would pull over to the High Standard Café in downtown East Liverpool. It would be the only place open at that hour. Here, too, he would help deliver milk, cream, and butter, trying to avoid Aunt Rho's glance so as to be part of Mr. Wilkins's "team" and not just her nephew. She would be making flapjacks and gently frying sausages on the large grill behind the service rail. He and Mr. Wilkins would have coffee and share a cinnamon bun just from the oven. At first, it had embarrassed him to sit there, almost like a stranger with Aunt Rho cooking right in front of them in a businesslike way. She had pulled him out of bed only a couple of hours before. But then, he liked the idea that they were all the same: Aunt Rho, the other women who helped her, Mr. Wilkins, and him. People doing their work.

Then, the dairy farmer would drive him to school, handing over a fifty-cent piece on the way. A morning's work already done, his book bags on his shoulder, and a half-dollar in his pocket. Sam relished the look on his schoolmates' faces as the truck pulled up to the curb and he swung off of it to step onto the pavement with a nonchalant hop, Mr. Wilkins never completely stopping.

Before they made their rounds, the farmer would have to finish the morning milking. Young Sam Emerson observed the farmer pour the creamy suds into a cooler to be pasteurized later. The cows swung their boxy heads round to stare back over their bony rumps to see what was going on, what was being done to them, and gently mooed their approval, gave off blubbery sighs. Some vented or pushed out steaming gobs of feces that plopped at their feet. Young Sam thought their eyes beautiful, large and deep, and with long lashes, but he considered for a time giving up milk.

By that school year's end, he had stacked up several columns of fifty-cent pieces on his bureau top. He counted them every night—146. Almost seventy-five dollars. His mother arrived to take him to a camp in the Poconos, where she had a job as a drama counselor, and she took the money. "These shirts are frightful and too small. You need some new ones." She never paid him back, but he had needed new shirts.

"You like chicken?" The aged Chinese woman broiling skewers of meat and vegetables asked as she looked up at him blankly. She offered her delicacies on a corner next to the Full Moon Grocery. If she had an expression on her lined face it would be one of suspicion. The brazier had been set up on the sidewalk, and the smell of the food cooking, ginger and cloves, had pulled Emerson up short. But he was barely aware of where he was.

"You like pork? We have all," the woman at the brazier said. She shifted her feet, uneasy under his blind stare. "Very nice," she said again. "All done nice." Cinnamon, cumin, and ginger flavored the tasty meat. He bought a skewer, though he wasn't really hungry, but his mouth filled with crunchy textures and flavors. He usually took a small espresso at La Prima at this point of the shopping trip, but the incongruity of sitting in the small coffee shop holding the Chinese chicken on a stick seemed to embarrass the unity he had been attempting. He did take up several armfuls of black-eyed Susans from a flower stall nearby. Cynthia would arrange them on the tables. He remembered his mother had liked the flower and had introduced them into Aunt Rho's garden, where they flourished, spread like weeds. But his mother rarely saw them in bloom. She had only planted them there, her presence in absentia. Good enough.

A plumbing contractor had held him up at the restaurant to talk about redoing their waste system. Sterling had forgotten to tell him of the appointment, and afterward Emerson had hurriedly scratched off a prep list for the line cooks, unpacked his marketing, and then sped across the West End Bridge to Phoebe's back garden. It was late afternoon. She once teased him that this small plot of land between her kitchen door and the alley was the real reason for his interest in her. Here, while meeting the challenge of the deep shade cast by the ailanthus tree, he could putter and dig in the earth as he could not do on the penthouse balcony. He had even attempted to grow a couple of dwarf apple trees that he had espaliered against the wall of her neighbor's house. The trees had never borne fruit, and their top branches stretched out toward light with an arboreal yearning.

And she was right in a way—the place eased him out from under the demands that often gripped him. The simple-mindedness of the garden chores dissolved the rigid lines of his other routines, and today, to transfer the fragile, green fledglings into the large planter boxes pulled up a harmony from within him. If he could sing, he would have. He inspected the planters: their panels showed no sign of decay. He had put them together a few years back, and they were holding up. He relished the idea of these delicate bits of basil becoming sturdy thickets of lustrous leaves, so green as to be almost blue, to make a kind of hedge around the back porch, leaving their scent of aromatic oils on the fingers that touched them. The flavors of pesto and *caprese* mingled in his imagination. Usually, he and Phoebe would enjoy a first harvest of the basil with buffala mozzarella, a tomato, olive oil, and some crusty bread—it had become a ritual they celebrated on her back porch.

He had finished one tray and had lifted the second one from the back of the station wagon parked in the alley when the kitchen door opened and Nick appeared. "Hi," he greeted Emerson. He was in the full regalia of his lacrosse uniform, shoulder pads and lined shorts. He even carried the stick and with a weary nonchalance tossed the thick gloves onto a metal chair.

"How'd you do?" Emerson asked, hiding his amusement with Nick's outfit as he placed a tray of the herb next to a planter.

"We won. We could go to the finals," Nick replied as he eased himself into a metal chair. His cleated shoes clubbed the wooden deck of the porch. He sipped from a can of soda. "Basil time, huh."

"Yeah, basil time. I don't know a whole lot about lacrosse," Emerson said. "They have different positions on the team, I guess. Goalie and such."

"I play mid," the boy offered.

"I see," Emerson said, not knowing what the position meant. He continued transferring the new plants, conscious of the other's surveillance. Doubtless, the boy had asked to be dropped off at home rather than at school, but for what reason? Probably to show up looking like a medieval page striking for knighthood to impress his mother. Or to impress him. Emerson reviewed and dismissed possible conversation entrees—questions about school, the team, movies. His trowel made another space in the soil and he put in a plant, gently pressed it down so it would stand upright.

"You want something to drink? Coke or iced tea?" Nick asked as he stood up.

"No, thank you, Nick. I have to get back to the restaurant."

The murmur of traffic enclosed them, the going-home sounds of the city. The garden was both a sanctuary and an anomaly. Emerson noted the clematis he had put in last year was doing well, but it needed a framework. Nick's cleats scraped the deck, sounding like the hooves of an impatient pony.

"That's awful about Jimmy Overstreet," the boy said hurriedly.

"Yes . . ."

". . . he could have played for the Steelers."

"It's tragic," Emerson said, thinking how inadequate he sounded.

"What did those cops think they were doing? I mean, four against one?"

"We don't know the whole story yet. I guess there will be a trial. It has to be looked into thoroughly."

"How's Sterling doing?"

"Good. He's busy with his family. I guess they're thinking of bring-ing suit. That reminds me, he's out for a few days so I have extra duties at the restaurant. I can't make the game on Wednesday. You can take a friend along with your mom. Three tickets."

"That's cool," Nick replied.

He had almost finished the transplanting, but Emerson sensed Nick wanted to talk more. Their times together alone had become less awk-ward, but he still felt a sort of testing occurring. Each felt out areas nei-ther was yet ready to traverse. "I'm sorry to miss the game—not to see it with you. The Cardinals are the team to beat."

"Your mother's pretty old, isn't she," Nick said, as if he had been hav-ing another conversation elsewhere.

"Yes, I guess she is," Emerson replied, thinking the boy was probably computing his age as well. "Why?"

"Well, I mean her dying. When she does. That will be like a new chapter."

"You mean, how will I feel?" Nick remained silent, though his expression anticipated an answer. "I can't feel sad, honestly. She's had a long life. I'll be moved up a notch." Nick's gave a slight grin. He won-dered if the boy was really asking about himself and Phoebe. He remem-bered himself at that age, having such worries that swept through him like sudden line squalls. Not so much about his mother dying, but about Aunt Rho. "I wish I had an answer for you, Nick. There's none that makes sense. We make do, that's all."

"You're going to water those new plants?" Nick asked abruptly, obvi-ously wanting to change the subject. "Can I help?" He got up and leaned the lacrosse stick carefully against the porch railing.

"Sure," Emerson said, feeling a little light-headed. The two of them filled watering cans from the hose at the side of the house and carefully applied the water around the soil of the small plants. The boy's attention to the task was earnest and reverent. Emerson started to hum.

PROGRAM NOTES

Some Scenes in Ohio

"Ladies' Day at the Players Club is on Shakespeare's birthday—April 23rd. It's the only day women are allowed in the place." His mother hands them the information in Aunt Rho's kitchen. She sips minted iced tea from a tall glass. Sam has picked the mint himself from the back-yard—has run out and back with it, holding stems of it in his hand like a bouquet. It is summer and the temperature has got into the 80s. The Ohio River nearby makes the heat heavy and wet. Her suitcase is on the linoleum floor by the back door. Just like his father, young Sam thinks, the two of them dropping their stuff on the floor in different places like part of a returning army. This time it's East Liverpool, Ohio. "Dennis King invited me," his mother is saying.

Neither Aunt Rho nor he knows anything about Dennis King, but he must be important. Sam imagines the Players Club to be a big hall with lots of people shuffling cards. All men, of course, and this King guy is one of the players. This guy named King brought his mother to bring him luck, just like in a movie Sam has seen at the Vista. "Yes, Dennis King," she repeats with a sad smile. She's aware the name means nothing to them, but that's her fate, isn't it? to be talking to people who don't have the same knowledge about her world. They have failed another test, as she knew they would and maybe—this possibility has just begun to take shape within him—she has meant for them to fail. The test was designed for their failure.

He and Aunt Rho have met her bus from Pittsburgh. Edie Olson looks wonderfully out of place in the front seat of Aunt Rho's Ply-mouth. She wears more makeup than usual, he thinks, or perhaps the cosmetics, especially the crimson slash of mouth, stand out more in the Ohio light. Her perfume, the same scent that rises from the suitcase next to him on the small back seat, makes him giddy. Her several bracelets clatter as she talks, waves her hands, and the amber beads his father brought her from Finland clash together. She could be an advertisement for something not yet available in Ohio. Sam figures that if people in East Liverpool who see her get off the bus had to guess what his mother was, they could only guess right. There's an actress, they'd say and nod; there goes an actress, and Sam stifles a chuckle in the back seat of Aunt Rho's car, like some joke has just been played on everyone. He and his mother have pulled off a funny joke together.

These appearances in Ohio, as some would call them, were like his father showing up in New York. One difference is that Sam has no place to roller skate in East Liverpool. Aunt Rho's farmhouse lies west of town, beyond sidewalks, and on the last corn lot of what is still called the Olson Place. The Vista movie theatre, a Montgomery Ward catalog store, several markets, the usual churches, two funeral homes, several bars, the Traveler's Hotel, and the High Standard Café—that is East Liverpool.

A small park down at riverside is a favorite haunt of Sam's when he is in town, waiting for Aunt Rho to get off work, and then she'd drive them both home. He's acquired a certain familiarity with the river and is drawn by the mystery of its current, so placid on the surface yet so swift and dangerous underneath. One of his classmates drowned in it just last year, and the boy's body was recovered far downriver at the village of Fly. Sam can identify the different paddle wheelers chuff-chuffing against this current, then later idly wheeling on the return trip. He waves to the captains perched high in the wheelhouses, and they wave back. Some even give him a quick toot of whistle that makes him dance with joy. Strings of barges, low in the water, are pushed by stubborn tugs toward Pittsburgh, and he's proud he can recognize these same barges on their way back, now empty and riding high, like the walls of a great city that have been torn apart, broken off to drift silently toward the Mississippi and then out to the sea. The men on the tugs also wave to him.

Sam doesn't mind these solitary vigils, alone with the river's sound-less energy and flow. On warm days, he dozes on the weedy bank, hummed to by insects. He feels included by the river, though he knows he's apart from it too. He can't explain the sensation, but it happens over and over to make him both happy and sad.

Rhoda Olson is the youngest sister of his mother's father. The Olson family settled in Columbiana County before the Civil War, and they had a reputation for hard work and slow decisions, not a successful combination toward the end of the nineteenth century. Banks and seed merchants gradually pieced the original acreage, so by the time Edie Olson was growing up her father had begun to improvise more than farm. Yet, at tables at Cavanaugh's or Bleak's she would proudly proclaim, "My father's a farmer," as if it were an exotic calling, even though others at the table could make the same claim.

Kurt Olson tried beef cattle, sheep, and finally potatoes. By then, Aunt Rho had moved in to do the housekeeping. Edie's mother had died of cancer. About then, her father had begun his experiments with potatoes—Edie was in high school. His idea was to make breakfast cereal out of potatoes. The Kellogg people had done it with corn—why not potatoes? He had set up a crude laboratory in one end of the barn, and every morning he would march out there, wearing clean overalls, to start up his machinery and conduct tests on the vegetable. One morning, he brought in a bowl of his latest concoction for them to taste. "It looks like white scabs," his daughter Edie is supposed to have said.

"Put on cream and sugar," he advised with a knowing light in his eye.

"Mashed potatoes," Edie said after taking a spoonful. "Cold mashed potatoes." She could eat no more.

So, back to the barn for more experiments. Then, one morning, the people from Kellogg showed up. All of East Liverpool knew about Kurt Olson's experiments, and the town was taut with excitement. The Olsons were going to be rich for sure. "All you have to do is add hot water," family lore has him saying to the food people. "And—presto, you have a healthful, nutritious, hot breakfast." He had even supplied them a name for the new cereal. "You can call them PRESTOES." But the Kellogg people weren't interested. Kurt Olson never gave up, never stopped going out to the barn every morning in his clean overalls until one morning he didn't wake up.

"That cereal business just broke his heart," Aunt Rho is fond of saying. "But I'm happy he didn't live to see what some fool has done with his idea—these instant potato mixes. We tried them out at the Café. More like instant glue."

"Yes, I remember," his mother says and sips the iced tea. She's been looking around the kitchen. The pieces of Haviland are still where they should be, and the blue Delft clock in the shape of a windmill yet hangs over the stove. The stove is from Montgomery Ward, and its creamy enamel resembles polished ivory. It's all as she remembers. Yellow canisters of flour, sugar, and coffee are lined up under the dish cabinet overhang. Before Edie left for New York, for her life in the theatre, the electric refrigerator had replaced the icebox, also from Monkey Ward, and it still hums by the back door, solidly white. Sam used to believe the round coil on top contained a big cake. "Everything looks wonderful, Rho," his mother is saying. Her approval comes with the smile.

"Sam helps out a good bit. He's a fine boy, Edie."

"He certainly is," his mother agrees. "He's a wonderful boy." She wrestles his arm and gives him a couple of whacks on the butt. Sam is embarrassed to be so singled out, even here in the kitchen. Almost more affection than he can handle. But he's also a little peeved that his mother would say such a thing. How would she know how wonderful he is? She hasn't been around all that much to see him being wonderful. But the attention makes him happy. He looks out the window over the sink. The road to Wellsville follows the river south, on its left. Farther down are bluffs and Steubenville, and then comes Wheeling, West Virginia, across the river, and then Fly, and even farther down and west is Marietta. He makes this excursion, here in the kitchen with his mother's arm hugging him, because it makes him feel better, but why, he couldn't tell. "Oh, do I need a bath!" his mother suddenly explodes. She stands up. "I had to sit next to a man on the train, all the way from New York, who smelled like a butcher. He stank awful."

"I'm doing away with the corn lot," Aunt Rho says. "The farmer what's been renting it has gone to different silage. I'm putting in berries." It's like a report and she speaks hurriedly as if she has only a limited time in which to make it. "Takes care of itself. You let people pick what they want and pay by the pound."

"Sounds fine," Edie Olson approves and turns down the hall to the stairs to the second floor. Aunt Rho follows.

Sam stays in the kitchen and looks over the puzzle his mother has brought him. Her gifts also included cologne and fancy soaps for Aunt Rho, with the Macy's price labels still on them. But the puzzle was in a separate bag, as if it was special, as if she had made a special trip to find it. He recognizes the store's name on the paper bag. The toy shop is located in Pennsylvania Station, and he has lingered before its window on one of the trips to New York he made to visit his parents. Aunt Rho had put him on the train in Pittsburgh, and a conductor had looked after him, gotten him a sandwich from the diner and a glass of milk. His mother met him at the other end.

"Dr. Thorndike of Columbia University has endorsed this game," she said when she gave it to him. So, Sam figures it's going to be interesting as well as fun. It's about multiplication tables, which he knows already—has for a couple of years actually—but there are cartoons to illustrate the different factors and answers. Some business in the theatre had made her almost late for the train, and she had rushed into the toy store and grabbed up this game, recognizing Dr. Thorndike's name on the cover. So, she knew it would be good for him. Good enough. She always brought him such board games and puzzles, and some of them were fun to play with. Stories with blanks to fill in. She has complained that the school in East Liverpool is not as good as when she went there. So, she's supplying the difference, boosting the quality of his education. One time she brought a book called *A Child's History of the World* and had him read a couple of chapters to her, which hadn't seemed fair, because he had read aloud already that week to his class at school. Sam is always excited by her arrival in East Liverpool, but he misses the gypsy he played with, made tea with—holed up in odd corners of New York that smelled of sandalwood and incense.

"I sent you his teacher's report." That's Aunt Rho's voice, and it comes from the heat register near the kitchen floor. She's talking over the rumble of water filling the tub. He kneels on the linoleum; it's a perfect listening post. Then his mother says something. Sounds like a complaint, and his great aunt replies. He leans down closer to the grill. He's sure they are talking about his father. "When?" Rho says startled. He can see her back stiffening the way it does when she's surprised by something.

The taps are suddenly turned off, and he holds his breath. Both women are silent. But he's certain they are talking in some way, maybe using sign language. They always have secrets. Water sloshes and his mother gives up a long sigh. He tries not to picture her, but his imagination speeds on. He sees her sinking into the bathwater wearing something like the women in the pages of the Monkey Ward catalog. Of course, he knows she is naked, but at this time of his life, he has only a vague idea of how that looks.

"I've made fried chicken and scalloped potatoes," Aunt Rho says finally. "Just relax yourself." He hears the bathroom door close, and he quickly takes up a studious pose before Dr. Thorndike's puzzle.

Earlier that morning, he sat on the back steps and watched Aunt Rho chase down a chicken in the wire roost built to the side of the barn. She held the chicken by its feet with one hand and whirled it over her head to slap it deftly on the stump, momentarily stunning it, just as the hatchet she held in the other hand smacked down to sever the head. The chicken, a small fountain of blood spewing from its neck, ran blindly about the backyard like a crazed toy. Later Sam helped her pluck the feathers and then gutted and quartered the bird as Aunt Rho had taught him to do.

One time, they drive up to Pittsburgh to see his mother in a play that is touring the country. *The Man from Cairo* sounded interesting, but it turns out to have no mummies in it, doesn't even take place in Egypt. Most of the actors wear formal clothes, like he has seen in movies. His mother got them seats for a matinee, down close to the stage, and he keeps waiting for her to walk onstage, to come through café doors in the first scene, or through the heavy drapery of a fancy living room. Halfway through the second act, he whispers to Aunt Rho, "Where is she?"

She nudges him, points a discreet finger. "There," she whispers. Curiously, he has been watching his mother all along; he has been drawn to this actress playing the snobby, rich girl, but he didn't recognize her as his mother. She wears a blond wig, and he feels dumb for not catching on. Then, the teasing smile becomes familiar, the catch of eyes that clearly makes this society girl his mother. He wishes the play would stop and back up so he could relish her moving across the stage, moving and talking and taking stands by the piano as his mother. She gets a lot of applause at the curtain—a lot more, Sam thought, than the other actors.

She's arranged for them to come to her dressing room after the performance, and they gingerly make their way backstage. The fancy drawing room looks pretty drab in regular lights, and the area behind the scenery is like a warehouse. Someone is singing, and stagehands and actors talk in loud voices like kids at recess. The place seems to make Aunt Rho look different too, and for some reason, he is a little embarrassed by how she looks, which makes him feel sad. She has pinned her dress-up black straw hat to the crown of her hair. It has fake red cherries on it. Her shoes look clunky, square boxes almost. She holds her best purse to her large bosom. When she got ready for the trip, she carefully looked through a bureau drawer for a brand new handkerchief, folded it up neatly, and placed it next to her red leather wallet and the car keys.

"Up those stairs, first landing," a man in vest and shirtsleeves tells them.

Emerson would always be able to call up the smells of that dressing room. The air is layered with the odors of sweat and perfume and singed hair like a cake. "Hello, darlings," his mother cries gaily when they appear in the open doorway. She is wearing her red kimono and sits before a mirror with many lights. She talks to their reflections in the mirror. A net holds her auburn hair tightly to her head, and on a stand is the blond wig with bangs that once disguised her. Sam feels dumb all over again. Then, just like a movie he'd seen, she gets up and goes behind a folding screen in one corner to take off the kimono and put on her real clothes. She keeps talking. The red kimono is looped over the top of the screen.

"Edie, darling." A man's voice startles them, and they move to one side. It is the actor who played the jewel thief who wanted to be a poet. He looks pretty ordinary standing next to them. "We have to pick up the pace in the third act. The poor lambs are wandering."

"You're quite right, Craig. I totally agree." Her voice is muffled by the dress she pulls over her head. Her bare arms reach toward the ceiling. "This is my little boy . . ."

"Hello, little boy."

". . . and my Aunt Rho."

"Hello, Aunt Rho. Up from West Virginia, are you?"

"Ohio," Aunt Rho corrects him. She has pulled her purse in tight and is standing especially straight.

His mother steps around the screen and looks beautiful. She fluffs out her hair. The print dress has an open collar that reveals her throat, around it a gold chain and locket. Sam knows his picture as a baby is in there. High heels give length to her legs. She grabs at her hair before the mirror, giving it several vigorous strokes with a brush. "We're just going to have a bite to eat," she tells the actor's reflection.

"Good luck. We're in Pittsburgh, you remember."

"What I mean, Craig darling, is that we'll have to go over the scene later. Let's go everybody." Sam's hand in hers, she leads them down the steel staircase, like a fire escape but indoors and then outside into the dirty gloom of the afternoon. Stagehands and members of the company nod to her, seem to make way for her, and Sam feels a little important. He skips ahead. Streetlights burn like sore eyes in the smog of Pittsburgh; it is only a little after four o'clock.

"Has your father written you lately?" his mother asks when they get settled. The restaurant has booths and is in the basement of an office building around the corner from the Nixon Theatre.

"He sent him a check for his birthday," Aunt Rho reports. "I put it in his savings account."

"I saved the stamps," Sam tells her. "They had a bullfighter on them and a bull. I took them to school to show my teacher."

"He's in Germany now," she says. The wave of her hand indicates Spain is old news. "He says there's going to be a war with Germany again. It just goes on and on, doesn't it." She looks at Aunt Rho and gives half a laugh, but it isn't funny. There is an odd pause between them that Sam can't figure out. Aunt Rho checks the pins in her hat and looks off.

"Owen says the thing in Munich was a joke Hitler pulled on the English. Right now, he's doing pictures of the German steel industry for *Look*."

Aunt Rho studies the mound of lettuce and raw vegetables that have just been served to his mother; then she cuts a wedge of the hot roast beef sandwich on her own plate. She cuts up the whole order into similar portions and then begins to eat them in some sequence she has already figured out. Sam has ordered Hungarian goulash because it sounded interesting, and is not to be found in East Liverpool, but it turns out to be like Aunt Rho's beef stew except spicy. It's okay, but he won't order it again.

Edie Olson took command of the setting; she was in charge of the basement rathskeller. It doesn't matter that they are the only people eating at this early hour. She swings her arms, waves her hands, crosses and recrosses her legs. Sam hears the buzz of her stockings scrape together underneath the table. She chomps her salad as she talks, biting whole sticks of raw carrot in two with her large front teeth. Her energy fascinates them, as it always fascinates them, and they are smothered by it, give in to it, for she is like a person coming out of a spell. Her color high and her eyes fired up. Young Sam had not recognized her onstage, but the woman sitting across from him is also different. It is like she is playing another part, one he doesn't recognize either.

He figures it had something to do with the applause at the last curtain. The sound of it closed a door on the long afternoons in back rooms he remembers sharing with her. Later, Emerson would consider that the successes that came to her filled out the crimps the times had put upon her as a woman to release the vivid personality that custom and bad luck kept under wraps.

"Owen will be back at the end of the month," she tells Aunt Rho. A few more people have come into the restaurant. "Just about when this tour ends—that is if we get this wagon as far as Kansas City. Pretty creaky play."

"I thought it was very interesting," Aunt Rho says, wiping some brown gravy from her lips.

"And then—then me boyo," his mother continues. She reaches over to squeeze his arm. "Your old man has rented us a little house in Bucks County. And we'll have a wonderful summer together. We'll grow our own tomatoes and . . ."

". . . and carrots," Sam jumps in, looking sideways at Aunt Rho.

They have their private jokes about his mother eating raw carrots. She eats all vegetables raw, including green beans and cauliflower.

". . . carrots, you bet. I think I'll try to grow cosmos like you, Rho. I'm talking to the summer theatre there about doing *Reflected Glory*. If they can't get Bankhead, I might do the show. So, we'll have a ducky time of it, kiddo."

"Next summer," Sam says. It sounds like he's making her promise.

"Yes, next summer," his mother says.

The two of them are silent on the drive back to East Liverpool. A couple of detours on Route 30 take Aunt Rho's attention as she maneuvers the Plymouth. Young Sam thinks about his mother. He's sure her behavior has nothing to do with the actor who had been so snotty. He's seen in movies things like that can happen, but not with his mother. Anyway, wearing that blond wig, she turned the guy down in the last act, and when she held up one elegant hand, the audience caught its breath, then almost cheered when she eliminated him from her life with just a simple wag of her little finger. Probably traveling around the country with people like that guy changed her a little, made her seem quick or on edge.

In his own sadness, he often feels sorry for her being alone most of the time in New York City or traveling around from place to place doing plays like they have just seen. At least, he has Aunt Rho and his schoolmates. Maybe, plays like they just saw were a kind of hometown for her, but one that moved around, like the barges he watches on the river.

Years later, Emerson would appreciate her struggle, her demand for status, but only after he himself had gone from one place to another, one relationship to another, like a clumsy tourist having his language corrected at each stay so by journey's end his pronunciation had been improved and he could pass as a citizen.

The Facts of Life

In addition to the illustrations in the Montgomery Ward catalog, additional sources contribute to young Sam's knowledge of the female body. One day at school a schoolmate passes around cartoon booklets that were crude imitations of the Sunday comics. Dick Tracy and Popeye. The figures are naked and take gymnastic postures. Amazingly, in one of them Olive Oil is trying to swallow Popeye's pee-pee, and Tess Trueheart is trying to do the same thing to the Chief as Dick Tracy rubs himself against her fanny. A third booklet depicts the comedians Laurel and Hardy, one of Sam's favorites at the Vista.

"Give it to me, you fat old fart!" a naked woman tells Oliver Hardy in one picture. She has her legs wrapped around his big belly. He's naked too, except for his derby.

"Just because I'm fat doesn't mean I can't jazz," the balloon over Hardy says. Sam remembers his father saying one time, "Let's get up to Harlem for some jazz." He was pretty sure his father had been talking about music, so this cartoon confuses him.

In the third grade, Sam and two other boys bargain with Clara Mueller to show them her privates. They offer her a Clark bar, an Orphan Annie code ring, and a yo-yo. Clara, a good student with straw-like hair always neatly fixed with a bobby pin, tells them she can't use a yo-yo too good, so they substitute a small compass that came in a Cracker Jack box

This private viewing takes place in a wood lot in back of her house, which adjoins a cornfield. Clara carefully places their tributes on the ground after testing the compass by turning it in several directions. Then, very simply, she holds her dress up under her chin and pulls down her cotton panties to her knees. Her plump belly and the smooth inter-section of her thighs are revealed. The boys stare at this mystery in silence. A couple of crows call from the cornfield. One of them thinks Clara ought to give back the Clark bar.

Emerson would remember the girl's poise during this presentation, her dress held up and her feet planted evenly together. She looked out over their heads and into the cornfield behind them with just the shadow of a smile and maybe a recognition in her eyes that she had also uncovered something in them, as well as herself, which was just as mys-terious and perhaps to her advantage.

He would never see Aunt Rho without her clothes on. Even at night, going to bed, she seemed to put on more clothing than a lot of women wear during the day. But he knows the soft contours of her body, knows the fullness of her bosom intimately. Hugs in the morning and soothing comforts at night. The terror of a nightmare, the ache of a stomach crammed with crab apples, have often driven him whimpering across the dark hallway and into her bed. As he lay up against the warm, lenient shape of her, the knot in his belly would slowly come undone. Pillowed on her lavish bosom, his face scratched by the stiff lace of her camisole he would drift wonderfully back into sleep on the steady current of her heartbeat.

His mother rarely hugs him, and when she does embrace him she often breaks up the affection with a good-natured slap on his behind, as if he were an athlete being sent into the game by a coach. Edie Olson is embarrassed by the very feelings she could portray so aptly onstage. When she visits them in Ohio, she sternly lays down guidelines for Aunt Rho—what Sam should be eating, wearing, even to the choice of playmates, and she has a theory on the expression of affection. "There's been a recent discovery—he's a world famous psychologist at Columbia—that says all that gooey stuff smothers a child's natural inclination for independence."

Aunt Rho says nothing at such moments but stands, arms crossed, her face set plain, fixed in that small town mien prepared to greet astounding revelations. She is a founding member of an energetic and sometimes boisterous bridge club that meets regularly in the basement of the town hall. The game has been played for many years. She also sings in the Congregational Church choir, and her voice is a sweet soprano, often sharp. Sam has heard her several times, though she has never urged him to attend Sunday school. She also has the company, six days a week, of the five women who work with her at the High Standard Café. She is Kurt Olson's sister, and most everyone in town knows the story about Billy Brown. Sometimes, as Sam snuggles deeper into her embrace, he thinks she would be all alone if it were not for him, even with her friends and bridge players. "It's all right, dumpling." She would hug him tighter. "That mean old bellyache is just about gone. There it goes. I can feel it drifting away, drifting away. There it goes."

But she hasn't always been by herself. Sam, playing indoors on a rainy day, would often take down from her bureau the picture in a silver frame. Billy Brown stares back. He stands stiffly in his soldier's uniform and looks like the farm boy he was—off on an outlandish excursion and just a little sheepish because the jaunt might be fun as well as dangerous. He wears a forage cap cocked over one ear, and his large, square hands are attached to wrists like the naked sticks of a scarecrow. The picture was taken in Hoboken, New Jersey, just before he got on a boat to cross the Atlantic and join Pershing's First Army. He's killed two weeks later at the St. Milhieu Salient. Aunt Rho has shown Sam a photograph of his grave in a huge cemetery located somewhere in France. A family member of Billy's sent it to her. To Sam the cemetery looks like a huge lawn with many, many white crosses, all the same, but a red mark has been placed on a tiny cross in the distance.

Billy Brown is further defined for Sam one evening. He has rushed into the house and run upstairs to use the bathroom, and he comes upon Aunt Rho just as she is drying her long hair. It falls upon her shoulders like a luminous cape, the golden strands turning silver. She laughs and blushes to be so caught in disarray. Her eyes are the deepening blue of the evening sky. Sam is used to seeing her hair wound tight in thin braids and then into a coronet pinned to her head by long ebony pins.

But he has never seen her so unfastened, and there is something careless and younger about her. He imagines her like this on the arm of Billy Brown at the town Fourth of July picnic down at the river. That picnic has just happened, so it's easy for him to picture the two of them, Billy in his uniform like in the picture, and Aunt Rho with her hair loose and lifting in the river breeze. They made a nice couple, everyone agreed, and they were to get married when the war was over. He was a good farmer, and he could have brought the Olson place back. Sam has heard all this talk around town.

Once, the pain in his belly becomes serious and his fever goes high. Pneumonia. His mother is trying out a play in Boston, and she has to fly into Columbus, where the minister from the Congregational Church meets her. "I had hellfire and brimstone the whole way," she says. "Life on the wicked stage. I got an earful."

"I'm sorry, Edie," Aunt Rho says. "He's the only one I know with good enough tires on his car. And I couldn't leave Sam."

He half hears their talk through the fever, but he smells her in the room—a spicy, brisk smell. She's left something important to be with him, and her bracelets clink together as he feels her cool hand on his brow. "Yes, he's very hot," she says. Her voice carries no accusation but agrees with the reason for her being there, for her interrupting her career. Enough of a fever; enough of a reason. As the fever subsides and he hears more clearly, she sounds angry at something.

She and Aunt Rho bicker more than usual, one or two real arguments. It sounds like a radio dial being switched, and he can't tell if it is one long quarrel or several spats during the several days she's there. He gathers it has something to do with his father, but Sam's name comes up also. So maybe they argue because of him. One night, the sound of his mother sobbing pulls him from sleep, and he is frightened by the unnatural, foreign noise of it, the drowning gasps and halts in the dark so unlike her vigorous voice. He hopes she might be lying up against Aunt Rho, even as a grown woman but still being taken in and soothed by that boundless warmth.

The night before she rejoins the play in Boston, he hears Aunt Rho in the kitchen, talking straight out. "Put some clothes on, Edie, when you're around the boy."

"The ills of this society come from hiding," his mother answers. She is calmer now, getting ready to leave, and it sounds like she's speaking lines from her part. She could be rehearsing. "We are only as free as our inhibitions." She talks about some doctor disagreeing with another one. She says they have "broken"—that's the word she uses—over nakedness. Sam thinks that's pretty funny.

Actually, he's used to seeing her in various forms of undress. The hotel rooms and small flats they have shared have forced upon them an intimacy uncommon for mother and son but one that has become normal for them. She has studied scripts in the red kimono, washed out stockings and undergarments wearing only a slip, lounged in one of his father's shirts that hung to her knees. She hates to wear clothes, though she would never consider a part that asks for the slightest nudity. "I'll leave that to Gypsy Rose Lee," she would say knowingly. It's as if she keeps her personal and her professional garments in separate armoires, less in one than in the other.

On the morning she flies back to Boston, Sam is on the mend, and he wakes to find her in his room. She keeps a lot of her belongings with Aunt Rho, retrieving them each season so she can travel light with just the steamer trunk. Some blouses are hanging in his closet.

He watches her quietly as she looks over each garment, holding one or two up to the light. She is entirely nude but for a flesh colored brassiere. "Oh, you're awake," she says when she turns to leave. He now notices the thin pink ribbon around her waist and from this ribbon another one passes down over her stomach to disappear between her legs. The thick wedge of her pubic hair is dark. "How are you feeling darling? Much better, I'm sure." She's come to his bedside and tests his brow; a couple of the blouses drape over the other arm. "You're almost well, and Mommy must get back to work."

Close up, Sam sees that the pink ribbon bisects the triangle of the pubic hair and is fastened to a wider piece of material snugged between her thighs. She has noticed his stare. "Some rig, isn't it?" she says. Then, in the glare of the morning light, she tells him all about menstruation— when and why it happens. Even what it looks like. Her language is clinical, straightforward, and he understands all she tells him. She pulls the Kotex a little to one side so he can see the small stain on its white texture. "I guess I better change this before I get on the plane. So, Sam." She readjusts the belt. "You see what it's like now. You see what's it like being a woman."

Years later, honeymooning with Amanda in Florence, Emerson would come upon his mother's expression in one of the old paintings in the Ufizzi. The Virgin Mary getting the news of her pregnancy. It was the same smile—the same smile he remembered on his mother's face that morning in East Liverpool, puzzled but resigned all the same.

THREE

"IN CASE THE POLICE stop you for something," the undertaker had said, "show them this document." He offered Emerson a yellow form as they stood in the parking lot of Crestview Meadows. He had already handed over the rectangular brown box Emerson had wedged under his right arm. He felt like a football player ready for scrimmage. "She had a long life," the man said, and then just for a fraction of a second, he seemed to measure Sam Emerson, his eyes going oblique. The guy was trying to figure his age, Emerson guessed, because he didn't look like the son of an almost hundred-year-old woman. He looked more like a grandson, and that was his luck, his genes. A man of a certain age who didn't look it. At his last checkup: blood pressure: 120 over 60. Blood sugar: 103. Bad cholesterol: 114, and good cholesterol: 45. PSA: 3.1. Triglycerides: 122. He swam laps at the Y three days a week, lifted weights. "Biologically, you're about twenty years younger than your chronological age. All you have to look out for," his doctor had told him, "is a truck when you cross the street." But the box under his arm had nudged his mortality. Now, he was next, as he had said to Nick only the night before.

Route 220 was clear, and Emerson pulled out and floored the Ford, amusing himself with a possible encounter. "Mind if I look at what you have there, sir?" The state trooper would be youngish but commanding in height and uniform.

"Not at all, officer."

"Sir, mind telling me what's in that brown box?"

"My mother is in that box, officer, and here is the certificate to prove it."

He had tucked the declaration of cremation into the side panel of the car. It was a curious diploma, and he might just carry it around for a little while.

The nursing home had called him as the kitchen was being cleaned up for the night. "Your mother has slipped away," was how the nurse had put it. An unusually discreet exit for Edith Olson—slipping away. He sat down at Sterling's desk in the corner as the cooks and the new guy doing dishes hung up pans, washed down countertops, and wiped off the stove burners. Food was put away into the walk-in cooler. They had had a busy night. He pondered his new status, motherless—but was that altogether new? He was about to call Phoebe when the phone rang and it was Sterling to say he would be back at work the day after tomorrow. "Well, you were ready for it, weren't you?" his partner said when Emerson told him the news.

"Sure." He heard the subtext in Wicks's voice—he hadn't been ready for his nephew's death at age nineteen at the hands of white cops. That's what he was saying. That was their difference.

"Hey, listen, on your way back," his friend had suavely shifted the subject, "why not go by that place in Wilkinsburg and see how they're doing with the new cooler. Summer's a coming in, and our old compressor is beginning to huff and puff. Give them a push."

"Good idea," Emerson replied, and it was a good idea. The trip back would not just be a funereal task but would serve another purpose—mundane and distracting but serving life. Back to business. He credited his partner with the diversion—it was a kind of therapy. He walked through the dining room of the restaurant to the bar, where he poured himself a shot of George Dickel. Constance had already left for the night; her roommate had picked her up. Only the intimate lighting of the bar area glowed so the city's skyline illuminated the area, and it resembled the set of a mystery film, black and white. He used the phone at the bar to leave a message with a reporter on the *Tribune Review*. He had given him his mother's obituary months ago, and the guy had offered to put it on the AP wire. The news was out. He had done that for her, given her a closure, a sendoff. What else could he do? He sipped the bourbon. A final marker of some kind, but where? She had given him no instructions other than cremation. He was supposed to find the place himself, the last gambit of that scavenger hunt she had played with him in lieu of an ordinary relationship. Find Edie Olson. Like one of those cartoons in newspapers of years past where you connected dots and all at once the face of a movie star appeared. Linda Darnell. Bette Davis. Edith Olson.

When he reached Phoebe she did not suggest he come over to her house. "I'm flying to Seattle in the morning. The bank there has a legal matter I'm involved in." She quickly told him the nature of the business in general terms. It sounded hastily put together.

"Pretty sudden, isn't it? What about Nick? Who's staying with him?" he asked with a hopefulness that shamed him a little; he was just too damn eager.

"I told you—you just forgot." She sounded irritated. "I should be with you now, Sam, and I'm sorry not to be. But you've been expecting this for a long time. My sister is coming to look after Nick, but why don't the two of you take in a game?"

"The Pirates are going on the road tomorrow."

"Oh." The ensuing silence suggested she had given him her best idea. And yes, she should be with him at this moment. Goddamnit, his mother had just died, however sketchy that relationship had been—wasn't this curtain call in the nursing home just another abandonment? The last abandonment? His mind had raced the course of yearning and rejection and then around again to come up to his and Phoebe's own prospects, and his mother's mortal desertion he had been offering as if it were some kind of trophy.

But what the hell, he had only wanted to come over and sit on the steps of her back porch in the moist cool of the night, the two of them beside each other on the steps to talk quietly of ordinary things and listen to the night sounds of the city. "I'll be back in two days," Phoebe was saying. "I promise you my undivided attention then." He finished his drink, rinsed the glass, and made a final check of the kitchen. Everyone had gone. He turned out the lights.

So this morning, driving back with Edith Olson's ashes, he pondered the next move. "What am I to do with you?" he asked half aloud. "That's always been the problem, hasn't it, Edie?" His hand had fallen to rest on the box beside him on the seat. Not just any hole in the ground would do, and as Sterling had whimsically pointed out, he had no mantel on which to put her ashes in his apartment. He had just gone by THE TABLE-TOP—*This Is the Place*. Maybe the kitchen was open again; he hoped the cook had returned; in there listening to her radio and putting everything back the way it was. No questions asked, he advised the owner.

He clicked off the other landmarks and then left Route 220 for a road that led into Wilkinsburg. Stopping at the company doing the new cooler only took a few minutes. They were surprised to see him. Was anything wrong? No, he was just passing by, he told them. Just passing by with his mother's ashes, he didn't say. The job was going smoothly, they assured him, and the installation would be on schedule. Soon. Then he remembered a place he had discovered on an earlier trip to Mansfield, on another trip to see her. Rudy's Diner served biscuits with sausage gravy, and he found the business still wedged between a vacant bank and a string of dusty storefronts that looked even dustier than before. The cluster of buildings reminded him of Benson Falls and the boutiques Amanda had tried to make a go of.

Her most successful venture had been a ski shop with an inventory that changed to tennis and hiking accessories when the snow melted. Amanda looked smart in the different togs—she was her own best advertisement—and the place became a hangout for women who rarely bought much and were not very good in any of the sports represented but who vicariously basked in Amanda's appearance. It became an informal women's center, the members all about his wife's age and brisk with gossip. They would get together to talk and smoke and, in winter, gather around a pot of mulled wine she kept on a hotplate near the cash register. Sometimes one of them would bring a fondue to dip into. Emerson could never figure out where these women came from; they resembled no one in town. Their strident laughter often came into the kitchen, and now and then, one of them would wander in to watch him prep, a cigarette in her hand and a flushed expression in the eyes. She would ask about a recipe, peer into a pot, and say she wanted to bring her husband to dinner sometime.

The stools of Rudy's Diner were covered with a glossy red vinyl, and Emerson straddled one of them, halfway down the row. It was before noon, and he was the only customer. Mere protocol made him peruse the worn menu card; he knew what he wanted, what had made him make this detour. The counter woman stood ready, and the kitchen behind the rear partition purred expectantly.

"Tell Rudy I'll have some of that good gravy with a biscuit," he told her pleasantly.

"Rudy's not here," she said. "He went to Florida about ten years back."

"Well, that's too bad. But how about the biscuits? They still here?"

"Fresh made," she said. "I guess you want coffee."

She scrawled on her pad, tore off the sheet, and placed it on the sill of the small window that looked into the kitchen. A pinkish hand appeared in the opening and lifted the slip delicately, then disappeared.

Emerson's system craved the dish. All at once, he felt he had to consume it almost whole, cram the thick gravy and biscuit into his mouth, even though he wasn't especially hungry. He felt like he would turn inside out, come apart if he didn't. The dish had become an all-purpose antidote that could cure anything. The High Standard Café had served this homely fare, and that was where he had first tasted it. His clientele at Sam's Place would be surprised to see him on the stool of Rudy's Diner, eagerly waiting for this simple dish, and he laughed a little. The *Gourmet* chef exposed. His customers would never eat at such a place, not even pause as they drove by. But the heavy white gravy with chunks of sausage was plasma he needed from time to time to restore himself, though he would never dwell on the idea, for it seemed so sentimental and maybe a little snobbish. Too patently ironic perhaps, with a humbleness about it some might think showy. It was the sort of dish he and Amanda should have served. He had come all this way, Emerson thought, and made this detour into Wilkinsburg, Pennsylvania, to discover what would have been successful in Benson Falls, Vermont, those many years back.

The combination of gravy and biscuit just tasted damn good—that's all there was to it—and this version at Rudy's Diner was passed through the small service window from the kitchen piping hot and redolent of sage. Some other spice he couldn't identify but wouldn't ask about. The biscuit was first rate, too, straight mixed, he could tell, not from a box—buttery and crisp around the edges and clearly just out of the oven. The food and his sudden appetite were made for each other, a perfect fit. Several years ago, he had talked to Sterling Wicks about doing a version of this dish as an appetizer, but his partner had only looked at him wall-eyed. The biscuit and gravy on his plate compared well with the combination he remembered Aunt Rho turned out at the High Standard Café. But, of course, hers could never be equaled.

So, Sam Emerson got back on the road feeling fortified and ready to handle whatever might be waiting for him around the next turn. Even the contents of the brown box were no longer a problem, though he still had no plan. The container lay beside him harmless in its simple dimensions. He patted its cardboard surface. He did not dwell on the contents or on the sediment of memories they represented. What he looked forward to as he drove through the tunnel entrance to Pittsburgh was a swim to loosen him up. Especially after that biscuit and thick gravy. He just had time for some laps before he had to get to the restaurant. The water temperature in the Y pool was on the cool side lately, just as Sam Emerson liked it. He sometimes thought the management heated the water too much to accommodate or even attract older swimmers. "How's the temp on the water, Mr. Emerson?" the lifeguard asked.

"Just about right. It could be cooler." And everything else seemed just about right, too. Sterling Wicks would be back in the kitchen tomorrow, bantering with the line cooks, directing the hectic pace of their preparations with off-handed flair. Emerson imagined him with the sky blue toque cocked jauntily over one ear, but he worried that Jimmy Overstreet's death had loosened the grasp of their friendship. Their talk the other morning had been stiff, almost formal, as if the nephew's death had reminded both of them of the differences they had worked to ignore all these years.

Emerson pulled himself through the water with enthusiastic strokes and a heavy crash of his hands that sometimes annoyed other swimmers if the pool was crowded. It was his style, lumbering but efficient, and he imagined the smooth ghosts of Buster Crabbe and Johnny Weissmuller swimming beside him, keeping up with him, as he shaped the arc of his arms and made clean kicks with his feet. He played with the idea that each lap reduced the distance between him and Phoebe. He was swimming across the Monongahela, then down around the point into the Allegheny, and across its current to the North Shore, where he would pull himself up and out and walk the several blocks to her house. He'd read a story like that—someone swimming home by way of neighbors' swimming pools, but he couldn't remember if the guy had made it. In his version, Phoebe would be waiting to towel him off, and then they would have a nice supper and make love. A near perfect day.

"This is how you seduced those coeds at Penn State," Phoebe had accused him playfully. It was early in their affair, and she was still a little uneasy about Constance Ho and the other restaurant staff seeing her disappear into the penthouse above—even if only for supper. Emerson had promised her a quick meal on her way home from work, and the muffled sounds of the restaurant below being readied for the evening business made the apartment feel even more snug. An April rain splattered the glass wall to pull a scrim across the skyline of Pittsburgh.

In the penthouse's small kitchen, he had stirred a risotto sprinkled with fresh peas—just come to market—slices of roasted red pepper and slivers of finocchio he had crisped in butter and olive oil. The Barbaresco was light and radiant, and Phoebe's pink and blond complexion glowed before the blurred image of the city. She liked to eat, which delighted him—always a good sign in a woman.

She resembled a Renoir flower girl. Emerson was always surprised by how different she was from the subtle and mannered women who had usually attracted him. His infatuation tickled him—yes, more than that. Her appearance had instantly fascinated him and continued to do so. Nor did Phoebe seem satisfied with the natural flamboyance of her hair and coloring but added elaborate costume jewelry to this exuberance, often with a décolletage that mocked the severe cut of her business suits. All of it somehow worked, and rather than making her look cheap, the overall effect suggested she carried out a joyful prank, a kind of pull on the nose of those who might want to determine how a girl from Turtle Creek should comport herself. Moreover, she was at the top of her profession. Her success appealed to him as much as her appearance.

"How did you get interested in cooking?" she asked early in their relationship.

"The woman who raised me, my great aunt Rho. She was a great cook. Nothing elaborate or fancy but solid food. Worked as a cook in a small town cafeteria. There she is. The woman in the middle. I guess she was the reason."

He had directed her attention to the large framed photograph that hung on the wall of the small kitchen and bar. She studied the picture of six women who huddled together to lean on a counter. Their eyes met the camera, and they were laughing, a little pleased to have their picture taken but little shy about it, too. Frilly blouses burst from the bib of their uniforms. A large-faced woman in the center held a spatula that clearly signaled her authority. He pointed to her again.

"Basic stuff," Emerson had continued. "Chicken and dumplings. Pot roast. Meatloaf. Biscuits and gravy. Pies. Nothing complicated, but that's the most difficult food to cook well, to make interesting. She made it interesting." He added broth to the risotto and stirred it. "My father took the picture."

"And your mother? Was she a good cook?"

"Not that I remember. Never had a real kitchen. She was in the theatre, so we ate in restaurants when we were together."

"Did you ever cook for your mother?" Phoebe had returned to the barstool to watch him prepare the rice. She used what he had begun to think of as her quiet voice. He could imagine her talking to patients like that.

"She ate here a couple of times. Downstairs in the restaurant. When I was little, I sometimes fixed tea for her. She'd come back from making the rounds, auditions. She worked at Macy's too. This was when I lived with her in New York. A brief time. I'd boil water on a hotplate and drop in a tea bag. Voila!" He laughed, but Phoebe had remained serious.

"That's sweet," she finally said. "Then Penn State."

"Yes, the Hotel School. This was before they called these places culinary institutes. It seemed like a good way to make a living. And I have. But I guess Aunt Rho probably gave me the idea. Before I tell you anything more, Doctor, perhaps I should find out your rates. Are you expensive?"

"Yes, but I'm worth it." Phoebe laughed, and then a lull came between them. "Then marriage," she continued again in that voice that softy probed.

"Yes, marriage."

Phoebe leaned forward again to look at the photograph of the six women on the wall. Emerson stirred the risotto.

He had served their supper on the low black lacquer table set beside the window wall. Several thick futons surrounded the table, so it was a little like eating in bed, a perception that sometimes was not far off of the mark. He had made an appealing setting on the glossy surface of the table. The bottle of wine in its silver salver, a bowl of mixed greens, a basket of crusty bread, and the two plates of risotto, redolent and colorful. A single candle burned in a heavy silver candlestick. Phoebe had gracefully folded herself onto one of the cushions and pulled a napkin across her lap. She was ready to eat.

"That's where I met Sterling, but we hooked up much later. Did this place together much later. Also," he paused to raise his glass to her and then sipped the wine, "that's where I met Amanda. My former wife," he added perhaps a little too quickly. Phoebe's eyes had passed over him discreetly.

She had noted a detail about him and put it away for further consideration, to be placed within the overall profile. A loose edge not quite tucked into his narrative had been caught up by her quick mind. Or it might have only been her contact lenses, Emerson thought. The lenses gave her most random glance an unusual intensity, as if she might be taking in not just the immediate object but also the whole field around it, all in focus. Just then she had heard a door close within him, and by habit she was urged to toe it open. "Go on."

Emerson encapsulated his marriage, the failed country inn, and the attempt to work together here in Pittsburgh. The slow drain of their intimacy. He hoped he was giving a fair report, balanced, but he began to feel uninteresting, stereotypical. He could have been giving another's history—not his own, which he had always thought to be unique, and the sense that it might not be saddened him. "It's like I'm one of those people down in the street." He nodded at the vertical shafts of the city's center. "I can see myself walking around another time or maybe that figure of me is still doing business down there, and I'm up here."

"And which is the original, the first copy?"

Emerson smiled. His own imagery had trapped him. "Why here, of course," he said at last. "Right here," he had almost added. He questioned how much of this speech was a line, a routine patter made up for another dinner guest. He couldn't deny it.

"And Amanda? What of her?"

"We used to talk now and then, but no more. She didn't like it here. She was happier in Vermont." Phoebe took a bite of the risotto, her eyes lowered. He could tell she was evaluating his words and that they had been inadequate.

"But the real story, Doctor, is to be found at the High Standard Café." He gestured toward the photograph on the wall. "I'd go there after school. Do my homework in one of the booths, and have my dinner. Around nine o'clock, Aunt Rho would clean up the grill—dinner hour was early in East Liverpool—and then we'd drive home together. Wonderful smells in that place. Generous smells of fresh food. Old guys sitting around, talking and smoking. Town regulars. A few old ladies by themselves. Families with babies. High school kids hanging out, eating pie. Everyone taken care of and served a decent meal. Affection and care poured over everything, like the gravy. To serve someone food was a way of showing affection. I guess I learned that. Looking forward to the next meal—that's a kind of optimism, isn't it?"

Phoebe had smiled. Her look was agreeable. Then she put her fork down and gave a small laugh.

"What?"

"Oh, I'm thinking we could be something of a team. I treat people who have problems with food, who eat too much or not enough, and you think up new ways to get them to the table." She took a sip of wine and looked merrily at him over the glass rim.

"You know we really could be, Phoebe. We really could be a team." Emerson was suddenly faced with the full measure of his feelings for her, and the urgency of these feelings stunned him a little. He was afraid she might feel their heat and be scared away. She might have noticed the flare of his thoughts, for she had drawn herself in, looked a little uncomfortable, and turned to regard the skyline. The drizzle had lifted, and a mournful shaft of sunlight caught up with the day just as it disappeared over the horizon.

They silently agreed to turn to other topics. Her son's school projects. She was amused to find herself standing on the sidelines cheering Nick playing lacrosse, a game she had yet to understand. Her ex-husband's late night phone calls had forced her to get an unlisted number. She opened her purse and fetched Emerson a card from it with the new number. She had all the legal lines drawn up, and if they didn't work—well, she'd do something else. Emerson talked about the restaurant. He related a funny incident with a customer. The mundane exchanges relaxed them; even the occasional pauses did not embarrass them or urge idle chatter upon them just to fill space. They were easy in the silences. Meanwhile, Emerson had brought dessert to the table. Phoebe looked down at the wedge of chocolate mousse as if it were a summons. She fell back on the futon, arms dramatically stretched out. "Oh, Sam, I give up. Come. Undo and do me so I can get home."

Emerson eyed the clock on the wall above the pool. He'd give himself fifteen more minutes because of that little snack at Rudy's Diner, and he selected a passage to review from a more recent talk with Phoebe. "Let's get off this ferry boat back and forth across the rivers and get married," he said.

"What a splendid offer." Her voice had become sly. "And so elegantly put, too." She was just back from a night meeting at the bank.

"The whole picture is out of focus. The rivers will start running backward."

"My goodness." She paused, and he imagined her removing a large earring. "If we lived together, you would feed me and make me fat. Fatso Konopski. Be patient."

"I want you in the rest of my life. I want you to share this view with me forever."

"Oh, Sam, you're going to make me cry. Now listen, darling, please understand how difficult it is for me to put both you and Nick into my one life right now. I don't want to lose him. I will not lose Nick, do you understand? I won't risk that. Ever."

"I understand," he replied quickly. Too quickly perhaps, "But, awful things are happening here. You remember the young woman I saw at the 7-Eleven, talking about God's will. How things would even out? She had a little boy with her."

"I guess so. The little boy stared at you, you said. As if he knew you."

"That's right." Hearing Phoebe say it startled him. "Well, she and the kid were murdered last night. It was on the late news. They lived on the other side of the slope on Olympia. Her boyfriend took a hammer and bashed their heads in as they slept. Both of them."

"How awful. Are you sure it's the same woman?"

"I'm certain."

"You can't protect everyone, Sam," Phoebe said softly. "You can't protect me. I'm not sure I want protection. We've been over this."

"Why not? What's wrong with that? Goddamnit, has *protection* become a dirty word? Must it be a synonym for prison? I guess I'm sounding like a bad tune in the Feminist Songbook."

Phoebe said nothing for a little time. Then, "Sam, I understand how you feel. It's wonderful, and I am grateful that you want to help me. You being here for me means a lot. Believe me." Her tone was the same she used when she opened a gift from him, say, a sweater or a pair of earrings. She would study the article, considering not just how it might fit into her wardrobe but also what terms·might accompany the gift. Then she would say she would wear the sweater. Yes, she would accept the earrings. Thanks. "And I do love you," she said finally. "Heaven help me, I do."

A tugboat nosed upriver under the bridges that glinted with rush hour traffic. A jetliner banked over the Northside. On another late afternoon—a Sunday—the two of them had stood on the balcony to witness a similar panorama, arms around each other. Emerson had raised his other arm to encompass a different airliner, the rivers, and the barge traffic—the whole amazing prospect of the city. The two of them had become part of one of those murals found in a post office, he suggested—they had become players in a larger picture, a history. Pittsburgh's history. But on this evening, he worried he was running out of things to say. In fact, he may have said too much and had only given her reasons to keep the distance between them. The roar of the jetliner's engines gradually faded away.

Phoebe's reluctance, her unfathomable woman's will to seek her own solutions, frustrated Emerson. He wanted to be good for her. The subtle bantering that had often challenged him in the best of ways—an important ingredient of her appeal—was now being used against him and against a plan he was certain was good for her and for Nick—in their best interests. Well, best for all of them. It really wasn't fair. She was just being plain stubborn, even mulish, he decided as he swam. He had offered to put her future beside his and lift her into a lair of security and plenty he had created high above the city, and she waved the offer away. He became a fly pestering her. At the same time, he understood that this plea from his heart might sound to her like the drumbeat of a forced march, but still her rejection hurt him. *Lack of closure,* she had said the other night about his mother, and the phrase suggested to him the unfinished and incomplete situation between them. He swam an extra ten laps, thinking some watchful god would reward him with an answer.

Sam Emerson had always sought the approval of young, ambitious women like Constance Ho. He was aware he responded to them as if they were surrogate daughters, though with a flirtatious sexual tinge sometimes that bothered him a little, but he really did want to help them. Just the other night, his front, Cynthia, had received his attention. Her boyfriend was becoming more of a problem for her—and her personal situation could be a problem for the restaurant as well. If she couldn't work, he'd have to take over her duties. All of them—these women who attracted him—were serious about themselves and worked hard. Amanda had seemed to be of that mold at first, but it wasn't fair to say she had deceived him. She had been trying to tell him the truth about herself in her own way; he just hadn't wanted to hear her message.

He could select the right ingredients for a dish, so why couldn't he correctly weigh the elements of his life? True, he had grown up with artifice: the residue of that make-believe waited for him in his car in the Y's parking lot. And it had been fun mostly, but that life hadn't prepared him for how events really took place, the vagaries of the human will.

The younger Sam Emerson had fallen in love with the idea of falling in love with Amanda Benson. The whole town in Vermont bore her family name. "They have this old inn," he told Sterling Wicks, "that's been vacant for years. It's been in their family for generations." His whole future seemed to have been arranged by this girl who had been put beside him in class, both of them learning to cook. He could not believe his luck, for she also routinely gave him her trim, athletic body— she captained the women's field hockey team—cheerfully marching up the three floors to his apartment, diaphragm in place.

"She's a nice girl," Sterling Wicks said when Emerson announced their marriage plans. They were in the last week of school, and the two friends lounged in the booth of their favorite off-campus dive. They would soon be certified cooks, diplomas in hand, and Wicks already had an offer from a casino in Las Vegas.

"Nice girl. What does that mean?"

Wicks made a face. "Don't pay me no mind."

"Come on, out with it."

"Just not my type, pal. She makes me edgy." He sipped at his beer. "Too hale and hearty. I'm used to chicks looking for a little novelty. I always think Amanda wants to loan me some of her equality. Probably my own brand of prejudice."

"She's just eager to be friends. She likes you a lot."

"Uh-huh. Well, I like her too. She's nice. Like I said." The offer from the hotel in Nevada had puffed up Wicks. He was always a little cocky, but this afternoon his smallest gesture crackled. "So you lovebirds are going to fix up the old family inn? Don't forget to tidy up the manger."

Emerson had mentioned their plans for the old place. They would have to redo the kitchen, but no trouble getting a mortgage. Her uncle ran the local bank. They'd start with a small menu. Maybe a prix fixe with corresponding wines. Amanda would do the desserts—she had developed a flair for them already. They'd use only the freshest of local products—nothing better than Vermont dairy products—Vermont cheeses, they're becoming famous. Some very good chevre was being made up there now. Trout from the region's streams, lamb from its hillsides. Going over this future the other afternoon had gotten them so excited they had fucked themselves silly on the floor of the apartment. And they would have kids, he told Sterling. Vermont was a great place to raise kids. He might even take up skiing. Amanda had been skiing since she could walk. A glow had come into Sterling's eyes as he listened. He held up one hand.

"Then one snowy winter night, and everything's cozy by the fire. Chestnuts crackling. Sleigh bells ting-a-linging outside." Sterling had leaned across the table, confidential. "Your register is *complis*. You are cooking up a storm, and Amanda is flaming the pears. Then this dude wanders into your place, and he strolls over to the piano and sits down and starts singing. He's singing 'White Christmas.' Man, it's Bing Crosby! It's Bing-Fucking-Crosby, and you've got it made!"

His friend's teasing often returned to haunt Emerson in the following years. Once a card arrived from the Bahamas, "Bing showed up yet?" Amanda had asked what he meant, and Emerson had shrugged. "Sterling is nuts." After cooking in Las Vegas, Wicks had become the sous chef on a cruise ship, while the Benson Falls Inn continued to post losses. Emerson had begun to wonder if her parents had sent Amanda to the Hotel School not so much to learn how to manage the business as to bring someone back who might. But the place frustrated his best efforts. It was too far from the major ski areas, and the train that brought up city people for the tranquil air and fall color had been discontinued the year they took over the inn. The rural roads were often closed down in winter. Local residents were not very interested in what Emerson cooked, and when he finally put hamburgers on the menu it was too late—the place was considered too high-falutin' for the village. He and Amanda gave a party five nights a week, and almost no one showed up. She stood at the entrance in the evening, menus in hand as the recorded strings of Mantovani plied the empty dining room. Even her family and relatives had stopped coming.

"I sometimes feel like the hired hand," he told her one night. Amanda had given up playing hostess and had begun to open different shops in the inn's creaky lobby. She tried wooden salad bowls and wooden toys, then a real estate business followed by a health food store. The latter seemed a contradiction to the foods saturated in butter and sauces he turned out in the kitchen. They joked about it. He often gave much of his evening's work to the old veteran who washed the dishes, a turkey-necked alcoholic who kept hounds. Emerson suspected the dogs ate well. Amanda accepted their failure, almost cheerfully, as if the Benson Falls Inn was supposed to fail—part of her family's tradition. He had been brought into the family, he began to think, to make the inn fail better.

"Of course, you must take it," his mother had said. They had come to East Liverpool together for Aunt Rho's funeral. She had left the house and the six acres to them both, but his mother had signed over her half to him. "Do you expect me to grow strawberries in East Liverpool?" Edith Olson had drawn herself up into the intimidating persona she played in television soaps.

"Well, do you think we're going to sell strawberries?" he asked her.

"No, but you can do something with it. Be sensible. That place in Vermont is a dump." Her voice took on the matriarchal timbre that had become her signature. The East Liverpool VFW was doing a ham supper to feed all the people who had shown up for Aunt Rho's funeral.

How different Pittsburgh looked this afternoon after his swim from that other afternoon when he had walked over to the Greyhound bus from the train station on that final leg to East Liverpool. It would be his last trip to Ohio. Today, the city's skyline was polished, the air clean, but on that other trip, the soot of the steel mills had charged his lungs. The thick air had made him strangely light-headed, or had it been his sudden inspiration? It was several years after Aunt Rho's funeral, and he had been going to Ohio to close the deal with a developer who was building a shopping center. The steel mills had closed down, thirty thousand men out of work, but Pittsburgh was somehow coming back. And so was he. The Olson place was a parcel of land that would complete the developer's plan. In the street, on his way to the bus station, he had looked up at Mt. Washington as it loomed above the city, across the Monongahela River. The city excited him, and in a flash, he knew he was right.

"This is the place, Amanda." He called her from a pay phone in the bus station.

"Really?"

"The money I'm getting from the farm would give us a fresh start. Here in Pittsburgh. The place has been waiting for us. Right here."

"Don't do anything rash," Amanda said. What had she been afraid of, Emerson had wondered—success?

They originally called the restaurant The Tables on Mt. Washington, a name that began to sound foolish to them, though its hint of elegance had pleased them initially. The spectacular view had attracted business, and then a feature story of the young couple cooking together on the height above the city put them in the Pittsburgh spotlight. When Sterling Wicks showed up one day with his silent laughter and way with fresh fish, their reservation book filled up and they had so much business they began turning people away. Their achievement amazed them, caught them unprepared—it had seemed so easy after the fruitless toil in Benson Falls. It was amazing, Sam Emerson reflected—somehow he had become successful.

Why not call someone at Mansfield College about a memorial for his mother—a place where her ashes could be deposited? The idea had come to him as he showered after his swim. It would be the right place for her, fitting. She had put the place on the map. The theatre festival she had started had brought distinction to the college and the community. He could help pay for the memorial, even offer a scholarship in her name. The Edith Olson Fellowship in Drama. Something like that, and he was pleased with himself as he pictured her fingering those amber beads and smiling over the honor. He stepped lightly into the restaurant's basement, where the wines were stored. He would call Phoebe tonight to try out the idea. She had given him her hotel's number in Seattle. He was certain she would approve.

Upstairs, the restaurant was quiet, a hush at this time in the late afternoon that was different and bothered him a little. One of the prep cooks was whistling in the kitchen. Emerson came face to face with Constance, just inside the door. "What are you doing here?" She had startled him. "You're early," he managed to say.

A sliver of a smile noted his surprise. "Cynthia called me, boss. She's not feeling well. So, I came in to take reservations. Then—," she paused. The fall of long black hair gently swayed as she shifted her head toward the bar.

"That be Sam Emerson?" the customer announced. He was a sturdy figure, his voice torn from the larger amusement he obviously was keeping to himself—for now. It was a ragged sound and uneven. "That be the master of these revels?" Emerson was trying to place the voice and its speaker so teasingly familiar as he took the fleshy hand thrust toward him. "It takes you back a little, do it not?" the fellow continued. "I had hair in those days, but this be Teddy Pennyworth from the old days in Greenwich Village. Our moms were friends."

The man snorted once and then again, a clearing of the sinuses that apparently indicated amusement or perhaps some satisfaction with the amusement. He held Emerson's hand in a firm grip, but his head had swiveled owllike to take in Constance as she stood at the front desk, filling the reservation register. She had leaned against the writing surface with a schoolgirl's concentration.

Sam Emerson felt removed from the moment, as if some aberrant gust had sucked him up from the spot, so he was looking on from above. The light pouring through the glass wall normally etched the skyline across the river, but in his mind's eye he saw that hand in Rudy's Diner appear, pick up an order, and hold it to this light that bathed the interior of Sam's Place, and then disappear.

PROGRAM NOTES

Buying Some Stamps

Why didn't she use the ladies' room at the bus station? Young Sam knows the answer. And stamps were stamps no matter where you bought them. Why did she have to march him across Eighth Avenue to the main post office, him dragging his suitcase against the back of his legs, to this huge mausoleum of a place with walls and ceilings of marble that echoed in a way that made you sleepy? Multiplied every voice—her voice especially. He expects to see Roman senators lounging in their togas after a bath, like in his social studies books. But here, she's going into one of her routines. He hates it when she does these things, and he tries to look like someone not connected with her, like another person in line waiting to buy stamps. It is Christmas time, and long lines of people wait at every service window. People mailing packages and buying war bonds. Buying stamps.

"Ooh-ooh-ooh." She's jiggling up and down, almost going from one foot to another. "If I don't get to a restroom soon, there's going to be an ac–ci–dent." Her tone is merry, like everyone should be happy about the emergency, and though her words are ostensibly just for him to hear, the people around them turn to stare. One or two smile sympathetically. His mother holds the tip of her tongue between her teeth, a good-natured grimace, perhaps a self-abuse intended to distract her from a larger distress. To young Sam, she looks like one of those Indian masks in the Natural History Museum.

He wants to walk away. He wants to walk out of the building, down the steps, but then what? He can see himself walking down the enormous flight of steps outside, somehow getting smaller and smaller as he descends. He has no place to go. His schoolmates were still asleep when he took up his post on the porch of the Village Variety to wait for the early bus to New York City. The store had not opened yet, and the clock face of the town hall was a second moon in the black sky. When he had passed through the darkened dormitory, he smelled sausages cooking in the kitchen on the other side of the dining room, sausages and pancakes being made for the other kids and their parents just before the Christmas break. It was a school tradition—kids and their parents, who had come to pick them up, all sitting down to pancakes and sausages.

Later, his classmates would throw their suitcases into the trunks of the family cars and jump onto the cozy upholstery of the back seats that smelled of a mother's perfume or the musty odor of a family dog. But he is taking the Greyhound bus and will be on the road most of the day, the bus grinding down to stop at every railroad crossing in Connecticut, spending hours, it seemed, parked in front of little stores like the Village Variety, where passengers waited.

If she had only told him she needed stamps, he could have gotten some at a couple of the post offices where the bus had stopped to pick up more passengers. But not many, because everyone was already home, he figured, trimming Christmas trees, wrapping presents. But here he was, almost the only passenger, and he half expected the driver to pull up some place, going no farther because it was his hometown, and his own family was waiting at table. And young Sam would have to fend for himself, get the rest of the way on his own. Also, he hadn't been able to sleep much that night either. Thinking about Nancy Wilson.

During the Christmas Hop, they had slipped away from the gymnasium and found a corner in the girls' locker room, where they had ground against each other like serious lunatics. "I'll help you out," she had whispered and gently pushed him away. Deftly, as if she had done the trick many times before, she unbuttoned his pants and pulled his raging hard-on out into the cool air. With just a few flicks of her wrist, similar to the wicked backhand that was the secret weapon of the girls' tennis team, she milked him, holding his jetting penis away from them, away from her dress. She looked upon the event with a mixture of fascination and disgust. Replaying the moment had kept him awake most of the night, his own quick hand a poor substitute for the girl's velvety grip.

"Oh, now what's the matter?" His mother is saying in that weary way. She hugs herself tightly to contain the anguish within her. "They have to buy money orders," she says pleasantly to no one in particular—but really to everyone. "They're unable to understand checking accounts. But of course, it's wonderful the government provides this service for them." At the front of the line, a black woman is carefully counting money at the window, one bill at a time. "Of course, it's not their fault, is it?" She seems to be addressing a larger audience now. Sam looks away. "Some things are just beyond them. Oooh-ooh-uh." More vigorous up and down hops now. He would laugh if she weren't his mother. She's almost like a clown. She looks like one of those dancers in Africa he'd seen in a school film. All she needs is a big shield and a spear. "I hope the janitor has a mop handy," she says and laughs good-naturedly. She's including the woman behind them in the joke, who looks blankly back at her.

Others in line have stepped away from them just a little. Then a dapper looking man at the front waves to her. His gesture meets with unanimous approval, because the customers between her and him quickly pull back to give her an open passage to the front of the line. Everyone wants to help her out in this emergency. Or they want to get rid of her—both, the two of them, Sam thinks.

"How lovely of you," his mother says to the man, pulling Sam along by his coat collar. One hand on her bosom, she's going to make one of those curtain call bows, he fears. "Thank you so very much—so very gracious of you. It's such a bother since the operation," she confides loudly to a woman now behind them. "The doctors promised me everything would be all right." Her smile was bold and courageous and could sell rice to China.

Now they are behind the woman who is still carefully counting her change. She inspects the money order, turns it over to read both sides. Sam is terrified his mother will offer to help, read it to her, and explain how the money order works. But she has become calm and composes herself pleasantly to encounter the clerk, maybe going over her lines. Then she quickly buys the stamps. "Nothing too religious," she tells the man. "I don't have time to send many cards, and we're nondenominational." Sam wasn't sure what that meant, but he didn't want to be included.

On the bus downtown, Sam asks, "Are you okay?" Her desperate urgency has miraculously abated.

"Of course I'm okay, darling, and thank you for asking. I'm even more than okay with you here." She hugs him, and he smells Mary Chess, her favorite perfume. She gets it discounted at Macy's. "We're going to have a ducky time together. It's Christmas after all. Your poor father so far away. How he would want to be with us. With you. But then we're used to that, aren't we? You're going to have such fun staying with Hazel Pennyworth. She has a boy just your age, and the two of you can explore Greenwich Village. She lives right in the middle of it. On Grove Street. Not far from Romany Marie's. Remember? Where that lady read your palm?"

He remembers the spicy stew. "Why can't I stay with you?"

"Well, I'm mortified about that, sweetheart. But times are hard. Parts are few and far between. I just have a tiny room at the Riverside Club. I don't even have my own bathtub. Hazel is a lovely woman. Her husband was a noted anthropologist, and he lives in Queens now. They are divorced. My little place is close to Columbia, and I can pop over to the university, use the library. And I have papers and books all over my bed, the floor. You should see the mess."

"You're going to school, now?"

"Just a little insurance. Hedging the bet, as your father would say, darling. Oh, my, this awful war. Seems like there has always been a war. It's been one big war the whole century, and your father in the middle of all of them."

"Where is he? Have you heard from him?"

"He's in Italy. He's all right—don't worry. I got a phone call from a friend of his—just back from there. From Italy. But what waste. What a waste." She peers out the bus window. It has begun snowing again, and the traffic is snarled. Sam is not sure what she's calling a waste, the war or his father taking pictures of it.

"What did he say?"

"Your father? Oh, that he's all right. Yes, something about bears. He said to tell you he has a bear story for you. What's that about?"

"Just some funny stories he used to tell me when I was little." Suddenly, Sam senses he's about to cry, and he hugs the suitcase to his chest. The bus is very dirty. A chewing gum wrapper has been ground into the ribbed floor. The highs and lows of his parents' lives are familiar to him—they are always broke or flush with money, but this time seems worst of all. He never understands why they have so little money, why they don't have a regular house or an apartment like other people. They always borrow places. Nancy Wilson has invited him to her parents' apartment on Beekman Place for a Christmas party.

He used to enjoy their way of life: the big steamer trunks opened up in this room or that, pulled open to set up an instant home place in whatever odd corner. The three of them had seemed self-contained and impervious. When he was smaller, he used to think of making up his bed in the drawer of one of those big trunks—like that kid in the cartoon. Then they could pack him around with their underwear, and the idea always made him giggle. Underwear.

But lately, a dark, messy grimness has come over them, like the weather outside the bus. Choices seem to be made for them by others now. He looks at his mother covertly. Even her hair looks different; it is darker; the auburn accent more black, and he guesses she must be dyeing it to get roles. And she's using a lot more makeup these days. She has always looked different from everyone else, but she does even more so now, and that bothers him, too.

"Your poor father," she is saying. "Somewhere in Italy. Near Bologna, his friend said. With the partisans. Naturally with the partisans. He could be hurt, Sam; as we ride downtown on this bus, he could be lying hurt, but . . ." She abruptly turns away and pulls a handkerchief from her purse and puts it to her eyes. Sam is not sure if it is an act or not. "I'm sorry, darling. What a bad show I'm giving you. Regrets."

She had talked his way into the prep school, even got him a scholarship. It wasn't a top place, but it was good enough, she had told him. As important as the education, maybe more so, he would have a roof over his head and food to eat. A place to stay. Whatever education came with these basics was incidental. He can picture her in Headmaster Talcott's office, threatening to pee on the floor if he wasn't enrolled. Sam hugs the suitcase tighter, but a snort of laughter escapes him. She hugs him happily, grateful that he might be having a good time.

"What's funny, darling?"

She has turned to him quickly and hugs him as if to draw off some of his good humor for herself. Her eyes are bright and her mouth is wide and held slightly open, expectantly. He sees, not for the first time, that girlish part of her, the part that has always wanted to have fun but has been mostly denied the party. "Hazel's boy is named Teddy, and he's loads of fun."

Sadly, Sam reviews the scene of Eighth Avenue and Fourteenth Street. It's a grungy view, like some old painting—snow on the tops of cars, slush underfoot, people walking hunched over against the cold. A Salvation Army Santa clangs his bell beside a black pot on a tripod. The sound is muffled. Sam knows he will never make it to Nancy's party, that even if he brings it up, his mother will find some way of getting herself invited too. He imagines the scene. She'd say she was just delivering him to the door. *Oh, but why not stay—come in*, Nancy's parents would say. *Oh, I wouldn't think of it*, she'd say—one hand at her throat. Hesitant eyes fluttering. She'd take a half step back, arms poised to embrace the moment. *Oh, well, then just for a moment*, and she would be in the place and immediately the center of the party, and he had only come with her. They were together—like a couple on a date. Looking at the stalled traffic on Eighth Avenue, young Sam Emerson knows that when he gets back to school, Nancy will be very different. He hates his mother.

Adventures with Teddy

Hazel Pennyworth, his mother's new friend, keeps a pair of parakeets in the living room windows of her basement apartment. The steel casement windows look out on a garden that features a cement figure of a Greek goddess and a table and two chairs of cast iron. The furniture is painted lime green, and rust is working through the paint. The apartment is strangely familiar to Sam, for its layout is very like a couple of places his parents have lived in—places he had hoped would become permanent. Instinctively, he knows where the bathroom is, halfway down the narrow hallway on the left, with two smallish bedrooms beyond that. The kitchen is off the living room and opposite the door to the garden. Even the arch that distinguishes the cozy foyer is familiar. He's traced its graceful curve in his memory many times.

The couch he is to sleep on is roomy and piled high with pillows in colorful cases. Like a sultan's throne, he thinks. Hazel Pennyworth has a promiscuous eye for color; the great variety of hues in the rugs, wall hangings and drapes—none of them congenial to the other—makes up a surprising vitality that is warm and vaguely artistic.

"She had to give up biochemistry and become a pharmacist," his mother fills him in as they trudge down Greenwich Avenue. "We all have to make do," she adds and laughs shortly. He gets the message—the prescription includes him. "I told you she's divorced. Teddy's father was an anthropologist, but he now imports tea or maybe silk. One of those. He's English. Or was."

The day has become darker and colder. German subs lie in wait off New York Harbor, so there are few lights. Because of the blackout, the streets look a little scary. Taxis wheel around with only their parking lights on, but his mother walks straight across intersections without pausing or looking. The importance she makes of herself crossing the street is meant to protect them, and somehow it does. Sam's hand holding the suitcase handle has gone numb. He will receive a pair of leather gloves from Macy's for Christmas. They pass a large movie theatre. Store windows are festooned with tinsel and cotton snow. He tries to look at these as they walk quickly by, for he has yet to get a present for his mother. He's been able to save four dollars and some change from his allowance. He has already sent Aunt Rho a pincushion filled with fragrant herbs, and he sent her a card with a big wreath on it. "Merry Christmas. How are the chickens? Love, Sam."

He's been thinking of those chickens in Ohio—how one of them would smell roasting in Aunt Rho's oven. The yellow enamel stove would radiate heat and the luscious aromas of chicken fat, pepper, and rosemary. The small farmhouse would vibrate with the warm flavors. Mashed potatoes, smooth and buttery. All the way down from Connecticut on the Greyhound bus, his memory has feasted on these images, so that he arrived in New York famished and aching with anger that he had been separated from such wonderful food.

So, the smells in Hazel Pennyworth's apartment somewhat appease these hungers, which only frustrated him more, because he had wanted to pick at his anger, toy with it longer. He can tell quickly the spices that permeate the rooms are different from those Aunt Rho uses. The smells of garlic and tomato are prominent. Other herbs he can't identify, but they seem to go with the colorful materials on the pillows. A tasty energy percolates in the small kitchen.

"Here you are," she has welcomed them at the door. She takes his mother's arm, then reaches for his hand. "Teddy. Come meet Sam."

She's a large comforter of a woman who wears her light hair pulled back into a black snood. Her face adds a final concentric accent to the rest of her, the eyebrows drawn on in a permanent surprise. Or interest. The perfect small teeth of her smile nip at Sam's dark mood, and he finds himself smiling back in spite of himself. Her legs are very heavy, which saddens him for some reason—unnaturally thick and out of proportion to the rest of her.

"Now you're staying for a little supper," she says drawing them into the foyer. Sam puts his suitcase down. Her tone is almost stern but good-natured.

"Oh, my dear, we couldn't." His mother's eyes have rolled with the line. "Sam and I will just go around the corner to that little Chinese place. They're always so filling. We just wanted to drop off his suitcase."

"Nonsense, Edie. There's plenty to go around. Teddy!" she yells over her shoulder. "Where is that boy? How about a drink? One of my customers gave me a bottle of Four Roses. Mix it with some Coca-Cola, and it isn't half bad. Now give me your coats."

"Oh, very well," Edith Olson gives in and laughs nervously as if she's just agreed to some risky adventure and not only dinner.

Sam likes the atmosphere immediately, feels instantly at home in the apartment's ragged clutter. Cream-colored walls, piles of pillows, and several leather ottomans are distributed around the carpets. The tapestries on the walls look like elaborate gardens. Footfalls come from within; a sort of off-stride shambling precedes Teddy Pennyworth. Then he looms into view and approaches Sam with his right hand held stiffly out.

"Hello, old man," the boy says and gives a peculiar snort as if to signal that neither of them should take the moment too seriously. He is about the same age as Sam but seems older and even larger, though he is no taller. Something about the cadence of his stride. A peculiar lurch, as if his feet abruptly have become too large for him, or perhaps a counterweight within his pudgy torso has swung off its normal arc. "Yes, amusing," Teddy says, "but here we all are, making the best of it." He grabs his mother about the waist. "Aren't we, old girl?"

"Now, Teddy—now Teddy." She giggles and blushes deeply, the color seeping down her neck. She looks at Sam's mother, who is laughing also. The two women share a secret of some kind. "Why don't you show Sam your stamp collection," Hazel Pennyworth says.

"Capital suggestion," Teddy agrees and thumps Sam on the shoulder. "Come with me, my boy."

"Now, Edie, I'll fix us some drinks," Sam hears as he follows Teddy down the hallway. "You must tell me everything."

Sam recognizes Teddy Pennyworth's room as the room he might have had if his parents were different. More pillows and comforters. A single bed with a Navajo blanket, and a similar blanket on the floor. Two model airplanes of tissue and balsa wood hang from the ceiling on nearly invisible thread, and a globe rests on the top shelf of a small bookcase. No window. A school banner from Fordham Prep slants across one wall, and tinted prints of sailing ships hang on another. A portable Remington typewriter sits at the center of the desk. A sheet of paper sticks up from the roller, and Sam tries to look at what Teddy has written, but the boy quickly snatches it from the machine.

"Just some of my elevated trash," he snorts and crumples up the sheet, throws it into the wastebasket. "My version of *Forever Amber*— some of the scenes elaborated you might say. Obviously, not for tender eyes." Sam notices how Teddy uses that word *obviously* as if what comes after was a waste of time.

He has pulled open a lower drawer of the heavy maple dresser and lifts out a large stamp album and places it on the bed. The two boys kneel on the floor, side by side, to look at the neat rows of different stamps. Teddy turns the pages, and Sam is impressed. "These airmails are especially interesting. They belong to the series where in some of them the plane was printed flying upside down. Those are worth a fortune. Obviously, I don't have any of those. I got these Greek airmails with Wheaties box tops. You listen to Jack Armstrong?"

"Sometimes," Sam says. He remembers in Ohio, sitting on the floor next to Aunt Rho's big Emerson radio. That was like another life, and in a sudden understanding, he knows he has changed and that he could no longer be part of that life. The idea makes him sad.

"You send in Wheaties box tops and they send you stamps," Teddy is saying. He's turned a new page. "Ah, here we have the ill-fated queen of Romania. Quite a beauty. Note the black border around the stamp. In mourning, you see. Killed in the Alps in a car crash. A tragic accident."

Sam is enjoying the guided tour, and Teddy's language amuses him, his way of talking. He's like a master of ceremonies, introducing magic acts he doesn't really believe in. At the same time, Sam tries to keep half an ear on the conversation in the front of the apartment. Instinctively, he's certain his mother and Hazel are talking about his father—a conversation like the ones he used to hear through the heat register in Aunt Rho's kitchen.

"Killed, you say?" Hazel Pennyworth has just said.

Then his mother talks very low, her voice rising to the surface of his hearing.

". . . Sicily. She was with some general. In his plane that crashed."

Then Teddy is telling him the history of some Confederate stamps. The women's voices have dropped, become confidential. Ice cubes clink against a glass—that would be his mother, he figures. She always swirled a highball glass round and round when she was keen on a subject, then she would pop one of the cubes into her mouth and crush it with her molars to punctuate her statement. Teddy has snorted several times as he makes a point about the poor registry of the Confederate stamps.

Teddy's mother explodes. "Edie, you don't mean it! Not with her mouth?"

Then his mother's voice is low and level and reasonable. She's explaining something in that dismissive manner he's heard her use when talking about certain actresses. He imagines her holding her hand up, for her bracelets clink. *Therapy.* She uses the word a couple of times. "It's just therapy," she says off hand. Has his father been sick? He's been hurt and she hasn't told him, because it's Christmas. "It's like a therapy for them and nothing more." He hears her clearly. "But I'm not playing nurse." The two women laugh uproariously. Gasping for breath, Hazel Pennyworth repeats his mother's words about playing nurse, and another spasm rocks her.

"The old girls are having a jest," Teddy says and nudges Sam in the side.

Sam is thinking of the last time he saw his father. It was the summer before he was sent to the prep school, and they had had a big seafood dinner in a restaurant in Brooklyn where Owen Emerson got on a ship in the navy yard. He had seemed okay then. He hadn't looked sick. His soft camera bag on one shoulder and duffel in the other hand. His mother and father had talked gaily, as if he might be just steaming across the harbor to New Jersey. His father sang a line of a song to his mother. "Good-bye dear, I'll be home in a year." His mother was bright-eyed and smiling, but Sam could tell it was a role she was playing, because there was a shadow on her, a dark reflection she couldn't elude. "And as for you, Mister Sam." His father pulled him up, the slender arms surprisingly strong and his cheek scratchy, "You're going to be just ducky."

"Your dad takes pictures," Teddy has just said, startling Sam in his reverie. Has he heard his thoughts just now? Teddy has turned back to the bureau to lift out another stamp album, but two magazines have been placed between its pages. *Beach Beauties.* He puts the glossy journals on top of the stamp albums and resumes his place, kneeling next to Sam. "Here's some choice material—very choice." He snorts.

The photographs in the magazine are of young women running and jumping on a beach. Some throw and catch large balls. Others kneel beside sandcastles or flee from waves. Inside shots pose them in swimsuits beside columns and pillars or leaning against doorways, which puzzles Sam, for the backgrounds don't seem to go with what they are wearing. It's like they have come in from the beach to a party in a grand house. Some of the pictures remind him painfully of Nancy Wilson, because the models are wearing shorts and sweaters and tennis outfits much like he has seen her wear, but none of them is as pretty as Nancy. "Here's a choice one," Teddy says and turns a page. He's familiar with the contents. "What kind of pictures does your dad take?"

"He takes war pictures." Sam hears his own voice through plugged ears. "What he really likes to take are pictures of old barns and roads."

"Surely, you jest." Teddy snorts and draws something down from his sinus cavity.

"Sure, roads. Going off into the distance. Roads." He can't say it any other way and has no language to say it differently. He's a little upset to feel odd about his father's liking for roads and barns and is sorry that Teddy has made him feel so, because he has liked him a little. Also, whatever is cooking in the kitchen smells wonderful.

"I'll just check on dinner," they hear Hazel Pennyworth say, and her slippered steps approach them.

"Cheese-it," Teddy whispers and deftly closes the album over the magazines just as she comes to the door.

"How are you boys getting along?"

"Just swell, Hazel. Sam and I have discovered a mutual interest."

"Do you like stamps, Sam?" she asks cheerfully, and Sam nods. Teddy winks broadly and replaces the albums in the bureau drawer.

Green peppers stuffed with rice and some kind of nuts are the main dish. Tomato sauce is poured over everything. A large dish of cooked greens is also served—not spinach. The square end table that holds a short lamp made from a copper jar has been opened up, magically becoming a small dining table. Four woven place mats in bright colors have been arranged precisely on the polished surface, and cutlery and glasses sparkle in the living room's subtle light. The heavy drapes on the windows are pulled tight, even though the windows face the inner garden. "Hazel is worried about the blackout," Teddy apologizes.

"Well it's the law," she says forcefully. But the drawn drapes only add to the cozy snugness of the apartment. Sam wants to pull the atmosphere over his head, lave himself with it. His mother stands to one side, smiling pleasantly with one hand at her waist. She is playing the honored guest patiently waiting to be shown her place; she doesn't want to be treated differently but will accept any deference graciously. Hazel Pennyworth is preparing their plates in the kitchen.

"I used the last of the meat coupons for Teddy's first vacation dinner. So I used walnuts instead of hamburger for the stuffing."

"And what worthy pork chops they were too," her son says and makes a deep bow. Sam laughs.

"Wallace Warfield Simpson is an expert," Sam's mother says, as if she's continuing a conversation with herself. "She's famous for it." She laughs scornfully.

"Why, Edie, how do you know that?" Hazel brings two plates of food to the table.

"Oh, everyone knows that." The bracelets shake to validate the statement. "It's common knowledge in London. Theatre talk, you know."

"And just for that, he gave up the throne." Both women laugh like school chums, then regard their sons and quickly become sober. "Come now, everyone. Edie, please sit here, and you next, Sam."

"That leaves me next to the old bag," Teddy says heavily and sits down. Everyone laughs.

Sam has not seen his mother look so happy in a long time. Joy suffuses her face, and she squeezes his thigh. He guesses some of her manner is due to the whiskey or to the expectancy of a home-cooked meal. She is radiant. "How lovely, Hazel." Her fork has picked at the stuffing in the pepper. "What good food!"

"Do you like the mustard greens? That's what they're called. I found them at the market yesterday. Funny how this war is making us eat different things. Only colored people used to eat these before."

"I say it's spinach, and I say to hell with it," Teddy loudly proclaims.

"Oh, Teddy," his mother almost shouts. Her complexion turns red again as she laughs. Sam likes the taste of the vegetable, a little bitter but interesting.

"And when next will you illume the Great White Way, Edie?" Teddy Pennyworth asks.

"Soon. Yes, very soon," Edie Olson replies. Her voice becomes measured and level. She takes a large forkful in her mouth and chews vigorously. Sam thinks it's the best meal he's had since he left Ohio.

Left to themselves during the day, the boys poke around Greenwich Village, touring Teddy Pennyworth's favorite places. They visit a magazine and tobacco store that is redolent of cigar smoke on the corner of Seventh Avenue and Twelfth Street. The sick-looking woman at the front counter gives them about a half hour each time to browse the comic books and the pulp magazines; Teddy casually works his way toward the rack holding magazines like the ones hidden in his stamp album. He always seems surprised to find them on display. "All right, boys, buy one or go to the library," the woman eventually says. Sam carefully replaces the copy of *Popular Mechanics* he has been skimming, and Teddy closes up the bathing beauties.

One regular pilgrimage is to the street below the women's prison on Sixth Avenue. Sam is astounded by a prison just for women, and he doesn't want to expose his ignorance by asking Teddy what a woman could do that would land her in prison? Sam and Teddy stamp their feet on the frigid pavement before a pet store and look up at the barred windows, expecting to see a face—a woman's face—at one of them. "I suppose they have heat in there," Sam says.

Teddy looks at him, his eyebrows waggling. "Of course they have heat. This is New York." He snorts. "They are mostly whores. I saw one once that could have been a movie star. Like Hedy Lamar. Choice."

They also sit through double-bill matinees at the Greenwich Theatre. War films and romantic dramas about people giving up something—often their lives—for duty and honor. Going blind or getting killed. But somehow the pictures have happy endings too. Teddy snorts a lot and laughs at all the wrong moments, and Sam learns to anticipate these responses at certain turns of dialogue or heroic developments in the plot. He often joins in, laughing, though he's not always sure why. They both agree Sonja Henie's round behind is perfect, and they sit through one of her films twice just to see her skating backward making the short skirt of her costume flare up over her tight rump. She always smiles and looks pleased. Actually, Sam prefers Joan Leslie, but he doesn't tell Teddy. She doesn't look like Nancy Wilson, but she is sweet and straightforward and quiet—a nice-looking girl who might let you do things if she had a chance.

In a store on Sheridan Square, Teddy helps Sam look for a present for his mother. The place has stuff women bring in to sell from their own closets. But better than the usual secondhand, Teddy has promised, and that's true. The purses and fur pieces and hats cost a lot more than he has to spend. Four dollars and some change. While looking at some scarves, Sam learns more about his mother taking classes at Columbia University—why he cannot stay with her.

"How do you know that?" he asks Teddy.

"She told Hazel. She's getting a degree so she can teach. She didn't tell you?"

"Teach?" Sam is astonished. She is an actress. People come up to her in restaurants, ask for her autograph. If only Teddy had seen her just once onstage, come out onstage so the lighting catches her eyes, he wouldn't even entertain the idea. She always looked as if she might rise right up into those lights. But another part of him knows it must be true. It was so cockamamie; he knew it probably was true. She was going to be a teacher. But why hadn't she told him?

They begin a bashful retreat from the store's finery under the amused observation of two women at the front counter. A display of bracelets catches his eye. One is ivory with a Chinese pattern carved around its circumference. He could see it on his mother's right wrist, slipping against the others his father has given her.

"How much is that one?"

One of the women holds up the bracelet and turns it carefully around, studying it. "This one. Let's see, this one is two dollars," she says slowly.

"Two dollars!" the other one exclaims. "Mrs. Tompkins says she wanted . . ."

"She was in yesterday and reduced the price. She wants to get rid of it," the first woman says. She holds the bracelet out to Sam.

"I'll take it," he says quickly. His heart jumps in his chest; he cannot believe his good luck.

"May I wrap it for you? I just have some nice Christmasy paper. Is this for your mom?" Sam nods, and the other woman shrugs and lights a cigarette, blowing a column of smoke toward the ceiling. She's amused about something.

He has two dollars and some change left over, so he treats Teddy and himself to chocolate ice cream sodas at the Jumble Shop on Eighth Street. "This is awfully grand of you, old sport," Teddy says as he sucks on the straw. Sam feels older and experienced, like one of those guys in the movies who take Joan Leslie to a fancy supper club. He's thinking he might look up Nancy's phone number and call her. It would be Wilson on Beekman Place, and he has a dollar left over.

One Saturday afternoon, Sam strides beside his new friend, and they abruptly turn into Bank Street. The name is funny because there's no bank. All the street names in Greenwich Village amuse him. Teddy dodges into the overheated foyer of a small brick apartment building.

"This is the afternoon I visit my little sweetie," Teddy says and winks like Jack Oakie in the movies. He punches a button on the panel by the mailboxes.

"Yes?" The woman's voice is a little annoyed; she's in the middle of something important.

"Western Union," Teddy says, leaning into the mouthpiece on the wall.

"Oh, give me a moment. I'm just out of my bath."

"Just out of her bath," Teddy whispers in Sam's ear and elbows him. His eyes roll.

Seconds later, Teddy is jangling the key chain that hangs from his pants pocket and the door lock buzzes. Sam follows him to a small elevator at the end of a narrow corridor that smells strongly of Clorox. The two of them just fit into its cab. They rise several floors in silence, save for a couple of contemplative snorts from Teddy. Then, down another narrow hallway, metal doors closed on either side. Stale cooking odors and something else Sam can't place. The door at the very end is slightly ajar, and Vaughn Monroe is softly singing on a radio inside.

Teddy punches the bell and pushes through the doorway and into a room Sam quickly understands composes the whole apartment except for the bathroom and a corner cupboard, where the basic elements of a kitchen have been installed. A small electric hotplate, a sink, and a pint-sized fridge look like articles from a dollhouse.

"I'll just be a minute," the same flat voice says from behind the bathroom door.

"Take your time," Teddy says. He motions Sam to the one armchair, and he sits down on the edge of the daybed. Sam understands Teddy is at home here.

"That's not very funny—that Western Union business," the voice complains. "It could be a message about Johnny."

Teddy makes a face. "You're right. My apologies."

Sam has been looking around. Over the sofabed hangs a tinted picture of a figure bending over another lying on the marble floor of what seems to be a temple of some kind. The building is in the middle of a lake. He cannot figure out the gender of either figure, even though both are naked, and he decides the picture is dumb. A desklike bureau is next to one window, and a photograph of a guy in a sailor hat sits on top. Another picture shows the same guy, in uniform, with his arm around a young woman. She is smiling and has one foot turned in on the other. The two boys sit in silence. A faucet is turned on and then off. Sam sneezes; the place smells of dingy laundry.

Teddy has pulled from his coat pocket two fresh packs of Chester-field cigarettes and places them neatly on the top of the black tin trunk that serves as a coffee table in front of the daybed. Sam has been looking at the trunk, for it reminds him of his mother's trunks. A lot of people must live like that, he thinks, not just his parents. He is also amazed Teddy could produce such cigarettes. Name brands like Chesterfield are almost impossible to come by now. Schoolmates smoke brands with odd names they say taste like rubber tires. Not real tobacco. Teddy is humming to himself as he carefully aligns the two cigarette packs, like a card player in a movie. A car honks in the street below, and the sound seems to come from a far distance, from underwater.

Then the bathroom door opens. It is the same woman as in the picture on the bureau, but she looks pale, rinsed of definition, and her eyes are tired. Her nose is a vertical line between the narrow-set eyes of almost no color. Gray, he decides. The face of the young woman in the picture seems to have grown smaller.

"Hello there," she says and reaches a hand out to Teddy. A weariness in her voice suggests she has made the greeting many times already that day. She pulls the sash of the chenille robe tight. Soiled, fuzzy slippers are on her feet, and the striped pajamas are much too large for her, making her look even more diminutive, waiflike. She wears her long, brownish hair over one eye like Veronica Lake, and she is stroking this fall of hair regularly with a hairbrush, keeping a rhythm.

"This is my friend, Sam." Teddy makes the introduction.

"Hello, Sam," the woman says in a low voice and takes his hand.

"His dad is in the war, too."

"Oh my," she says. She slowly perches on the edge of the daybed, near Teddy, continuing to brush her hair. "My Johnny is in the navy. In the Pacific. Your father is in the army?" She has leaned forward a little and the robe and the pajama top dip away.

"Not really," Sam replies. The room has become very hot, and he wants to slip off his outside coat, but that might look like they were staying for a while. He wonders if he should be here at all. "He takes pictures."

"Oh." She brightens and her brush pauses. "He's a correspondent."

"Something like that," Sam says.

"Our moms are friends," Teddy explains. "We just thought we'd drop by and say hello. How are things down at the office?" Teddy's snort signals a familiarity with her situation.

"Oh, the same old story," she says with a half a laugh. She has curled up on the sofa, legs tucked under, so Teddy must twist around to talk to her. The pose makes her even more diminutive. She continues to work on the long fall of hair, holding her robe together with the other hand. She could be huddling in a doorway, Sam thinks—his father has made pictures of people like that. "That Ruby person I told you about has been moved up to Specialty Items—just as I told you she was gunning for. That's the name for her all right—'specialty item.' She spent almost an hour in Mr. King's office—with the door closed. It was scandalous, believe me."

"Doing some specialty, perhaps," Teddy says. He wipes his nose with a finger and hoots.

"Oh, aren't you the wicked one?" she says. "Isn't he just awful?" she asks Sam as she leans toward Teddy and playfully taps him on the shoulder. Then she tells Sam, "Mr. King is our office manager. He's Jewish and can't keep his hands to himself."

"He's bothered you, has he?" Teddy asks seriously.

"Oh, I've felt his paws here and there."

"Here and there."

"Well, yes. The other morning I was filling the reservoir of the ditto machine. The reservoir is in a very awkward place, just behind and over the machine." She seems fond of saying *reservoir*. "I have to go up on tippy toe and bend over—it's so very awkward, you can imagine—and I hear Mr. King come up behind me, asking if he can help, if he can do anything, and then I felt his hand on me."

"Scoundrel," says Teddy. "Put his hand on you, did he?" He looks half-asleep.

"I guess I don't have to tell you where."

"That pig. And what did you do?"

"Well, what could I do?—in the position I was in. I said, 'Mr. King, my husband is in the navy fighting for democracy, and I would appreciate it if you removed your hand from my person as I fill this reservoir.'"

"That told him. And did he?"

"Yes—but not quick enough for my appreciation."

"Then, Ruby got the promotion."

"That's easy to understand. She can have it, for all I care. Just imagine all the filthy things she has to do."

"Yes, filthy," Teddy says and jiggles his nose with one finger. The three of them sit silently. On the street below, a truck grates its gears, and a man's voice shouts hoarse directions. Sam's imagination has played out Ruby's ordeal at the hands of Mr. King, assisted by the glimpse he has of the bathroom. Several pairs of stockings hang from the shower curtain rod. Also a brassiere.

Teddy clears his throat and scoots toward the front of the daybed. "I know you prefer Old Golds, but the drugstore only got Chesterfields this week. I managed to slip a couple in my pocket when Hazel was busy. So, Merry Christmas!" He tries to sound hearty.

The young woman looks very surprised, as if she's only just seen the cigarettes lying on the trunk top in front of her. "For me? How very sweet of you, Teddy. They certainly taste better than the awful things they call cigarettes. But, then I think my Johnny is puffing his Lucky Strikes in the Pacific, and so it's okay. Yes, Chesterfields—they satisfy." She says the slogan through her curtain of hair. "I see that Robert Taylor smokes Chesterfields. I saw a picture of him in *Life* magazine, and he was saying that he prefers Chesterfields. Of course, it was an ad, but I don't think Robert Taylor would say that if it wasn't true."

"Certainly not," says Teddy.

"I like Robert Taylor," the woman reflects. She has picked up one of the packs and turns its fresh squareness over in her hands.

"Sam likes Joan Leslie," Teddy says.

"Oh, she's keen," the woman says.

"And his dad takes pictures for *Life*, too," Teddy continues.

"He must be famous." She turns to Sam and pulls the brush through her hair.

"I don't know," Sam says.

"Johnny and I went to a lot of movies before he shipped out. Our first date was a movie. I gave him my all." It is the sort of line that would make Teddy snort and cough in the darkness of the Greenwich Theatre, but here his face becomes intense, and he leans forward attentively, waiting for her to say more.

"Well, here I am just being an old silly. Let's light up and say Merry Christmas to one and all." Her small, sharp nails have neatly sliced the cellophane top of one pack and torn off a corner of the package. The fresh pungency of tobacco rises into Sam's nose. She taps out several cigarettes, offering one to Teddy. She takes one for herself. "I bet you don't smoke yet, Sam. Well, then, you'll just have to sit there and watch the two of us. How about a doughnut? I have a doughnut left over." She has been laughing at something and looks sideways toward Teddy. Sam notices a good-size bruise on the pale shin of her right leg.

Teddy has picked up the Zippo lighter next to an ashtray of green glass and flicked it open and snapped the flint. He holds the light out to her. The woman holds aside the curtain of hair and leans the cigarette into the flame. She inhales and blows a stream of smoke toward the ceiling. "Ah, they satisfy." Both she and Teddy laugh.

"They satisfy," Teddy repeats, laughing even harder, as if the slogan were a peculiar wisdom he had just introduced into this ordinary room. Sam watches him smoke; his friend holds the cigarette in a strange way between a finger and a thumb, sticking straight out. They talk about movies, and sometimes he joins the conversation. Teddy's friend tells more stories about her office. Some of the other women have also betrayed her—that's her word for it. *Betrayed.* She has to redo a lot of their work because they are so careless. Then she rubs out her cigarette, only halfway smoked. It is a signal of some sort, because Teddy is on his feet, and they leave quickly. She closes the door behind them. As they wait for the elevator, they can hear the lock turn. On the way back to his apartment, Teddy stops off at a cigar store on the corner to buy some Sen-Sen. His pace is relentless—long, loping strides that veer as much as they advance. "Choice," he says to himself. Sam has trouble keeping up with him.

More Facts of Life

The third night of his stay with the Pennyworths, Hazel announces at supper—scrambled eggs and fried Spam—that she has to go back to the drugstore for a few hours. "You boys will be all right. But I don't want you to go out."

After Hazel leaves, they listen to some radio shows. *I Love a Mystery* also turns out to be a favorite program of Teddy's. He likes the spooky organ music. Sam listens intently to the voices of the women in the story. One of them could be his mother with an English accent. So, he's a little irritated when Teddy lurches to his feet before the program is over and checks the wall clock in the kitchen. "It's time, old man. Get your coat on. And you'll need a cap. Take that brown one in the closet."

But Sam is surprised when they don't go out the front door. Teddy has opened the door into the garden, putting a cautionary finger to his lips. They pass into the frigid night and creep across the carpets of light thrown down upon the frozen earth by the windows of the adjoining apartment. Teddy crouches down beside one of the iron chairs, holding on to one of its legs, and motions Sam to do the same. "We're just in time, I think," he whispers. "Show's about to start," he says and sniffles.

The windows look into a living room very similar to the Penny-worths' but for the décor. The place is crammed with odd objects. It could be a storeroom for the Museum of Natural History, Sam thinks. Big shields hang from the walls along with crossed spears and clubs with fuzzy tops. Huge Chinese vases stand sentry in the room's corners, and statues carved of wood stare fiercely with eyes of shell.

A man and a woman sit together on a large overstuffed sofa. Both wear velvet robes. The woman is reading the *World Telegram & Sun,* holding the large paper open wide as she concentrates. The sleeves of the robe fall away to her elbows. The man watches her read and plays with the sash of his robe. The woman continues reading, slowly turns the page of the newspaper. The man looks over her shoulder, then shifts his gaze to a large mask with feathers by the doorway. It is very cold in the garden, and Sam is getting a cramp in one leg.

"Any minute now," Teddy whispers. "Usually he waits until she's on page five. You can see he's impatient. She's a slow reader tonight."

Then, as if to act out Teddy's commentary, the man reaches over and pulls aside one lapel of the woman's robe. Her right breast is exposed. It is smallish but juts sharply out from her chest to end in a pointed pink nipple. Sam recognizes it as the breast of a Varga girl in *Esquire* magazine he has sometimes used for his solitary pleasure in school—before Nancy Wilson had showed him the difference.

"Choice," Teddy says in his ear. "Choice."

The woman continues to read the newspaper. It's like a ritual, some plan the couple have agreed upon, because the man casually reaches across and lifts back the robe to reveal her other breast. "A perfect pair," Teddy says softly and sucks the frigid air up his nose. The woman slowly turns the page to the next section, then turns back quickly as if she has missed something in the story, an important point or a transition. The man next to her and the two boys in the garden study the conical perfection of her breasts. They rise and fall evenly with her breathing, their taut nipples nosing the air.

"Here we go," Teddy says dreamily.

The man pulls himself up straight and leans forward to delicately tongue the nipple closest to him. His companion adjusts her right arm to facilitate his attention, though the hands holding the *World Telegram & Sun* do not waver as they spread the large sheets of newsprint wide. The man now engulfs most of the woman's right breast, and Sam can see the muscles in his throat work as he sucks. His cheeks hollow. It's like a frog he watched once in a pond trying to swallow a salamander—half in and half out and trying to figure out how to gulp down the rest. The guy pulls away with his tongue out, and he laps at the hardened tip. His other hand reaches across to fondle the left breast. He'd have to lean across her to suck on this one, Sam figures, and that would interfere with her reading the paper, which she has continued to do. But the man seems satisfied with the one he has.

"Really choice," Teddy is saying, rocking back and forth on his feet and hugging his knees. Sam's feet have become numb. They must have knelt on this frozen ground for half an hour; yet he doesn't want the scene to end. But just then, it does.

Abruptly, as if she's just finished the particular article that has interested her, the woman closes up the paper and tosses it to one side. She looks down pleasantly, even a little amused maybe, at the man glued to her right breast. She gently pulls the robe closed over her nakedness, and puts a finger on his nose to push him away when he looks up. She stands up and walks through the doorway. He follows. The room is suddenly empty with only the artifacts and sculptures to look at. The wooden figures with their eyes of shell stare at the boys. The blue jars stand in the corners. It looks as if no one has ever been in this room, that what they have just witnessed has been in their imagination, but then there is the newspaper, spilling its pages off the sofa, slipping to the floor.

"Show's over," Teddy is saying. "But one time, she came back in completely stark. Like she had forgot something while they were doing it and had to come back and get it."

"What was it?" Sam asks.

"What?"

"What she forgot."

"Oh, something, I can't remember. But you could tell she was getting it done to her."

"You could?" Sam is shivering uncontrollably.

"Of course," Teddy snorts. "Easy to tell." They wait several more minutes. The room remains empty, illuminated like a display window.

"I'm getting cold," Sam says at last, and they go back into their apartment. They make hot chocolate, using a lot of Hazel Pennyworth's sugar ration.

Men of the World

Edith Olson has brought a bottle of Virginia Dare wine. Hazel Penny-worth has made salmon cakes and boiled potatoes with a white sauce that has chopped green onions in it. "Imagine it's dill," she says and laughs girlishly. The molded lime Jell-O has canned peaches trapped in it, everyone has had wine, and Teddy has stood to ceremoniously pour the last of the bottle into their wineglasses.

"Oh, please, no more for me." Edie Olson waves him away. "And no more for you, Mister Sam."

"Oh, let him have a little more, Edie," her friend protests. "He's here for the night, after all."

"Well, just a little more, then," Sam's mother says. It hasn't been a hard decision. "A lovely dinner, Hazel." The large white beads around his mother's throat are like candies; her nails are trim and polished.

Earlier Edith Olson has told them about turning down a USO tour of a play in order to be close to Sam at Christmas, and Hazel is very sympathetic. She knows all about raising a boy by herself. All this talk makes Sam uncomfortable, and all three of them, even Teddy, look at him as if he's to blame for something. His mother has a radio show lined up—some sort of a program that dramatizes the year's events. She will play several parts in it, using different voices and dialects. "Aren't you amazing," Hazel says.

"Oh, it's just a job, the tricks of the trade," Edie Olson says and shrugs. She has carefully put her knife and fork on her empty plate. "Shall we do the dishes?"

"Oh, not yet. It's so nice to sit here," Hazel says. And Sam agrees. The food, the wine, the steam hissing comfortably from the radiator in the foyer. His mother has changed her perfume—the new scent smells like meadow grasses, warm weather. She's working almost full time at Macy's, and everything seems to be going okay with them. Except for his father being away. It must be cold where his father is in Italy. "Sunny Italy" is a phrase he heard somewhere, and that sounds like it is warm, but then he saw a newsreel that showed American soldiers having snow-ball fights in an Italian village. The radiator in the corner knocks and exhales, and the four of them drowse at the table. Having eaten dinner, they all seem puzzled as to what to do next or even how to get up and leave the table. Abruptly, Teddy shoves his chair back and slaps his thigh.

"Well, have you heard the one about the old lady in the old soldiers' home."

"Oh, Teddy, not now," his mother admonishes.

"Oh do," Edie Olson says. "Let's hear it." She leans forward eagerly, one hand holding the white beads to her throat.

"Well," Teddy says, "this old lady goes into the old soldiers' home and holds up this small paper bag, and she says—'Anyone guessing what's in this bag, gets to see me naked'—and an old geezer in the corner pipes up—'An elephant'? And the old lady says—'Close enough.'"

"Oh, that's good," Edie Olson says. "Yes, I get it." She is laughing only a little, her large front teeth exposed. Teddy's mother has turned deep red.

"Where do you hear such things?" she says, but she is laughing, nervously, but also a little proud that her son has heard the joke somewhere. Almost admiring, Sam notes.

There's more. The little encouragement has inspired Teddy Penny-worth to re-create a treasury of similar jokes—each one becoming more scabrous than the last. The mothers shake in their chairs and hold their sides and bend low over the table to fall back in their chairs gasping for air. The jokes are terrible, but the image of this man-child telling them so confidently rattles them. His audacious vulgarity makes them nearly hysterical.

"I have one," Sam suddenly says as they catch their breaths. The women turn to him, their eyes wet, their mouths ajar expectantly. "Have you read the new book titled *The Yellow Stream* by I. P. Daily?"

"Oh yes, that's a good one," his mother says and nods at her friend. The two women laugh just a little. He knew it was an old joke, but he thought he'd tell it anyway.

"Oh sure." Teddy leans back in his chair. "Then there's *Trouble in the Morning* by I. P. Early. And so forth." He sucks air and seems to get an idea. "Don't forget the famous Russian novelist, I. Bit-er-titsoff."

The two women whoop; their limbs seem to come unstrung. Sam is happy to see his mother enjoy herself so, though the hilarity appears a little strained as it goes on. He has rarely seen her laugh with such full-throated energy, but it's a little scary too, as if a cord within her is about to snap. Teddy's jokes are not very funny, but the women cannot control their laughter. Hazel even pounds on the table. They seem trapped in a type of torture that resembles revelry. Teddy's face glows with delight, and his eyebrows jump up and down happily. He keeps telling more. "No more, no more," they cry helplessly, but they cannot stop listening.

"Then there's the one about Mae West," Teddy continues. "She's sent her clothes out to the Chinese laundry down the street, and it's late getting back. So she calls the guy up and says she's in a hurry for her laundry." He pauses to drink the last of his wine.

"Yes, go on," Sam's mother says. She's wiping the tears from her eyes with a napkin. "She wants her laundry." Edie half laughs.

"The doorbell rings, and she goes to the door, and there's this Chinaman holding the box, and he says, 'I bring laundry lickety-split.' And Mae West says, 'You don't have to go that far, but come in anyway.'"

The two mothers look intensely at each other, holding their breath like in a contest between them as to who would let go first, and both explode in an even wilder hilarity, louder than ever. But there's something harsh and unpleasant in the sound, Sam thinks, though he also laughs—Teddy's imitation of Mae West was pretty good—though he's not exactly sure why the joke was funny. He thinks he knows.

Then he remembers a joke a classmate told him. The kid has an older brother who's in the Army Air Corps who told him the joke, and Sam is trying to remember it. He remembers the punch line but not what comes before.

"There's this army airfield, and they have secret codes for landing planes. This pursuit pilot is coming in for a landing, but he doesn't know the password. Maybe he forgot it. The guy in the control tower keeps asking him for the password, and the pilot says he's running low on fuel. Finally the pilot asks for a hint. 'What's it got to do with?' he asks." Sam has come to the part he can't remember. Everyone is looking at him. His mother's eyes shine. Hazel has been quietly lining up her glass and plate.

"The guy in the tower radios back, 'It's like a sandwich. What goes on a sandwich?' and the pilot says back, 'Mustard, custard, and you, you big turd—I'm coming in!'" A dog in the apartment above gives a few yaps and scampers across the floor.

"I get it," Sam's mother says and looks around. Her smile is too magnificent. "Yes, I get it. It's the words. How they sound—mustard and turd."

"Yes, very clever. It's the words," Hazel Pennyworth agrees and laughs a little. Teddy looks confused, his brow furrowed.

A Christmas Dinner

Edith Olson disguises her disappointment with a bravura Sam finds especially winning. "Why, of course, you must do that," his mother urges.

"I'm really sorry," Hazel Pennyworth is saying. She is coloring and looking guilty. "I haven't seen my sister in a year, and Teddy is supposed to spend Christmas with his father."

"In Queens," Teddy says mournfully. "Can you imagine Queens in winter?"

His mother ignores him and continues. "Of course, you're welcome to stay here. I have a bottle of Swiss Colony, and you and Sam can make your own celebration—just the two of you."

Sam considers that the woman is tired of them. His mother has eaten most dinners with them, and her stories of the near misses of her career are probably becoming less interesting. He knows; he's begun to get bored with them. Lately, she's also added stories about Jews and the reds who get the parts she should be playing. She also brings up this woman called Mary who was killed in a plane crash in Sicily, and he can see Hazel Pennyworth has begun to only half listen to the tale.

"You can use my bed, Edie. In fact, I've just changed the linen."

"That's lovely of you, darling," his mother replies, "but we've been invited to a rather nice party at the National Arts Club. On Gramercy Park, you know. One of those events where I have to show up, just to look in, but I think Sam might enjoy it. Jimmy Cagney will probably be there and dear little Helen Hayes."

"No kidding, Jimmy Cagney," Teddy Pennyworth exclaims. He seems genuinely impressed, which gladdens Sam, and he nods casually to suggest that seeing Jimmy Cagney was old hat.

At the same time, he is chagrined to be taken in by his mother as well. It is Christmas Eve, and Jimmy Cagney never shows up at the National Arts Club, nor is Helen Hayes anywhere in sight. In fact, as he expected, they have a hard time getting into the place. The attendant in the lobby insists they show an invitation, which his mother is vainly looking for in her purse. "You saw me put it in here somewhere, didn't you, Sam?" she says. Then, she is suddenly waving at a dignified older man crossing the foyer ahead of them. "Here we are!" she shouts over the doorman's shoulder. It is her girl's voice.

The man stops and looks bewildered down into the gloom where they stand, and then he suddenly smiles and fingers the lapels of his dinner jacket. "How extraordinary, Edie, to see you there. Yes, do come in. Come in." His wave commands the doorman to step aside. His mother changes from the perplexed innocent and passes before the attendant with a queenly dip and side step to ascend the several marble steps, one hand out to the old gentleman waiting at the top.

"Oh, Everett, so happy to see you and Merry Christmas. You know Sam, of course. Darling, this is Everett Bledsoe, one of the great Cyranos of all time."

"Walter Hamden be damned," the fellow says and chuckles.

His mother takes the man's hand in both of hers, and her eyes are glowing. She looks like she might fall to her knees right there in the foyer. "Silly me, I've lost my invitation."

"Oh bother take invitations. You have no need of invitations, Edie." He escorts them into the large room of the party. Sam's awkward feeling is doubled by the imposing nature of the club's interior and by the people standing around, drinking and taking little things to eat from trays being passed by Negro waiters. He recognizes no one, sees no movie stars. Jimmy Cagney is nowhere to be seen. Even the waiters wear tuxedos. Enormous portraits of men and women in extraordinary costumes hang on the walls and over the mantels of several fireplaces. Some of the guests pause in their conversations to look them over, also to wave to the elderly actor who guides them. They turn back to their own group.

"Well, just one, thank you," his mother says to a waiter. She takes a glass of wine from the offered tray and sips at it. She looks at the actor over the rim of the glass. "You're such a dear, Everett." It seems to be a cue, for the man bows and slips away into the crowd as if he had performed his part. "Dear old letch," she says to Sam out of the corner of her mouth. "There's the grub, over by the fireplace." She leads the way.

As she plows through the crowd, wineglass held high, Sam notices she moves in a peculiar shy posture, a hunched up attempt at anonymity that largely succeeds and at the same time seems ready to be singled out. One or two people pluck at her dress sleeve to receive a boisterous greeting, a kiss on both cheeks. But the buffet has been thoroughly ravaged. A few crustless triangles of bread with some sort of cream cheese on them are all that remain on large trays. Three shrimp float in a bowl of melted ice water. She becomes an innovator, a mother full of invention. "Here," she says to Sam quickly. "Let's put these shrimp on these pieces of bread—and—voila!" At the far end of the table is a bowl of olives and some celery stuffed with more cream cheese. Sam is famished, and these bits of food only make his hunger more painful. It claws at his stomach. The quick march through the bitter cold from the Pennyworth apartment in the Village has turned his stomach inside out. "Why can't we take a taxi? Like everybody else."

"It's just a short walk," she'd told him at every street crossing. Intersection after intersection—there seemed no end to them. Now the party at the National Arts Club is thinning out, and he has just gotten warm. The tweed material of his pants has become flexible. Bunches of the membership bustle into long coats and furs at the front door. This party hadn't meant to be dinner, he understands. That's what the people are all going to now. They are all leaving to eat dinner somewhere else. Huge logs crackle in the fireplaces, and several men all but disappear into giant chairs, holding drinks and talking. They look ready to spend the night, even all winter maybe.

"Well, that's that," his mother is saying. She sounds like she's just finished a four-course meal. She puts down the empty wineglass on the table and starts toward the foyer. He follows her down the wide marble steps and out into the winter night that has become even colder. His pants instantly freeze again; he fears the material might splinter as he walks.

"We're going uptown, Edie," someone says from a Checker cab at the curb. The warmth of its interior gushes over them, laced with perfume and soft leather smells. "Can we drop you?"

"Oh, how kind of you," his mother is saying. "But we have a dinner date just around the corner. So very kind of you though. And Merry Christmas!" she cries out, waggling her fingers. She sets a good pace down the street and around the corner on Irving Place. A restaurant called Pete's Tavern lies ahead. "Here," she tells him suddenly, as if she has only just remembered their destination, and pulls him through the establishment's several outside doors.

Sam immediately feels at home. Dark paneling sheathes the walls, and a long bar runs down the left side. It is crowded deep. Cozy booths are on the right. Several brass spittoons punctuate the floor, which is composed of small white tiles. Red bells and green wreaths of cardboard hang from crepe paper strung across the width of the place. The people at the bar laugh and talk. He can imagine his father as one of them, and he knows instantly his father has been one of them. Has stood there.

Others bend over their dinner at tables or within the semiprivacy of the high-backed booths. Photographs of racehorses decorate the walls. Huge radiators pour out a heat that prickles Sam's near frozen flesh, and the aromas of hot food are pushed out from the restaurant's kitchen through swinging doors at the far end of the room. Waiters in long white aprons rush the laden plates to the tables. The smells are both wonderful and cruel. He thinks his stomach is a deflated balloon, never to be full again.

His mother makes a beeline for an empty booth by the side door. "O. Henry used to come here," she explains. "You remember 'The Lady or the Tiger'? Also that boring business about a couple at Christmas pawning watches and so forth and so on."

"'The Gift of the Magi,'" Sam says quickly. They have just read the story at school in English class. "She cuts her hair off to sell it." He takes the seat opposite his mother.

"Yes, sentimental poop. One more disfigurement that men think so appealing." Her laughter is short, a flick of amusement at most, and then seeing the confusion on his face, she hands him the menu. "Order what you want. Your father likes the corned beef and cabbage."

He's still angry about the long, cold walk to the National Arts Club—it must have been twenty blocks at least—and then only for a couple of shrimp and droopy celery. Surely, she could have done better for them somehow. It is Christmas Eve, after all. So, he avoids her eyes, the keen excitement in them that relays the fun she is having in this odd scavenger hunt. She's performing these tricks for him—he knows that—and it is the best she can do, but he looks away to keep his resentment inviolate, even as a part of him chides his petulance and gives her credit.

"Long time no see, Edie." He's a short man with a paunch and very dark hair cut in bangs across his forehead. His nose is strongly made, and Sam can imagine him poking it into pots in the kitchen, for he is obviously the proprietor.

"Hello, Pete," his mother says. "This is Sam."

Pete puts out a fat hand and stares at Sam. "Looks like his dad, too. And where is Owen these days?"

"He's playing the hero in Italy," she answers. "Last heard from, he's with the partisans north of Bologna. Up in the hills, eating spaghetti and meatballs." She stiffens in her seat, a strengthening all along her spine as she lifts a smile toward the tavern owner, a posture that carries courage and humor all at once. It is a Joan Crawford pose. Sam and Teddy Pennyworth have just seen one of her movies. But he thinks his mother does the smile better. His throat suddenly grows thick, and he wants to cry. His mother still holds the man's attention. "I'm between shows, Pete, but I expect the tab is still open."

"Not only open, Edie, but it's Christmas. You and Sam are my guests."

"The Gift of the Magi," Sam says, feeling wise and happy to amuse the adults. They both laugh at his remark.

And it's a great meal. Slabs of succulent turkey, mashed potatoes with gravy almost equal to Aunt Rho's. The dressing has oysters and chestnuts in it. That was new to him. Side dishes of squash cooked with honey and brown sugar, and brussels sprouts, which Sam doesn't like very much. He eats them anyway. Warm soft rolls with butter and gooseberry jam. The waiter brings him another helping of turkey, potatoes, and his own bowl of gravy. Sometimes with his mouth full, Sam catches the owner watching him from the bar, nodding and slightly smiling. Sam promises himself he will come back to this place again, when he gets older, and it will always be the same. He would make it one of his places, like his father has. His hangout; he'll stand with one foot on the brass rail.

"What's this about you going to be a teacher?" he finally asks as his hunger is slowly put down.

"Oh that," his mother answers. Her bracelets slip and rattle. She's eaten sparingly, as if to compensate for his gluttony. Nor has she finished the glass of red wine Pete served her. She seems to be somewhere else. "I'm just looking ahead, Sam. Your father is in a risky business right now. And so am I. We have to be straight about it. I'm no spring chicken any longer. I can't play Ophelia anymore. Astor asked me to take over the part when Barrymore was getting too much for her, but that was a long time back. Also, the commies and the Jews are giving the good parts to their pals." Her profile has become fierce, a mask of some kind. For some reason, he doesn't like to hear her say such things. She talked like that with Hazel Pennyworth, and it made him uneasy. Sad, even.

"So, what are you studying?"

"Shakespeare, the Greeks." She brushes one hand through her hair. It is the gesture of a much younger woman. "Of course I know the plays backward and forward. But I just need the credits for my degree. Schools only hire people with degrees."

Sam's a little winded by the idea that his mother is going to become someone like old Mrs. Paige at school. The idea stuns him. Moreover, his astonishment is accompanied by the unexpected recognition that her being an actress has been important to him. He has reveled in the distinction of her career, which had set him apart from his classmates in East Liverpool and now in the new school in Connecticut, where mothers all look like ads in the *New Yorker* magazine. Especially lately, her profession gives him a sort of immunity, an impervious shell, like the old heroes he has read about, while it also makes sense of the way they lived, out of trunks and borrowed sofas and with deprivations disguised as escapades. Now, she is ditching all that to become just a teacher. Nothing special. He thinks her decision amounts to a betrayal; that he has been given no voice in the matter makes it worse.

"Cheer up," she is saying. "Take off that dumpy face. It's not the end of the world. We have to keep going, Sam."

Just then, Pete wheels a small cart to their table and personally prepares the plum pudding. He pours a liberal amount of brandy over the dessert and lights it. Sam carefully observes how others in the room have paused to take in this special treatment. The flame of the burning liquor rises and dances, and his mother claps her hands and throws back her head to laugh. She's redoing some scene from a play, he's pretty sure, for the benefit of the audience at the bar. She turns to the other patrons and, in a silent appeal, begs their understanding of why Pete himself is preparing their dessert. She must get used to such treatment herself, her expression suggests, so they have to ignore this excessive display—if they can. The thick slab of hard sauce slowly melting on the warm confection is so enriched with sugar and butter that it burns all the way down Sam's throat.

"Pete has his own black market," she confides when he leaves them. "Butter, sugar, booze. He has a warehouse full of stuff over in New Jersey where he keeps his horses. He owns racehorses too. Your father knew him when he was a bootlegger." She takes a large bite of the pudding. Then she tells him of a recent job on the radio. She plays a girl from Wyoming who comes to New York and meets a successful architect at a drugstore lunch counter. The cast is just she and the other actor, and they read from a script in a room with no windows. No audience either. Just the engineer at the control booth, who watches them through a pane of dark glass. And, in another room, another guy does all the sound effects. He plays recordings of people talking, car horns, typewriters, phones—even footsteps as the two of them pretend they are walking along the East River. The soundman plays records of gulls crying and a tugboat whistle. But she and the other actor hear none of that. The room where they read their scripts is silent as a tomb. The rest is all made-up.

Sam listens intently and takes in her face. High cheekbones, wide mouth, demanding eyes, and prominent smile—still a striking image in the warm glow of the small table lamp. Sam is aware she is happy right then because she has pulled it off—given him this Christmas Eve. She has made it up, and he knows he must love her.

Camp Lackawanna

"Camp Idontwanna is more like it," Teddy Pennyworth grouses. Their mothers are in the back bedroom of the Pennyworth apartment, and it is the following June. Teddy's mother goes over the list of clothing the camp requires. Sam's things are already packed in a small suitcase of woven fiber, which sits in the foyer.

"It's so very wonderful of you doing this for Teddy," the boys hear Hazel Pennyworth say. Teddy rolls his eyes and sticks a finger down his throat. Sam snorts too. "A month out of the city."

"Not at all," Edie Olson replies. "After everything you've done for us. Putting Sam up last Christmas. Everything."

She's been hired as a drama coach by a large corporation that operates several summer camps in the Poconos. She's to stage plays for the older campers and tourists at the establishment's casino. "They own a thousand acres, all fenced in against snakes," she assures Hazel. "Also, no Jews or Negroes are allowed and just a few Catholics." She's wangled what she calls scholarships for the boys.

On the bus ride down from New York, Sam shares two seats with Teddy in a row behind his mother. She has told them more about the camp. Camp Lackawanna is directly across a small lake from the girls' camp—Noowackie. There will be cookouts and canoeing and hikes that will be joint activities. "Secret rites at midnight," Teddy says wisely when they talk about it. But Sam has become a little shy around girls. As he had feared, Nancy Wilson would have nothing to do with him after the Christmas holidays—he knew he should have showed up at her parents' party. She has taken up with the captain of the tennis team, and the rumor was that she was doing it with him in the woods next to the courts. "We'll have to stick together, old man, us two against the designs of the encamped female," Teddy tells him.

Oddly, Teddy is nervous, and Sam is surprised how the increasing distance the bus puts them from New York puts his friend on edge, diminishes his confidence. He also smells bad and complains the bus doesn't make restroom stops often enough. He farts a lot. His cockiness has come unstrung. Then, counselors assign them to cabins in different sections of the camp. They hardly see each other and have little opportunity to talk, and as Sam looks at Teddy at mealtime across the vast dining hall, the boy's usual round-faced irreverence becomes more and more sullen. He seems to be looking at something inside himself even as he sits at table, shoulder to shoulder with other campers. With a stab of heart, Sam recognizes Teddy sits alone. He's heard talk about his friend's bragging and the noises he makes when he sleeps that keep his cabin mates awake. He's gotten the name "Gas Bag." The others don't think his stories are funny, and Sam wants to come forward to say that the stories Teddy tells about Greenwich Village are true—that there is a big jail just for women who do sex for money. That he does have a girl friend who's married to a sailor and she washes her underwear in the bathtub and hangs it up for you to see. But he pulls back, partly because some of the boys making fun of Teddy have also become his friends and partly because he finds he enjoys Teddy's being laughed at. Just a little. He's surprised by this feeling in himself and at times is sorry for it.

One night, Teddy Pennyworth doesn't show up at the mess hall for dinner. The whole camp turns out to look for him. Flashlights sweep and poke through the dark woods around the lake. Counselors in rowboats efficiently crossing each other in a prescribed pattern inspect the lake. Everyone calls his name in the night air. "Hey, Teddy—Teddy!" Only frogs answer, "Ted-ieee!"

At daybreak, he's found tied to a tree near the girls' camp. He's been gagged by his own underpants and he is naked. His pale, pudgy belly has been decorated with Mercurochrome and large circles have been drawn around his nipples. GAS BAG has been scribbled on his stomach. He has cried himself to exhaustion.

Teddy Pennyworth is the only passenger on the afternoon bus. Sam has waited at the administration building to say good-bye—to say something, he doesn't know what. But they do not speak, because Teddy hurries up into the bus, clutching his small duffel to himself, his gaze determined and held away from Sam. His face is still swollen from all the tears he shed during the night, and his cherry red mouth is twisted into what might look like a grin but for the pain the expression harbors. Inside the bus, he quickly finds a seat by a window, and then he looks down to meet Sam's eyes. Teddy's expression is blank, and Sam is even more bewildered. Sam raises his hand to wave and then thinks it would be ridiculous to do so. He does not understand what has happened or why it has happened, but he is certain Teddy is blaming him, and he recognizes that wouldn't be completely wrong.

FOUR

"I LIKE THE MOUSTACHE," Emerson told the other man. It had been a quick reunion once he recognized this older version of Teddy Pennyworth and had sorted out their former relationship.

"The ladies say it contributes to the moment." The round face slanted into a leer as the whole head swiveled to take in the bartender. Constance was putting up wine goblets, humming to herself as she prepared the bar. "Makes up for the empty ballroom above," Pennyworth said and patted his baldness.

The thin line of hair above his mouth resembled a party disguise hastily pasted on. Together with the magisterial baldness, the moustache gave Pennyworth the appearance of one of those so-called medical experts in newspaper advertisements that promote cures for psoriasis or incontinence. His reddish lips twisted to one side as he took in a succulent breath.

"It's been a long time," Emerson said. "What brings you to Pittsburgh?"

"We're hoping to make Jimmy Overstreet a national martyr, second to none. I refer to the *Weekly Agenda,* the newspaper that gives *Right the Might.*" The flourish of his language was ambiguous; the boast could be taken seriously or not. He continued, "I was just telling—what do they call you, Connie?" The round head swung around once again to look over the bartender.

"I am Constance," she said simply and continued setting up her station.

"Constance, eh? Maybe Con too—eh?" He continued to stare at the young woman, then his head turned back toward Emerson, and he winked. "You speak French? Parlez-vous?" He didn't wait for an answer; he hadn't expected one. "But it's just outrageous—four against one. Four white cops against a lone black kid on a street late at night. Is that

America or what? And what's being done about it? That phony hearing for the cops. C'mon, you got to be kidding. Is that what Martin Luther King Jr. died for? Never mind answering that—I'm sure you are embarrassed enough," Pennyworth said.

"It's an unhappy time," Emerson said. "How did you find me?"

"Flying down here, I open that slick airline throwaway, and there's a whole story about Sam's Place. Pictures and everything. Your chef is a black guy—way to go! Could this be the same Sam Emerson who was my pal in Greenwich Village, I ask myself? Could this be the brilliant imago of that feckless pupa of those golden days, I ponder? You should have seen this guy then, Con-stance. Not quite the ladies' man he must be today." The journalist had been watching the young woman as she hung up wine goblets, and to include her in the conversation was clearly an excuse to look her over again.

"How long have you been in town?" Emerson asked.

"A few days, and that's enough. What do they say about a day in Philadelphia?—well, Pittsburgh gets a week. No offense, old man."

Over the years, Pennyworth's voice had deepened to give weight to the quirky manner of its delivery; the posturing of his youth had now filled out. The sound had matured, but the rhythm had not changed, for certain words in a sentence would be arbitrarily stressed like wrong notes abruptly hit on a piano. The snorting rasp of the man's voice struck a chord in Emerson's memory.

Homer, the busboy, was methodically setting up the tables, arranging crisp linen napkins and aligning the heavy silverware with the china especially created for the restaurant. The profile of the city was eerily defined by a light Emerson knew to presage a storm coming in from the west, from behind them. A jetliner in its landing pattern passed over the skyline, close to the US Steel Building. In the kitchen, a hot pan sizzled in water, and the sound seemed to echo in the glassware behind the bar.

Pennyworth had been observing Emerson taking in the view as he continued talking in his taunting manner. That same tone had amused and astonished Hazel, his mother. *"Now Teddy,"* she would say. "But I expect up here in the clouds, in this eagles' aerie, that is, if Pittsburgh has eagles—let's say pigeons . . . ," Pennyworth clucked and sniffed over his own correction. "Up here you might not be all that aware of what's happening down on the street below. You might be divorced from the quotidian. The times they are not changing—they're getting worse. Our Leader diddling the stenos—can you believe it? I am shocked—shocked," the man said and rolled his eyes toward Constance.

"If it happened, it was before he was president," Emerson reminded the journalist while thinking that just a few steps behind the padded, swinging door, Jimmy Overstreet's uncle—that black cook Pennyworth had mentioned—was at this very moment putting his own touch to some dish in the kitchen. The airline magazine had included a picture of Sterling to make a not so subtle point of their interracial partnership. Emerson enjoyed playing with this information, holding the fact of Sterling's proximity and his relationship to the dead athlete over the journalist. But he figured it would be only a temporary edge. If he were any sort of a reporter, Pennyworth would discover the connection soon. In fact, he might know it already, and it could be he was playing games. Emerson saw himself smile in the mirror behind the bar.

At checkout counters—such as the 7-Eleven up the street—Emerson had sometimes perused the *Weekly Agenda*. The tabloid seemed to have no single political identity but swung wildly both left and right to punch worthy issues at its readers with the same ferocity that other tabloids pursued the follies of celebrities. The pummeling of a particular cause was often so aggressive it seemed to Emerson the coverage undercut the very issue the newspaper was ostensibly claiming to champion.

"Yes, just a few days," Pennyworth answered the question again. "Just to get the lay of the land—if you'll excuse the expression." Constance Ho continued to polish champagne flutes and line them neatly on a shelf. Her face was without expression.

"It's perhaps early, but may I offer you a drink?" Emerson asked.

"That would be splendid. It is early, but I will accept some of your local water with just a slice of lemon perhaps. If you please, Connie."

"Constance," the bartender corrected him evenly. Her eyes had become slivers of ebony.

"Of course. Mea culpa. Con-stance." When Pennyworth sucked in some air, his moustache tilted to the left. "Isn't this just super? Here I am in Sam's Place, a gourmet landmark high above Steel City. And with the old companion of my flaming youth in Greenwich Village. When I read that magazine piece, I asked myself, could that be the old Sam Emerson I knew? The son of the famous Edith Olson—Everyone's Mother on the Big Tube." He paused to clear his head and swallowed the results.

"How I envied you your mother, the glamorous actress." The man sounded sincere.

"That's funny," Emerson said. "I used to think your mother was pretty special too. I often envied you."

"Did you know about his mama, Constance? Her glory days were before your time. A Queen of the Soaps, they called her. The Sarah Bernhardt of afternoon melodrama," Pennyworth continued. "But I guess she's no longer trodding the boards."

"Actually she just died," Emerson said. The words were new to him and pronouncing them startled him a bit.

"Oh, I am sorry, old man," the journalist said.

"And what of Hazel?" Emerson asked quickly. "I only knew her that one winter, just a week, but the time of it has stretched out in my memory. Fabulous apartment—all those pillows. The lamp glow. Your mother coming out of the kitchen, smiling, with plates of wonderful food."

"Baked Spam and overcooked pasta was the usual *plat du jour.* Wartime of course." Pennyworth lifted the glass of water to his lips. He drained it thirstily and chewed hungrily on the lemon slice. "Old Hazel filled her last prescription about ten years back. I tried to get her obit in the *Times,* but of course I could not. I expect your ma will make it. In the *Times,* I mean." He eyed Emerson quickly, an equivocal assessment, then continued. "She was a good old gal. So, you and I are alone in this cold world—orphans in the storm, my boy. We're next to step up to the plate and answer the phone." His laughter was heavy as he cleared his throat.

The Pennyworth apartment had been a cozy outpost in the arctic landscape his mother had paraded him through that one Christmas holiday. She had enlisted him in her attack on fame and success, and Sam had been a willing recruit. However, Teddy and his mother also made him sadly aware of how much he missed his life with Aunt Rho and how far away he was from the homely simplicity of her house in Ohio. Though plainly furnished, it radiated the same offhand affection that had briefly warmed him in the Pennyworth apartment. Yet, as Sam grew up, so grew a knot in his heart. He scolded himself. The very simplicity of that life in East Liverpool went begging for his loyalty, only to become a memento he might come across now and then in a drawer rarely opened.

"How long did you say you'll be in town?"

"A couple of days," Pennyworth said soberly. "I've got just about everything I need for a piece."

"Boss." Constance delicately dried her hands with a small towel. Her nails were long and crimson. "I need some Chablis and a few splits of champagne."

"Right." He turned back to Pennyworth, whose round countenance had sharpened a little. The journalist had obviously just made a quick study of employer and employee and come to a conclusion. "Excuse me for a minute, Teddy. But you're to be my guest for dinner."

"Hey, I got a place to stay. I can make my way. You don't have to put me up on your sofa." He thumped Emerson's shoulder. "I won't embarrass you. I'll just hang out here with Connie—oops, *excusez moi,* I mean Constance. Hit me again." He pushed the empty glass across the bar top. "It felt so goo-ood the last time." She filled the glass with mineral water and slipped a new slice of lemon over it.

Emerson spent more time than he needed to pull out the bottles of wine in the cellar in the basement of the building. He knew exactly what champagne to bring back up, where the Chablis was located. But he took his time. He chose a white Burgundy from Servin, not the best of the lot but adequate for the single-glass customer. The wine was a Grand Cru, five years old, and he could charge a good amount for it. He had stopped offering California versions of the grape; they had too much oak for him. His customers readily accepted his taste.

He enjoyed turning the bottles within their orderly racks. The wine cellar of Sam's Place was not the largest of Pittsburgh's restaurants nor even the most valued, but the inventory had been assembled with care. His customers drank what Emerson liked to drink. He had constructed this soundproof, windowless room with its temperature kept at a steady sixty-five degrees in the basement next to the parking lot. Many times he had come down here after returning from a visit to Mansfield, to shift and rearrange the vintages until the melancholy that had accompanied him all the way back to Pittsburgh disappeared. He put himself into quarantine among the Bordeaux and the Barolos, so that his mood would not infect the atmosphere upstairs. He did not come out (come up for air, he often joked to himself) until he felt and looked normal, with a bottle or two of something interesting in hand.

"You know what she said to me today?" he had said to Phoebe after one of these visits to his mother. "You're like me—we both have a talent for being left."

Phoebe had dressed and brushed her hair, fixed her makeup, and sat on the edge of the sofa with her purse in her lap, the briefcase under one arm. With few preliminaries, they had made love quickly on this large sofa that faced the city's panorama, and their satisfactions had lingered upon them. But now she leaned into her departure, knees and feet primly together, ready to get home. She was a runner who had finished one race and was ready to start another.

"Well, that's a kind of alliance, isn't it, sorry as it might be? She was reaching out."

"Yeah, but who left whom?" Then Emerson paused and looked down at her. "Who's leaving who?" He had not meant his voice to sound so significant, gratuitous emphasis, for Phoebe gripped her briefcase and laughed as she stood up briskly. All business.

"It's 'whom,' isn't it? Who's leaving whom?" She kissed him and sighed. "How did I ever meet you? What am I doing here?" She shook her head and laughed once more.

After he had selected and put the wines into a wicker carryall, Emerson went out the back door to the parking lot and his car. He retrieved the box of ashes from the front seat and returned to the wine cellar, paused, and looked around. It would have to be something special, appropriate. Several bottles of a Chambertin from Drouhin seemed right. The wine was intense, a little rough but fragrant—aged remarkably. Just right. "There you go, Ma," Emerson said as he placed the brown box upon the bottles of Burgundy. "For now, anyway."

If only the different seasons could be held up to the light as easily as one of these wines, opened, and then digested. Upstairs a character out of one of those seasons waited for him to emerge, rightfully expecting him to be familiar. And maybe he was the same, though he fancied he had reinvented himself, particularly on that afternoon in Pittsburgh after the sale of Aunt Rho's farm. He had gone to the heights of Mt. Washington to create Sam's Place, only to keep this residue of himself in the basement of that success.

"There's a guy out front from the *Weekly Agenda*—that tabloid, who's here to do a story on Jimmy." Sterling Wicks accepted the information without a pause as he pre-sautéed some sweetbreads in butter. One hand reached into a bowl of chopped parsley to sprinkle the flakes of it over the meat. "It also turns out he's a guy I knew when I was a kid—in New York. Greenwich Village. Our mothers were friends."

Wicks turned from the stove and took up one of the bottles of wine from Emerson's basket to check the label—to see what sort of wine was going to accompany his cooking. He was interested but not completely invested in the choice. A yellow rosebud was fastened to the neck of his smock. "So, we're going national." He put down the wine. The two line cooks worked and chatted behind them. "What about the new cooler? What's the story?" His look was a little stern. He had been needling Emerson about replacing the old one for almost a year now.

"Not to worry. It's almost done. About ready to be installed." Emerson leaned over the stove and spooned a bit of risotto from a large saucepan. The rice grains were hard yet, yielding only a little to his bite. Their finish tonight, done per order, would include saffron, sun-dried tomato, and grilled sardines. Wicks and his family might use the kind of publicity Teddy's paper would give the case.

Suddenly, Cynthia pushed through the swinging doors and marched to the bulletin board near the walk-in cooler. She leaned close to the wall to check the evening specials Sterling had neatly penciled on a sheet of paper. Both men silently followed the woman's entrance, discreetly looking her over. Emerson could see no new bruises. Finally, the chef spoke.

"What's the book look like?"

"We have forty-eight, mostly parties of four," she said without turning around. Then she joined them at the cooking station. Her Slovak ancestry rounded the young woman's face into a moonlike sweetness, though her eyes slanted above the high cheekbones. "Oh, goodie. Can you save me some of that?" she asked Sterling. Rita had just unmolded a lemon mousse cake. "That would be especially tasty at the end of the night."

"Cynthia, my heart is yours, and so is my mousse," Sterling Wicks replied. The woman's laugh was a little sardonic, but Emerson was glad to hear the sound. She returned to the dining room.

The chef placed the large sauté pan on a cool burner and walked toward the far corner to a small cubicle near the pantry that served as his office. On the desk was the menu for the next day, printed in his open lettering. Another sheet of paper lay beside the first, noting the items required. Emerson's shopping list. With the exception of a small electric clock, the rest of the metal desktop was bare, stripped down. As if to compensate, a corkboard fastened to the wall above the desk was thickly shingled with notes, scribbled phone numbers, clipped recipes, two dried-up carnations, photographs, several arrays of ribbons, an invitation to a charity event, and a page torn from a date book. *Encore, s'il vous plaît* was scrawled in loops of lipstick on it.

Over the whole board reigned a headline from the *Pittsburgh Post-Gazette*. OVERSTREET TO PITTSBURGH. A picture of Sterling Wick's nephew wearing his high school football uniform was attached. The newsprint had yellowed and curled at the edges, but the look in the boy's eyes remained fresh, alert. He had been a good-looking youth with a wide forehead over eyes that seemed ready to take in much more than an offensive formation. A gentle, almost girlish line of mouth countered his reputation as a vicious tackler. He was known to risk injury, throwing himself into running plays with a fierce recklessness. Lately, Emerson had studied this picture to catch some glint in the printed resemblance to connect the violence the boy so ardently had practiced on the football field with what might have happened on the night of his death in Upper St. Clair. The police had called his behavior "bull-like" and "ferocious." He had resisted arrest and put up a fight. Yes, he may have been fighting for breath, Emerson decided. For his life.

"He was a great kid," Wicks said.

"They're going to bring in a jury from outside, I hear," Emerson said.

Wicks nodded, sat down, and wiped the back of his neck with a large white napkin. "They're talking about people from Harrisburg, maybe so as to reproduce the purity and ethnic distribution of our own suburbs. So the cops will get a fair trial, you understand. A jury of their peers." His laughter crawled around the bottom of his throat.

"Someone downtown told me the local fed attorney is taking depositions. So that should bring some pressure on the local authorities," Emerson said.

"Sure. Everybody's getting into the act." The chef had picked up the shopping list and passed it to Emerson. The gesture was meant to change the subject, Emerson knew that, but then Wicks ignored it himself with a sudden shift in his chair. "Let me tell you something," Sterling said casually. "I've never told you this, I don't think. My great-grandmammy had been a slave, and during Reconstruction—this was in Atlanta—she and some other black ladies, all former slaves, did the city's laundry. I mean all sheets and shirts and underpants were washed by these women, ironed neat, and delivered back to white families. Excellent work, too. You can believe it. They had learned the profession on the old plantations as girls. Broken in, you might say. Learned how white folks liked their things pressed. They learned more about white folks from the secrets left on the underwear. You dig? Before DNA, buddy." Sterling leaned back and put his feet on the desk.

"They were paid pennies, of course," he continued. "So what do you think these women did? They organized. They called themselves the Neighborhood Union—I guess *union* was the word then—and they went to the white families and said they wanted more money to do the laundry. I mean, the whole city of Atlanta. The white people said no, and my great-grandmammy and her friends went on strike. I'm talking turn of the century. They'd read about strikes and such, so why not them, washing white folks' tablecloths and skivvies? Great-grandmammy was right there, too, in the front line. In the front tub." He stretched out his arms and smiled broadly.

"Well, Atlanta was outraged. The laundry wasn't being done. The newspapers had angry editorials. The mayor and the governor had meetings. But the strikers held fast. Poopy drawers piled up, and who was going to wash them? Not the National Guard, you can believe it. So, they won."

"No kidding," Emerson said perhaps too quickly. He sounded as if he had only been half listening.

"They got their raises and went back to the washboards, but—guess what? Rub-a dub-dub. Mysteriously, all over Atlanta, house rents for black families were jacked up. You see what I'm saying, Sam?"

"This guy—Teddy Pennyworth—could probably get your family some money for lawyers' fees and such. These tabloids pay well for interviews," Emerson said. "You know, an exclusive interview. Might as well get their side—Jimmy's side of the story in print."

Sterling Wicks rolled his head to look at Emerson; he almost seemed to be smiling, but it wasn't a humorous expression. "You're saying our side of the story has not been printed enough?" he asked quietly. Emerson couldn't tell if that required an answer. "And by the way," the chef continued, in the same easy voice. "What's this crap about there not being enough salt in the humus? If your taste buds are so deadened, then pick up the nearest salt cellar and invert."

Now they became playful, like boys kicking at each other's feet. This sudden comradeship was genuine, and their horseplay cheered the kitchen crew. It looked like the real thing, and it might have been the real thing, but if it was only a slipcover, Emerson thought later, pulled over a worn situation, it was still important.

"Jimmy's folks don't have a whole lot. Their lawyers are talking about suing the township. The county. Everything white. They might could use some help." Wicks took off his cap and scratched his scalp. "Well, why not? They'll pose, give a little talk for a good fee. That's the way it goes."

Emerson had been looking over the shopping list. "The asparagus looked a little woody yesterday. What about broccoli instead? I hate brussels sprouts."

"I remember," Wicks said. "Find what's fresh. I'm adaptable."

When he gave the wine to Constance, Emerson looked around for the journalist. The bartender pointed to the far corner of the restaurant. Pennyworth was outside on the balcony, one hand on his bald head as if he might be keeping the breeze from blowing something off. The journalist surveyed the panorama of the city and its rivers. "I hope he didn't hassle you," Emerson said to the young woman. "He's someone I knew a long time back. In high school."

"No problem, boss." She shrugged. "I was busy, and he just wandered off."

"When will you start calling me Sam instead of 'boss'? You've been here almost three years. You sometimes make me feel like I'm in an old Charlie Chan movie."

"Well, that's your problem, isn't it? And I will overlook the faintly racist subtext of your remark." She finished fitting goblets upside down into the rack above her head, but she was smiling. She had never missed a day at Sam's Place. She would be getting her degree soon, and then she would leave to take up a position in some economics department. Professor Constance Ho. He liked the sound of it and was momentarily pleased with himself for contributing to her achievement. Yes, a very small part, he edited his thoughts, maybe too small a contribution to even think about. Constance had become a feature of the place, chatting sweetly with customers as her delicate prettiness was reflected several times over in the mirrors and glassware around her. Emerson was more than aware how her exotic appearance contributed to the ambiance of the restaurant, but the thought troubled him sometimes. That he would even think of her as exotic was a fault he admitted to himself.

Teddy Pennyworth had been moving along the balcony, perhaps seeking different angles on the skyline, and Emerson turned back to the front of the restaurant where Cynthia worked at the high desk, accounting the reservations, taking more by phone. "We're getting a good number of people from the play at the City Theatre," she told him. "Looks like the prix fixe may be taking off."

Only a few restaurants served late, which always surprised Emerson, considering how Pittsburghers liked to eat, but their stomachs apparently closed down early. Maybe something left over from the old days when the steel mills were going. So, he had been experimenting with serving a late-night supper. It meant keeping on a line cook and one of the serving staff. He took over the bar himself. But he wasn't yet convinced the venture was worth it, so he appreciated Cynthia's optimism. She was a team player.

"So how are you?" he asked her.

"Me? I'm fine."

"No, I mean . . ."

"Oh, I know what you mean, Sam." She became quickly busy with the sheets before her. She ignored his steady look. Finally, "Look, you and Sterling just have to back off a little. I'm a big girl, and I can take care of myself. I can make my decisions and will if the situation gets to be more than I can handle. I promise you. I appreciate your concern, but you guys are not my daddies, okay? In fact"—now she was looking directly into his face with all the boldness of a Southside urchin—"this solicitude of yours could be downright suspicious. If you know what I mean." Something like a smile curled her small mouth.

"Right. I understand," Emerson replied and took a couple of steps back, his hands open in front of him. He did know what she meant. Their concern for her—his and Sterling's—could be something else, their own designs on her, if only in an occasional fantasy. How can women tell the difference, Emerson wondered? Some signal goes off, a scent in the air? And was there a difference? The male impulse to keep the female from harm—keeping her safe—probably always had a selfish motive. The impetus partly explained his urge to marry Amanda maybe.

The poor girl never had a chance to escape his concern for her. She might have been perfectly happy to leave their affair at State College and go back to Benson Falls by herself. But he had insisted on protecting her. It had been a dictum of the era. Yes, she said she loved him—and probably did—but how much of that love had been to accommodate social circumstances that, as a female of the period, she could not avoid?

When the storm broke, the dining room's subdued quality was radically changed as patrons entered drenched and complaining about the sudden deluge. They made good-natured alliances with others in the restaurant's vestibule. Good sports at Sam's Place. The anticipation of their dinners served up in the midst of this natural havoc sharpened their appetites as it somehow exalted them. They felt chosen, and Emerson's easy manner moving among them anointed the calling. He wore the dark blue shirt Phoebe had given him. The torrential rain lay siege to the city's battlements and kicked up white divots in the normally placid surfaces of the Monongahela and Allegheny. The downpour lashed at the restaurant's giant windows and cascades of rolling thunder loosened tremors underfoot. Lightning stabbed at the Northside. No fireworks display could equal this extravaganza. Emerson became very busy tending to his customers, even bringing out towels for the women to dab at their hair. "Oh, Sam, you think of everything," one of them said gratefully.

"Yes, everything," he replied, and the woman laughed flirtatiously.

The recorded impressions of the Ravel piano pieces he favored were overwhelmed, yet the rage outside only seemed to enforce a sense of the refuge within the restaurant. Or it could have been a feeling of privilege among those who pulled the heavy napkins across their laps and took up their menus. Confusing privilege with security is an old error. Older diners recalled a time earlier in the century when some of them supped in the first-class salon of an ocean liner as it resolutely steered through a tempest.

"Should we send it back?" Sam Emerson asked his guest when he was finally able to get back to their table. Pennyworth had stuck his nose deep into the goblet and inhaled deeply. The server had just poured a sampling of the Chateau Neuf du Pape. Emerson had chosen the heavy Rhone because he had already decided what Pennyworth's dinner would be. The journalist rinsed his mouth with some of the wine and smacked his lips.

"It will do nicely," he said and looked up at the woman holding the bottle. "Be your name Hebe, cupbearer to the gods?"

"My name is Mary," she said evenly, "and I'm ready to tell you about our specials."

But Emerson ordered for them, choosing the lamb navarin, one of Sterling Wicks's signature creations. The stew was accompanied by a cake of couscous with almonds and currants, surrounded by pan-smothered mustard greens. For starters, Pennyworth chose oysters, and Emerson told Mary to bring him some of the black bean humus. It was a dish he could leave and come back to as he rose to greet customers, show them to their tables.

"You do that really well," Pennyworth observed after one of these interruptions. "Where did you pick up that savoir faire? It amazes me, old sport, that you could be running a place like this."

"You mean feckless me?"

"Well, yes." Pennyworth laughed with a charitable heartiness. His frankness, however insulting it might be, was always meant to be useful. He sucked an oyster from its shell. "And these handsome wenches you've hired."

"Mostly students, graduate students from different schools in the city," Sam said.

"That dusky maiden over there. The girl at the front. And the unique creature at the bar."

"You better watch it," Emerson said with a smile. "The women in this place will hand you your head."

In fact, Teddy Pennyworth's head seemed about to spin off his shoulders as it swiveled left and right to follow different wait staff passing their table. "Want to run a test? I bet if I stare at one of them long enough, I mean at her behind, she'll turn around to look at me. We've sensitized them over the years—part of the Darwinian selection process, no doubt." Pennyworth paused to clear his head. "They can feel us looking at them. It's become part of their defense—they know whether to run or not without looking. Often, I've walked behind a woman on the street and stared at her derriere, and eventually, without turning around, she'll reach her hand around to cover the spot. They have sonar built into their nethers."

"That never occurred to me," Emerson said. He was thinking this corner table had just become a strange annex to that back room of

Hazel Pennyworth's apartment, the two of them on the floor looking at girlie magazines. Outside, the storm had lessened; the sky had gone from navy blue to purple.

A party of four had just entered with that expectant look that always cheered Sam Emerson. He was about to satisfy their appetites, and he greeted these familiar customers, spending several casual minutes with them at their table. Cynthia sidled up to him gracefully and waited her turn to describe the special suggestions of wines for the entrees—her part of the performance.

When Emerson returned to the corner, Pennyworth had finished his oysters, and the shellfish seemed to have stimulated his thinking. He fussed and fiddled with the silverware, organizing his thoughts and was clearly impatient for Emerson's return, for his audience. "I have no time for these phonies who claim to be feminists," he began as his host sat down. "Can a male be a feminist? That's the question." Emerson tasted some of the humus as Pennyworth described a novel he had just read. "And you know what, this guy is touted as a feminist because he supposedly can picture the woman's point of view." The journalist snorted and stuffed a piece of sourdough roll in his mouth. "And what is this point of view—all the women in his book get on top? That's what his feminist point of view amounts to." Pennyworth appeared to be genuinely outraged. His brow surged and unfolded several times.

"That's amazing," Emerson said as Mary brought their service plates.

Pennyworth looked after the server's retreating form, followed her until she pushed through the swinging doors of the kitchen. "That's what I hate about these guys. I see them in my business, putting on these phony poses just to get their fingers in the ya-yah."

"The ya-yah?" Sam asked laughing.

"Sure, the jam jar. Nookie. Pretty pucker. The fold of heaven. The little nightingale that never sings. The pink. The gash. Surely, you have some words for it in Pittsburgh?" Pennyworth paused to suck in a breath, and Emerson felt he could see the word taking shape in the back of his throat, roll along his tongue to clash against his teeth. "How about cunt?" the journalist added finally and lifted his glass to drain its contents as if he had made some point.

Emerson poured more wine for them. "I remember you as a kind of passenger," the journalist continued. "I expect having that steamboat for a mother must have kept you in the back seat." Emerson wondered if the metaphor had been inspired by the excursion paddle wheeler that had just edged into the wharf below.

"Don't you think we are the sum of the people we encounter, the figures that surround us? We absorb and reflect their images," Emerson suggested.

"Whoa, this is heavy stuff. Sam the Mirror," Pennyworth conjectured. "So who are you in that mirror?"

"I'm just an ordinary guy, going about my business and trying to do what's right."

Pennyworth patted his mouth with the napkin and surveyed the dining room. "It's you ordinary guys trying to do what's right that make the problems for the rest of us. But let me disabuse you of that conceit. This is not the domain of an ordinary guy. And tell me about Anna Mae Wong over there behind the bar."

"What about her?"

"Well, is it true what they say—that their yum-yums go sideways? Oh, don't look so stricken, old man. It's a creaky joke. Do I have to list the number of historical routes that have been detoured through that little tunnel? You know, of course, that *vagina* means sword sheath in Latin?"

"I guess I didn't know that," Emerson said, wondering what connection Pennyworth was making.

"Now take this Paula Jones woman," Pennyworth said as he lined up his silverware and leaned over the table. "She's just another variant on the old story."

"Clinton said nothing happened. Doesn't remember the episode," Emerson said.

"Well, whether it did or not, she's become part of the myth. And as a registered voter, I'm not so happy about that myth—I mean a president who only asks for a blow job? What kind of an equivocation is that? Is that the kind of evasion—the passive pussyfooting, if you will—we want in a leader? Guiltless compliance? We want someone in there who knows how to pound the pound cake. Hey, you remember when JFK got elected, the sigh of relief that went up because, after Ike and Mamie, Harry and Bess, and FDR and Eleanor, we finally had a couple in the White House who were actually doing it?"

The imagery the man had called up made Emerson laugh, though he was about to raise more of a defense for Clinton when Mary appeared. She held the earthen crock of lamb stew in mittened hands and placed it down carefully on the table. Emerson served them both, spooning the navarin onto large plates. "Lately, I've been trying to make myself agreeable to a particular woman," he said. Emerson spoke carefully as he tested the couscous. It was a little dry, and he made a mental note about it. And the humus had still needed a little more salt. He quickly sketched his relationship with Phoebe, trying not to give Pennyworth too many details. He only wanted to get the conversation onto another plane. "My hope is that she'll make an honest man of me. I gather you have never married?"

Pennyworth shook his head. "Like the man said, happiness is whores. What does this lady do?"

"She's a therapist."

Pennyworth's eyebrows went up, then down. He put a forkful of meat into his mouth and chewed. "You know, our mothers ruined us for other women. Extraordinary women in their different ways."

Emerson wiped up some of the rich gravy with a scrap of bread and ate it. Just an edge too much bay leaf, maybe. "Your Hazel was very special, as I told you."

"You don't hold it against your mother that she wasn't Helen Hayes, do you? A hard worker for sure. A hearty laugh as I remember. Of course, something of a bigot, but then who isn't? Bigotry has brought me to Pittsburgh. Only the bigot in America sleeps soundly these days. Here's to bigotry—it has sponsored our reunion." He raised his glass in a toast. Emerson tapped his glass but did not drink.

"But your mother made a place for you. My parents were always living out of suitcases," Emerson said.

"That's the way they lived." Pennyworth spoke as he chewed. Some brown gravy dribbled down his chin, and he dabbed at it with his napkin. "By the way, I saw your father's pictures at MOMA last month—part of a large show. I guess you know about the show."

"My mother gave all his negatives to the museum years ago. Yes, I knew about it."

"Something about a cafeteria in Ohio. Not the war pictures you'd expect, but this small-town restaurant. Food again. Did you ever think, old fellow, that your history is one long meal?"

"We spent a summer—all of us—in East Liverpool. Just down the river from here." Emerson pointed out the window. The sky had begun to clear, and the rain had stopped. Pennyworth turned around a bit, as if to see the river town.

"But your mother did settle down near here, didn't she? Isn't this Mansfield College close by?"

Of course, Pennyworth had been doing research. Looking him up. As if to verify what facts the journalist might already have on file, Emerson found himself telling the man about his mother's teaching at Mansfield College, the Shakespeare festival, and the theatre named after her.

Pennyworth's face had somehow managed to grow long; the heaviness in his eyes was that of the professional mourner. "Happy her last years there? No desire to be nearer to you? To live in Pittsburgh?"

Emerson looked around the restaurant. Everything was going smoothly. A satisfied hum floated above the tables. Knives and forks clinked against china. Glasses of wine sparkled. Laughter and talk rose in the room. "You might say we had learned to live apart," Emerson said.

For a moment, Pennyworth looked a little taken back, but then he snorted and guffawed. "Hey, that's the sound of abandonment I love. I love it; I love it! Don't give up the slight. I'm all for it." He raised his glass again, but Emerson did not meet the salute this time.

"I had a great aunt who cooked in this village café. The High Standard Café it was called. My father took pictures of her and the others who worked there."

"Yes, those pictures were in the show. Your destiny was cooking. You couldn't escape."

"I remember one summer especially," Emerson continued as Mary came up to the table.

"Can I get anything for you?"

"What do you have in mind?" Pennyworth drawled. His mouth hung slack in an attempt at cleverness. The young woman cocked her head and smiled sweetly with an expression that had been obviously rehearsed.

Just as swiftly as it had arrived, the bad weather reversed itself to bring a brilliant clarity to the atmosphere, as if a dark garment had been turned inside out to reveal a dazzling lining. A rainbow arched over the rivers and the skyline to draw diners first at one table and then another, and then yet another, from their chairs to saunter out onto the dripping balcony. Some held their napkins, others a glass of wine. They stared at the rainbow, exclaimed over the bands of color.

"The sophisticated mesmerized by natural phenomena," Pennyworth snorted. "See Fellini."

"My partner is Jimmy Overstreet's uncle," Emerson said simply. Pennyworth gave a slight smile to suggest he had heard and that the information might not be new. "The family is planning civil suits and could probably use some money," Emerson went on. The journalist continued to nod, his face lowered over his plate. "I could introduce you to Sterling."

"That would be super, old bean," Pennyworth replied and glanced up shortly. He had known the connection all along, Emerson was convinced, and had only been waiting for this gesture from him. The journalist's countenance had become less amiable, professionally serious—he would have talked to Sterling Wicks on his own anyway.

Several patrons were taking their leave, and Emerson got up to follow them to the door, to shake hands. Constance leaned into the bar to converse with a couple waiting for a table. The Pirates mug that held her tips was stuffed with currency. The restaurant had settled into a pleasant stir—the outside noise of the storm abated—and this murmur within the room produced its own energy. The piano pieces on the sound system celebrated the turn. It would be a good night after all, Emerson estimated. From this side of the room, Pennyworth was a lumpy silhouette against the luminous skyline. The skyscrapers looked scrubbed by the storm, the facets of their architectural diversity newly made. Pennyworth's figure was cut from another background and pasted onto this brilliant display, Emerson thought. The silver dart of a jetliner banked over the city.

Unexplainable sadness touched him. In a flick of remembrance, he pictured the two of them pacing the streets of Greenwich Village in winter, looking for adventure if not romance. He saw himself endeavoring to keep up with Teddy Pennyworth's lumbering, offbeat steps that had been a demonstration of the boy's seriousness. He was feeling sorry for the two of them then in that past, a vain exercise, he knew.

"Ring me when you're leaving," he told Constance. "I'll come down and do the final check. And please do the setups for the prix fixe." What sort of a gift would be appropriate for her when she got her degree? She had family in Taiwan. He would miss her, and he felt a little guilty about using her image in an occasional reverie, her sleek and glistening figure turning in the Jacuzzi. He would have to get her a really nice gift, something to remember him by.

"I've got some stuff to do upstairs," he told Pennyworth. "I recommend the plum torte. It's contributed to our fame."

"Super," Pennyworth replied. He had just emptied the last of the wine into his glass. "Thanks so much for the repast. It was super. I'll just paddle back across the river. No need to worry—I won't harass your help. I'll leave a note for Mr. Wicks." He swung his head toward the bar and smoothed down his moustache. He meant to look sly. "I'll be in touch. Hell, the *Agenda* is paying the bills. So, I'll come back and buy my own dinner. Just to stay honest." He sucked in a large amount of air.

Few patrons of Sam's Place noticed the small door fitted smoothly into one side of the restaurant's foyer, for it was covered with the same tweed fabric that finished the walls. Nor was there a door handle. Just a discreet brass lock. Phoebe had her own key. Behind the door, a tight iron spiral of a staircase went straight up to the penthouse, and as Emerson took the steps he played a familiar game—he was a diver rising in a slow chandelle to the surface of the sea, to break finally into the open, dark shelter of his apartment, where he took a deep breath.

He turned on no lights. The Pittsburgh skyline had moved closer, as if it had been transplanted across the river to shoot up from just beneath his building like an enormous amusement park. Emerson splashed some George Dickel into a glass and stretched out on the leather sofa that faced the view. He called the hotel in Seattle where Phoebe was staying. She was out. Three hours earlier there; she was probably at one of those corporate dinners he had seen her reign over. He hated voice mail, hated to talk to a machine, though he did like to hear her voice. But this was a hotel humanoid giving him options. He rambled. "This is Sam Emerson of Pittsburgh," he said. "It's a night of heavy rain and even heavier nostalgia here. An old pal from yesteryear has shown up. I'm thinking of you, babe. I have an idea for the lady's disposal. Taking care of things. Sweet dreams."

As he talked, he ran a sort of movie in his head of Phoebe. It was a home movie of her and her family when she was a young girl, and though he had never seen such a movie, wasn't sure that a movie like that even existed, all of its details were sharp in the perfect lighting of his imagination. It was Christmas morning, and the family was opening presents around the tree, Phoebe in her nightgown and furry slippers, her siblings on the floor around her. Then, suddenly her arm reaches straight out; she takes a step forward and one finger points down at a particular package. "What's that?" she was asking, though there was no sound in the film. She had made that same stiff-armed gesture, a finger abruptly aimed, the other night in the garden, pointing at the foxgloves. "What's that?" He replayed the image, the sound of her voice again as he looked at the skyline. He had transplanted her directness of the other night into her history. He was certain the scene had happened.

He would talk to someone at Mansfield tomorrow. Surely they would be interested in doing some sort of a memorial, especially if he paid for much of it. It was typical of his mother, scattering the parts of herself for others to pick up. He had often admired her selfish trajectory, was certainly amused by its energy, but he also hated to be captivated by her gaudy business. He had learned very early that all those exciting and glamorous appearances were always matched by disappearances, and here she was again, just as obstinate in death, waiting for him below in the wine cellar to do something about her presence. Maybe Pennyworth would go with him; the man would add some amusement to the long trip, to its sorrowful task.

He had learned to live alone. Edith Olson's wacky theories on child rearing—one of her favorite examples described Spartan babies being put out into snow to toughen them up—were actually only to validate her casual handling of him. Perhaps, her offhand regimen had given him an unique but sad resolve. Sam Emerson had learned that discipline, and every woman who may have been initially intrigued by his seeming indifference eventually left him when they began to suspect their leaving him had been his expectation all along. And then, one time, he had opened a dresser drawer to select a new shirt and discovered that Phoebe had neatly arranged the shirts so they looked like a display at Brooks Brothers— looked fresh and made new by her care. And in fact, one of the shirts was new. She had bought him a shirt, the dark blue one he had put on tonight. No woman had ever bought him a shirt, not even Amanda. Its design was different from what he usually wore, the collar less formal, the thick Oxford weave of the fabric in a color he would never have thought to buy for himself, but it looked and felt just right. He had put it on and worn it with a pleasure he could not identify and was new to him. So Phoebe was different. She really seemed to care for him, but the old fear would sometimes slip into his happiness. "You're taking advantage of me, aren't you?" he half joked one evening as she left for home.

"You better believe it," she replied and kissed him. One hand had dropped to his trouser front and playfully squeezed him.

The late news on the TV showed Jesse Jackson announcing a prayer-for-justice to be held on the courthouse steps in the morning. Jimmy Overstreet was lauded by former teammates and teachers. President Clinton had dismissed the allegations made by Paula Jones. A special defense fund had been established to pay his legal expenses; meanwhile, Clinton was performing his duties in the Oval Office. The president announced his intention to overhaul the FBI and the CIA so the two bureaus communicated better. Boris Yeltsen looked drunk as he shook hands with Chinese diplomats. The Pirates were shut out by Atlanta. Emerson hated the Braves.

In the dim light, he could make out Aunt Rho and her colleagues at the High Standard Café. The photograph hung in the kitchen-bar alcove. What were their names—the other women? He used to know when he was a kid. All of those women, as well as the man who took the picture—and the woman who stood next to him when he took it—all were gone now. He gave a Pennyworth snort to the sentimentality that threatened him. It must be the bourbon. He had been pleased when the Modern Museum notified him that this picture and several others would be included in the exhibit, THE CENTURY'S IMAGES. The photographs of violence Owen Emerson's camera had been known for had been replaced by this simple shot of five women in starched uniforms. It could have been a picture one of the café's customers had taken with a Kodak, but it wasn't—it was different. That's how he wanted to remember his father, making something simple into something unique.

He had dreamed of his father lately. Young Sam Emerson as a boy is standing on a hillside, looking down at a small house below. Then this figure who is himself though not himself is walking through this farmhouse that is much like Aunt Rho's house, yet it isn't. The interior is empty and very quiet, but he knows his father is there. The wood floors glisten, squeaky with polished wax. At the end of a long hallway is a small door that opens into a narrow room with one window at the end. It is like Aunt Rho's sewing room, except it has a bed and his father is lying in the bed.

"Hello, buddy," his father says. "Good to see you."

"What are you reading?" Sam asks. His father holds up a book that had a photograph on the cover of a straight road between rows of tall trees. The road disappears into the distance. He recognizes it as one of his father's pictures, but in the dream he knows it is not. His father is very happy to see him, and he's laughing. Then they are embracing, and he feels his father's arms around him. He notices long white hairs growing from his father's nostrils, and that is strange because the hair on the man's head is still coal black. Glossy. This part of the dream makes him sad and happy all at once. He will never see his father age.

"I'll have to trim those," Sam says to his father.

"Be my guest."

Sam Emerson knows—in his dream—the small, round-nosed scissors he uses himself are in the kit in his bathroom in Pittsburgh. So, they are unavailable in the dream, though everything should be available in the dream. He looks through every empty room of the sun-washed farmhouse but finds only a small nail clipper. His father lies back on the pillow, a wary look in his eyes. Sam carefully grooms his father, and the man's arms are still around him. A phone rings in one of the vacant rooms. It rings and rings.

"We better answer that," his father says finally.

"Hey, boss, I'm closing down."

"I'll be right down, Constance," Emerson said.

PROGRAM NOTES

A Winter Scene

"Your father has been killed." Snow began to fall before breakfast and continues to drift across the tidy campus of Cornwall Academy. Some kids were talking about a toboggan party after classes, and Sam has been thinking of Nancy Wilson. She might show up. He might be able to be with her only with other classmates, but he could enjoy the frank look in her eyes, the way she moves. She might recognize how really good he was. How deserving he was of her affection. They could be friends.

But then, his mother shows up. The winter crispness has sharpened the pungency of her perfume, and she's all bundled up in a fur coat he's pretty sure she's borrowed for the occasion. She's playing the role of a woman of the theatre forced to ride a common carrier—four hours on the Greyhound—up from the bright lights to this obscure corner of

Connecticut. As always, she's a startling contrast to her surroundings, dressed for the wrong party. In this monochromatic landscape of winter, in this dun-colored sitting room, the vermilion slash of her lips is a banner from another season. Sam catches the tight look in the headmaster's eyes as he escorts her out of the cold and into the room, utterly polite but with a strained appreciation that she is someone slightly out of place who still must be handled carefully. Tolerated for an hour or maybe two.

Afternoon classes have already begun. Sam had waited for her alone in the sparsely furnished reception room just off the school's dining area. Dishes and pans scrape and clatter in the far kitchen as luncheon is being cleaned up, and the smell of corn chowder still cloys the heated air drummed out by steam radiators along the wall. He wishes he had taken one more of those biscuits. They were his favorite. Then the heavy outside door had opened and closed. He hears voices, feet stamping. Her voice, almost cheery, is muffled within the enclosure of the storm entry, and then the inner door opens and her heels smack across the parquet floor. Her talk fondles the headmaster's murmured courtesies. She sounds oddly gay, unusually good-spirited. Later, he would think it was the voice of the courageous woman carrying on, the solid front of the character crying within.

And while the two of them sit in this dingy sitting room of this fourth-rate boarding school, the rest of his class is working through a story by Maupassant in French II, and Nancy Wilson, sitting up front, is maybe thinking of giving him a second chance now that his father has been killed.

"How?" Sam asks.

"In France," his mother replies and unfolds a letter. "They say only that he's missing, but well, it's . . ." She smoothes the paper across her knees as she sits on the sofa beside him. The letter shows many such handlings and ironings. "Some place called Pont-à-Mousson. Must be a bridge of some sort. He was with Patton's tanks." She glosses the letter's information, digesting the contents to save him the trouble. He notes the stationery. *Look* magazine. "This is from his editor. I also got a wire from the government. So it must be true. We have to believe it."

She draws herself up straight, and the fur slips from her shoulders. Sam thinks she looks magnificent in her grief, her courage unsheathed, and she takes his eyes into hers with an eloquence that envelops and measures him all at once. "My, but they do keep you warm here, don't they?" The letter is folded and put away in her purse, replaced by a handkerchief she holds to her eyes. "You mustn't distress yourself on my account, Sam. I've lived through this moment many times over. It's been in rehearsal for a long time." She laughs a little, and her eyes become tattered around the edges. "It could have happened many times over. Even before you were born. But here you are. Here we both are—just the two of us. Now." Her mouth twists to one side, and the arrogant flamboyance of her lipstick is abruptly discarded like a used tissue.

"But how? I mean, was it the Germans?"

"Yes, of course, the Germans. You've seen the papers. The fighting is terrible. He was with some tanks. Last seen riding on one of them. Taking pictures. Bronco Billy." She laughs a little, and it is a strange combination—her laughter and the silent tears on her cheeks.

"Last seen. Maybe—"

"Don't even think it, sweetheart." Her voice has regained its projection. "He's gone. It's over. Finished. Finito."

"But, I mean, is he buried somewhere? Wasn't there a funeral or anything?" Sam fights back tears; his throat has filled up. It all seems very unfair. She is shaking her head and puts one arm around his shoulders. Her scent stings his nostrils, and he chokes back the clots of mucous in his throat. "Like Billy Brown. Where he's buried?" Sam asks.

"Who is Billy Brown?"

"Aunt Rho's fiancé from the other war."

"No, probably not."

"Nothing?"

"Well, maybe. Listen, Sam when this awful war is over, I promise you we'll go there and find him. I promise. How about that? We'll go together."

The room's radiator gurgles and clangs, and the ensuing steam heat smells like washed stones. It penetrates his clothes and gets into his bones, making him drowsy, and he wants to sleep. He wants to go up to his room on the third floor and crawl into bed and go to sleep. He wouldn't mind missing the toboggan party or even dinner, if he could wake up on the other side of this moment where everything is back to where it was. His mother puts away the handkerchief, opens and snaps shut her purse to release a puff of powdery fragrance that makes him sneeze.

"I must look a bloody mess," she says with a trouper's good humor. "And speaking of Aunt Rho, have you written her lately?"

"Yes," he says, which is a lie, but he figures the truth would only complicate the situation. "Are you staying for dinner? It's only pot roast, but I have to tell the kitchen."

"Thank you, darling. How I would love to stay and meet your chums. But Snookie Watson has a place in Sharon, and she's up here getting it ready for the holidays. Why she bothers, I don't know—her family is simply dreadful. But she's meeting me here in about an hour." She pulls down one glove to peek at her watch. Opens and snaps her purse shut again. "She's driving me to Millerton, where there's an afternoon train back to the city. I'm in rehearsal. You wouldn't believe how complicated this trip has been for me to make. The bus up. The train back. But, of course, it was important." Her smile seeks his understanding, his approval. Then, as if she has just remembered a piece of business, she puts her arm around him again and squeezes. "Steichen said your father could have been another Jacob Riis."

A Summer in Bucks County

In memory, that summer stretches on and on like a swing at the top of its arc, hanging in the light, never to come down. Sam never wants it to end, though he misses Aunt Rho and his friends in East Liverpool. All three of them are together—his mother, father, and he live in a little cottage by an old canal. He's never seen his father so relaxed. He wears old pants and short-sleeved shirts unbuttoned so the boy sees, for the first time, the thick hair on his father's narrow chest. "Harry Ape," his mother calls him sometimes or "Tarzan" when he loafs about in baggy swim trunks. Though that doesn't make sense, because Johnny Weissmuller, who swings around in a jungle at the Vista Theatre, has no hair at all on his chest. His chest is as smooth as Sam's.

It's like school being out all the time, save for his mother's schedule at the summer theatre. The Bucks County Playhouse. But his father hasn't carried back a camera since a couple of weeks one summer in East Liverpool when they were together for a little bit. In the meantime, he's been away to Greece and has just returned from France, which has just surrendered. He's brought Sam a beret. The photographer ambles about this stone cottage—it came with his mother's job at the theatre—coming to rest on the steep staircase by the fireplace that goes to the second floor. Or, he lounges on a bench just outside the door against the whitewashed wall of the building. Taking the sun. Sam thinks he looks like one of those old people in East Liverpool who have just missed the bus to Steubenville and who are waiting for the next one. His father looks older, though it has only been a year.

When he must put on more clothes for a party at the Playhouse or when someone invites them to dinner, Owen Emerson pulls on a pair of worn twill slacks and a rayon shirt the color of ripe cherries. Thick-soled sandals made of rope are strapped to his feet. His toes are crooked and the nail of one large toe is black; it takes the whole summer to come off.

"If you don't care how you look to my friends, you might set a good example for the boy," Sam hears his mother say. "That shirt is hopelessly vulgar."

"I certainly don't want to offend your playmates," his father says. Sam is outside, practicing yo-yo tricks. He can't do walking-the-dog on the uneven ground, but he has gotten pretty good with rocking-the-cradle.

"My playmates, as you call them, are among the leading intellectuals of this country. They have causes and believe in them strongly," Sam hears his mother say.

"Sure."

"I recognize such belief or the capacity for such belief is an anathema to someone like you, who has no cause."

"Yeah, that's right." Their voices are not angry; in fact they sound to Sam as if they are making jokes, having fun. "All those causes look alike to me, Dimples. I've made too many pictures of them."

"Oh, let's hear it from the wounded hero. The sensitive soul in an unfeeling universe. You've been boozing too much with Hemingway. You sound like one of his trashy novels. Show us your wound, Roberto."

"As you wish, Miss Olson." It sounds like his father gets up; the chair has scraped on the floor. Then Sam hears his mother laugh low in her throat, and then silence.

"You villain," she says after a little. Softly. The yo-yo spins within the string lattice Sam has made of his fingers. "I have a matinee today, remember?" She seems to be talking against something. Sam releases the yo-yo, and it falls and then snaps back into his hand perfectly. He wants to hear more, but he's nervous about listening, so he moves toward the old privy as he hears their steps rapidly taking the stairs to the second floor.

But most days, father and son have to themselves. His mother is always busy at the theatre, rehearsing or meeting with different people.

It's an exciting time for her. She looks like she's about to jump into a wonderful lake, and contrary to his father's appearance, she has become younger looking. All of her has been refreshed, and the light tan she's acquired gives her a sultry look. She spends a lot of time with the writers and theatre people who summer in and around New Hope. His father calls them parlor pinks, which is a funny name that makes Sam think of wallpaper, but he knows it has nothing to do with wallpaper. Occasionally, just to please her, his father accompanies her to some of these get-togethers, which remind Sam that his father is a little famous too and that people want to meet him almost more than his mother.

"Me and Sam are going to look for some hats in Hatboro," he might say.

They survey dry creek beds, roadside ditches, old barns, and the weathered tumbles of deserted homesteads on back roads. Sam captures salamanders for a terrarium he's started in a large round tin that held chocolates, a gift to his mother. They spend drowsy afternoons by the canal, fishing poles extended over the still, mucky water. They eat chunks of bread and cheese—provisions, his father calls them—beside a pond they discovered at the end of what seems to be an all-day hike through scrub pines and juniper bushes and over carpets of moss laid over levels of slate. High pussy willows curtain the pond, patrolled by dragonflies, sporadically pelted by the commentary of frogs. Sam wakes from a nap lying against his father, his face deep in the man's sweaty body, pressed against the damp undershirt that smells of burnt wood. The fireplace in the cottage has the same smell, and it is an odor both obnoxious and addictive all at once.

Sam is embarrassed to have fallen asleep in the middle of his father's story about bears, but Owen Emerson is smiling down upon him. The thin, bony face has softened, and the falcon eyes look hooded in the afternoon haze. "A good dream, boyo? You missed some excitement."

"What happened?"

"What's happening is that the frogs have revolted. They have united, held a convention, and formed their own party. They say they are no longer going to beat their butts on the ground. History demands that they be given wings. You missed all that."

"Will they?" asks Sam, still half-asleep. He isn't always sure when his father is joking.

"Get their wings? Come the Revolution, boyo. All God's chillen will get wings. But the Revolution may have come and gone." He starts singing something like a hymn in the meadow by the frog pond. His voice is light.

The order of everything is turned upside down—topsy-turvy. Aunt Rho would not approve. They eat pork chops for breakfast and Wheaties for supper. Or at any hour of the day or night. Clocks don't seem to matter, except for his mother's time at the theatre, and Sam wears the same pair of shorts and the same shirt, and his mother never says anything. They eat thick slabs of the local tomatoes on white bread with mayonnaise and onion. The tomato's juice burns the skin of his chin. Surprisingly, his father knows how to make clabbered biscuits with buttermilk. That his father can cook is an amazing discovery. Owen Emerson stands easily at the small coal oil stove in the kitchen—as the kerosene burns the stove makes a glub-glub sound like the frogs croaking, and the sound accompanies the smell of the pancakes to wake him on mornings. He sees his father flipping the pancakes over and dropping in a handful of the raspberries that grow wild along a fence line. The pancakes are lathered in butter and Caro syrup spiked with local honey bought at a road stand. They live like gypsies—his mother's schedule at the theatre the only rule to be observed.

"Holy Mother of God," she says and starts up from the late breakfast. "I've got a tech in fifteen minutes. What are you bums doing today?"

"The president has commissioned us to collect specimens of dinosaur droppings," Owen Emerson says.

Sam is caught off guard by his father's answer and chokes on some pancakes going the wrong way down his throat and up through his nose. He can't believe his father has said such a thing. Droppings? He's pretty sure he knows what that means.

"Well, please no more weed specimens. That last bunch made me swell up like a pigeon. I could hardly get through my lines."

"Never fear, my little pigeon." His father croons his W. C. Fields imitation. "Rest assured. Yes, indeed-ie, rest assured." The two of them kiss and embrace, and Sam briskly swabs the syrup on his plate with the last piece of flapjack.

Someone must have loaned them the Chevrolet roadster. His mother can't drive, and his father driver's license has expired. But it doesn't seem to matter—Sam imagines his father could get in a car anywhere, China or Russia, and just drive off. The car is cream-colored with orange spiked wheels and a rumble seat that is his alone to ride in. He is a prince on tour like in the newsreels. His father sits in front, holding the steering wheel firmly in both hands, and his mother sits close to him, her arm around him like they were high school kids. She usually sings different show tunes as they bounce over back roads. Her voice has expression but not much range. They take jaunts to historic sites and roadside taverns that smell of old wood and stale beer. Valley Forge. Washington's Crossing. King of Prussia. They stop at antique fairs and farm stands or pause beside meadows that stretch to the sky. Sometimes they park to picnic by a creek or a small stream, and his mother wades in the water, holding her summer dress around her knees. Her auburn hair is gathered and falls over one shoulder and across her front. Her naked feet splay pinkly in the clear water. His father sits on the bank, his bony knees drawn up to his chin, his dark eyes sharp beneath the bill of a cap he had gotten in Spain. Sam looks for salamanders.

"What?" she asks suddenly. She is blushing, as if his father has caught her doing something slightly naughty.

"What?" he asks.

"You're studying me."

"Making a picture."

"Without a camera?"

"The best kind. Here." His father taps his chest.

But most of the time, it's just the two of them, and Sam rides up front, next to his father as the photographer grasps the large wooden steering wheel and pushes the gearshift back and forth, to make satisfying grinding noises. He laughs, as if his own expertise has surprised him. The Chevy clucks-clucks along the road, and the smells of hot oil whisk into Sam's nostrils to meet an appetite he never knew he had. It must be like the pilots his father has told him about, flying their pursuit planes over Madrid and London, their heads stuck out of the cockpits to smell their engines heating up. Outside the car's windows are ditches filled with goldenrod, wire fences, barns, and dairy cows beyond.

The barns interest Sam most because many have strange, round designs painted on them. Hex signs, his father explains, supposed to keep off lightning and other evil things. In a five-and-dime in Lambertville, his father buys him a notebook and a box of colored pencils. Then they stop at some of these barns and Sam carefully reproduces the hex sign in the notebook. He colors them. "It will be your journal," his father says. "Every explorer worth his belt keeps a journal. This will be yours. Of this summer."

"Where's your journal?"

"My journal is different. In pictures."

They see not only hex signs on their travels. One time, his father pulls to the side of the road and stops. He turns off the ignition key. "Look at that," he says quietly as if not to startle an animal.

Sam looks but sees only some pasture going to sumac and clumps of thorn bush. The shambles of a barn dissolves into the ground next to some abandoned farm equipment. Owen Emerson is out of the car and motions for Sam to follow. They cross the ditch and duck under the sagging wire fence and walk directly toward the random shuffle of siding and fallen timbers. His father appears to be on a mission—the way his nose sticks out. Sam has never seen this kind of eagerness in him before, and it makes him think of hunting. His father's angular features are concentrated, pulled to a point, almost as if he's smelling something.

Abruptly, they stop before the weathered side of the old barn, the section that encloses a small door. The planks of the door have shrunk, and the knots in the wood have fallen out to offer peeks into the emptiness on the other side. Nothing but old ground, Sam discovers. He can't figure why they are standing there. A couple of grasshoppers play in the weeds nearby. Finally, he says, "I left my journal in the car."

"Have you now?" his father replies and strokes Sam's neck and shoulder. "But that's all right. Just look. That's all-important. To see—look at that door. The wood. The light on it."

Years of sun and weather have silvered the grain of the wood and made it into a landscape of itself, one that runs perpendicular with vertical riverbeds long gone dry. The shoals and shallows are exposed and shrinking back from the old carpentry. Three hinges, mere stencils of their original utility, transfer their rusted patterns at the door's edge. The slant of midafternoon light scores the brittle texture with the precision of a crosscut saw.

Several crows call just beyond where they stand, reminding Sam of the crows in the field back of Aunt Rho's house, and he wonders how she is right now. By herself in that house and hearing those crows, he thinks, but his father's arm closes around him, and the hot flesh becomes uncomfortable, sticky. One of the grasshoppers has just flown away and disappears into tall grass. He turns his head to look up at his father and becomes a little frightened of what he sees. Owen Emerson has become like one of those wax statues that have glass eyes that are too lifelike for the rest of the figure in the Ripley Museum in Times Square. These are not the same eyes that twinkle and laugh, making jokes with him, or warm to a story or even look funny at his mother. They are stones of eyes, totally occupied with what they see and hardened by it.

"Okay." The sound is calm, content. "That's enough." He pats Sam and caresses his shoulder. "Okay."

Mary of Hatboro

"Do they really make hats there?" They have made tuna fish sandwiches and put grape Kool-Aid with chipped ice in a thermos.

"All kinds," his father answers and cranks up the roadster. The morning air is cool on Sam's face, and the early sun warms his bare legs. It will get really hot in a day or two, for it's August. "We're doing research for the WP and A."

"What's the WP and A?"

"That's what President Roosevelt has made for people who can't find jobs."

"Find jobs," Sam repeats. It sounds like collecting specimens, looking for things along the road or the brilliant orange salamanders that come out along the canal after a rain. Their bodies are so delicate and soft, and their little feet tickle his hand when he picks them up.

"Yep, find jobs. Everyone has to work, Sam. All work is good and honorable. If you can't work, you lose your honor."

"What's honor?"

"That's what you live by. It's the gas that keeps the buggy rolling."

"Mama works."

"You bet she does. Mama is a hard worker."

Sam thinks of the little rooms he used to share with her before he went to Ohio, and how she would come back to those rooms with swollen feet and collapse on the bed. From work, he understood. Sometimes he would boil water and make her a cup of tea. She had been auditioning and then standing at the counter in Macy's. Even trying to work can be hard work, he thinks. "And you work hard," he says.

"Oh sure. I have a job," his father says. "Whatever it is."

Hatboro is a pretty little town with frame buildings that come right down to the road along the main highway, but there's not a single hat store. A sign outside the village limits does feature the picture of a top hat. Something Fred Astaire might wear. His father slows down and crosses the main intersection, drives to the next street, and makes a right turn to put them immediately back into the countryside. This lane takes a steep dip, and at the bottom is a stone house, set back, and mostly hidden by a high hedge and vines that grow over its roof. Morning glories. Sam recognizes them because Aunt Rho has some growing up one of the posts of her back porch.

Sam expects to see a small stream on the other side of the house, maybe with a waterfall, but a vast flower garden stretches into the distance. His father quickly leads him around the side of the house. The boy's even more amazed by the large, white-tiled swimming pool right in the middle of the garden. It's a real swimming pool, in the open, not like the one in the YMCA in Steubenville, which is in a basement. He has to skip to keep up with his father, minding his feet so as not to trip. The clusters and profusions of blossoms make his head swim, and the forests of stems and leaves, with their compounded aromas engulf him. Rounding the corner and coming into this tumult of color and shapes is like walking into one of those seed catalogs Aunt Rho looks at all winter. His father continues his brisk pace, straight ahead and toward a woman who stands within the arch of a white trellis.

She wears a large straw hat and carries a basket of straw. It almost could be another hat, Sam thinks, but held upside down from her arm, and this basket contains the flowers she has been cutting. Her dress is loose about her with a wide top that bares her shoulders and the top of her breasts. Her dark hair falls sleekly from the hat's halo, and she wears earrings, large loops of silver with green stones that catch and mill the light and make him think of Romany Marie, that gypsy who runs a restaurant in New York.

"We've brought our own lunch," his father is saying gaily.

"How perfectly splendid," the woman says, though she doesn't sound like she really thinks so. "And what a pleasure to see Master Sam." She doesn't sound happy about that either.

She has put the flower basket on a stone bench and walks past his father with her hand out. She almost bends low to reach down to him, then stops herself which Sam instantly likes her for. She shakes his hand standing up straight. But he has begun to feel awkward and little—in the Chevy, he and his father seemed to be the same size.

"Hello Sam." Her hand is small but firm, hard even. Her almond-shaped eyes are intensely blue, like the morning glories on her house. Her mouth is wide, and her front teeth stick out just a little to give her smile a prankish look. She knows lots of jokes, Sam figures, but doesn't tell them.

"This is Mary, Sam," his father says behind her. "An old friend of your mama's and mine."

"That is certainly the case," she says a little out of breath. She still grips his hand. "Certainly the case." He wants to pull away, but her eyes hold him as well. "So, let's go into the house where it is cool. My poor cosmos are wilting, and we need rain badly," Mary says.

"We have tuna fish sandwiches," Sam says.

"How splendid. I love tuna fish sandwiches," Mary says. Her hand gently propels him ahead of her on the path toward the house. "I hope you brought enough for me."

"We can share," Sam offers.

Behind them, his father gives a little cough and clears his throat. "Right," he says.

The layout of Mary's house inside is not that different from the interior of their cottage in New Hope or of others he has visited with his parents. A steep stair is carpentered into the wall by a fireplace and rises to the upper floor. There are wide board, bare floors and white plastered uneven walls whose thickness is indicated by the deep set window wells—three in front and one beside the fireplace. A horsehair sofa faces the fireplace, and a large wing chair sits to one side with a reading lamp crooked over the top. The kitchen is minimal too, with a kerosene stove as well, but Mary has a refrigerator like Aunt Rho's. A long wooden seat takes up one wall of a side room off the kitchen, and a screened-in porch is at the end. The most unusual feature is a table in one corner of the living room with a small portable typewriter surrounded by manuscript pages, a gooseneck lamp, several books, and a Mason jar of pencils.

The familiarity of the place eases Sam's nervousness, and he goes to the long settle and sits down. He opens his journal that he has held at his side and begins to draw the statue of a woman's head that sits on a table by the window. It doesn't look like a real woman, everything's stream-lined, but the lines marked into the stone mysteriously add up to a real face. As Sam tries to sketch it into his notebook, he slowly perceives that it might be Mary.

"How about some cider?" Mary asks. Her smile is instantly genial. "Fresh pressed by Farmer Brown down the road." She has removed her hat and shakes out her hair that has chestnut brown highlights. A little like his mother's. She wears tied around her largish feet the same sort of rope sandals his father is wearing. And her toes are brightly painted with red polish.

Mary lifts out a ceramic jug from the fridge, and while she takes down three glasses from a shelf over the sink, Sam has been secretly watching his father. Owen Emerson has become restless again. They have only arrived, are about to have some cool cider that smells delicious, and his father wants to pick up and go. His father steps around the room, poking into corners. He picks up and shakes a dried gourd. He thumbs through the magazines on the table with the statue. *New Masses. Life. The Nation.* Sam reads their names as his father idly flips through the pages as if he has already read them, knows their contents. One is a newspaper, the *Daily Worker,* which impresses Sam because he and his father have just been talking about work, and here is a newspaper all about it.

"So, thanks to Uncle Joe, the Nazis are eating knockwurst in Paris." His father is smiling.

"Oh, well," Mary says airily. "Circumstances sometimes require odd arrangements. The French are a mangy lot anyway—serves them right. Look what they did to us in Spain. It's a long-term matter and will be for the best."

"Sure, that's what the Poles discovered last year. Now it's lesson time for the French."

"Oh, Owen. Sometimes that pessimism of yours just doesn't do for an ideology." Mary is sounding strangely like his mother—a sort of affectionate picking at his father, though his mother is usually talking about his father's clothes. "Let's go out on the porch. Everything's ready."

Sam is surprised to find a table there already set up with napkins and plates and glasses. Lunch has been planned, though Mary carries with her a third soup bowl and a glass, a napkin, and a set of silverware. She gracefully adds them to the table setting. He is saddened by the intuition that the tuna fish sandwiches may never be eaten; they had never been needed in the first place. The wicker furniture is painted white and creaks when sat upon. One broken strand of wicker pokes into the back of his left knee when he sits down. As Mary returns lofting a large tureen, Sam carefully bends the fiber until it snaps, loudly clearing his throat and staring blankly at his father across the table. Owen Emerson leans forward on his folded arms, his profile turned to one side, his expression thoughtful.

The screened-in porch is full of flowers also, as if Mary may have planted the room along with the garden outside. Sprays of blooms of many varieties erupt from vases, old milk pitchers, and jugs in different shades of brown and white. The tablecloth is freshly white with an elaborate floral border in blue, and the plates are edged with red and yellow clusters of ceramic vegetables. Sam identifies squash and tomatoes. The soup bowls are similarly decorated. The wineglasses are of a heavy green glass.

His father has just reached into a basket covered by a napkin with an easy certainty of what he will find. He pulls out a roll and offers Sam the basket. "Crusty bread, Sam," he says, and the boy takes a warm roll and bites into one corner of it. It's about the best bread he's ever tasted.

"Here we are, men," Mary announces. The soup she ladles from the large tureen is mostly tomato, but it also has other vegetables, a lot of cucumbers. And it is cold. Cold soup, Sam thinks. The idea seems backward, but it tastes very good, and he takes another large spoonful. Maybe they have arrived too early and not given her time to heat it up, but it doesn't matter. Spicy, too. The flavors combine with the crusty bread to make a special lusciousness in his mouth.

His father and Mary continue to talk about the war in Europe, and Mary seems to know a lot about it. His mother and Aunt Rho never talk about the war, not like this. Mary not only explains the events to his father—his father clearly knows the explanations already—but she also talks like she knows some of the people in the explanations.

"More soup for Master Sam?" she asks him. She turns from her political talk to him without a change of breath, her voice all the same. Her look makes him feel scrawny and tongue-tied. "And what's this? I forgot the fabulous tuna fish sandwiches." Sam had put the small package on the table beside his plate. *Qué tonto! Me perdonas, camerads.*" She leaps up with the sandwiches and trips into the kitchen.

His father has a huge smile on his face. The luminous field of the tablecloth, the plates, and the odd glasses all play on his features, and he looks very happy. And at rest, it occurs to Sam, and that makes him feel more comfortable.

"Now then," Mary says. She returns just a little breathless. She has neatly cut the sandwiches into triangles and small rectangles and squares and passes them on a plate, exchanging a look with his father. Something amuses them. "And how perfectly splendid they taste, too," she says after biting into one of the portions.

"Where did you get this rosé?" his father asks. He has taken a mouthful of the wine and swishes it around in his mouth.

"Not in Pennsylvania, that's for sure," Mary answers and laughs. "This state has liquor laws that wear black socks."

Sam starts to laugh and can't stop. The idea of putting black socks on things like speed laws and crossing the street is too much for him. Some of the soup backs up in his throat and dribbles from his nose. He's embarrassed and uses the napkin. Neither his father nor Mary notices.

"Your gazpacho is better that the Florida's," his father says as he helps himself to more. Sam also holds out his bowl.

"Well, I would hope so." Mary sits up in her chair. "The Florida had terrible food; the chef turned out to be part of the fifth column. Do you remember?" Her smile opens wide at the memory. "They shot him in the courtyard, just before dinner one night."

"And not a moment too soon either." His father's laugh was low and quiet. "The son of a bitch always overcooked the lamb. We should have known he was a spy." Both laugh, which makes Sam wonder about the cook. Had he really been shot?

After the soup, Mary serves them a hard cake full of figs and walnuts. More cider for Sam, more wine for them. He is getting full as a tick, Aunt Rho would say.

"Sam has been keeping a record of our travels," his father says and nods toward the notebook.

"Oh, do let me see," says Mary. "I am a passionate admirer of your father's travels." She turns the pages carefully, inspecting each hex sign, and Sam is glad his drawings seem to get better page by page. His colors keep within the pencil lines. "How perfectly splendid," she says, and it sounds like she means it. "I bet I could find something interesting for you to draw in the garden. Would you like that, Sam? Oh, I know; there's a Chinese temple with a yellow roof out there that I bet you could do it especially well. But mind you—" Mary stands up with the notebook, and Sam gets to his feet also. He's pretty sure they're going to talk a lot more about politics and different people. "—mind you, don't get too near to the pool. Promise?"

He never locates the Chinese temple. He's gone down every path in the garden, but the temple never appears. He does come across a huge ceramic toadstool large enough for him to sit upon, so he kneels on the grass and opens his notebook and uses the toadstool as a desk. Two rabbits tentatively cross the path at the far end, and bees continually toil around him, visiting and revisiting the blooms that tower above his head. Finally, he walks on and comes to the pool. The water is very blue, and he wonders if Mary puts some kind of dye into it. He's a little afraid of water; he's only had a couple of swimming lessons at the Steubenville Y, and last year one of his classmates drowned in the Ohio River just off the town landing. A lot of people had stood on the bank and watched the kid trying to swim out of the current that carried him away.

The sun's warmth massages the back of his neck as he sits on a folding chair by the pool. His stomach is full. Insects hum and wheeze in the foliage. Two hawks idly play tag in the sky above, and his eyes grow heavy as he looks up at them. He's awake, and then he's asleep and then awake, and it is no longer so hot but a little cool, and his father is calling to him.

"*Hola,* Sam."

When he gets back to the house, both his father and Mary are in a hurry about something, and she is laughing nervously, as she plumps up the pillows on the sofa. They are continuing some conversation. "Maybe not, maybe," she is saying. "Maybe at the Schwitzers'. I can't say right now," she says. "Yes, maybe at the Schwitzers', but I can't say for sure. There's that picnic in Philadelphia about then. Browder will be speaking."

Sam and his father leave by the same kitchen door they came in. He gets the idea that nobody ever uses the front door here. They walk around the house to the road where the Chevy is parked. Mary comes to the screen door to say, *"Adios, amigos,"* sounding like a little girl, Sam thinks, and then they hear her beginning to do the dishes. He visualizes Mary's small hands putting the beautiful bowls and plates with the colorful vegetables on them into the soapy water.

"Why does she call me 'master'?" he asks on the way back to New Hope. Now a fierce western sun covers his bare legs on the hot leather seat. His father has to squint and pulls the brim of his Spanish hat low over his brow.

"It means she thinks you are a solid citizen," his father replies.

"Is she Spanish?"

"Sometimes." Owen Emerson lets loose one of those low laughs.

"Mayperdonaz," Sam says to himself.

"Yes—forgive me."

His mother is dressed and ready to leave for the Playhouse. "I was about to hoof it." She's not happy, though she sounds cheerful.

"I'm sorry, kid," his father says and kisses her on the cheek.

She bends down to hug Sam, to kiss him, but pulls back sharply. "What's that I smell? My membranes are having conniptions."

"We dropped by Mary's," his father says quickly. "I guess we got too close to the garden."

"Oh, really?" his mother replies. Her hand closes on Sam's shoulder. "And how is old Red Mary?"

"Perfectly splendid," Sam says wisely. His parents catch their breath, then explode in laughter. It must be the best joke he's ever told.

A Star in Summer

Sam has lost count of the number of times he and his father have attended the play. The performances seem to go on all summer, as the summer seems to go on and on. They may have been in New Hope for only a few weeks. Maybe just a month. The three of them being together day in and day out seem to stretch every day and night beyond the ordinary parameters. Clocks have lost their hands.

The Bucks County Playhouse looks like one of the old barns with the hex signs he's been drawing, but it has no hex signs on it. Inside, it smells a little barnlike too, but the seats are like those of a city theatre, it even has a balcony built into what may have been a hayloft. Also, the audiences dress up like the ones he's seen in Pittsburgh and New York, and there are real programs with his mother's picture on the front. "They're using the one Arnold Genthe did," she says to his father, with a funny laugh—like she was teasing him. He only nods and looks away and shrugs. "So, what's the matter with that?"

"Nothing's the matter with that," he says. "If you want to be an advertisement for gauze plasters."

"Well, you never take my picture, Mr. Social-Realist. I'm not plebeian enough for you."

Now his father really looks hurt, but he gently puts his arms around her. "Your mug, my little Swedish meatball, is too wondrous for my camera. I could never see anything like it again."

Reflected Glory is a comedy in two acts by George Kelly. Actress Muriel Flood contemplates giving up her career to accept one of the marriage proposals of two wealthy suitors. One is from Chicago, and the other is from Baltimore. In the last scene she declines both and goes on with her career—the show must go on. Curtain.

Tallulah Bankhead created the role of Muriel Flood when the play opened on Broadway in 1936 where it ran for 167 performances. Miss Bankhead has since performed the play with several important summer stock companies, but is unable to appear at the Bucks County Playhouse in August of 1940. The role will be taken by Edith Olson, a veteran of many Broadway roles, most recently in last year's much-acclaimed Emily's Cousin. *She and her husband, the photographer Owen Emerson, are the parents of a son, Sam.*

"Wearing your clown getup, I see," his mother said earlier.

"I am a clown," his father replied and made a funny face that wasn't really funny. He'd fried two small steaks for the two of them in a black iron pan. His mother ate nothing before a performance.

She had started to say something and then inspected her nails after glancing at Sam. She was painting them a light pink this afternoon. Sam was embarrassed by the sudden quiet and walked outside. His mother only wore a slip as she sat at the table to do her nails, and her legs crossed every which way, lolled openly.

"Quentin will be there. Also George and Ruth, a whole bunch of people from New York."

"I look forward to seeing them," he heard his father reply.

"My vagabond lover," his mother sighed. She was chewing gum and cracked it a couple of times.

The program falls between Sam's bare knees to the floor beneath his seat. His father doesn't notice. It is opening night, and the theatre is full. Not an empty seat. Everyone has come to see his mother, and he feels people looking at him, falling silent as he and his father move through the crowd outside. One or two call to his father and wave, or his father quickly shakes someone's hand. Then Sam is pushed ahead. It is like a big party.

Back in Ohio, he and Aunt Rho sometimes listened to *Mr. First Nighter,* a favorite radio show. Every week this person, Mr. First Nighter, went to a different play, a different opening night. He always took a taxi to the theatre, and in East Liverpool, they knew the route by heart.

"Here we are traveling up the Great White Way," the voice told them from the radio's speaker. Sound effects from that guy his mother told him about—all by himself in a small room with different gadgets. Car horns, a policeman's sharp whistle, brakes screeching, car motors. *"And our cabby has just turned off of Broadway and the lights of our theatre beckon just ahead. And here we are. Thank you, cabby."*

"Good evening, Mr. First Nighter." It's the voice of the theatre's porter as he opens the taxi's door.

"Good evening." More sound effects: the bustle and murmur of the distinguished audience filing into the theatre.

"Good evening, Mr. First Nighter. Here is your program." That is an usher speaking. *"I'll show you to your seat."* Background sounds of a pit orchestra tuning up, seats being turned down, more talk in the background. The audience's hum of anticipation is dissolving. A few coughs.

After taking his seat, Mr. First Nighter speaks in a low voice. *"Let's look at the program. Oh good. Tonight we will be seeing Les Tremayne and Barbara Luddy in the leading roles."* It is always the same names every week. *"And now the house lights are dimming and the curtain has begun to rise."* Sound effects: the audience has become quiet. Dead silence. Then, a telephone rings.

It's just like the radio program, Sam thinks. He knows how to behave, what to do at this theatre in New Hope, Pennsylvania, because he has listened to *Mr. First Nighter* in Ohio. He pretends he is Mr. First Nighter when his father leads him through the crowded lobby, and he fashions modesty from the radio actor's manner—not wanting to take advantage of his importance. He understands how difficult it must be to be famous and inconspicuous all at once. His neck almost burns from people looking at him. They've come to see his mother, and they know he is her son. It's in the program after all. He walks head down into the crowd, enjoying the warmth of their recognition. His father doesn't help. He's wearing that cherry red shirt again, and people put their hands out to him.

They want to touch him, it looks like. Some call him by name. "Back from the front," they joke. His father speaks quickly, passes on, uses single words, a shake of the head as they slowly progress into the theatre.

The house lights dim—just as he heard them do in Ohio—and the theatre becomes completely dark. The audience holds its breath. The curtain pulls back to reveal what looks like a hotel room. The telephone rings just like on the radio. Then his mother suddenly enters from stage right, and the applause is tumultuous. His father makes huge clap-claps that counter the assembly's rhythm, and his different cadence makes Sam uncomfortable. But no one notices. Meantime, his mother is standing, one knee on the sofa, holding the phone to one ear while adjusting an earring in the other. A shoe dangles from her raised foot. She rolls her eyes and waits prettily for the applause to subside. She is adorable, and Sam falls in love with her all over again.

The set absorbs him. He knows about hotel rooms, and this one looks real. His father's picture of the road lined with trees should be on the wall. His mother always hangs it up first thing when she unpacks in a new place.

Of course, he knows he would not find such items on the set for *Reflected Glory*. He knows this hotel room within which his mother turns and tosses her hair, one hand at her throat, is all painted canvas, make-believe. But still he finds himself sitting on the edge of his seat looking closely at the furniture—say, at the thick-cushioned sofa, where there might be a comic book he has left behind somewhere else.

Edith Olson is a great success. She has the audience in her spell, and they love her. She gets them laughing with the merest twist of her mouth, with a single glance or the merest gesture of her hand. At one point, the wriggle of her pinky is just too much, and the walls of the barn shake with the volume of their laughter. At the end, everyone stands to applaud her. She comes forward into the footlights, an armful of flowers held to her bosom. Her eyes glisten and sparkle in the diamondlike glare. They keep bringing her back, and she returns good-naturedly, though she also admonishes the audience with a charming gesture for not letting her go. They only applaud louder. Cries of "Brava" rise in the darkness. Sam has never seen her more beautiful, and it nearly makes him cry to see how everyone loves her. She locates him and his father in the darkness and blows kisses at them. Someone behind them says, "husband and son," which makes Sam want to get under the seat. But he's happy also. She is mostly looking at his father, her eyes are fierce with happiness, but she also seems to be questioning something. She is crying and laughing and blowing them kisses all at once, and his father is shouting, "Hurrah! Hurrah!"

Party Time

The parties go on past midnight, and Sam usually falls asleep in a corner somewhere. They go from one festival to another, and each group of partygoers applauds and cheers their entrance. The night air is heavy with honeysuckle and the wheeze of locusts in the trees. The Playhouse throws the first party after the show. The entire audience seems to attend. Tables with food and drink are set up on the grounds outside the barn. His mother whirls within admirers, autographing programs, signing right across her own face, her face taken by Arnold Genthe. She is a blur, saying, "You are too kind," or "I'm ever so very grateful." He and his father lurk around the food trays, testing small bits of dark ham and nibbling on slices of sharp cheddar cheese. His father carries a bottle of beer by the neck and takes sips from it.

The second party is at someone's house, and a third is at a place on the banks of the canal with a boat dock and paper lanterns strung out from the house to reflect like street lights in the water and attracting squadrons of gnats. A smaller, subdued crowd is served food and drink by men and women in servant dress. One of the guests plays the large grand piano in a corner, and someone pushes a woman forward and she sings several songs. Sam thinks the guests are impolite because no one stops talking to listen to her, but the couple performing don't seem to mind.

His mother is not so busy now, but has become serious, and stands, feet apart in conversation with older men near some bookshelves. The house has walls of books, and there is something strange about the place Sam cannot figure out. The guests move easily from room to room, dressed like people in the movies, but they talk about the war and President Roosevelt and about workers. There's that word again like the newspaper in Mary's house. One of the men is saying to his mother, "The play presents its own paradox, don't you think? Because it's not a choice available to most women, but, at the same time, it's the choice the system forces upon all women."

"Yes, that's right, you're exactly right," Edith Olson agrees wisely and turns graciously to someone else who is waiting to speak to her.

Eventually Sam finds a quiet corner in a small annex, another room with a lot of books and small statues on tables or on the bookshelves. He's become adept at finding such corners, and he settles down to wait for his parents. This will be the last stop of the night. He's very tired and wants to go to sleep.

"Comintern? You say, Comintern?" It is his father's voice raised inside somewhere, and he sounds both angry and amused, his patience lost. Sam knows the sound. The piano music grows louder in a series of chords, then disappears into the muddle. The young actress who plays the maid in the play's dressing room scene darts into the room, leading an older man by his hand. He's wearing a tuxedo and smiling. "Oops," she says and pulls her companion back and out of the room. Then Mary appears in the doorway.

"There you are, Master Sam. I've been looking for you." She is a carrying a plate of something and looks happy to see him. He is happy to see her too. Her hair is swept up in an old-fashioned way and pinned with two very long brass rods. Her ears are small and pink, and long earrings of brass hang from them. Her dress is scooped out in front like the one she wore the other day. Her eyes are the blue of the Chinese vase on the low glossy black table by the sofa. She kicks a leather hassock toward him and sits down on it, knee to knee with him.

"I've brought you some crème brûlée."

"What's that?"

"How keen of you to ask. What, indeed, is crème brûlée?" Her perfect white teeth show just a little as she smiles. "It is really only egg custard, but it is turned upside down and called something else. It's the world we live in, Sam. But you and I will always know egg custard when we see it. Here." She rests the plate on her knees between them, and she produces two spoons. So, she really has been looking for him. It is like sharing the tuna fish.

The silky sweetness of the custard melts wonderfully on his tongue. He's never tasted anything quite like it, though Aunt Rho makes egg custard too. But this dessert is different, and each bite makes him hungry for more. Mary carefully spoons tiny portions for herself, letting him have most of it, as if she's only keeping him company. Sharing. Sam has the feeling she is also collecting a lot of thoughts, putting them in line to make a long speech, but then she says simply, "I want us to be friends, Sam."

Noises in the Night

"You mustn't."

The two sounds, simply made. In the dark, the two sounds fall into his ear, into his head, and he is quickly wide-awake. It was his mother's voice, coming from above on the second floor; then, silence. He thinks maybe he has imagined the sounds. Outside, tree frogs shrill. The cold light of an August full moon is thrown across the foot of his bed. The round tin with his salamanders is safe on the kitchen table. He snuggles back down under the quilt.

If he were back in Ohio, he could walk down the hall and get into bed with Aunt Rho, although he's almost too old for that now. In sleep, she would hear him coming and would have the covers lifted, the warmth of her flushing his face at bedside, and he would settle against her and instantly fall back into a dreamless sleep. In this small bed in New Hope, Pennsylvania, he goes over this path he has taken in Ohio. First out the door of his room, the bathroom opposite, the sink and one side of the toilet dimly illuminated by the small lamp she keeps burning. The lamp is a celluloid Donald Duck with a small bulb inside. Turn right. Go along the hallway wall. To the left is the dark stairway going down to the first floor. He fell down those stairs one night, early in his living with her. So, turn right. Hug the wall. Next comes the rough pattern against his bare feet of the iron heat register in the floor. In winter, his pajamas would fill out like sausages when he stood here to warm his feet. Next came the closed door of the room reserved for his mother when she visits, and then at the end of the hall, in the front of the house, Aunt Rho's room. The door is always partway open, and he smells the clean soap smell mixed with lavender.

In New Hope, he follows this route, half-asleep, and his face is wet and his nose snotty. He's been crying and he hasn't known it. The ache in his belly is from nothing he's eaten. He knows that. If he goes up to his parents' room, he will have to climb the steep stairs, and their bed is not very large. He likes being with his mother and father. They have fun together. But he also wants to be back in Ohio with Aunt Rho. He pictures her chasing a chicken for dinner and that makes him giggle and then, somehow, laughing makes him cry more. He looks up at the rough boards of the ceiling above, the several braces that look like the limbs of trees. His parents' floor is his ceiling, and he pretends he's one of the salamanders in the round tin, listening very hard and his eyes flat in his head.

Above, bedsprings creak. Bedclothes shift. A foot is put down on the floor. "Yeah.'" His father's voice. He sounds tired. He hasn't been sleeping well either. The feet move and the ceiling boards creak. "It's not just that."

"Then what?" The tree frogs pause in their chorus. They may be listening too. Then they commence again, even noisier.

"I don't have any more pictures in me."

"Everyone says—"

"Fuck everyone." Sam has seen the word in dirty cartoon books, eight pagers they're called, which someone passes around, at school. It's strange to hear the word in his father's voice, not different from his normal way of saying *thank you* or *please*. "Here's the truth, Dimples. I can't look at it anymore."

Sam is wide-awake now in the ensuing silence. Intent. Something different or important has happened—he's pretty sure, but he can't figure what. He tries to picture them in bed, the same moonlight shining on them from the same angle. Not talking. Then, some rapid shifts and turns of bedclothes. "Listen." That's her idea voice, when she is about to make a suggestion that's just come to her. "Why not do landscapes? Go west, young man. No one does them like you do. You need some different scenery, that's all."

His father is laughing gently, a rustle of a laugh, a mouse clawing paper. "That's what I've been doing, Edie. Landscapes. That's been my scenery, and I've lost my eye for it."

They stop talking, though Sam knows they are awake. They haven't finished what they want to say—he somehow knows this—but they have stopped talking. His mother begins to hum, then sing softly, a little flat, but confident.

"Shine on,
Shine on harvest moon. For me and my guy.
He ain't had no lovin'
Since January, February, June and July.
This time,
Ain't no time for . . ."
Sam is pulled wonderfully into his mother's off-key singing and

begins to feel weightless. Like a leaf on the surface of the old canal. He gently slides beneath the surface just as someone's rooster crows.

A Bear Story

"One morning Bear was enjoying himself in the berry patch," Owen Emerson begins.

"What kind of berries?"

"These were the best berries. Some people called them luscious berries. He was just tasting a delicious mouthful of these best luscious berries when he smelled something on the air. He remembered this has happened once or twice before, but he can't remember exactly when. He raised his head and took several sniffs. It wasn't exactly a smell but more of a something else, like a change of air. Just about berry time too, he remembered from below, and the light falling on the birch trees was different too. He looked close at their white bark, and they looked even whiter. 'Ralph will know about this,' Bear said to himself. 'I'll go ask Ralph,' and that's what he did.

"Now Ralph was very wise and knew about everything because he slept all the time in his cave up above the pine forest. Ralph had the answer to every question, but Bear knew he had to be careful asking Ralph questions. Not just any question would do, because Ralph's nap was not to be disturbed for just any question. It had to be an important question.

"So Bear chewed some more of the luscious berries, to consider the importance of his question, whether he should disturb Ralph with it. Just then, the ducks and geese paddling in the pond all rose together and flew way out over the mountain and disappeared. It was like they had never been on the pond at all, though Bear knew they had been. 'That does it,' said Bear. 'I'll have to ask Ralph about these strange events.'

"As always, Ralph was snoozing at the opening of his cave, making a kind of easy-going, relaxed sort of snoozing sound with his front paws over his eyes. He was lying half out of the cave, though some might think he was lying halfway inside the cave. Bear was too interested in his own question to worry about the difference—even if there was a difference. He walked carefully near Ralph, trying not to kick up little stones on the ground, but Ralph still turned over and made a muffly awake sound. First one eye, and then the other eye opened, but neither went wide open. They squinted over his paws. He looked at Bear. Bear looked at Ralph. 'You've been down in the luscious berry patch again,' Ralph said softly and yawned. 'The unmistakable smell of luscious berries is on your breath. But gathering honey from the nest in the old sycamore is risky business. The branches are dead, and you'll have a bad fall one day.'

"Ralph's wisdom astounded Bear once again. How did he know everything? In fact, he had climbed up for some honey earlier, and it had been delicious and easy to gather because the bees had been strangely drowsy. 'Elementary, dear boy,' Ralph explained without being asked. He knew Bear couldn't figure it out on his own. 'That bit of vine wrapped around your left rear leg could only have grown on the sunny side of the sycamore, the side you obviously chose to climb so the sun would not be in your eyes.' His eyes closed and he sniffled once or twice. 'So, what's your question?' Ralph asks out of nowhere.

"Bear has a hard time putting his question into words. He wants to make it interesting for Ralph—to make it worthwhile waking him up for—and second, now that he has Ralph's attention, he's not sure what the question is. So he tells the wise old bear about being in the luscious berry patch and noticing the air was different, about the light on the birch trees, and the geese and ducks suddenly flying off.

"'I understand,' Ralph says, and Bear is happy that he does so. 'You find the luscious berry patch different today but it is also the same.' Ralph yawns deeply. The question has been too easy. 'The berry patch will always be different. It is the same luscious berry patch, but it has to be different sometimes in order to be the same.'

"'So it is sometimes different?' Bear asks.

"'That's the old bull's eye,' Ralph replies. He rolls over to a more comfortable snooze position.

"'But it is always the same?' Bear asks hopefully.

"'You have it in the proverbial nutshell,' Ralph mumbles and falls into a deep, deep sleep.

"Bear feels a little sleepy himself. It has been hard work talking to Ralph, as always, so he thought he would tiptoe away from Ralph's cave and find a snug place among the soft grasses by the stream. He could curl up for an afternoon snooze. And so he did."

"Tell me another," Sam says after a minute.

"Later," his father replies. "I'll tell you another later."

FIVE

"WE HAVE TO FACE THE FACT that Western industrial society as we know it is coming apart," Pennyworth announced to Constance Ho as she prepared a tray of drinks.

"That sounds like one of those apocalyptic, liberal visions meant to scare us into another constraint," she replied calmly. "Just another form of cultural bondage tied up with pretty rhetorical ribbons." As she talked, she deftly tended two martinis, a glass of Chablis, and one of sherry. It was a busy night, and Emerson stood nearby waiting for a party of six that was running late.

Pennyworth blinked rapidly as if to ward off the young woman's lecture if he could understand it. He had apparently eaten elsewhere on his modest expense account and had shown up to have a drink and to flirt with Constance. He lounged against the bar in an attempt at nonchalance, but the overall effect was of a discomfort endured. Emerson noted the journalist's attention seemed only to amuse the bartender. The man's wild pronouncements reminded him of the lumbering cadence of the boy as they had patrolled the streets of Greenwich Village, and for a moment a curious affection for Pennyworth was reborn within him, though he could not be sure if it was only because of that time past his appearance had called up. Even as the man's egregious behavior made him wince—his off-the-wall theories and goatish commentary—Emerson found himself perversely enjoying Pennyworth's presence, for the journalist had not only been a witness to that guileless kid Emerson remembered himself being—someone who slept on borrowed sofas— but now had shown up to verify how that same kid had turned out. An indisputable success. That Pennyworth might be unaware of this latter role was irrelevant—his ignorance was even a fillip to Emerson's enjoyment, for it revealed a core obtuseness that had been part of his character all along, disguised by the lumbering assault of his personality.

The journalist's eyes narrowed as the young woman continued her argument. "The genius of the market system is the way it has of reinventing itself. It has absorbed all the threats and attacks—and has incorporated most of them into its own dynamic. It continues to be the most effective distribution system of resources and incomes. So, what you see as an unraveling may only be a reweaving of the existing fabric into a new pattern of allocation of the same amount of resources and products. A *refraichment,* as some observers call it." She deftly twisted a scrap of lemon peel over the clear surface of a martini as if to emphasize her point. Her smile was winning, and her dark eyes seemed to be set at a sharper angle. "Now then, if you are referring to the so-called Eastern experiment, then you might want to consider the events in Asia to be only one more configuration of the original hypothesis presented by the ancient Greeks."

"Quite so," Pennyworth said quickly, his eyebrows waggling. His mouth pursed as he smoothed his moustache with one finger.

"The bar is open upstairs," Emerson interrupted. He expected to see a glimmer of appreciation in Constance's expression for his interruption, but she only turned to fill another drink order, as if to demonstrate that neither of them was more important to her right then than pouring some house Merlot into a goblet.

"Splendid," Pennyworth agreed and finished his drink.

"Take over for a little, will you?" Emerson asked Cynthia at the front desk.

"I have taken over." The young woman laughed. "Haven't you noticed?"

He led Pennyworth up the corkscrew stairway to the penthouse. "She calls you 'boss,' your delectable bartender." The man's voice had become knowing as they reached the top floor. "How very quaint."

"I don't know where she got that. Something she came on herself. Natural."

"I think you may be making my point."

The night was clear, and the cityscape below looked like the metropolis of a newly discovered planet that bore a likeness to the known world but was also strange and just come upon. Emerson did not turn on any of the room's lights. He was aware his guest moved carefully through the shadowed contours of the living room. The journalist was evaluating the setting as he made his way through it. He stopped before the enormous pane of glass. "You've done well, old man. Living off the lamb, you might say."

"More brandy?" Emerson moved to the small bar in the kitchen area.

"I cannot refuse your hospitality, though my sugar numbers are through the roof. Every night when I take off my socks, I expect to see little black dots on my toes." Pennyworth wiped his baldness with one hand as he placed the other against the glass as if to touch the skyline across the river. "I expect the inscrutable Miss Ho has enjoyed this magnificent view on more than one occasion."

"In fact, she has never seen it," Emerson said. "Not from up here, I mean." He joined his guest and handed him a snifter of brandy. He had chosen a glass of soda water. "I keep business and private separate."

"Of course." Pennyworth nodded. "Absolutely correct. Enough said."

"Let's go outside." Emerson pulled open the heavy glass panel and led the way onto the balcony. The sounds of the city at night drifted up to them, almost humming aroma. The stadium was dark. The Pirates were on the road. "The woman I've been seeing is away," Emerson said. "On the coast, on a job. She's with the Mellon Bank." It was a credential he enjoyed offering Pennyworth and then felt a little guilty. It had not been necessary.

"Ah yes, the therapist. You mentioned her. Sounds serious."

"Yes, I guess it is. I want it to be."

"And the lady?"

"She says she loves me, and I believe her. I have a few years on her. That may be a problem."

And there it was. The phrase—"have a few years on her"—floated out on the night air as effortlessly as one of those model planes he had glued together as a boy that would carry a wish, or a dream of a wish, into the sky on wings of tissue paper and balsa wood. It had almost been a throw-away; he had just launched the expression without thinking, and he saw in the darkness what had been visible all along, and he followed the path of its truth down and then further down to land in a clearing of recognition.

His own words had surprised him; had he ever said them aloud before? He couldn't remember. They had just slipped out, their meaning chased into the open by doubts he could no longer keep secret from himself. It could explain a lot—Nick's awkward affection, the boy's stiff, almost formal manner, and Phoebe's management of their affair that never seemed to contemplate how the fun they were having might lead to something more serious, even permanent. She gave no sign she recognized what he had lately begun to worry was the flaw in their affair— his age, a cruel fact like a gravy stain on a silk tie that she had overlooked so far but that lay in the back of his mind, waiting to soil his happiness.

Last week at her house, he had suddenly taken her in his arms to pleasure her—right there in the kitchen—Nick wouldn't be home until late from a lacrosse match in West Virginia—and this unwieldy truth of them had inflamed Emerson's abrupt passion as much as Phoebe's sexual appeal. She mistook his desperation for ardor, though the distinction was moot. Later, Phoebe cuddled on his lap, her clothing charmingly disordered, all her ribbons undone, unaware of this sense of a finitude that had bitten him. "My goodness," she had murmured against his neck, still a little breathless. "We're like teenagers."

So, they were not practical; that's all there is to it. Call it bad timing, call it worse luck. Sam Emerson stared into the darkness below the balcony as his throat filled with the downright meanness of the calendar. That frantic lovemaking in Phoebe's kitchen had prepared the ground for the understanding he had just reached standing next to Teddy Pennyworth; yet, he would not be turned back by so feeble a factor as the shift of a few seasons. She loved him, and she often said some of that love was inspired by the hope that lived within him, that he now summoned on this balcony above the darkness with all his might.

"Experience has its value," Pennyworth was saying with a ponderous gravity. "The female always wants to put herself into trustworthy hands." Pennyworth snorted. "It's part of the natural selection," he added and scoured his sinuses.

"Whatever happened to that woman we visited? You took me there one day—to her apartment. I remember you brought her cigarettes."

"Ah yes, my Esmeralda," Pennyworth said. "That wasn't her name— something like Mary Lou or Betty. Goodness, you remember that?"

"I remember the place. The tiny apartment. Cozy. I envied you a good deal—the times you must have visited her by yourself." Actually,

Emerson only remembered the stale smell in the hallways and the dankness of the woman's apartment; the odor of soiled laundry pushed into the back of a closet. She was almost featureless in his memory.

"I was no more than a courtier, old man. A youth on bended knee before the pale chalice of that forsaken damsel. A war widow—soon to become one anyway—a victim of history bereft in the cold workplace. Ah, the romance of it—only Edith Wharton could do it justice."

"You go in for the romantic business, too."

"It is the gaudy raiment we hang over our quotidian hard-ons."

"I'm sorry not to have read anything you've written. I just don't have time. I can only glance at the headlines," Emerson said. He had become impatient with the other's posturing.

"Perhaps you'll catch my interview with the Overstreet family. I spent the afternoon with them. Got some yummy pictures of Jesse Jackson talking with them, sure to increase our black readership. Heavy stuff. Choice." He took another sip. "Well, print is coming to an end anyway. Did I tell you I have my own web page? People actually send me money for my ideas. My slant on the fatuity that surrounds us. People like strong opinions. No ads, no commercials. Just me and my unadulterated vitriol." Pennyworth snorted and took a swallow of brandy.

"What do you call it—Pennyworth's Pennyworth?" A siren wailed in the distant tangle of the city.

After a little time, Pennyworth finally said, "Clever. Really not bad."

"I've often thought of that Christmas your mother put me up. How warm and comfortable she was. The smells of her cooking. What a generous woman she was."

"Fried fish and macaroni and cheese. Stuffed peppers."

"As I've told you, I envied you your mother."

"Ah, but you had *the* Edith Olson. Everyone's favorite mother."

"Yes, everyone's," Emerson said and watched the traffic on the parkways and bridges. "How did our mothers meet? I never knew that."

"A simple answer to that. Your mother came into the drugstore one day to get a prescription filled. She was living in the Village then, I think. Absent husbands perhaps made for a bond. Then the two of us—incipient studs—brought them closer." Pennyworth snorted. "You can almost hear them compare notes."

"The friendship didn't last. My mother had problems with relationships. All kinds. She saw people as an audience. She could be charming, funny. But she eventually wore people out, and she had to move on to a different audience," Emerson said.

"But that wasn't it," Pennyworth continued quietly. In the dark, Emerson felt the other's curious glance. "That wasn't it. You don't know? About their quarrel?" He pretended to give his host's puzzlement more consideration than it merited, but then he went on.

"First some background. Hazel's father, Granddaddy Jones, had been one of John L. Lewis's aides when the CIO started to organize the coalfields of West Virginia. We were a union household—strong on plebeian rights. You never noticed that even the casseroles were served from the left?" Pennyworth's short laugh had been held back just long enough to see as if he'd catch Emerson taking the joke seriously. Old guileless Sam.

"So when your mother talked about testifying before the House Un-American Committee, it riled old Hazel. Brought up all the old bugaboos about company goons and gumshoes. You do remember this, don't you?"

"But she never testified," Emerson said. "She never testified. I remember that much."

"Only because they never asked her to testify. That was what was so—so pathetic." He had reviewed the word before he used it. "Her information wasn't all that important. So sad. She wanted to volunteer— say nasty things about her thespian buddies, and that upset Hazel. The disloyalty of it. So they broke off, or rather Hazel turned off."

Emerson found nothing to say. The information was new but did surprise him. He could remember his mother talking about a congressman from Ohio, an old schoolmate from East Liverpool, and going to see him. Also her complaints about the Group Theatre, its Communist Party connections that supposedly denied her jobs, had been part of her conversational repertoire but tossed off lightly it seemed. So she had been serious, had been seriously piqued. He counted the bridges that crossed the Monongahela. He knew their number by heart. Then the Three Sisters crossing the Allegheny. Others lay upstream, at least five more within the city's prospect.

"Tomorrow I'm taking my mother's ashes up to this college where she taught. I'm hoping to find a place for them there. Something appropriate. I talked with the college's president today, and he agreed something should be done to recognize what she did for the place. We're to meet with some of the administrators and an important trustee. How about going with me? You have a good sense of strategy." Pennyworth remained silent. "I mean you might as well be part of the family," Emerson added. "What family I seem to have."

"Well, old sport, I'm touched. I was planning to work up my story on the Overstreets tomorrow—the paper wants it for next week. I suppose I could finish this brandy and put it together tonight. The designated mourner, eh?" Pennyworth snorted. "I like it, I like it. So I better get back to the hotel and be serious. Can you get me a taxi?" He became very businesslike, the working journalist. Even his voice hardened. "There might be a story in it tomorrow as well."

On the way down, they made arrangements for their meeting tomorrow, and Emerson put him into one of the several taxis that were always parked outside the restaurant. The dining room had thinned out; only four tables had customers, and he made an affable circuit of these, signaling Cynthia to bring complimentary liqueurs. In the kitchen Sterling had already changed clothes and was on his way to his sister's. "Final plans for Jimmy's funeral," he explained.

Then Emerson told Cynthia and Constance to go home, and he sat down on the stool behind the front desk, nodding to the departing customers, rising to shake hands with some. The last of the wait staff cleaned up. He reviewed tomorrow's reservations, made notes for the cleaning people who would arrive in the morning. They had been slacking off cleaning the bathrooms. The large windows looked a little grimy in a certain light today; he asked about the sponges they used—should they change them more often? Someone in the kitchen whistled, and once again he wondered which of the line cooks made this melodious sound. He always meant to ask. He got up to peek through the door to find out when a red light on the phone panel started blinking. It was his personal line.

"It's you," he answered, taking a chance.

"It's only me." Phoebe's voice was fresh in his ear. "How are you, sweetheart? What's been happening?"

He brought her up to date on the case against the police by the district attorney. His idea about a memorial at Mansfield College. "You've caught me downstairs. I've sent most everybody home. Just waiting out a few lingerers. This evening before we opened—I want to tell you—I went over to your house to check the garden. We've had some heavy weather here lately, and I thought it might need attention. And guess what? Nick was watering the plants. Doing a careful job of it too, though they didn't need it."

"Was he? Isn't that wonderful?"

"We had a swell time together."

"That's sweet. I am so happy to hear it."

"So when are you getting back?"

"You miss me?"

"It's not like I'm walking around with a boner."

"You disappoint me." She paused wickedly, and he smiled. "Well, I have one more thing to do tomorrow. It's an interview." She had slipped the information in, placed the words into the conversation as if they were a receipt for something unimportant. Quickly, she turned a corner. "And you've talked to the people at Mansfield about the ashes?"

"Yes." Emerson briefly recounted his talk with the college president and his plans for the next day with Pennyworth. "I'm hoping I can get them to fix up something on campus. Something that's right for her, you know?"

"Oh, Sam, you're going to make me cry." And she did sound a little tremulous, a softening around the edges of her voice.

"Why is that?"

"You're so good," Phoebe said.

"What's this interview about?" he asked after a moment. An excursion paddle wheeler passed under the Duquesne Bridge.

"Well, it's a clinic. A women's clinic. I've met the director before at a couple of conventions. They're looking for someone who does addictions. It's a great job. Pays awfully well."

"And it's in Seattle."

"Yes." Her voice was thoughtful. "That's right." He waved to the last customers. Emerson was now alone in the dining room. The lights in the kitchen went off, and he heard the service door open and pull close, and then pulled closed again as if to be sure it was securely locked. "Oh, it's a very long shot," she said quickly. He wondered if she could hear the heaviness settling within him. "Lots of complications, things to think about. Nick's schooling. The house. It would take a lot of doing. I'm really just seeing how I'd stack up in the competition." The silence between Pittsburgh and Seattle pulled even tighter. Finally, as if catching her breath, she said, "You, of course. Us."

"You're a winner," he told her. "By the way," he felt he had to change the subject. "All that stuff you talked about Pascal and souls in Purgatory—how did you know about that?"

"Oh, I guess I must have remembered it from school. I took a couple of philosophy courses at Duquesne. Are you surprised this girl from Turtle Creek knows about such stuff?"

"No, of course not."

"And how, may I ask did you know it was Pascal?"

"I Googled it. I got on the Internet at the Y's computer. When I went swimming yesterday."

"So there," she said and laughed shortly. Then after a pause that worried him a little, "I love you, Sam. I really do."

"And I love you. But it's unfair, isn't it?"

"What do you mean? What's unfair?" Phoebe asked, and Emerson regretted his question. He could almost visualize in the soundless ether that presently enfolded them, the woman's quick intelligence fastening on this new topic that was a flicker of his own anxiety—something she may never have considered. "Are you accusing me of exploiting you?"

"Well, your garden needed a lot of work."

"Is that some kind of a dirty metaphor? I love you, Sam; that's all I can say."

"Then, let's do something about it." He shouldn't have said it—it was the same old petition that must be tiresome for her to hear. She fell silent. He could imagine her expression, a shadow moving over the brightness—the excitement about being taken seriously, her hard work and expertise receiving new value in Seattle—thousands of miles away from Pittsburgh and him, and he had spoiled that prospect by being stupid, by baring his own doubts about their future that may never have occurred to her. What a clumsy oaf—something out of a farce pushing around his swollen need in a wheelbarrow ahead of him. "So, I'll let you know what happens at Mansfield tomorrow."

"Oh, yes, please do that." She was grateful he had changed the subject, her perplexity dissolved. For the moment. "And be careful on the road. Goodnight, darling Sam. I love you."

"I love you." The small refrigerator behind the bar pinged. "And good luck in the interview," he heard himself say. The dishwasher in the kitchen growled through its final rinse. Emerson had Sam's Place all to himself.

"Part of the source of this catastrophe," Pennyworth said the next morning, "this catastrophe we live in, is that we are trapped in our own bad habits. That's the catastrophe. The world is going down as we continue to pamper our digestions." Teddy Pennyworth sat beside Emerson in the station wagon. The sky was overcast, the road not too crowded.

"Like the Roman Empire, you mean?"

"I prefer the image of the *Titanic*. Even the name invites disaster. The hubris of it."

Teddy Pennyworth's buoyant manner amused Sam Emerson, and he was glad he had invited the journalist on the drive. The box with his mother's ashes sat on the back seat. The man embraced his own opinions with an enthusiasm so unbridled as to be almost contagious. Emerson remembered the young Pennyworth dismissing an idea or an act with a fervor that contained some appreciation for the rejected concept—condemning a crime while reserving admiration for the criminal's attempt to get away with it.

"But how to escape the shipwreck?" Emerson spoke slowly. "These bad habits, as you call them, may be part of our genetic profile. From the beginning. Look at me—I cater to a kind of addiction. I make my living by enforcing this bad habit people have for eating well. That hunger—not just for sustenance—but also for the perfect meal. The perfect martini. Such perfection exists only in fantasy."

"But look at what you've done. You've created an island in the sky. Sam's Place. You can be apart and yet a part as you look down on the shipwreck."

"It's a pretty view." Emerson laughed. The strip club was just ahead, around a bend in the highway.

"Topless and Bottomless," Teddy Pennyworth exclaimed as the red neon sign came into view. "Which do you prefer?"

"I like it all."

"Ah, the holistic male." The journalist turned in his seat to look back as they passed the strip club. Emerson kept the station wagon at a steady sixty. "How appropriate to our discussion. You couldn't have timed it better, old man." Pennyworth thumped him on the arm.

Several pickup trucks and a couple of cars were nosed into the parking area of the cement-block building. The midday routines were in progress—the luncheon show. "How do you mean?" Emerson asked.

"It must have occurred to you, old man, that the vulva is an icon of the Twentieth Century—certainly the American twentieth century. It's become *the* holy chalice, presented in glowing color from every perspective and mostly open for business. Not so much a centerfold as a centerpiece—if you forgive the expression." Pennyworth wiped his nose, then rubbed his head.

"A centerpiece," Emerson repeated.

"Not to mention a centerfold." Pennyworth hugged himself and kicked his feet against the floor of the car to underscore his inventiveness.

"Yes, I get it. Perhaps on a par with the perfect martini? The quest for perfection again?" Emerson took a chance with the idea.

"Touché!" Pennyworth exploded. "Our knack of transforming a subject into an object; it's our Cartesian sleight of hand—or should I say, sight and handling." Pennyworth's pleasure in his own cleverness further cleared his nasal passages. He sniffed several times and looked out the window. They passed the Two-20 Diner. Emerson reviewed the happy afternoons there with Phoebe and Nick. The journalist continued. "Such contemplations are all we have left as the catastrophe overtakes us, as that final big rock knocks us senseless or some goon lights a fuse that brings it all down. You remember your Plato—the contemplation of the eternal and all that?"

Farmland stretched out on either side of the highway. Pennyworth had stopped talking. The highway had gone beyond the fringe developments around the city and into the countryside speared by realtor signs. Silos and grazing dairy herds took up their appropriate places in the perspective. "There we have another example of our topic," Pennyworth said.

"Do we need another?" Emerson laughed, but Pennyworth was not to be diverted.

"I bet some of the audience back there are men who milk those cows every morning. Every morning and evening they look into the kazoos of these Holsteins. It's basically the same arrangement on display back at the strip joint."

"Yes, I've thought of that. A fundamental curiosity," Emerson replied.

"Yes, basic. Tell me, Sam—man to man, now. All these years you've driven back and forth to see the estimable Edith Olson—herself a possessor of this holy chalice—you were never tempted to spend a few moments in that arena, that paradise back there? Never tempted to so some impersonal pondering of pussy in the dark?" His own laughter pulled Pennyworth up from his slouch and just as quickly pushed him back into the seat.

"Maybe curious," Emerson replied. "About the place mostly."

"You mean to check their bill of fare, to inspect their kitchen? Of course."

The journalist's face became broad and knowing. "Why don't we stop on the way back? Spend a little time sighting some snatch after we dispose of Dame Edie Olson. Like a celebration. Show business and all that. Very appropriate, I think. Death and sex—it's a prime study."

"I have to get back to the restaurant," Emerson said. "We've got some people coming about our new cooler. Final measurements. I have to get back." They passed a road stand with fresh cherries. He would look them over on the return trip.

The vice-president of Mansfield College was full of cautious pleasantries. The president had talked to him about Emerson's suggestion, and there had been some complications since yesterday. "I regret the trustee that President Rollins wanted to join us is away on vacation. We want to do something special for your mother's memory. She meant a great deal to this college. Important to our history."

Emerson wondered if the man's compliments were being read from a notepad on his desk. Pennyworth seemed to be vibrating with impatience in the armchair next to him.

"We've named the theatre after her," the administrator reminded Emerson rather sternly. "And then there is the very valuable trove of papers and memorabilia—theatre programs and such—which she so generously gave our library," the vice-president continued with an odd merriment in his eyes. "We were so very happy to acquire them."

"Quite so," Pennyworth snorted. He was playing his role to perfection, Emerson thought; the important friend and family advisor. When he had introduced him and mentioned his newspaper's name, the administrator's eyes had made a quick, almost playful inspection—someone to handle carefully but not take too seriously. Emerson had been a little irked by the man's expression.

"So a place for her remains on campus would be fitting then," Pennyworth said. Large, multipaned windows behind the official looked out on the handsome grounds.

The vice-president's expression became troubled. "Worse luck that old Hal Jones is away. He has a way of swinging the board, and he was a great admirer of your mother. Didn't know her of course. Placing her remains on campus is problematical. Might set a difficult precedent, too. Other deceased emeriti might ask to be buried on campus." He laughed good-naturedly, inviting them to share his joke. He looked as gray as his superior had sounded on the phone—suit, socks, and tie all gray— though he was a youngish man with a slight pompadour, a calculated attempt at uniqueness within established lines. He reminded Emerson of those earnest undergraduates at Penn State who took on joyless callings to become class presidents and student senators while being good fellows all the same.

"Then there's a problem with the town, putting her remains here. Ordinances and so forth. We're not a cemetery after all." He looked regretful but was still amused.

"But Old Hal could have helped you with that," Pennyworth suggested with a winning smile. "If Old Hal were here, I mean." The vice-president glanced briefly in his direction.

"I would pay for it," Emerson said. "Something useful, say a small gazebo of marble that students could use in good weather. She was happy here. The college was important to her. It gave her a last act, if you will. A final curtain call. Or even a bench with her name and dates chiseled into it. We could put the ashes under it and no one need know."

"Yes, we could come up some night and pop her into the ground." Pennyworth had now gone too far, and Emerson was momentarily sorry to have brought him. On the other hand, he understood the journalist's practiced eye had already deduced the college's position, and so why not have a little fun with their stiff protocol?

"I've been holding some discussions with the art department," the vice-president said, leaning toward Emerson and obviously ignoring the journalist. "They've suggested a profile in bronze, part of a plaque that could be mounted in the lobby of the theatre. You could supply us with information. If you have a favorite photograph, that would be useful." He had picked up a pencil and tapped it against the notepad on his desk. He had covered all the points in his agenda for their meeting and the interview was suddenly over. His intercom had just buzzed.

Emerson stood with Pennyworth on the steps of the Edith Olson Theatre. Above them stretched a banner proclaiming A MIDSUMMER

NIGHT'S DREAM. He felt like one of the fools in that play, changed into an ass by his own fantasy. What was he doing on this silly errand? The refrigerator engineers were coming this afternoon to make the final preparations, and he was also supposed to meet with the linen suppliers about a new contract. He had compounded his folly by bringing the ashes with him. They were still on the back seat of the car. What had he hoped to do, march into the college president's office and plop them down on his desk?

His companion had become restless and climbed to the top of the steps, then entered the theatre. After a moment, Emerson followed. Inside the darkened theatre, the curtain was open and only two work lights burned on the stage. As their eyes became accustomed to the low illumination, both saw that the set design reproduced the interior of a large greenhouse. Potted ferns and artificial small trees, shelves of plastic plants, garden accessories and bags of topsoil and fertilizer artfully filled out the stage design. For a silly second, he entertained the possibility of finding something interesting for Phoebe's garden here. This version of Shakespeare's magical forest had particularly appealed to the *Times* reviewer, not so much for its novelty, but because someone in the mountains of western Pennsylvania had had the idea. On the other hand, one of the Pittsburgh reviewers, who had seen plays not just in New York but even in London, had expressed impatience with the conceit.

Teddy Pennyworth had already climbed onto the stage to take up dramatic positions around the dim set. He struck a pose and tried a line. "Oh that this too, too solid flesh should something and so forth and so on." Emerson let himself be entertained, expecting his companion to knock over a potted plant as he trundled here and there among the artificial vegetation and the jumble of the stage greenhouse. Pennyworth moved with that odd rhythm Emerson remembered from years ago, a gait that always seemed to pull him back just before a mishap.

"You know, old sport"—the journalist had walked down to the center of the stage to talk to Emerson, who stood in an aisle—"this is where the plaque should go. Up here somewhere. She was always onstage. Whenever she came to dinner, Hazel always said to me, 'I hope you remember your lines.' And we'd laugh."

"I can see that," Emerson said. He had sat down in a seat on the aisle with an expectancy both strange and familiar—strange because it was familiar. A grief fell over him in the darkness as he remembered the entrances and exits he had watched from similar posts—that failed star tossing off her lines and following her blocking. Pennyworth continued to patrol the stage, picking up and examining different props as if he were on a kind of scavenger hunt.

"Here we are," the journalist said suddenly. "This fills the ticket. Look!" He had just lifted a large artificial fern from its ornate pot. Emerson was puzzled. Pennyworth waved the plastic plant and then scooped up a handful of the filler from the pot to let the granules sift through his fingers. "Who could tell the difference, and talk about sight lines! She'd always be onstage. Hallowed ground up here—isn't it?"

"What an idea," Emerson exclaimed and laughed loudly. "Hallowed ground. You're right. Yes, hallowed ground."

"See?" Pennyworth continued his promotion, playing with the material in the pot and looking pleased with himself. He thought Emerson was agreeing. "Who could tell the difference?"

How simple it could be. The ashes were in the car. It would take only a few minutes to make the transfer. No one would know, and Pennyworth was right, she would be onstage, in this production anyway. And he would be done with it—his mission accomplished. But the man's ghoulish humor—he had begun to look a little embarrassed holding the fake plant and the pot. He had given Emerson an idea. But it wasn't hallowed ground, not on this stage. "Thank you, Teddy," Emerson said standing up, a silent ovation. "Hallowed ground it is. Thank you." And then he clapped his hands.

The distance back to Pittsburgh seemed shortened, made more direct somehow, though the return took the same amount of time. The two of them spoke little, as if the trip up to Mansfield had exhausted the reserves of their familiarity. Emerson was eager to get back to Pittsburgh. They passed the Highway Paradise without comment. Its neon arrow stabbed the empty air.

He invited Pennyworth to dinner. Emerson felt he owed him something, and it was Pennyworth's last night in Pittsburgh. The *Weekly Agenda* had done all it could for Jimmy Overstreet, and the journalist had another assignment. Something about the Whitewater investigation and the Clintons. The journalist said mournfully, "Think of it—I have to spend a whole week in Arkansas."

At Sam's Place, Pennyworth immediately made himself comfortable at the bar. Emerson went into the kitchen, where the engineer from the refrigeration company was waiting for him. He and Sterling talked over the final plans with the guy. "They can do it next week," Sterling said. "What do you think? We can close the place down for a few days. Let's get it done; it's been hanging fire too long."

"Fine," Emerson said, his mind working. He walked the engineer to the front door, and when he came back Wicks threw an apron at him. "Here! Give me hand and sauté these mushrooms while I get the shells ready. I'm running late."

The two of them worked back to back in a tight corner of the kitchen, and it was like the old days. Their offhand expertise and the pleasure they shared in that expertise added to Emerson's good spirits. He had hummed to himself on the drive back to Pittsburgh, and putting this recipe together with his partner was a good omen. Their intimacy was restored. The awkwardness that had begun to come between them disappeared in the sure moves of this joint preparation. Moreover, this dish was one he had created, and because Sterling had chosen to feature it this night, Emerson's optimism was bolstered. In the early days of their partnership, Emerson had created this starter that used four kinds of mushrooms, separately sautéed in herbs, then placed in puff pastry shells with a Madeira sauce, and finished in a moderate oven. Grated Romano and parsley made for a final dressing. They called it Fungi Fantastico, not the best title but inventive menu language had never been their strength.

"Pennyworth said his paper has donated some money," Emerson said as he chopped.

"It's a goodly amount," the chef replied. "The minstrel show wasn't all that bad. Your friend did well by them. He surprised me a little. He's a pretty cool dude for all that." Emerson was strangely gratified by Wicks's evaluation of Teddy Pennyworth, and his mind wandered. Finally, the chef asked, "What's on your mind?"

"While they install the new cooler, I want to take some time off."

"Hey, it's holiday time for all," Wicks said. He carefully folded the cooked mushrooms Emerson passed to him into a large bowl to be sauced. "You could go to Seattle."

"No, she'll be back soon. I have a better idea. We never found out where my dad is buried in France."

"Oh yeah," Sterling Wicks said. His eyes had brightened.

"Well, I've been thinking of calling in some of those free cognacs we've been pouring Senator Daniels—putting him to find out. He ought to be able to find the place. Then I'll take her ashes there. Put them together."

"Sounds good," his partner said.

"There's more." Emerson had only just come up with the plan. "I'll take Phoebe and Nick with me. To France. What do you think?"

"I think you got it bad. Take as much time as you want. We can manage without you."

"I don't know that I like that," Emerson said and hugged his partner's shoulder.

"Pas devant les enfants," Wicks said, motioning toward the two line cooks who hadn't been too interested.

Teddy Pennyworth was entertaining Constance and another woman who sat on a barstool beside him. His story was an elaborate account of a Kennedy family embarrassment. It had been an exposé he took credit for. Both women were laughing at the anecdote, a little too eagerly, Emerson thought. The Kennedys were old history to them. He decided not to join them. He'd go upstairs and try to call Phoebe, though she probably wouldn't be in. It was early afternoon in Seattle, and he imagined her sitting forward during the interview—alert, poised. A winner and on her way without him.

PROGRAM NOTES

Seeking the Dead

The train from Paris to Metz takes several hours. Amanda sleeps most of the way, curled up on the seat opposite them, going backward during their progress across central France—as if to match the retreat within her that has begun to worry Sam Emerson.

"Poor lamb," his mother says. "The jet lag has really hit her."

Edith Olson sits perfectly poised by the train window, commanding the passing landscape. He hopes Amanda is sleeping soundly. His mother's voice has been loud enough for everyone else in the car to hear, though few would understand English.

"I'm not in such great shape myself," he says.

Her cologne heavily layers the air in the coach, one more intrusion into everyone's space, he thinks, then bites off the thought and stretches his legs. How sad—how ridiculously sad that he, a grown man, would continue to raise these trivial complaints. It was like arguing with the change of seasons, perhaps an outrageous event but still perfectly natural. He didn't want to claim the phenomenon, but there she was, sitting beside him. Amanda had lost the child, and in the passivity of their disappointment, they had allowed Edith Olson to take them over, to take them into this heartland of France that unrolled alongside the train's advance.

She had invited them—if that was the word—to accompany her to hunt for Owen Emerson's grave in Alsace-Lorraine. It had seemed like a good idea to put some space between them and what had happened—as if the great distance between Benson Falls and this part of France might somehow stretch their sadness into a despair light enough for them to bear. Moreover, Edith Olson was treating them to the trip. She had landed a good part in a daytime serial on TV, and the old days of scraping by had been left behind. She wasn't quite sure where his father's grave was—she had a few directions, but they would have to seek out its location she told them with a challenging merriment in her eye. He guessed her motivation for this journey was to cure the hurt of their loss by searching for the remains of another.

Almost as soon as they had landed at Orly, his mother had doused herself with Chanel Number Five, her perfume of choice these days. A refreshment, she called this baptism. "Come," she had said to Amanda. "Let's find the ladies' while Sam waits for the bags." Off they went, his wife a step behind his mother. Edith Olson looked older than she had appeared on their television set in Benson Falls. If business was slow—as was becoming typical—the two of them would watch her program in the Inn's front parlor—the rooms upstairs empty, a *boeuf bourguignon* slowly simmering in the kitchen. His mother's role in the soap seemed to have been written for her. She played the matriarch of a Park Avenue family who by turns spirited and wise, imperious and sentimental, patiently oversaw the impulsive misdemeanors of the other cast members. Jessie Royce Landis had been supposed to do the part but had become ill. His mother's years seemed to pause within the television frame. The camera softly digested her appearance in close-ups as the music swelled for a commercial break, and Sam Emerson noted how her face over the years had reduced itself to a compact version of the flamboyance he remembered as a boy. Here in France, he sees the years have settled around her as she walks across the terminal's floor, feet splayed out in sturdy shoes. A heavy belt of age had fastened around her body to thicken and make it tubular. The resolute alacrity that still might reside in her knees can no longer spring the rest of her.

Their arrival had spun in a whir of false starts and wrong turns. "Here we are." Edie Olson had led first one way, and another, and then to a halt, confused and just a little perplexed by her own confusion. "No, it's this way," she would finally decide, and off they tramped behind her. They were dependent on her willful ignorance, but guided by the force of that will to go in circles, until Amanda finally went to a ticket booth and, in halting French, asked for the correct connection for Paris. "Yes, that's right," Edith Olson had said, as if to certify this information, as if all along her own wrong directions had been meant to test the two of them.

Now as the train glides across the multiparallels of track near the Metz station, Amanda rouses and stretches. Her taut posture rouses Emerson as well. Their sex life has been minimal lately, but his appreciation of her trim figure within the slacks and sweater has not lessened. Smallish breasts firmly molded on the ribcage and the swell of a slight belly just at the sharp indent of the waist. A brown mole on one thigh, near the groin, is a sentry he has bribed on more than one occasion with kisses. Amanda, innocent of this inventory, yawns and pulls herself into consciousness.

As the train slows to a halt at the station, Amanda is saying she has to get some sleep. "You two get on the road, if you want. I'm crashing at the nearest hotel."

"Excellent idea," his mother agrees. "We all could use some rest." But she looks as if she is ready to push on, to survey the list of military cemeteries someone has given her. She's shown them her research. But Amanda's partial fluency with French has convinced Edie Olson they should stick together.

The Hotel de la Gare is directly across from the station in a block of buildings that is a hodge-podge of architecture. Two or three old buildings, survivors of the several wars that have passed through the city, are wedged between newer, more modern facades like old teeth in a shiny mouthful of plastic implants. Their room faces the station and has large windows shuttered against the afternoon light. They can hear the scarflike murmur of trains coming and going and the stationmaster's muffled announcements preceded by what sounds like the chimes of a nursery. And rightfully so, Emerson thinks, as they drop their bags, for they are behaving like sleepy children. They collapse fully clothed onto the twin beds as Amanda apologizes sleepily that she hadn't asked for a double bed in French, couldn't remember the term.

Emerson had done a little research when his mother announced their trip. Metz had been the point of the German advance in 1918—Verdun was nearby. And if that hadn't been enough, history had put the city on the route of the Nazi retreat in 1944. Amanda is interested in none of this history. She has kicked off her sneakers and now stretches out on one of the narrow beds. Her white-socked feet are reflected in the mirror of the armoire just before him. Emerson wonders if she had purposely forgotten the term for a larger bed. "Maybe we shouldn't have come," he says after a bit.

Also in the armoire's reflection and beyond the end of the beds and Amanda's feet, he notes a small washbasin in the corner. The wallpaper has a faint pattern of castles and towers. Her feet uncross and then recross. "Of course we should be here." Her voice behind him is startling in its assurance. She doesn't sound sleepy at all. "We need to close this chapter. Your mother is right, and you should give her credit."

"We both have to close a chapter." He waits for her to say something more. He continues, "Anyway, business was slow." It was a dumb remark, and her feet disappear from the mirror in consequence. He hears pillows plumped. He knows she's sitting up, alert, but he's too tired to even turn over. The miscarriage had been very hard on her in every way.

"Do you think we'll make it?" Her voice is light. She could be asking about the Inn, but he guesses not.

"Of course," he answers both questions. His fatigue piles up within him. Not just the trip, the time lag, but the whole passage of their lives has fallen upon him. Parallel endeavors—the Inn and their marriage. Similar renovations and fixing-ups that have been continuous work for the two of them, that have kept them busy and unmindful of the cracks in the foundations. They pooled what they had learned at Penn State to create a menu no one has wanted in Benson Falls. And what about the marriage? The stultifying atmosphere—her family's continual presence, the interference in the guise of generosity—has worn down their joy and enthusiasm. So losing the baby seems to be the final failure.

They could have been lovers in college and then gone their separate ways, he has begun to think. They would have had some good memories and little hurt. "I guess it was my fault. Some kind of romance," Sam Emerson says.

She is getting up. "I could have said no. But I wanted to be with you. And I wanted my family. And I still want to be with you."

Amanda walks into the bathroom, leaving the door almost closed. He hears the toilet flush. Then it sounds as if she's running water in the sink, but he recalls there is no sink in there. "What are you doing?"

"I'm using the bidet," she answers. "I feel like one of those women in Henry Miller. They were always sitting on bidets in Paris either before or after doing it." She sounds amused and a little pleased with her allusion.

Sam Emerson sees himself smile in the mirror. "Is this a before?"

The rasp of a motorbike saws at the thick lull of the siesta hour outside their window. A train pulls into the station. The chimes go off, and a woman's pleasant voice makes an announcement. It is an inviting sound. Even if you didn't think of it, Emerson considers, that voice would urge you to travel, tempt you to turn away from whatever you are doing, and get on the train that's just pulled in. Go some place. Drowsily, he wonders if the French railway people hold auditions to hire station agents with just that note of seduction in their voices.

Amanda has remained silent. He pictures her sitting on the bidet. How her legs look, how her feet in socks are set down a certain way on the floor. Initially, she wasn't enthusiastic about the trip. Spending time with his mother was not appealing to her. Finally, she agreed it might be time to put some distance between them and that afternoon when she doubled over. Her stricken look would always be with him—as if she just did something terribly wrong and hoped he would forgive her.

"You know when I came to Paris on that student tour . . . ," Amanda has been talking, "we all thought using a bidet was wicked. It verified the idea that sex was dirty. The French were into sex and were therefore dirty. Some of us thought that."

"But not you. When was that? Before . . ." Emerson stops. She's told him about losing her virginity—about some of her sexual history—but he can't remember if it happened in Paris.

"My freshman year," she supplies the answer—maybe to both questions. "Just before we met. It seemed to me the French were right. Practical. Like washing your face. Just the other end of the proposition, you might say. I thought of putting one in our bathroom when we redid the inn, but I was afraid it would shock you."

"You're kidding," Emerson says. He feels strangely rested, as if the easygoing nature of the talk in this dim hotel room has refreshed them. But he admits he might have been shocked. He too read Henry Miller, but then all the women in those novels using the bidets seemed to him to be either whores or nymphomaniacs. At the same time, Amanda Benson's offhand, matter-of-fact attitude toward sex amazed him. Nobody could tell by looking at her—he used to tell himself—that this pert, winsome-looking coed came equipped for worry-free sex and was eager to practice it. Amanda Benson just liked doing it. How lucky could a guy get? On the bed in the hotel room in Metz, Emerson cringes at this image of his younger self, and he smiles sheepishly at the man in the mirror.

"I'm lonely." Amanda's voice is quiet, and the two words fall gently on his reverie. It takes him several moments to comprehend them. She continues, "I'm pretty much alone with you these days. You have needed me, Sam, and there have been rewards in that—being needed, I mean—but that's not everything. I don't think you love me, Sam. I think you want to love me, you hoped to love me, but you don't know how. I think the woman across the hall has trained you to do without love. What a strange discipline. And I must say, I didn't know much about love either, but I knew it when I felt it. So I know what's been missing with you."

He's about to make some sounds of denial, a defense of his feelings for her, but she has somehow picked up these impulses to interrupt them. "Look. We had our reasons for getting married. I had mine. All of them can be grouped under one heading—I wanted to be with you."

"Why was that?"

Amanda doesn't answer immediately; she is choosing her language. "Because you were so hopeful. Even in that sad childhood, you were hopeful. Something inside of you worked against the sadness to produce hope."

"You make me sound like an oyster."

After a moment, she gives a small laugh. He stretches out on the bed and looks at the ceiling. An ornate plaster finial extrudes from the smooth surface like a clump of bland fruit under many coats of paint. A chandelier may have hung there in former times.

"So we have this history now—" Water runs and drains, clothing is arranged. "Here's what I'll do." She appears in the doorway holding her slacks that she neatly fits over a hanger to put in the armoire. Emerson's reflection momentarily disappears as Amanda stands before the open cabinet barelegged, her small feet in the white socks. The tails of her blouse hang just below the tight curve of her butt.

"Here's what I'm going to do," she repeats. Her dark eyes solemnly study him when she turns around. "I'm getting out of the kitchen. I can't work beside you—it's a pro forma thing anyway. You're not there. Where you are, I don't know, but I feel it's outside the city limits and into some kind of angry place. I don't want to be near that anger, and I can't handle the distance in you either." She pauses to take a ragged breath, and Emerson thinks he should rise and take her in his arms, but her expression keeps him seated on the bed.

"You're leaving me?"

"I'm leaving you in the kitchen. I think if we're apart for most of the day, that will be better. And not so unusual. Most people have different jobs. Aren't together all the time. If we get busy, I can come back to cook with you. I'm going to fix up that one end of the lobby that has always been a horror. Start a little shop. Sell sweaters and caps. Knitted things. We'll be in the same building, but we'll be apart. Maybe we'll learn to miss one another. It will be fun." She gives him that brave, toothy grin, a familiar ironical look that used to make him laugh but lately has nearly moved him to tears.

She sits beside him on the bed, and he puts one arm around her. He leans forward to kiss her, but she does not turn her head to him, and his lips come to rest on the pulse in her throat. She is small and stiff in his embrace; the two of them in the mirror look like a couple dressing for a meeting. Maybe a PTA meeting, Emerson thinks, then turns the idea away. "I love you, Amanda. I really do."

"Poor Sam. I think you've lost more than I." She takes one of his hands in both of hers. "You've lost an image as well." They sit quietly for some time. The soft garble of an announcement at the railroad stations filters through the slats of the window shutters. The chimes ping and ding. "Now then, if you are really interested, the time on the bidet could be a 'before.'"

She kisses him hard, her tongue an angry dart that instantly fires him. Smiling faintly, she complies with the relentless disorder he makes of her, amused by his fumbling with her woman's fastenings—after all these years of undoing. But his very awkwardness somehow feeds her desire until he has stripped her completely in the gentle afternoon light of the hotel room. Her nakedness is at once familiar and exotic to him—always different—and he gasps and quickly pulls off his clothes, freeing his erection that rises hot from his fatigue. Amanda hums at the jut of his cock as if it was her own accomplishment and pulls him quickly to herself and into her mouth. She is rapacious, a desperate sort of greed that is not really pleasurable but somehow required of the moment. He slowly pulls her away then lifts and folds her around himself, and a coiled spring within her unlocks. She cries out, and her intensity frightens him a little, and then he joins its rampage.

Later, Sam Emerson would consider her frenzy, the near mindless grinding that had little to do with love or lovemaking, but could have been a sort of punishment—of both of them. She had made both herself and him into objects in that hotel room in Metz. He remembers in college Sterling Wicks telling him of certain white coeds who apparently sought him out because of his blackness in order to work out some kind of retribution, a payback made more exciting for the women by their lingering sense of superiority while turning in his embrace. He wonders if Amanda's hot usage of him just now has been invented from a similar lust.

Their final release wrings them senseless, and they fall into a deep slumber, the sweat cooling their naked bodies. The bluish light of early evening spills through the shutters, and they are gradually pulled awake. They might have slept straight through, but something has disturbed them. The doorknob turns and rattles. Turns again, left and right. They think it might be a maid and prepare to ignore the disturbance.

"I'm just going down to dinner." Edith Olson's voice rings from the hallway outside. "Dinner is on our plan, you remember. I'll wait for you downstairs." They are fully awake now.

Pont-à-Mousson

George Patton's Third Army came to the Moselle River only to be stopped by German Panzers hidden in the forest west of the city. The bridge across the river had been fought over in World War I and was again in September of 1944 in the repetition of horrors the century seemed to require. The American advance was also complicated by German artillery in place on the butte across the river, and it took several weeks for Patton's infantry to clear the area. The town was mostly destroyed. The Germans blew up the bridge, so the Americans crossed the Moselle a few kilometers upstream to establish the first bridgehead south of Thionville. The Rhine River and Germany were just ahead, and the photographer Owen Emerson was last seen on top of a Sherman tank, two cameras dangling from his neck.

"But Dad was killed in December. I remember you came to tell me when I was in Connecticut. There had just been a heavy snowfall."

They have rented a small Renault through the hotel in Metz. Emerson is at the wheel as they follow N57 south, along the Moselle River. The freshness of June lies upon the peaceful landscape. Pont-à-Mousson is only thirty kilometers from Metz, and it is a lovely day. On either side of them, fields stretch out warm and indolent. The trills of blackbirds pierce the dusty roadside. Edith Olson sits in the passenger seat, looking neither left nor right.

"No, in September," she corrects him. "I didn't tell you until December because I didn't want to bother your school work. You weren't doing that well as it was."

Emerson doesn't remember not doing well, but he glances quickly into the rearview mirror. Amanda is looking out the window at the landscape, and he can't tell if she's been paying attention, if she has heard this evaluation. Large black ovals of sunglasses give her expression a blank indifference. She could be asleep.

"What difference did it make?" Edith Olson declares as she sits straight in the passenger seat. "He was no more dead in December than in September."

Emerson figures theatre work might have delayed the information. "So, he was probably only missing in September. I mean not officially dead yet."

"Your father was always missing."

"Were you in a play then? The fall of '44?" Amanda asks becoming interested.

"Yes, that's right." His mother is grateful to be reminded. "That's right. *Outrageous Fortune* with dear little Elsie Ferguson. It was about wealthy Jews living in the suburbs. What was that you had for dinner last night, Amanda?"

"A sort of veal stew. *Blanquette de veau*. Sam does it better."

"I'm sure he does. My omelet was just perfect—just what I wanted."

She hugs herself with the memory of the choice. "With those mushrooms."

The road has taken them to high ground above the river. On the left the Butte de Mousson abruptly pops up from the terrain. Then the road curves to the right and dives sharply down. The town lies below in the center of the panorama at the river's edge.

"Here we are. Here it is," Edith Olson says suddenly. "Stop!" She waves her arms as if her gesture alone will halt their progress. One of her hands nearly hits Emerson in the face. A small military cemetery has appeared on the left, in the bend of a tight curve downward, and Emerson pulls into the tidy parking lot. Hundreds of white crosses ascend the hillside. Many graves bear a different symbol with Arabic lettering. The French tricolor flies from a pole.

"Muslims," Emerson says. "Colonial troops, probably from Algeria. This is a French cemetery. He wouldn't be here." He has not turned off the engine, and they stare at the lush dune stapled with white markers. Not a sign of life, well, of course not, it's a cemetery, Emerson chides himself. But it seems especially quiet.

"Yes, that's right," his mother replies, as if his comment agrees with something in her head, something entirely different. "This is it," she announces and opens her door. Her tongue is caught between her teeth; it's a gleeful expression.

"But wait a minute." Emerson considers reasoning with his mother when Amanda pokes him in the back and opens her door. He turns off the motor.

"It was all mixed up," his mother is saying. "Nobody kept accurate records. The fighting went on for several weeks, and people were buried quickly." She has already passed up the hill and has started to review the first line of markers.

"C'mon," Amanda is saying. "It's a beautiful day. We can get some sun." She pulls his arm, and Emerson catches her good spirits. The picture of the two of them making love yesterday aftternoon stirs him a little. She skips ahead. She wears shorts and a light sweater draped over her shoulders. A T-shirt leaves her arms bare. It wouldn't take them long, he speculates wildly. Just dodge behind some of the shrubbery for a quick one to celebrate these fallen warriors. What better way to honor these ancient remains? But they have climbed to the very top of the burial ground, and the day has become warm. Below them, Edith Olson relentlessly moves back and forth across the sloping ground, inspecting the names on the markers, gradually moving up the hillside one row at a time. She's tied her scarf around her head so she resembles some old peasant woman searching for firewood, and she might even be playing that role.

"She's amazing," Amanda says. They follow her example, working down the incline, row by row. The air is pleasantly scented, and the day has become immensely still—perpetually still maybe, he thinks, or perpetually expectant of sound. Not a single birdcall. Maybe all the sound that has ever occurred on this spot, all the horrendous noises that have put these bodies into the ground, has also been sucked into the graves with them. Emerson takes Amanda's hand, and he knows he is preparing himself for the chance that his mother might be right, that his father might be buried here, and they are about to come upon the chiseled name OWEN EMERSON among the Raouls and Phillipes and Alis. He prepares his feelings for this event. The thin face with the flat black hair hanging over the intense eyes—he can see that face.

He considers the fact that his father was dead for several months before he knew of it. Maybe that was like the old philosophy question of the tree falling in the forest. If nobody heard it fall, had it? Maybe his not knowing of his father's death gave the man an extra three months of life, more time to focus his camera, to find the right moment. His father took pictures, to find the truth of things. That's what he said one time, but what truth was he trying to seek out here? A horrible truth. Amanda hugs him to her side, and Emerson guesses she might be visiting her own casualty.

"They will know in town," Edith Olson yells up to them, across the exact parallels of the gravesites. The cemetery is meticulously maintained. "They will have records in town."

But when they cross the bridge and enter Pont-à-Mousson, they drive through empty streets. The populace has disappeared. The citizenry could have fled one last barrage, a final attack miraculously delayed for decades, taking its time to fall upon the town. But it is just the lunch hour. All the shops are shuttered, and the Hotel de Ville is closed until two o'clock, but, thankfully, the building's restrooms remain open. "How civilized," Edith Olson says and leads the way quickly to the WC. Emerson has parked the car near the central square, Place Duroc. His mother appears confused. Not finding her husband's grave in that roadside cemetery where she was certain it was located has spun her off her confidence. "What should we do now?" She is lost.

"We shall have some quiche," Amanda says. "When in Lorraine, eat quiche."

And they find a small restaurant that does serve quiche, and it is very fine. That his wife and mother are getting along pleases Emerson. They have found some affinity as women and seem easy with each other. It may be only gender deep and only expressed by using a public toilet together, but he is grateful for the mellow mood and enjoys watching them walk around the closed-up square arm in arm. This feeling is further flavored by the ambiance of the small café, the honest quality of the meal, and the pride taken in its service. The *pichet* of the *vin maison* is just right, and the meal's portions fall into a larger bowl of well-being Emerson imagines holding, warm in his hands.

Like many men, Sam Emerson sometimes wants to gather all the women in his life into one congenial community. Mothers and grandmothers, favorite aunts, cousins, sisters, wives, and lovers—meeting in companionable assembly in a kind of heavenly pattern, a meadow of common gossips about the one man they have shared. At lunch, the ordinary Burgundy rolling on his tongue, he notes the countenances of the two women who sit opposite him. Surely, he is partly responsible for these happy faces; it couldn't just be the food?

Amanda has perched her sunglasses atop her forehead so she resembles an old-time aviatrix after a historic flight. She is very relaxed, with a confidence she has not shown in some time. She indulges his mother's arrogance and handles her with an amusement that does not offend the older woman. He guesses her manner is related to her talk yesterday, her announcement. She resembles a woman who has radically changed her hairstyle to signal an important decision, and this profound alteration of mind and style out of the way, she thinks no more of what has prompted the change.

His mother's attitude toward Amanda is generous, and the light of appreciation in her large eyes seems genuine. She becomes the matriarchal figure she plays on television. Certainly, Amanda is a new audience to win, and she turns toward her with a dip of head to recognize her facility with the language—Amanda has ordered for the three of them—but there is something else he cannot figure. Here in this village café in Burgundy, Emerson remembers other tables in rooms that seemed to wait upon Edie Olson's next outrageous act, her next outburst. This old behavior often embarrassed him, but her plain manner with Amanda now attracts him, and he wonders if there was a shyness in her all along that has only just worn through the glossy finish. She makes him think of Aunt Rho. At the same time, he reminds himself she is out of her element, outside the television format that has lately composed her, where her lines are all written for her. Now she is at the mercy of Amanda's knowledge of French and his handling of the Renault.

After lunch, they walk toward Place Duroc in the silence of the midday. It is still early; they are the only people on the streets. Emerson sits down on a bench at the edge of the square, and the two women set off to review the store windows within the roofed arcade. The arches of the facade are repeated around three sides, the city hall behind him making up the fourth side of the quadrangle. He does not know the age of the place. They have left the guidebook in the car. The original Moorish facade, demolished by Patton's artillery, has been replicated, and the setting makes him think of a Shakespearean play. He can envision characters in tights moving in and out of the columns to appear in the different apertures. Delivering soliloquies. The same expectant silence he felt in the cemetery strikes him in the Place Duroc, but here it is because a play seems about to commence.

In the center, a marble plinth rises from a fountain pool, probably dedicated to Duroc, a figure of the Revolution, and just over Emerson's shoulder is a corner house with elaborately sculpted figures sticking out from the second floor. The figures seem to be looking down the street, anticipating more violence on its way into town. The enormous clock above the city hall's portal shows a few minutes before the hour. A Cross of Lorraine is supported on the wings of eagles.

The figures of Amanda and his mother intermittently show themselves in the arches across from him. They pause before one shop whose windows are splattered with the bright scraps of summer clothing; bikinis explode within the antique frame. Then Emerson becomes aware of the readying whir of the town clock's huge gears. The hour is struck, and, almost simultaneously, the large wooden entrance doors of the Hotel de Ville fold back as if they have been powered by the clock's mechanism.

Emerson gets up to walk across the square to meet the two women, who have turned to come to him. The vacant area between them is rapidly repopulated, as if the town's citizens have been patiently awaiting their entrance cues in nearby alleys—women with shopping bags, men and women with briefcases, children with book satchels. It's a large and steadily growing cast of characters. Young and old, singly or in twos and threes, or in larger groups, walking fast or slow, the population of Pont-à-Mousson floods the square. He has lost sight of Amanda and his mother; they have been swept away by the tumult, so he stops at the center, at the monument.

The citizens of Pont-à-Mousson have raised this memorial to honor American ambulance drivers from the war of 1914–18, American volunteers, so eager to throw themselves into the misfortunes of others. A dubious altruism, Emerson reflects—almost an American pastime. One more example of that peculiar generosity nurtured in the security of the Continent's isolation so removed from the world's hatreds. How the world must be weary of such charity, such a heavy debt to be paid off, if ever. And how envious and angered by the geographic isolation that affords America's generosity; surely some must yearn to soil the luxury of that detachment. The Vietnam War has only just ended, and before that conflict the century records a long list of wars in which Americans gave their lives defending land that did not belong to them. Something arrogant in that, Emerson thinks. Would any foreigner volunteer and fight so fiercely to defend Benson Falls, Vermont? Somewhere around here, Emerson thinks, his father perished focusing his camera on the horror of this battle, making one more picture he had begun to believe was no different from the rest. Being an undertaker, he remembers him saying.

Missing in Action

Edith Olson unfolds the Michelin map as if it is a secret document while the clerk in the city hall in Pont-à-Mousson marks the locations of military cemeteries where Americans are buried. The man speaks some English and is evidently used to such questions. The exchange restores Edie's confidence, puts her back on the bearings of her assurance, and she now directs them as she sits next to Emerson in the Renault. She calls out road numbers and tells him where to turn. She is in charge once more.

They have stopped several times before small cemeteries. "This is it," she has claimed each time, before they get out to walk among poppies and wildflowers and crosses. Emerson has made no objections. It's become a fool's errand, and he's decided to enjoy it. Amanda sometimes picks the flowers and distributes them in an order only she knows. The burial grounds look severe and a little absurd, pointless in the aromatic landscape that surrounds them so casually in the perfect light.

"It's becoming embarrassing," he says to Amanda as they stand in yet another cemetery. "Maybe that's not the word, but all these graves so well taken care of is like holding on to the awfulness that goes with them. Not being able to let go of it."

"But aren't we supposed to remember so we don't do it again. Isn't that the popular wisdom? All those speeches we've heard?"

"No worry about that." He takes one of the wildflowers she has picked and places it on the top of a headstone. "It's a continuing education."

On another day, the patron of a small hotel in Clermont en Argonne marks their map, and they drive as far west as St. Mihiel, to the Meuse River, and then northward to Verdun. A few miles west of Verdun, they come to a place where fourteen thousand Americans are buried.

"But this is the other war. The First World War," Emerson explains uselessly. They have stopped before an enormous quilting of white crosses thrown over the greenness of a huge park. Two groundskeepers ride on muffled grass mowers.

"That's right," his mother says. She sounds half-asleep, dazed almost.

"We might find Billy Brown in here somewhere. But not Dad," Emerson tells his mother

"Who is Billy Brown?" Edith Olson asks. She seems to be counting the number of crosses before them.

"Aunt Rho's sweetheart. They were going to be married."

"Oh yes, I forgot." She nods her head, then nods again as if she's come to some understanding of what they have been about, that they have been destined to fail from the beginning. The car's cooling engine pings, and a nearby blackbird responds merrily in the brilliant sunshine.

"I bet there's an agency someplace," Amanda says from the rear, "that has it all down. I bet in Washington the army has such records. We can find out when we get home, and then we'll come back."

"Oh will we? Will you come back?" His mother turns in her seat, reaching a hand out, which Amanda takes. Edith Olson's smile is dazzling. Emerson hates himself, but he cannot help but think his mother is filing away this moment and its attendant expression for use in some episode of her soap opera. Or, perhaps she's pulled it out of the files for this moment in France. He can never be sure when she is acting. But he is grateful to Amanda, who continues.

"I know what." She's still holding his mother's hand. "We have a couple of days before our plane leaves. Let's get back to Paris. I remember a little café near St. Germain des Pres that I'd like to see again. How about it?" Amanda looks bright.

"Yes. What a good idea." Edith Olson turns around and claps her hands. "Let's have some fun. We must have fun."

The accumulated weight of the dead has worn down their spirits and made them weary of each other as well. They say little on the drive back to Metz. They eat a rather ordinary dinner at the hotel but drink a whole bottle of wine. Sam and Amanda create conversation out of critiques of the food and service. Edith Olson eats her meal silently and pays no attention to them. "I thought my little steak and French fries were excellent," she says finally, as if she wanted to defend the hotel's cuisine.

"I'm turning in," Amanda announces. "Too much Côte du Rhône."

Sam Emerson and his mother go into the small salon off the hotel's bar. He gets a brandy, and she takes another coffee. Without speaking, they observe the locals talk and smoke. Several enjoy a card game.

"I'm still glad we made this trip," she says at last. She is obviously tired but also relaxed. "We needed this time together. You and Amanda to get away for a little. Do you remember your father much, Sam?"

"Of course. I have many memories of him. Playing with his cameras. Taking trips together. That summer in Bucks County—or was it a whole summer? He was fun to be with. A great talker."

"Yes, a great talker. He told you stories, too, I remember."

"The bear stories."

"Yes." She seems to be scrolling through the past to find a memory they can share. "Steichen said he could have been one of the greats. What a waste. What a terrible waste. He got pulled into all those wars."

"It was his subject. Let's face it—it's the century's subject."

"He was so idealistic as a young man, and it was like a weakness. Others saw it in him and used it to pull him from his real subject." She sips her coffee.

"What was his real subject?"

She does not answer for a bit. "There," she says finally. She nods toward the men playing cards. "That was his subject." They watch the card players in the corner for a few moments. "I'm not coming back here again," she continues quietly. Another conversation has just concluded in her head. "Sweet of Amanda to say those things today, but maybe someday the two of you can find him." Then, as if she has gone on to a different scene, she says, "I'm getting out of the acting business."

"How come?" She has surprised him.

"More like it, it's getting out of me. These women I play are boring. Silly creatures. I just don't have the fire for it anymore."

"You always lit up the stage," Emerson says. "You were wonderful."

She pats his hand. "Let's hear it for the home team, eh? Well, thank you, dear boy. Well, like the man says, it's been a living. A life."

A sudden notion stabs him. He envisions her holding court in Benson Falls. "So what next?"

"I'm going to try teaching. You remember my work at Columbia. My degree certifies me as knowing something about Shakespeare. Can you imagine?" Her look ridicules the idea. "I've had an offer from a foundation that runs a theatre school in Greece. And there are colleges here that might use an old ham like me on their faculty."

"You're amazing."

"No, just hungry. I've always been hungry."

"I can see you at some college." Emerson likes the idea. "You'd be very popular."

"Yes." She appears to be ready to spend the night on the tufted seat of the banquette. "I will be." Her eyes are open, but the rest of her is dormant. Her mind is elsewhere. He thinks of Amanda upstairs.

"It's time for bed," he says.

Their rooms are on the third floor, and the lift is not functioning. Mother and son slowly climb the wide, carpeted stairs. Edith Olson's steps are resolute but slow, and, at each landing, she pauses and looks around for someone to approve her progress thus far. At the door of her room, she embraces him and pats his arm.

He makes out Amanda's silhouette in the dark.

The streetlights from below faintly illuminate the room. The railroad station is quiet. "Hi." Her voice is sweet. She's been waiting for him.

He undresses and slips into the narrow bed beside her. They find a comfortable fit for their legs and arms. She's very warm, and when she puts one arm across him, the material of her cotton nightshirt tickles his bare chest. She's been crying, and her tears fall quietly now. She sucks air through her nose and gives a soft cough.

"We've been tending graves," he says. Her arm hugs him tight. Emerson does not trust himself to continue.

"She meant this trip to be some kind of a remedy," Amanda says evenly. It sounds like she's been thinking through the idea, putting the words of it together as she waited for him. "Do you really think she expected to find him? That she wanted to find him? The search was for us. I think that's what she had in mind." How long, Emerson wonders, had she been saving up these thoughts to tell him, cramped in the back seat of the small Renault as they rolled along the back roads of France. For having said them, as if relieved of their weight, she slipped into a deep slumber. She becomes heavier upon him, and he surrenders to the lovely imprisonment. He follows some voices and a few footsteps in the street below the window as they become absorbed by the night. The city of Metz takes a deep breath and becomes still.

Aprés le Bain

In Paris, couples embrace on benches and lean against each other on bridges or on traffic islands in the middle of busy boulevards, oblivious to the trucks and cars racing around them. It's a cliché, Emerson thinks, something seen too many times in movies. But here it is happening. Actually taking place right before them.

"What was it called?" Edie asks again.

"Les Trois Something or Other." Amanda is embarrassed and laughs a little. She has led them through the narrow side streets around St. Germain des Pres. Each alley has looked familiar to her, but the restaurant she remembers from her school tour never appears.

"This looks attractive," the older woman says. She's stopped to look at a posted menu. She's looking for an omelet.

"Let's try the next corner," Amanda says and turns toward the Seine. Her eyes have grown large, and her color is high. It's just after six o'clock, and they are not very hungry. But eating together, they have discovered produces an intimacy that seems natural whatever the fare.

Finally, they choose a small place near Notre Dame with fresh white paper covers on its tables and a respectable *vin ordinaire* by the carafe. Two waiters and the chef are just finishing their own suppers at a table in the rear when they enter. They look them over with that Parisian regard that has measured tourists for centuries—not an unwelcoming look, but one that verifies their strangeness, that they are out of place. And too early for dinner. But the staff efficiently serves them without comment, and the bread is delicious, the lamb chops seared just right. Edith Olson claims her omelet is the best yet.

They walk back to their hotel along the Seine, stopping to buy ice cream at a confectioner's. The slanting western sunlight is a ceremonial sash hanging across the massive front of Notre Dame and other building fronts. Their hotel is nearby on rue St. Julien le Pauvre. They have satisfied their itinerary but have time left over. They don't know what to do. Their flight is in the morning, but to explore one more picturesque street is not on their timetable. They are tired.

"I have some packing to do yet," Edith Olson says. "You children go play if you want."

"I'm for a bath," Amanda says. "I'll come with you." She takes her mother-in-law's arm. She looks at Sam, but he cannot read the message in her eyes.

"I think I'll take a last look at Notre Dame," he says. Amanda nods, and the two women step off in the direction of the hotel. They make a graceful pair, and he watches the them step in tandem around a corner.

He has no real interest in the cathedral; it is an excuse to have some time alone. He walks slowly around its monumental structure in the deepening violet of the light, and he imagines he passes around the base of a huge cliff that has been grotesquely sculpted by wind and water. Or another fancy—it could be an odd space vehicle, its design fabulous in its own cosmos but curiously antique here on earth. It has come from a planet where technology is yet suborned by the mystical, and the gigantic vehicle has landed on the bank of the Seine River.

He takes a small coffee in a café next to the cathedral and enjoys being overwhelmed by the gothic busyness of the architecture. The screens and the filigrees could be rockets, waiting patiently for a signal that will ignite them and send the whole construction back to its own world. The huge buttresses that arch from the sidewalls support the apparatus, hold it upright on its launching pad. Emerson dips a sugar cube into the coffee and considers the possibility of the cathedral taking flight.

All the history of this place has been gathered into its great vault; all the events both glorious and despairing are kept within it, so it has become too heavy to fly. It lacks the power to lift this accumulated history from the ground. He sips some of his coffee, thinking their trip has been similar—they have tried to raise their separate griefs, to lift their different sad stories, but the ordinary turn of the earth keeps them here on the ground.

He realizes he has been absently looking at a carved tableau on the cathedral's side before him. The scene depicts Judgment Day, graves opening, their occupants spewing into the open air to make their joyous flight to Paradise. Some of them perch on the sides of their tombs, their plump behinds innocently hanging over the lips of the sarcophagi as if they lounge in a sauna.

He finds Amanda sitting in a chair by the large high window of their room. Streetlights join the fading daylight to fall across her nude torso. A bath towel lies across her lap as she passes a hair dryer around her head. Her arms are raised. He thinks of a museum picture, a woman by a window with the light falling across her—a woman just from her bath, her face flushed, self-absorbed. The dim light models Amanda's smallish square shoulders, the top curve of her breasts, the slight swell of her belly. The rest of her is in shadow. She turns to him, her face going from shadow into light. She shuts off the appliance and opens her arms. Sam Emerson kneels and presses his face into the damp towel and her lap. He breathes in the aroma of her bath-warm flesh. Amanda bends low to embrace his back. Her head rests upon him. Then abruptly, as if this interval has reached its determined course, he sits back on his knees like a supplicant.

"What?" Her smile is shy, expectant.

"What if we start over someplace."

"Start over?"

"I could sell Aunt Rho's farm. There's an outfit that wants to put up a shopping center. Remember? I told you. We could go anywhere. Start fresh."

"You mean leave Vermont? Benson Falls?"

"Yes, leave it all. Why not?" He puts his head back into her lap. Her fingers stroke his hair, rearrange the heavy strands of it.

SIX

Phoebe's interview had gone well. Emerson listened to the excitement in her voice as he followed the red beads of automobile lights strung on the golden strands of the parkways below his windows. The restaurant had closed, and Pennyworth was down there in the city somewhere with Constance and her roommate. They were going to a dance club in East Liberty. The journalist was flying back to New York in the morning.

"I think they might offer me the position," Phoebe was saying a little breathless.

"And then what?"

"Oh, I don't know." The anguish in her voice surprised him. "I just wanted to see how I matched up with the competition. You understand, don't you, Sam?"

"Yes." More than understand; Emerson reveled in Phoebe's ambition, her command of the profession. Her accomplishments complimented him, that a woman so on top of her game would be interested in him, but now that very success might take her from him. Nor was it only a matter of the distance from the West Coast. Lately, he had begun to worry their paths would diverge even here in Pittsburgh. "I have an offer for you, also," he said.

"Oh, I know you do." She laughed. "I know."

"No, wait a minute. This is different." He quickly told her about the trip to Mansfield and about Pennyworth's wild idea to put Edie Olson's ashes onstage. "Of course I would never do that."

"No, of course not."

"But how about this? We're closing down here in a week for some kitchen remodeling. A new walk-in cooler. And I'm thinking of going to France to look for my father's grave—"

"And you're taking her there. That's perfect, Sam. Wonderful! Yes, wonderful."

"Why don't you and Nick go with me? We could do a couple of days in Paris too. How about it?"

Her immediate silence heartened him. She was taking the invitation seriously. "Jiminy, that is an offer, for sure." He knew her eyes had become very bright, the light in them kindled by the idea. He had seen the look before when she talked about a patient or her son—any topic that really interested her. "Nick is still in school," she finally said.

"It's just for a week. It would be educational. His school might even give him credit."

"I do have some time coming to me," she reflected. "I won extra points out here."

Emerson started counting the cars passing over the Smithfield Bridge; if he could reach twenty before she said more, she would go with him. "It sounds wonderful." He had made it to nineteen.

"Passports," he suddenly remembered. "I have a contact—a customer—who can run them through in a hurry."

"We have passports," Phoebe told him evenly.

Just for a flick of a second the information startled him, a part of her life that was new to him, that he hadn't expected, but then his excitement rushed ahead. "Then you'll come with me?"

"I'm paying our way," she told him.

"It's a deal," Emerson exclaimed. His heart pounded, and he felt a little dizzy.

"I can't wait to give you a big hug," Phoebe was saying.

"And that's another idea I have. Hug shops."

"Hug shops?"

"Listen to this. Think of a fast food place, but just for hugs. Drive-in hugs. The franchises would spring up overnight across the country because everyone needs a hug now and then. Set them up near a McDonald's to satisfy the two hungers. People could drive in after a hard day or during midday stress, and have a snack and a hug. The menu would include Old Buddy Hugs. Favorite Teacher Hugs. Former Lover Hugs. Grandma Hugs. Favorite Uncle hugs. Think of all the unemployed actors who would find work as professional huggers. All those character parts to play. The possibilities are endless." He had her laughing gently, lovingly. He was working to make himself attractive, a demonstration of his congeniality, his infinite companionship—long term.

"Say you arrive at an airport in a strange city," Emerson continued.

"No one to greet you. You can go to the Hug Shop and for twenty bucks have a Welcome Hug. You could phone ahead, reserve a hug, and there would be your choice of character waiting at the gate, holding up a sign with your name on it, and you would go right to this person and receive a genuine, solid hug. It's a service whose time has come. We'll make millions."

He worked to entertain Phoebe to keep her from having second thoughts about the trip, though he was aware her mind could handle several ideas at once. That she allowed him to amuse her heartened him, yet he knew the important subject between them, this distance—if only just from across the river—had yet to be crossed. And now the long stretch to Seattle might be added to the problem. But Emerson found enough in her voice to make him happy. Phoebe then quickly became all business—she repeated her arrival time and flight number, and they hung up.

Earlier in the evening, the dark-haired woman at the bar had turned and put out her hand. "Hello, boss." He had met Constance's roommate a couple of times before. Noreen was her name, and she was some sort of a computer whiz.

Pennyworth sat on a barstool. "They're taking me dancing later." He wiped at his baldness and grinned knowingly. "To celebrate my last night in Pittsburgh."

"We have to treat the press right," Noreen said. "I read the *Weekly Agenda* religiously. Religiously. The things you people uncover. It makes a person think." Her voice was high and squeaky. Emerson couldn't tell if she was serious or merely mocking the journalist. She looked studiously at Pennyworth.

"We were just talking about Adam and Eve," Pennyworth said with mock severity. He put down his martini and smacked his lips.

Just then, something caught Emerson's eye. A man at a far table, in a party of four, had pulled out a cell phone and was punching in a number. Emerson left the bar and made his way smoothly to the table. "I'm sorry, sir. But we don't permit the use of cell phones at table."

"It's kind of an important call," the man replied. His large face was genial, expectant, and radiated the importance of the call.

"You're welcome to make the call in the foyer. But not in the dining room."

"Nobody said anything about this rule when we made the reservation."

"We suppose our guests understand without being told."

"And I suppose we'd be welcome to make the call anywhere outside too, say, if we were to leave your fancy restaurant."

The challenge in the man's eyes wearied Emerson. He didn't have to put up with this kind of behavior. "As you wish. Finish your drinks—they're on the house." He signaled the busboy. "Homer, clear this table, please, and set it up for the party of six that's arriving after nine."

"Hey, just wait a damn minute," the guy said. Homer had already picked up small plates and the complimentary pot of smoked bluefish paté.

"Safe home," Emerson said and turned on his heel. One of the women choked off an embarrassed laugh and started to get up.

When he returned to the bar, Noreen was sipping a glass of white wine and lighting another cigarette. Teddy Pennyworth leaned next to her, the look of a happy-go-lucky cavalier on his bald countenance. Constance prepared a tray of drinks for Cynthia, who stood nearby.

"What's your last name again?" the journalist asked her.

"Schmidt." She blew some smoke toward the ceiling and lifted the glass of wine to her lips, pinky finger extended. She seemed ready to say more when Constance interrupted.

"She's finishing her PhD in computer science." Constance supplied the information routinely as if explaining her roommate to others was part of their relationship. She had raised her arms to grasp the long, black fall of her sleek hair in both hands and pulled it up and around her neck and over her left shoulder. She looked at Emerson defiantly.

Noreen continued to stare straight ahead, blinking once or twice as Constance filled in her vita. This rendering of her biography seemed to amuse her, and she took a sip of wine and another puff on her cigarette. Her fingernails were bitten crudely, the polish neutral. She looked to be in some sort of hibernation on the barstool.

"So what's this about the Garden of Eden?" Emerson asked and checked the restaurant entrance. Some old customers were due to arrive.

"Mr. Pennyworth says the snake was irrelevant," Constance replied. She turned within the bar space, tidying up the area.

"Can you believe it?" Noreen looked at him. "No snake, no story."

"I didn't say no snake." Pennyworth leaned close to her. His face was flushed. "There's always a little snake to wriggle here and there." He wagged his index finger under her face.

"Ooh!" Noreen pulled back. "That's scary."

"You said the snake wasn't important." Constance Ho sounded like a child repeating a lesson.

"Yes, he did," her roommate joined in. "That's what he said. We heard you say it."

"Now seriously . . ." Pennyworth stroked his moustache and drew himself up, one hand grasping a lapel of his jacket. "Seriously, it's not about sex." He grinned and continued confidently. "It was Augustine who introduced the whole idea of the snake. The idea of sin. Fifth century. Look it up. St. Augustine," he pronounced the name emphatically, as if to benefit of the two women. "He made up the reason."

"Far out," Noreen gasped.

"So what was the reason?" Constance asked. "Why were they kicked out of the garden?"

"It's obvious. Eve had overreached herself. She wanted to know about herself, wanted to explain her own mystery. The Big Why."

"Our fault again, is it?" Noreen stared at Constance, and both women grimaced.

"Sounds like the old hubris to me," Emerson contributed. The people he had kicked out were leaving quietly, trying to look amused. He ignored them.

"Sure. Hubris." Constance nodded. "I remember him. Eddie Hubris. He had a sister who was a nun." Noreen's giggle had a hard edge to it.

"Sam is right," Pennyworth pushed on. "But hubris didn't sell well. By the fifth century it had worn out its effect. Augustine decided the church needed a strong image. A metaphor. Something that would instantly be recognized as bad. Evil and something to be feared. Ergo, a snake in a tree. Imagine reaching up to pick a nice, ripe apple and your hand encounters a snake."

"Oooh," said Noreen. "That's creepy."

Just then, the people with a table at eight-thirty showed up, and Emerson conducted them to their place. They were from out of town, and immediately began to ask him about the specials, requested water. Emerson signaled to Cynthia, who gracefully eased them into the protocol of Sam's Place.

"It's all very complicated," Noreen was saying when Emerson returned to the bar. She rolled her eyes.

"You want something, boss?" Constance asked. "The new Chablis is nicely buttered." He shook his head and asked for a glass of Pellegrino water.

"So, what's happening in the garden?" Emerson had begun to enjoy the talk and the nature of this odd seminar. "Bring me up to date."

"You won't believe it," Noreen said and laughed. She glanced at Constance, who was slicing a lemon. Cynthia had just brought the drink order from the new table.

"What I'm saying is that they would have been evicted anyway." Pennyworth finished his martini and put the empty glass on the bar with a flourish. He gave it a slight nudge. "Even without the snake, without the sex part. They were on the outs with the landlord."

"Get back to the snake," Noreen demanded with a laugh.

"We mustn't give it a Freudian twist," Pennyworth said quickly.

"Certainly not," the bartender said defiantly.

"Absolutely not," her friend agreed.

"There's a difference between original sin and the origin of sin," the journalist told them, his eyebrows waggling anxiously.

"I've always said that." Noreen also pushed her empty glass forward. Carefully.

"It's how the term *sin* is defined." Pennyworth spoke like a man with only a few seconds to make himself understood, before the firing squad took aim. "Augustine was trying to define it. Sex wasn't a sin, but self-knowledge was. That was the no-no Adam and Eve wanted, Augustine said, but he was misinterpreted. He wasn't talking about sex."

"Oh, pooh," said Noreen.

"Origin not original," Pennyworth persisted and looked at Emerson for help.

"I'm cutting you off, Schmidt," the bartender told her roommate.

Noreen pouted and looked wide-eyed at Emerson.

"Give the lass a wee drop more," Pennyworth pleaded.

"She has a delicate stomach," Constance explained.

"And a lovely one too, I wager." Pennyworth snorted.

"I don't need to have her barfing in the middle of the night," the bartender said, neatly folding up a small hand towel and patting it into place next to the sink.

"If you're having dinner, there's a table free in about fifteen minutes," Emerson told them. "My check."

"Noreen's my tab," Constance said quickly.

"It's my place and my check," Emerson corrected her easily. She shrugged and fiddled with the bar liquor. He felt generous, expansive. It was Pennyworth's last night in Pittsburgh. Phoebe was getting ready to fly to him at this very moment, and she was going to France with him. His idea for his mother's ashes. Everything was coming together.

"But the case isn't over," Noreen was saying. "How can you leave before the case is over? Don't those cops get sent to jail or something?"

"It's essentially over," Pennyworth replied and pulled himself up. "Justice has been done—well done. You can read all about it in the *Weekly Agenda*. In-depth reporting. Exclusive interviews." He seemed to be serious.

"It's not fair, is it?" Constance Ho said to no one in particular.

"That's what Adam said." The journalist raised a fresh martini. "To the Republic—and the Garden of Eden."

Emerson walked away to escort some regular customers to the door. They talked in the foyer with the lively intimacy the passing relationship afforded. When he returned to the bar, all three were laughing.

"They're going to take me dancing after you close up," Pennyworth said happily.

"You said that. Where are you going?" Emerson turned to Constance.

"Peaches," she named a lesbian disco in the East End. "You want to come?" The invitation was faint, and he was pretty sure his bartender hoped he would say no. "I have stuff to do," he replied. Then reassuming his role—the one Constance had just reminded him of—he turned to Noreen. "I recommend the seafood risotto."

Emerson wanted to plan a special dinner for Phoebe's homecoming; he would cook for her the first night back. Up in the penthouse. He'd have Nick there, too. So it would be like family—like the Two-20 Diner but with a view. He would do something simple but elegant.

"You are trying to enslave me," she had said one time. He had just whipped together a brunch for them. Her arms had spread wide with dramatic alarm. She wore his bathrobe, sleeves rolled up, and one of the pretty chemises he had helped her select. She always wore something out of bed, not that she was shy, but as if she permitted nudity only when that condition was required. The delicate coquetry of her lingerie was almost an art form that was oddly and wonderfully contrary to her professional exterior.

That morning, the flecks of white on Sterling Wicks's close-cropped black skull were discreet reminders of their partnership—the duration of it. Partners, maybe even friends. "Any suggestions as to what I could cook?" he asked Wicks. Emerson had picked up a large knife and joined the chef at the large butcher-block table to chop celery, carrots, and onions. Sterling was preparing a *court-bouillon* in which to poach sea bass for an evening special. The two men worked side by side, their knives relentlessly mincing the vegetables. It was too early for the prep cook, and Wicks wanted to get the broth done and cooled, because he had an appointment downtown with the law firm that represented the Overstreet family.

Working together reminded Emerson of the early days when the restaurant was called The Tables on Mt. Washington. A guy named Earl ran the bar. A procession of college students, never more than two at a time, marched the plates he and Sterling finished into the dining room. Amanda had handled the front, poured the wine. Earlier she had prepared the desserts. The arrangement had seemed perfect. Like something out of a movie.

But one evening Amanda said, "I can't keep up with you." They were sitting on the balcony upstairs after the restaurant had closed. The evening had finally cooled as the grip of the Ohio Valley humidity loosened. "I'm like one of those characters in a pulp novel who gets winded on the trail and is left behind."

"I'd leave you the last canteen and enough powder and shot to bag a few turkeys," he said, but he saw she was serious. He could find no answer for her.

"I am feeling odd here—out of place. I don't like being exposed up here on this mountaintop, though it's a great view. It's your mountaintop. I can come visit. It will be like we're having an affair. Maybe I can keep up with you from afar."

"But what will you do in Benson Falls?"

"Do? You are always so worried about my doing something. I hate making desserts, and I'm not especially good at it. Why should I do anything? What if I don't want to do anything? Oh, I'll keep busy. A gift shop. Wooden bowls and candles. Knitted stuff."

The list had made him feel worse. He had reached to touch her hand, to take both her hands in his, but she had pulled away and stood to go to the railing. Her silhouette against the city lights made him think of those times he had watched her dress in the dark to sneak back into the women's dormitory at Penn State. Unexpectedly, a sob caught his breath. She turned toward him. "And you should change the name. Call the restaurant Sam's Place. That's the truth of it."

Sterling Wicks had rinsed off the large knives, wiped them dry, and run both over a sharpening stone. Crisp peaks of chopped vegetables rose from the mellow wooden surface of the table. Each man waited for the other to speak, to make a move. It was a familiar lull. Over the years, they had learned to cross such awkward gaps without looking down too closely at the spliced-together friendship below.

Emerson took a deep breath. "What would you think about my spending some time away from the restaurant?"

"How much time?" Sterling Wicks had leaned back against the stove, crossing his arms.

"We're halves anyway. I won't take much. I'd like to keep the building for now and the penthouse. You could pay me some kind rent if it would make you feel good. Cynthia has become first rate in the dining room—she's gotten good with wines. And she's been helping me with the books. You'd need a new bartender, as you know," Emerson said.

"Whoa, hold on, Kemo Sabe. Wait just a minute. How long is this sojourn going to be?"

"I'm not sure. Phoebe may move to Seattle."

"How does she feel about your following her?"

"I haven't mentioned it to her. It's not certain she will move."

Wicks started as if the stove behind him had suddenly turned on. Emerson couldn't tell what he was thinking. Their offhand mastery at the chopping board—the intimacy of that moment—may have led him to say too much, before he had thought it through. Emerson changed the subject.

"What's happening with the case? I thought the feds were stepping in."

"Stepping in and stepping out. Everyone takes his place—it's an old dance. Wheels grinding slow and so forth." Wicks might have been describing a part of the stove that wasn't working. "Do I get to rename the place?" he asked.

The possibility had not occurred to Emerson. "You don't like the name?"

His partner opened his mouth in a silent laugh. "Don't worry, buddy. It will always be Sam's Place. Not good business to change the name. But on your way to Seattle, would you mind going down to the Strip and picking up the fish for tonight?" He began to whistle, and it was a melodious signal that his attention was moving away, and, in fact, he opened the door to the cooler and disappeared inside.

Emerson knew his partner pretty well, and he was certain Wicks was already making changes that would go beyond the menu. He had moved too fast, spoken without really thinking. He feared he had instantly exiled himself from the cozy rightness of this kitchen he had designed, not to mention the penthouse above. He had only meant to test out the idea on Sterling, on himself at the same time, but his idea may have become irreversible. He might have lost his place, just handed it away without thinking. Then, what if Phoebe didn't go to Seattle? Where would he be then? Who would he be?

At Weisberg's vegetable market, the heft of an Arkansas tomato restored Sam Emerson's confidence, his good humor. "To be honest, Sam, they're not on a par with the Mariettas," Sol Weisberg told him, "but they won't embarrass you either."

The wholesale market area was relatively quiet for a weekday morning, and the give-and-take of the area renewed the citizenship he feared he might have just given up. He belonged here, he told himself. He was part of this community, the handling and portioning of food. He was made for these discussions and making of deals, the direct, rough-sounding talk of the purveyors who all knew him. At the Macaroni Company, he tasted some new chevre and then bought some *pastore sini*—a cheese of sheep's milk from Rome he particularly liked. He'd add it to the restaurant's cheese board. The peppers at Jimmy Sunseri's were works of art, and the tang of the arugula stung his nose pleasantly. As he shopped, he imagined Phoebe on the other side of the continent beginning to choose the clothes she would pack.

"I'm picking up those stripers, Louis," he told the fishmonger.

"These are first class," the man said. "Look at those sides. Firm bellies. Just flew them in from Atlantic City. Our own plane."

Emerson gently poked the resilient fish, looked closely into the eyes that returned his stare. "Heads and tails on."

No, repetitious as they might be, he couldn't give mornings like this up. He'd make it up to Sterling some way.

PROGRAM NOTES

Keepsakes

All of the past, Sam Emerson thinks, can be kept in a stone. Just an ordinary flat, smooth piece of granite you might pick up by a stream and handle to feel its texture, its silent pulse and perfect weight, before you toss it into the water. There goes the Ice Age, and the dinosaurs, Caesar's legions, Lewis and Clark, and Frank Sinatra—the whole catalog of the planet going ker-plunk at midstream. But if you held the stone a little longer, all the sounds and flavors of the past fit themselves into your hand.

He's in the kitchen of the small house in East Liverpool, going through the closet and cabinets to sort out Aunt Rho's possessions. He's just come across the heavy black iron pan he remembers her using to make corn muffins or cup cakes, moist and redolent of vanilla, or walnut-studded honey cakes. This single ordinary pan had turned out all those extraordinary flavors.

His mother performs a similar rummage upstairs. Her every footfall clatters and resonates on the floor above his head, and the house seems to have shrunk since he was last here. The hallway between kitchen and front door has shortened—he could take the distance in only a half dozen steps—but the iron grill of the heat register set in the floor still marked the parlor entrance. "Look at this!" his mother exclaims. She sounds just outside the kitchen. No need to crouch down close to the outlet in the baseboard to hear her.

He can tell she's still a little put out. There's an edge in her voice, a forced gaiety, an opening scene in a Chekhov play, a covering over of real feelings her technique quickly and cleverly reproduces. He hadn't wanted the house and the land—what was he going to do with them? The lawyer assured him the house could be rented easily and suggested he might want to hang on to it for a little while. Everything is slowly disintegrating—the house and the small barn. The acreage is going to sumac; the berry bushes have rotted in weeds. Property always increases in value, the man said, and something worthwhile might happen in the future.

And what would his mother do but sell it? She couldn't look after it and certainly wouldn't live here. She wants nothing of it—no reminder of her days here in East Liverpool. She is doing well now because of television work, and she is even helping him pay his tuition and expenses at Penn State. So she quickly signed over her part of the estate—all or nothing, her gesture seemed to indicate.

Sam Emerson opens the tap of the kitchen sink and lets the water run until he hears the click and hum of the pump in the basement, drawing water from the well. He fills a glass and drinks it down. Good water. His mother's high heels tap and click across the floor above.

"Well, will you look at this?" she cries out.

"What?" he answers almost conversationally as if they were in the same room.

"There must be every bottle of perfume, every box of bath powder I ever sent her. All right here. Unopened. A whole drawer full of stuff I got her when I worked at Macy's."

He says, "But she preferred Evenings in Paris."

"Evening in Paris," she corrects him.

"Whatever."

They have just come in from the cemetery, and her behavior there yet makes part of him curl up, the way she spoke to the local people, old people who were friends of Rhoda Olson. One or two old classmates lingered at the open grave. His mother plucked at the grass around her father's tombstone, neatened the ground around the grave of the mother she never knew. Her rueful industry, as others watched, suggested a duty being fulfilled with the poise of a chore done regularly. He is sure she has not visited these sites since she left East Liverpool.

She took the role of the visiting duchess with all the old people who showed up at the funeral home. Some of the old ladies had worked with Aunt Rho at the High Standard Café. They had advanced themselves shyly. A former town mayor headed a delegation of courtly old men, who laughed and joked and jostled each other at her bier at Dawson's Funeral Home. Sam Emerson thought they resembled wizened schoolboys standing resolutely at roadside for a school bus that had failed to pick them up. A picnic was held in the afternoon. The Ladies' Aid of the

First Methodist Church filled long tables set up on the front lawn with ham, smoked turkey, potato salad and coleslaw, fresh biscuits and corn sticks. Homemade preserves and pickles were lined up on one side. Iced tea, lemon cake, and chocolate cream pie. "I was about to sit down," his mother joked, "when the next county showed up." Her enthusiasm, whether real or contrived, pleased them, and the same performance that flattered them only made Sam Emerson uncomfortable. So, he felt out of it.

In fact, he took a walk. At one point, he slipped away and strolled the several blocks into the center of town to the street where the High Standard Café had been. The building has become a store selling surplus army goods, fishing and hunting supplies. Guns and Ammo. The Vista Theatre next door now looks like it has been closed and boarded up for years, the facade dirty and the marquee falling apart. He remembers the hushed expectancy in the carpeted lobby, and the cloying, greasy smell of popcorn. Fred and Ginger dancing inside.

So, it hasn't been fair, Sam Emerson considers as he goes through the kitchen cabinets and shelves. This small town in Ohio up against the practiced wiles of a seasoned campaigner like Edith Olson. Some remembered his mother from high school; she had been a little different from them with that drive to get to New York. To chase fame. And right there was a problem. He has counted only a few TV aerials on the town's rooftops. How many in East Liverpool had seen her play Paul Newman's mother? They were staying at the Traveler's Hotel downtown—his mother had wanted to stay in town—and the picture on the set in the hotel's lobby frantically flopped with every passing vehicle.

No resident could have gotten a clear picture of *Playhouse 90* or *Studio One,* even if they had chosen to do so. He remembers the grainy image on Aunt Rho's TV—and come to think of it—where is her set? She must have gotten rid of it, maybe when his mother stopped appearing on its screen. In any event, her image on the local sets would be in black and white and not the full colorful collision of the woman in person. She would be unrecognizable, though her bearing and manner would be implication enough of her fame.

"You still in the acting business?" one of the old men had asked her politely. They were standing on the wide porch of the funeral home that afternoon.

"Oh, my yes," she replied, one hand at her throat, charitable deference excusing ignorance. "Keeping busy." She rattled off some names of plays and actors that meant nothing to the man. However, he accepted the credentials.

"Rho and me were bridge partners for twenty-five years. A quarter of a century," he said and tried to stand straighter.

"Think of that, Sam," she said and pulled on his arm, bringing him close to her. He knew she wanted to expose him to the full tedium of the town. "Twenty-five years shuffling all those cards."

"We won our share of the tournaments," the old fellow continued. His voice became weak and watery. "Rho had a great head for numbers. She could keep track of every card. She had a mind like that. She could have taught school, I always thought. And, if I remember correctly, you grew up here too for a little?" He turned toward Sam.

"Only a few years," Edith Olson replied for him. "When his father was overseas in different wars. His father was a photographer, you know. And I had a number of important engagements. It was no life for a boy who needed a stable home. Rho gave him that. But you were happy here, weren't you, Sam? We spent a summer here—or part of one. When was that, darling? I think it was the summer that gangster was killed. Pretty Boy Floyd wasn't it? The FBI killed him here. He robbed banks, didn't he?" Her smile was large and patient with understanding that such a person could be a hero to people like this old man.

"That would be in 1934," the fellow said. "October 1934." He looked a little uncomfortable supplying the fact.

"Well, I guess that wasn't the summer we were here then. It must have been later. My husband was just leaving for Spain. They had a civil war there."

"The funeral parlor that handled Floyd was the Sturgis place, just three blocks down on Fifth." The recall made the man eloquent. "Floyd's body was prepared there, and I helped with that. I was working part time for Mr. Dawson, who was the funeral director for the Sturgis family. He started this here place on his own later. We shipped the body to Floyd's mother for burial. Mr. Dawson bought the business later from the Sturgis family and moved it here. That would be 1939."

"Think of it—1939," Edith Olson said and touched the beads around her throat.

"When they caught up with Floyd he was sitting up against a tree. Bleeding to death. His tommy-gun was lying beside him. 'Are you Pretty

Boy Floyd?' one of the FBI agents asked him. 'I am Charles Arthur Floyd,' he answered and then died. He hated that Pretty Boy name."

"Yes, I think I heard that," Sam's mother said She looked around the large porch. "They're probably waiting for us to go to the cemetery." She pulled on Sam's hand. In the back seat of the funeral home's limousine, she turned and whispered in his ear. "Do you remember any of that?" She was holding herself together; blocking the outrageous laughter that flooded her eyes and seemed ready to burst her apart.

"Some."

In fact, all that fall, he and his playmates had played G-man and Pretty Boy Floyd, each of them taking turns to play the rural gangster so as to enact a glorious death before their playmates' cap pistols and broomstick tommy-guns. "I am Charles Arthur Floyd." Each quoted the famous last words in various attitudes of mortal agony. "Robin Hood is dead," Aunt Rho said one hazy morning in October. She had just pulled a pan of corn muffins from the oven. The town was full of strangers who had come to see the corpse laid out at the Sturgis Funeral Home. Thousands had come out of curiosity to pay their respects. Before that, grayish young men in city hats had wheeled into town in heavy, dark sedans. They resembled the salesmen who sometimes showed up at the door selling encyclopedias or promoting a Mormon heaven. But these were G-men. It was rumored J. Edgar Hoover was in town, too. Some of them took their meals at the High Standard Café. Aunt Rho told him they smoked a lot, drank many cups of coffee, but only picked at her corned beef hash.

His mother's high heels click-click overhead like some sort of signal being sent. He has just poured into one of the round molds of the heavy muffin pan the small stones Aunt Rho kept in a green glass on the windowsill above the sink. Before Billy Brown had gone overseas in 1918, the two of them had gone with a church group to Lake Erie. She had collected these pebbles from the lake beach. "How come he didn't marry you before he went to the war?" young Sam asked her one night in the middle of his homework. The Vista was playing a picture with Constance Bennett, and she had married this guy before he went to France. He was killed, too, but they had got married first.

"Billy said he didn't want to tie me down in case something happened." She poked through her sewing box for a button for one of his school shirts.

Sam Emerson considers filling each of the cups in the old muffin pan with other small objects from the house to make a kind of sampler, residue from his time in East Liverpool. He'd have to add the sound effects and the aromas on his own. The squawk of chickens out back and the smell of the lavender bush growing at one corner of the barn. The clunk of the furnace turning on in winter followed by the thick rush of hot air across the linoleum laced with the oily tang of coal. He could make up a small collection, things he could pick up and handle.

Party Time

She joins him in the kitchen as he prepares their supper. She's become almost flirtatious, for she is in her party mode. He remembers her in restaurants in New York, her show-biz charm going full blast, and this tidy kitchen is clearly too small for her. Has always been too small for her. "I'm in your way," she says teasingly and snaps a stalk of celery in two to chew half of it noisily. He's about to sauté the fillets of the black bass he bought from a fisherman at the town dock earlier that afternoon. As a boy he spent hours at this spot, watching tugs and barges pass by, and he and the fisherman chatted easily, as if they shared a history. He did some marketing after the cemetery ceremony, and without warning got the notion—the first of many such inklings that would eventually add themselves into an insight—that when he gathered and chose ingredients he also gathered himself, picked over his choices and the ways to solve a problem. The spontaneity of this self-awareness delights him, and he feels like he's learned something in his literature class at Penn State. An epiphany, the instructor called it, and that it has just happened to him—to Sam Emerson in East Liverpool, Ohio—makes him a little giddy. He's been *epiphanied.*

So, he is showing off the skills he has learned at the hotel school, but it will be a simple meal. The fish, small red potatoes pan roasted in their skins, and slices of zucchini sautéed in vegetable oil and garlic. Olive oil was not to be found, so he adds some butter for flavor, and then a handful of raisins from Aunt Rho's pantry. The local stores had only iceberg lettuce so he improvises a salad from sliced cucumbers with dill from the back garden, dressed with mustard and vinegar from the pantry. He slices up the red onion that was the sole occupant of the basket on the counter. No telling what Aunt Rho had planned to do with the onion, but he happily thinks she would have nodded as he adds thin rings of it to the salad. He could see her.

"I salute the chef." His mother holds up a small water tumbler containing the Portuguese rosé. The state store's wine inventory is modest.

"Not much for dessert." It is a mock apology, and he smiles. "I found a couple of pears that look decent."

"Couldn't be better," she says and smiles warmly. Her look upon him is luminous, and he begins to feel a little uncomfortable. The auburn hair around her face is professionally colored now, but she is a handsome woman—mature, though something youthful remains. He wonders, and not for the first time, why no other man has entered her life. She seems to have taken orders for a single existence. He almost tells her about Amanda Benson. After all, talking about dessert would be a graceful introduction.

By the way, he might say, there's this pretty girl at school who is specializing in desserts, and her family owns a rustic old inn in Vermont. He wants to confide in his mother, as if she might be an older sister—and to show her he has made a life for himself. That they are on equal footing. But their conversations have not been easy, and in the last several years, they have been together only three or four times. Neither is a good correspondent. They rarely use the telephone. When they are together, they observe a simple decorum, and Sam Emerson keeps his distance, unwilling to surrender his resentment.

"So," he asks after a moment, "how do you feel about all of this?" Her expression sharpens as she waits for more definition. "I mean emptying out this house you grew up in?"

"We have to move on, don't we? That's the cycle we're given, isn't it? Fall to winter to spring and so forth." She takes a last forkful of the fish. "Moving on. But you lived here, too. How do you feel? Who was that guy who spoke to you at the cemetery?"

"Just someone from my class in grade school. He owns a hardware store here now. Most of the kids I played with have left."

"There you have it—some run hardware stores, but most people move on. Of course they've left. What would keep anyone here? I left. I learned to travel light." Her laugh is quick, as if it has been a mistake. "With your father, of course, I had no other choice." The explanation is not an apology. "But now that you are a property owner in East Liverpool, do you think you'll live here? You could open a restaurant—

another High Standard Café. But I suspect the kind of cooking you've learned in school wouldn't go over well here."

The idea stuns him. He can see his whole life unroll on the red checkered oilcloth on the kitchen table. She has given him an idea, and he doesn't resent the gift. He could marry Amanda Benson, and the two of them could take over her family place in Vermont. He is watching his future as a movie. They have only become lovers, just the last week, and he thinks about her a lot. She seems to have memorized whole books of poetry and can come up with quotations at the right moment. He will call her tonight.

"I guess I'll rent it out until I figure out something," he says finally. "But I was talking about clothes. The knick-knacks."

"Well, I do want that Delft clock there on the wall. You don't want it, do you? You have no place for it." Her tone is defiant, as if he has been about to claim it. Early on school mornings, especially in winter as he waited for the school bus, the grind of its gears grew loud, as if the wings of the windmill had come loose from their ceramic cast and had begun to turn. He was afraid to look at it as it hung over the stove. This evening, the mechanism innocently spins the hour.

"Yes, I know what you mean," she continues. "Some civilizations burn the dead's possessions with them. It's sensible. Getting rid of the past. But we are tied to accumulation. We've made the right decisions." In the morning, a truck from the Salvation Army in Steubenville will back up to the house and clear it out.

"On the same subject, you might be interested to know that I've talked the Museum of Modern Art into taking your father's negatives for their archives. It wasn't easy. He didn't fit their idea of a photographer— not arty enough. They're gaga over Weston and Company. And that woman who takes pictures of freaks. But a couple of his old pals from *Life* talked up for him. So, they are safe now, and maybe someone will print up a couple sometime. You can imagine how relieved I feel. I've been carting them around for years."

"His war pictures."

"And also the beautiful landscapes he used to do. He had a lyrical side to him. I think you have it, too. He suffered because of it, and others took advantage of him because of it. Don't you be a pushover." Her eyes glint, and she bites the tip of her tongue. Sam recognizes this isn't the time to talk about Amanda Benson. "Also included are the pictures he took that summer we visited here. He was leaving for Spain then. That damn war changed everything." She sips some of the wine, not really tasting it, he's sure. He guesses she means their lives were changed by it, though she might mean more.

He's just aware that she is not smoking. "You've quit?"

"I never took it seriously." She waves away the whole habit.

After dinner, he sits on the back steps and watches her work in the small garden in the back yard. She bends low to pull weeds from around the dozen tomato plants staked out in a perfect line toward the barn. It is a curious stewardship, he ponders, like the one she practiced at the cemetery this afternoon and carried off with all the offhand familiarity of a regular routine. But again, as at the cemetery, he wonders if the activity is only a bit of business to accompany the scene. The hard green fruit of the plants nestles in the leaves. Some are changing color, turning red. In about a week they will ripen and burst in their ripeness and then rot on the vine, unpicked. He will pack some of them back to State College and let them ripen on a window sill of his and Sterling's apartment. Something of Aunt Rho's for Amanda to know about, to taste as he tells her about growing up in East Liverpool. Ohio tomatoes from Marietta, he will boast, can't be beat.

The long twilight stretches beyond the barn and the ragged chicken coop to irrigate the darkness between the rows of tasseled corn. Crickets send their signals from beneath the porch steps. The headless ghosts of chickens run amok in his imagination. Birds have made their final calls, and in the lull between the drone of trucks on Route 7, he listens hard for the running murmur of the Ohio River. As a boy, upstairs in the bedroom that faces east, he would drift into sleep on a night like this one, conjuring the river's endless narrative.

Earlier this afternoon, he tried to fit the stiff, rouged mummy that had been made of Aunt Rho into some of this chronicle. Happy stories mostly—the time here in East Liverpool—but these stories have ended, and looking down at her in the casket (she never wore much make-up), he sensed that part of himself would be interred with her, and he would hereafter suffer an incurable ache, a dull cramp around his heart.

"It's sweet of you to want to keep some of her things." His mother stands at the far end of the garden, a clump of dandelions in one hand. "That's your father's nature in you. He wanted to keep beautiful things too—in his cameras. But the choices were limited—the century reduced them."

"You mean the Spanish War. All wars are awful."

"Yes, awful, but Spain was different. He used to say the world lost something in Spain. Not innocence—that was knocked out in 1918—but he said hope and fair play were still left. The right side had won—the good guys, as he said. Good intentions were still rewarded. But Spain changed all that." She's almost invisible in the deepening dusk. He hears her bracelets clink. Earlier she put them in her purse at the funeral home. "Your father was never the same after that. He said he had lost an eye in Spain."

Slowly materializing as she approaches, she returns through the twilight to where he sits on the porch. Sam leans back against the steps, welcoming and enjoying this moment they have thoughtlessly fallen into. Two people talking about a person they once shared and becoming closer as they do. The darkness is a convenient shelter. "Those people changed him. They ruined him."

"You mean like Mary What's-her-name? Mary Splendid?" He expects the old litany to start playing, and the mood might change, and he is sorry to have thought of that woman.

"You remember her?" His mother's laugh is easy, a little sad.

"I remember you talking about her with that friend of yours in Greenwich Village."

"Hazel Pennyworth. Yes, I may have talked about her then."

Those evenings of that one Christmas flash in his memory as he sits on these back steps in Ohio. There was also a strange boy, Hazel's son. In recent years, the subject of his mother's complaint back then, fellatio, has become a commonplace, almost a custom. Every coed does it. Well almost. Just the other night, Amanda perched on her knees, her appealing nakedness slick with the sweat of their lovemaking, to tell him she wasn't sure she could do *that,* but she'd try. And it was the most amazing thing. He could almost believe how a king would give up his throne for the pleasure. How strange, Sam thinks, that human relations, perhaps even world history, could turn on this single act.

"I remember you talking about her," he says again. His mother pulls her dress tight over her knees and rests her head there. "And Dad."

"It wasn't just the physical part, though that hurt of course. But she and those other people did something to his perspective, made him feel what he wanted to look at was unimportant. That was terrible."

"Landscapes and barn sidings."

"Those people made him feel irrelevant. They tossed that word around a lot. Pictures had to *do* something. They could no longer be just beautiful. Pictures had to instruct the masses. You just couldn't look at them. You had to read a text that came with them. You can understand why I wanted to get back at them. They took away his hope. They took my lover from me. I had names and dates, too. Dear old Emmet Thornton and little Wanda Jordon never worked again because they weren't pink enough."

"Or Jewish enough." He holds his breath, afraid he's gone too far.

"Well, they stuck with their own kind, didn't they? Of course, that was natural. It didn't bother me."

"The play about the prizefighter. You said that was a gyp."

"Yes, *Golden Boy.*"

"The Commies kept you out of the play." He feels her breaking down his sentence, inspecting its component parts, syllable by syllable, for sarcasm or mockery.

"That was different," she says finally, and her voice is level. "Frances Farmer was sleeping with Clifford Odets. He wrote the play. And she was very good in the part, too. Very good. But Hollywood ruined her. I never did that, Sam. I got the roles I got standing on my feet."

"I appreciate that," he tells her. "I know."

"They told me I didn't have to testify." She slips back into the other subject. "My deposition was more than enough, they told me. So I got even for what they did to your father."

A truck downshifts gears on Route 7 and gradually slips into the heavy silence. All the times he has heard this story, her rationale and explanations, Sam still has trouble with the idea that she betrayed friends and colleagues. And what value was her information really—how did it change anything? Unaccountably, he feels sorry for her, and he puts an arm around her shoulders and hugs her tentatively.

"What's your next part?"

"Someone's mother on the *Philco Playhouse.*" Her laugher wells up in the darkness with a near girlish sound. "That's my role, isn't it? I wish someone would write a script for me I could use in real life. With me and you. I needed a script, I guess."

"You've done well," he finds himself saying, but he joins her ironic laughter. They are enjoying each other's company, as if all the skirmishes and deprivations have given them a camaraderie, a pension of sorts to reward their years of disaffection.

"You'd think I would have learned something from the typecasting. This new script is by one of those Southern playwrights who write about selfless women, weary with wisdom and a heavy foot on the love pedal. They mow everything down before them—no one can escape their affection. I bet my bottom dollar the prototype was hell to pay."

"What are you going to do with all that perfume and powder Aunt Rho saved?" She has already packed up a large box for shipment back to New York.

"Gifts I suppose. Some of them are antiques. Valuable." She laughs. But for whom, he wonders. She never talks of friends, and he wonders if she has any.

They do not look back when they turn out of the driveway later that night. They have washed the dishes and put everything away, arranged the kitchen, as if someone will rise in the house on another morning to start a new day. Boxes are stacked by the front door waiting to be picked up by the Salvation Army. Next to the box of perfumes in the back seat of the rented car is a strong canvas shopping bag that contains the iron muffin pan and jars of small stones, buttons, hairpins, and other small items Sam has collected. Three long ebony hairpins as well. For some reason, he has pocketed the small picture of the military cemetery in France—a small red check mark on one of the distant white crosses—but he and his mother tacitly agreed to leave the photograph of Billy Brown in his soldier uniform on top of the bureau in Aunt Rho's room. It might end up in an antique store, and someone might buy it to add it to a collection of such old photographs. They decided not to spend the last night at the house. "Let's leave it to all the old ghosts to have to themselves tonight," she said as they finished the wine.

At the hotel in town, they quickly bid each other good night. Her train back to New York leaves Pittsburgh at noon, and he plans to catch a bus back to State College later. When Amanda answers the phone, she sounds sleepy. He tells her about the funeral, cleaning out the house, and how he cooked the fish.

"Are you sad?" she asks.

"A little. She practically raised me." Amanda says nothing. "What did you do tonight?" he asks her.

She went to a movie with her roommate, and then they went for pie and coffee at the Corner House. The crust was soggy, she says, and obviously not made with real butter. She's just washed out some things and has been doing some reading for her paper on Escoffier. She fell asleep over the book. The ordinariness of her day stirs him. The lackluster recital is strangely exotic in its placid differences from the din and clatter of his mother's presence. He has never become accustomed to the commotion Edie Olson makes or the noise of her in his life.

As they talk, he pictures Amanda in her sweater and skirt with the strand of pearls around her neck, the white socks and loafers on her feet. She wears the standard uniform of the day. Then he imagines her without these clothes, as he saw her just the other night, shielding herself rather primly as she went to the bathroom after they had sex. Her figure was neatly formed, nothing remarkable, but he found her body powerfully erotic because it had only just been so conventionally appareled.

"We have to get married," he says abruptly into the phone.

Amanda gasps, then says, "You're pregnant?"

She is giggling, and Sam joins her merriment, a little irked that his impulse—his seriousness—has been turned into a joke. Her quick wit surprises him and puts him on guard. Just for a moment, he thinks he may not know her well enough, that he has been carried away more by the sentimental feelings raised by Aunt Rho's death and the conversation with his mother than by the girl's actual appeal. The idea of marriage, of wanting to share his life with someone—doesn't that count for something? "I'm serious," he says finally. "I think we'd make a great team."

"Making a team is important." He can't tell whether she is still being funny.

"I love you," he says, and he's pretty sure he means it.

"Let's talk when you get back," she says.

"So what else happened at State College today?" he asks her. Below his hotel window, the streets of East Liverpool are deserted. The bridge across the Ohio River is vacant and almost brutally illuminated. His question has unplugged a reservoir of details in Amanda, and he willingly lets himself be carried on their ordinary flood.

The Honeymoon

"She's a pretty thing," his mother says. "Perky." They are sitting in Edith Olson's apartment for drinks before dinner. Amanda has just excused herself to go to the bathroom. It occurs to Sam Emerson that his bride may be starstruck and that she might have married him for his mother. His stories about the ramshackle way of her life, her gypsy course, only increased Amanda's fascination. Perhaps her admiration.

This one-bedroom studio east of Madison Avenue in the Sixties has been the most permanent place Edie Olson has kept that he can remember. But the heavy wardrobe trunk sits half open in the bedroom, ready to go with the quick clap of its two halves. Some pictures have been hung on the walls, but most are stacked against the baseboard, at the corner of the hallway. "What's funny?" she asks.

Sam shakes his head. She's found a place for them to stay in Greenwich Village, in an apartment of a friend who is working at the Stratford Shakespeare Festival. Amanda is pleased, for it saves them money, and he's agreed to the thrift, but it also reminds him of the many borrowed sofas he has slept on. Amanda's entranced by the small, angled streets of the Village, the little shops and cafes. This is her first trip to New York, and she responds to Edie Olson with the same bug-eyed wonder, as if his mother were an item on the tourist agenda.

"What shall I call you?" Amanda has asked earlier. "Edith? Edie?"

"You may call me what you wish," his mother replies indifferently.

"Certainly not Mother Emerson," Amanda says and smiles.

"Certainly not," his mother replies, and the two women laugh together. Already they have found a commonality, formed some kind of bond. He can't figure out how that has happened and is not really sure he likes it.

"Edie. I'll call you Edie."

"So named," his mother says and raises her cocktail glass.

But what will he call her? He's very aware he has created a way of talking to her that avoids any naming, any reference to their relationship. His letters written from Ohio when he was a boy addressed her as Mommy. *Dear Mommy, Aunt Rho has bugs in her corn. School is good. I miss you. It is raining.* But that appellation would not suit him today. To say *Mother* would make him sound like one of those characters in her soap opera—who have only found the term in the script. He has practiced

237

the sound of *Maw*, and that seems acceptable, though he has not used it yet. He will have to come up with something. What if tonight as they walked to dinner he watched as she stepped off the curb before a speeding taxi? Would he stand silently on the curb, not shout a warning, because he has no name to call her? So he continues to address her around the blank.

She has mixed and serves daiquiris in cocktail glasses with silver rims. She invites no orders—it is the house drink apparently. A bowl of cashews and several paper napkins are on the glass-topped table. She has made reservations at an intimate restaurant in her neighborhood that, she adds with a winning laugh, will not insult their expertise. The furniture in the apartment is not familiar to him, but then his parents never owned any furniture he could remember. His mother is working steadily in television and occasional roles in the new Off-Broadway theatres. Recently, she was in a production of *The Lady's Not for Burning* at the Jan Hus house, once more doing a mother role.

"So tell me about this atmospheric little inn in Vermont," Edie says.

Sam Emerson is aware he is about to prove himself, but he goes on. "It's been in Amanda's family for generations. Empty about fifteen years, no one to run it."

Amanda returns from the bathroom. "More like twenty. My father has an insurance business. But the bar part has been kept open."

"It's a perfect spot. Skiers in winter. The autumn color people in the fall. Clean air, spring and summer," Sam goes on.

"A healthy retreat," Edie Olson says. Sam cannot read her tone. "And the two of you will bring it back to life."

"Yes, something like that," he says. Amanda sits on the edge of her chair and smiles broadly. "Amanda's uncle runs the local bank, so we've got a good mortgage to fix up the place. New kitchen. You'll love it. There's even a summer stock theatre a few miles away."

"How interesting," his mother says and sips from her glass.

"They couldn't find the right cooks, but now they have." He keeps talking and wants to stop. His salesmanship has become obvious. Amanda continues to smile and begins to look idiotic; then she stands up to look at the photographs hanging on the wall. She is wearing her hair cut like Jackie Kennedy's and the miniskirt suits her trim figure. She goes on tiptoe to peer at one picture, and the stretch lengthens her legs and thighs and compacts the roundness of her behind. The strangeness of the borrowed apartment has inspired them to experiment with different furniture, make love in its kitchen, the foyer, as well as the bedroom. They have been at each other almost continuously.

"Some of my husband's photographs," Edie Olson tells the young woman. She is no longer interested in Benson Falls or their project.

"Any of you? I mean in plays."

"A few."

"Sam says you appeared with John Barrymore, and that he couldn't remember his lines."

"Ridiculous!" His mother snaps and sits straight in her chair. She puts down the cocktail glass to assemble her outrage. "The Barrymores were very professional. Anyone who knew them can tell you that. Too many people talk of matters of which they know nothing." It is been a quick, surgical correction. "Now that next picture is interesting. You haven't seen this one, Sam. I just got it a month ago: the people at the Modern printed up a copy for me. Your father had never developed the film."

"The women at the High Standard Café," he says and stands beside Amanda. He puts his arm loosely around her. "A small-town cafeteria. In East Liverpool. There's Aunt Rho in the middle." Five women lean on a countertop and look straight into the camera. Behind them is a large stove with a flat griddle and a bill of fare chalked on a blackboard.

"Pie ten cents," Amanda reads.

"A long time back. Great pie too—crust almost as good as yours. This woman on the end—I can't remember her name—would come in at five in the morning and make a half dozen kinds of pie. Aunt Rho ran the griddle and did the heavy cooking. They had biscuits with sausage gravy. And grits," he adds.

"Oh yes, the ubiquitous grits," his mother says behind them. "I fear you'll find none on the menu tonight."

The women in the picture wear a neat uniform, a one-piece dress with a sensible apron, the points of a handkerchief accenting the top of the breast pocket. They pose for the camera with assurance, with an agreeable bemusement that anyone would want to take their picture but go ahead, they seem to say, suit yourself. They could have been a popular singing group, singing in a sweet harmony on an afternoon radio show. They could have posed for this picture to show their audience what they look like. Aunt Rho is smiling, but her attention is caught by something outside the picture. She holds a spatula. Sam half expects her to lift her other hand to confirm the tight rolls of her hair at the top of her head. He squeezes Amanda gently, remembering when the picture was taken.

"So you see, cooking is in the family," his mother says behind them. "How could that little inn in Vermont fail to succeed? You darlings."

When they are not making love, Sam gives Amanda a tour of Greenwich Village, shows her places he remembers from years before. She's interested to see the sites of these memories he often tells her late at night. She becomes a witness to his resentment that a certain bookstore has become a place that sells prosthetic devices or that the Gilbert Toy Museum is no longer there. Moreover, she's a little peeved with herself for bringing the wrong clothes—almost everything in her case makes her look dressed for church or for a dorm mom's tea party. Everyone around them is dressed so informally, a kind of thrown-together rightness.

"I spent some happy times here," Sam tells her. They stand on a corner near Sheridan Square.

"When to the sessions of sweet silent thought, I summon up remembrances of things past." She swings his right arm in a wide arc, and her eyes entreat his approval. She wants to be glad with him.

"Shakespeare?" he asks. It is a good guess, and he's a little pleased with himself for guessing right. He's been selfish, dragging her around these old neighborhoods that were actually never his—his need for them only made them seem to belong to him. He senses she's becoming impatient, but he can't seem to stop. "This was Edna St. Vincet Millay's house."

"'I only know that summer sang in me / A little while, that sings no more.'" Her voice lofts sweetly into the air. Her eyes are half-closed.

"I get the message. I've been piggish. What do you want to do?"

She is nearly skipping around him. "Really? Really-really? You won't laugh?" She pulls on his hand. "I want to go to Radio City Music Hall. I want to see the Rockettes."

Starting Something

"Pregnant? How can you be pregnant?" Amanda has pulled him down at one of the tables in the dining room. Carpenters work around them, hammering and sawing. The renovations of the old inn are under way, and the air is charged with the sweetness of freshly cut lumber. Their honeymoon trip to New York is months past. The windows are open to the crisp mountain air, and the gush of water outside from the falls pleasures the ear. Large books lie open to display swatches of different fabrics. Amanda's been choosing patterns for tablecloths and napkins—separate sets for each of the seasons. His dream kitchen lacks only the new automatic dishwasher that will require a new boiler. It's being trucked over from Rutland, but a teamsters' strike is holding up its delivery. She is sitting beside him, her knees together, her hands plainly folded in her lap. Her face is flushed, and she looks both anxious and happy.

"How can you be pregnant?" he repeats.

"Must I explain the process?" She grinned.

"But I mean—"

"We've been busy." She smiles and leans toward him. He sits straight. One of the workmen starts singing part of an aria Sam cannot identify. The whine of a power saw cuts off the carpenter's fine tenor. Amanda begins to fidget. Her hands clench, and she rotates them in the air as if she's tearing something apart, perhaps a prepared speech. "I can't lie to you, Sam. I wasn't wearing my diaphragm in New York."

Some workmen carefully put down a heavy timber on the floor beyond them. Nails are pounded and measurements made. A truck with wallboard slowly backs up to the building's entrance. Everything continues, but Sam Emerson feels everything has stopped, as if the industry that has been constructing his future, a future of his own design, has turned into an enclosure. He has been confined. "But you always have worn your diaphragm." He looks at her, and Amanda stares back him with a determined expression. Her cheeks are pink. "Always before. Even before you and me," he says and feels stupid.

"That's just it." Tears quietly appear in the corners of her eyes. "I wanted it to be different. I should have told you, talked it over with you. But don't you see? I wanted it to be new. Just us." She carefully places one hand on the table between them.

"Jesus, pregnant."

"No, not Jesus. Me. Us." She is trying to laugh, nervously, but takes in the stunned expression on his face. "I'm sorry, I'm sorry."

"No, it's okay," he says. "It's fine. It's fine."

SEVEN

THE SENATOR'S OFFICE regretted they could find no record of an Owen Emerson buried in any of the military cemeteries around Pont-à-Mousson. What battalion was he with again?

"He wasn't in the army. Like I said before, he was a journalist, a photographer." It was the third time Emerson had made the distinction, first to an assistant, and now he was talking to an intern. "Is the senator around? May I speak to him please?"

"He's in a committee meeting and regrets he can't talk to you. He hopes to get back to you soon."

"My father was taking pictures for *Look*."

"*Look*?"

"It was a picture magazine. Like *Life*. It's not published anymore." Clearly, his request had become a problem for them, and one not quickly solved with a phone call to a bureau next door. He had presented a balky knot their automatic protocol could not undo quickly, and they had lost interest. Their enthusiasm to be of service had cooled.

"Where are you from?" Emerson asked. Perhaps getting personal might help.

"My family lives in Ligonier," the young man replied. "My dad has a real estate and insurance agency there."

"I run a restaurant. Sam's Place. Ever heard of it—Sam's Place?"

"Far out! The place with the great view of the city. My folks just ate there. They had an anniversary."

"Tell them to come back. They will be my guests."

"Super. I'll tell them."

"What about hospital records? Maybe he was wounded and died in a hospital." Traffic on the bridges below was beginning to stack up.

"The data base is pretty inclusive. Nope. Nothing like that."

"So what does that mean—missing in action. He just disappeared?"

"I guess something like that."

"He'd have to have been noticed by someone before he could be missing."

"I see your point," the intern replied. "I guess *unknown* is the term. Some of the cemeteries have unmarked graves. Unknown."

"In that area? Do you have the towns where they are?" But missing in action was the appropriate term, Emerson considered. He remembered his mother trying to make a joke of it, how his father had usually been missing. That afternoon in Connecticut with the radiator in the dorm lounge hissing. The whole building empty but for the distant kitchen noises; the staff cleaning up after lunch. The sounds had isolated them even more.

"Here's a place—I'll spell it. N-o-m-e-n-y." The aide sounded very young—doing a lesson. "It's east of Pont-à-Mousson. Farther out, there's a smaller cemetery in a place called Delme. I guess that's how it's pronounced. I took German."

"They both have unknowns?"

"I guess they all have some unknowns."

"I could just pick one," Emerson said. He realized he wasn't joking. Why not just pick an unknown—a surrogate father? His mother would make do with that—hadn't she always?

Sam Emerson continued cleaning up the penthouse for Phoebe's return. He hummed about his labor, thinking how this relationship could become permanent. He'd call that architect who a few years back had sketched some ideas for expanding the restaurant, enlarging the penthouse. Or they could get a larger house somewhere in town; they wouldn't have to live near the restaurant, though he would miss the view. The logistics were daunting, but he was up to it. He called a travel agency and made reservations for their trip. But the more his good spirits lofted, the more they were restrained by the fact of her interview in Seattle. As he ran the sweeper, he heard again the excitement in her voice as she announced it. Something told him that interview hadn't been a spur-of-the-moment happening; she had the appointment before she went to the coast, and the bank's business may have been only secondary. Forces beyond their control, as the announcer sometimes said on one of his mother's melodramas, were pulling them apart. As he went about his housecleaning, his mind gathered evidence from the past to counter his fears.

"Nick and I would like you to go trick-or-treating with us," she had said on the phone. The fall weather had been balmy, a luxurious extension of late summer that graced the city. When he parked in front of her house, dry leaves scurried in the street, and the air was redolent with the aromas of backyard barbecues. Inside, he had greeted Nick, who looked embarrassed in his tramp costume—the boy was on the edge of adolescence and about to put away this kind of activity. Or his mother's getup may have unsettled Nick. Phoebe had scrounged around in her closet to find the articles for a shepherdess costume, including a rhinestone coronet that she had fixed in her blond curls. Disks of lip rouge were perfectly drawn on her cheeks. She resembled the third act of a folk ballet.

"I have to get back to the restaurant soon," Emerson told them. "Cynthia's running the show."

"We better get to it, then," Phoebe replied and gave him and Nick paper sacks.

They canvassed the streets of their neighborhood, going door to door with other children and their parents to receive candies and fruit. Nick went about the ritual in a perfunctory manner as if he were accompanying them—the adults—in a chore he would be happy to see finished. Phoebe's unself-conscious participation threw the boy off, Emerson could tell, for he had been a little embarrassed by it himself until her selfless good humor, her determination to make the event a happy occasion for her son—no matter his resentment—affected Emerson deeply. And she hadn't needed to invite him to join them. He turned off the sweeper. He had imagined they were a family, and he heard himself crying, "Trick or treat," in a stern voice that startled homeowners as they stood in their open doorways.

He had changed the sheets and plumped the pillows, vacuumed the carpet and put out fresh towels. Just in case. Trumpet lilies of pink and rose blared from a blue vase on the apron of the Jacuzzi. Ta-dah! Bouquets of daisies lavished the living room. His industry consumed him, kept his mind occupied, and he wanted everything to be right. Emerson paused to inspect the rooms for any stray thread, any particle that might catch her eye. But if he missed anything, he guessed she would smile indulgently, and he called up that smile, the dimples and the small, even teeth, the intense blue eyes that widen and shutter with amusement

Also in the small fridge were the little "birds" of veal scallopini under wax paper. He would brown them slowly in butter and olive oil and then finish them in marsala with some broth. He would prepare their supper in the tidy kitchen built into the half-round kiosk that marked the apartment's center. Phoebe would relax with a glass of something— say, a chilled Tocai. She would sit on one of the barstools, watching him cook, sipping the wine as he stirs the risotto. He would tell her about him and Nick talking easily in the garden—how he felt they had become more relaxed together. But did he really think a woman like Phoebe Konopski could be influenced by some scraps of veal in a sweet sauce? One of the qualities that had appealed to him was her resolute aim, keeping her eye on the mark; it was a factor in her success—in that history that he loved almost as much as the woman who had lived it. Could one be separated from the other? And now that very purpose could come between them. The mirrored sides of the PPG towers refined the sunlight to purify its radiance. Emerson stood straight in the glare and looked for his reflection in Phoebe Konopski's view of herself.

He wiped up some water from around the pantry sink and surveyed the living room. Below, an excursion paddle wheeler rounded the point and headed up the Allegheny. The Gulf Building resembled an Aztec pyramid that could have been the site of a recent sacrifice for good weather. And it had worked. It was a beautiful day in Pittsburgh. A passenger jet slipped into its landing pattern, banking steeply above and behind the black tower of the US Steel building. The proof of the city's success rose in the crystal air, and he was part of that success, of that picture on the other side of the penthouse windows. How could he go wrong? A good swim at the Y might discipline his unruly mind, and the steady progress of his body within a marked lane of the Olympic size pool would order his thoughts.

The midmorning period for lap swimming was never well attended, and he had the immense pool to himself except for another swimmer in the far lane. He broke the flat pane of the water feet first with a juvenile glee. Then back and forth, back and forth, he plowed the middle lane with a steady, easygoing crawl that could surely take him to Portugal if need be. He swam the laps, trying to turn gracefully with no wasted motion at each end. He conducted interviews with himself as he swam. "How do you explain the headway you make through the water? Your strokes don't seem very graceful." The questions would be asked by one of those bright young women the TV sports networks were now hiring. "It is due to the deceptively powerful stroke of my left arm that goes deep and unseen into the recesses of the water to grab momentum by the throat." Grabbing momentum by the throat; he liked the sound of the phrase as he pulled himself along. He made up such exchanges to pass the hour of the repetitious exercise. Sometimes he went over menus, changing their items. The questionable nature of a new white Burgundy, a Saint Veran—was it too heavy? What could be done about Cynthia's abusive boyfriend? Was Sterling Wicks content, or would he be moving on—to get away from the scene of his nephew's death? What then? He'd have to take over the kitchen until he found a new chef. Was it feasible to make their own yogurt?

Emerson tried to do the underwater somersault at the end of the lap he had seen others use, only to make a serviceable turn. He took a breath and continued his crawl. His palms struck the water explosively. He plunged ahead, kicking up waves with an off-tempo flutter kick and pulled up at the far end of the pool to eye the clock, adjust his goggles. Fifteen minutes to go. He saw himself as the character in the Chinese play Constance had invited him to attend with her. How foolish he felt—especially this morning—as he remembered being teased by her invitation. She had only wanted to share some of her culture, to indicate her respect for him by introducing him to some of her background.

A French theatre group performed this ancient folktale on a tour of the United States. The story was about a young man trying to locate a missing princess. There it was again, Emerson thought, resuming his swim. He could hear Pennyworth's interpretation—the pursuit of that particular chalice, however it is costumed. Or not. But the young hero in the play had to meet a series of challenges, and one of these was a baboon that turned out to be his half-brother lying across a mountain path. Emerson had thought it was meant to be humorous until he saw Constance's serious concentration. She seemed to inhale the drama onstage. But let's say Phoebe was the princess who waited for him at the top of the mountain. And this brown box had been put down across his way. He couldn't remember how the young man had handled the baboon, but he had overcome the problem and, naturally, won the princess. Happy ending. With a strong stroke, Emerson considered the obstacle that lay between him and Phoebe, and the progress he made through the water convinced him she would accompany him to France to help him finish the job.

Sam Emerson had done his laps and pulled himself up and out of the water. He had gone nowhere with some effort, made no headway in the monotonous swim while performing a sort of circuit that had kept him toiling in the same place. Nothing in a straight line. Back and forth, or in some view, from left to right, or even—his whimsy fed on itself—up and down if the pool were turned on end. The notion amused him as he pictured himself swimming up through a vertical casement of water, on an invisible ladder, as the famed power of his left stroke pulled him higher and higher. A legendary Olympic swimmer. Effortlessly. He could swim any length endlessly. Surely there must be more than just three ways to move in space. Of course, there's the fourth dimension, but could that be swum? A unique angle surely.

But his legs were still okay, full in the calf and well muscled. Emerson stood before the mirror in the locker room. The waist had thickened a little, but his belly was holding its own against gravity. Some lines of the old Herculean girdle yet remained. Phoebe's amusement at his defini-tion had cheered him once, and it did so again as he checked himself over. He should do some sit-ups, work on the abs. He tried to look at himself as Phoebe might inspect him. His arms had become odd at the elbows and looked as if their points might have been glued on carelessly. He had no time today to lift weights, but maybe he'd start a program with the Y's trainer that would firm him up.

Then, she was here! Phoebe had returned. She had emerged into the waiting area of the airline, looking left and right for him, flushed and a little breathless, her eyes brilliant and expectant. Emerson had purposely chosen a spot to one side, from which he could enjoy—just for a moment—the rosy, full-bodied Botticelli look of her as she searched for him. And that was probably wrong, he considered for a moment; the voyeur caught in his own surveillance, his motive maybe not any different from that of the audience at the Highway Paradise. He would have to plead guilty as he relished his crime. Her hair fell in gold ringlets that should be festooned with ribbons, and, in fact, she had braided two blue ribbons into the hair that framed her face. Beauty surprised, Emerson said happily to himself, as beauty should always be surprised, so he held back a little longer to relish her pretty puzzlement. Then he stepped forward.

"Oh you!" She embraced him tightly. "Spying on me again, are you?" She was a little piqued but laughing too.

"Many bags?" he asked, feeling stupid now. Then he settled himself. "You feel so good here, Phoebe. Here in my arms. We must work something out." He stopped himself, for he was going too fast. Steamrolling again. Foolish chatter at the wrong time.

"Yes, and I have missed you too, Sam. But here we are." She seemed amazed by the fact, by the whole series of inventions, including the airliner that had just landed her in Pittsburgh. Back in Pittsburgh. Her eyes danced over his face, his neck, and shoulders. A joyous reappraisal. "And yes, I have two bags."

Emerson covertly studied her as they stood by the baggage carousel. He looked for a hint of change in her appearance, some clue as to what she might have decided. "This clinic is in a building that overlooks the harbor. Spectacular views. The director was a Rhodes Scholar and something of a track star in college, too. She's very nice; I felt an instant rapport." Her voice had become high and enthusiastic, her thoughts tumbling out.

"So they have made you an offer?"

"No, they haven't." Her eyes were bright, expectant. "Actually, I worry they will. It would be a major move for me, as I said."

"Yes." One of her bags tumbled onto the conveyor belt.

"There would be all sorts of legal complications about taking Nick so far from his father. Out of state."

Emerson assessed the list of those complications as Phoebe held his arm and leaned against him so they joined hip and thigh. The dense aroma of her perfume enveloped him. She had changed to some kind of Estée Lauder, but he couldn't remember the specific fragrance. A mellow sweetness at once earthy and light. "I'm a little disappointed someone from the Hug Shop didn't meet me," she was saying. "I put in my order." A merry glint had caught in her eyes.

"In fact, they called me," Emerson said. "Their principal hugger called in sick, and they asked me to fill in." He took her in his arms. "I'm not as professional, but I'll try really hard to please you." Holding the dear form of her close, his face deep in the silky strands of her hair, Emerson smothered a catch in his throat.

He pictured how they looked to others in the terminal—this handsome woman leaning into him, intimate and frank. Phoebe stood out; she was a Technicolor image that had walked into a black-and-white movie. Large hoops of pink plastic swung from her ears, and an ornate gold butterfly was pinned to the lapel of her blazer. A heavy chain belt dangled from her waist. Her shoes were violet with a moderate heel. Several rings and bracelets adorned her fingers and hands, and her nails were long and polished with a pink enamel that went with the earrings. As always, the colors of her delighted him—nothing seemed too much when applied to the extravagance that was herself, and he was conscious of people taking them in. Some of these people, he mused, might talk that evening about this couple waiting for baggage—an ordinary-looking guy of a certain age—but still trim and clearly a swimmer—with this fabulous woman all over him. Light-headed and humming to himself, he pulled her second bag off the moving belt. At the station wagon, she put herself into the passenger seat, fastened her seat belt, and sat back, ready, it seemed, for a journey longer than the drive into Pittsburgh. But that might be only his imagination, he cautioned himself.

He waited until he had driven through the loops of the airport exit before he told her. "They're having trouble finding his grave," he said. "But I think, once we get there, we'll be able talk to the locals. But in any event, it will be a great trip. Paris. It will be good for Nick. Educational. He'll soak it up."

Phoebe remained silent, looking straight ahead.

Emerson kept his eyes on the road. The intimate scene he had imagined as he cleaned up the apartment could not be played out as they drove toward the city at sixty miles per hour. He played a game with himself. If they reached the tunnel entrance to the city before she said anything, then her response would be positive when they emerged at the other end—the magnificent array of the city's skyline and the rivers before them.

"But how will you know if it's him?" she finally asked and crossed her ankles. She held her purse in her lap. "If the grave isn't marked, how will you know?"

"I'll know, I tell you; I will know." Did he sound so desperate? "I'll buy a trowel somewhere and do the job myself."

Phoebe was sucking on her lower lip. Emerson took a deep breath. They had just entered the Fort Pitt tunnel. The roar of traffic echoed and enveloped them. As always going through the tunnel, Emerson pictured Sam's Place just above, over them, sitting on a thousand feet of rock and earth, tons of it above the tunnel. It was like traveling through a geological dig that was part of history. His history.

And then, they broke free of the noisy enclosure; the grand spectacle of Pittsburgh lay before them. "I'll run you home now," he spoke quickly. "Tonight, I hope we can have dinner together."

"No," she replied. "Let's go to your place now. Then I'll go home. Nick is at my sister's and doesn't expect me right away." His blood rushed through him, and his heart pounded. He should have swum more laps.

They left her bags in the car and went up through the restaurant. The two guys from the cleaning service bent over their roaring vacuum machines and didn't look up. At the penthouse, Phoebe walked swiftly to the expanse of glass as if to be sure the view was still there. He watched her tour the living area, touching a bowl or a lamp. He could tell she appreciated the flowers. She checked out the pictures on the walls, especially the photograph of the women at the High Standard Café—a greeting of some sort, Emerson thought feeling pleased. "How about a Jacuzzi?" he finally said, a little nervous. He wanted to revisit all the stations of their pleasures.

Phoebe slipped out of her shoes with a delighted laugh. "You silly man. You think I've come all this way to take a bath?" She removed her earrings and necklace and put them on the table. She held out one wrist for him to unfasten her bracelets.

Next came her blazer and she stepped out of her skirt. As she carefully folded and laid aside this proper apparel, he unfastened the buttons of her blouse, then the ties and snaps of the delicate lingerie underneath. She slowly became tousled and undone as he played the faithful retainer, always at hand to resolve a balky fastening. That she had costumed herself so for this reunion excited him. Her breathing caught as her breasts spilled into his hands from loosened lace. Her stockings pooled roguishly around her ankles. Emerson, not one to ignore an unexpected fetish, observed his double in the glass next to the bed idly playing with the clasps of the garter belt that dangled against her thighs. Then she was naked but for the wisp of her panties, which he took in his teeth and pulled down with a kind of growl that she graced with a happy sigh. Emerson sank into the musk of her to delicately taste and hold her on his tongue, and she opened herself, giving up little pants. Her arms went wide to make angels in the smooth sheets. Her hands vainly grabbed for purchase. Finally she held him to herself, her torso arched and straining in what seemed to be a ferocious contest, the goal line always moved just as it was about to be crossed.

Emerson's arms and shoulders ached as he pursued her ecstasy. He could sense her almost fighting it, coming close to pull back once, then pulling back once again, and then she held still, tensed, her breath stoppered. He heard her listen for some sound deep within her. Then she jerked, became limp, and cried out, the contralto register of her joy so different from her normal voice that it might have been another woman suddenly born within her. "Please," she pleaded. "No more."

Her pleasure gratified and endorsed him. Emerson slowly moved up upon her, tenderly enfolding her pliancy to bend over her and kiss her breasts. Phoebe watched him dreamily through slitted eyes. Looking down at the two of them joining.

"Oh, goody. There's more," she sighed and stroked his shoulder.

Emerson's passion had no method, no order, though the effect of his lovemaking would make it seem so. Phoebe's eyes had moved far back in her head, and she softly bit her lower lip, then her mouth went slack. Her ragged breaths marked the depth and pace of his stroke.

Suddenly, the fist of a cramp hit him in the back of his right thigh as if a steel clamp had been fastened around the muscle just above the knee. He tried to work it loose without losing his rhythm, shaking the cramp off like the bite of a mad dog. He attempted to brace his right foot against something, to force out the stitch, but there was only the smooth, unencumbered surface of the bedclothes. So far, Phoebe had noticed nothing different; she was cooing and moving her hands above her head. He could not quit the race, nor vary its tempo, but the pain in his hamstring was excruciating. He'd heard of football players, suddenly seized by such a cramp only feet from a touchdown and how they kept going to cross the line and how this team spirit, this determination to keep going for the sake of the school's honor, had made them into life-long cripples. It crossed his mind—even in the grip of his agony—that he must prove himself similarly. He experimented. If he raised his leg and stretched it straight back, pointing the foot out—in an attitude of classical ballet—the pain was lessened and made bearable, and in this position he continued his joyous humping. He caught his reflection in the mirror over the marble vanity, vigorously speeding over the reclining woman, his right leg straight out, the foot pointing into the wake of his exuberant passage. He was a figure from an ancient vase, maybe Mercury delivering a message or a bouquet of flowers. Western Union, Phoebe had opened her eyes momentarily to look down at them, to see what he was doing.

"Oh my," she said between ragged breaths. "You're doing something different," and the deep chords of her orgasm rose again. Emerson came, sweating and triumphant, the cramp slowly coming undone in the tumbling pleasure of his own release.

Phoebe gripped him and thrust him up and away from herself, though they were still joined, to study his face as if to identify him. Her scrutiny held him, a strange inspection that made him want to look away, but then whatever question had spurred this inspection seemed to be answered, or maybe found irrelevant, and she drew him close with a sigh. They slipped into a tranquil doze.

The late afternoon sunlight poured through the glass wall beside the bed discreetly curtained by the lacy foliage of the immense locust trees that grew straight up from the hillside outside. Phoebe's hair spilled loosely on the pillow to tickle his face and shoulder, but Emerson didn't pull away, didn't want to disturb their laze and coziness. As if struck by a sudden modesty, she had pulled the sheet up over herself and held up one wrist to inspect the loopy bow made from one of the blue ribbons she had worn in her hair. Earlier, as he had undressed her, he had playfully fashioned this knot on her right wrist, and she had dutifully held out her left one with a crooked grin to be similarly bound, but Emerson's attention had been drawn to her breasts. Now, she pulled at the ribbon so it came loose and fell into her hand. She wound it around a finger.

"I'm making those little veal bundles you like."

"*Fagottini de vitello.*" She pronounced the Italian carefully and with delight. He had taught her how to say it.

"And tomorrow night, I have tickets for the symphony. Previn is back in town doing Mahler."

"Sexy Mahler." Phoebe stretched. The sheet pulled away from one breast and Emerson leaned forward to kiss its appearance. "Let me catch my breath. I've been up since four this morning. I want a bath and then a little nap. Then you can take me home." She snuggled close to him. "You have worn me out."

Her flattery cheered him whether it was the courtesan part of her talking or not. "I'll draw you a bath," he said. He knew he made a comical picture bending over the faucets to adjust the water temperature in the Jacuzzi—flaccid penis and balls swinging like soundless clappers. Not the neat, tight apparatus seen on classical statues, so he wrapped a towel around his waist.

Phoebe had risen and selected two of Aunt Rho's long hairpins from the jar on the tub's ledge. She fastened them in her hair. She caught and swept up an errant curl to fix it with the rest. Her casual and familiar handling of the hairpins—she had used them before—made everything even more right. In a way, Emerson thought, she had refastened the memory of that other woman's unbound affection within the vapor of the warm bath water.

He went to her side and took her hand to help her step down into the bath. It was the manner of a Venetian beauty stepping daintily into a gondola, and she purred as she lowered herself into the hot water. She stretched out delightedly, all of her buoyant and incredible prettiness. Emerson sat on the edge of the Jacuzzi for a moment to relish the image of her. She motioned to him to join her, and the gush of water caressed and mantled her shoulders as she sank lower in the tub. When he had eased himself into the water next to her, she looked frankly into his eyes.

"Sam darling, I can't come with you to France. It would be a wonderful trip, and Nick would gain much from it, but his team is going into the play-offs, something called the WPIA, whatever that is, but it is a big thing. He's very excited. He told me last night when I called him. He can't leave and I have to be here to cheer him from the sidelines. You of all people understand why I can't leave him. Why I have to be here for him." She had taken one of his hands in hers and looked directly into his eyes, a gaze that implored his understanding, yet it was a plea unfairly made, Emerson was thinking. She was using privileged information to shake down his agreement; how could he—of all people, she had reminded him—urge her to leave her son to go gallivanting around the French countryside with him? That was the subtext in her stare, and it just wasn't fair. Yet he knew her appeal was just and that his need for her—his love for her—could make him into some kind of a villain. The unwanted perception chilled him. He pulled his hand from her clasp but then picked up a sponge, dipped it in the bath, and squeezed the warm water over her shoulder and neck.

"Also, I have a lot to catch up on here," she continued. "In fact, I'm asking you for a few days off from us right now. I honestly don't know about the job in Seattle if it is offered to me. I just don't know whether I will take it or not—if they make an offer. I actually did the interview only to see if I had the stuff, like I said. I'm almost sorry I did. A sort of test. Traveling with you in France would be glorious, but I have to be here. I have to be calm. It's so very sweet of you to ask us."

"If I found out where he's buried—would that make a difference? We could go right to the place and come back. Just a day or two away." Emerson was a little embarrassed by the plea in his voice. Phoebe shook her head slowly. It wasn't possible. Some curls at the back of her neck had become dark with moisture. Her face, nearly clean of makeup, had become almost plain as she regarded him steadily.

"Now you mustn't read into my decision some gloomy forecast about our future. Our future is here, right now. We must take each day as it dawns. We're together, aren't we?" She let herself float over him to settle in his lap. Her arms went around his neck. "Who is this in your arms right now?"

But when he parked in the alley behind her house he was making just such a forecast, his thoughts sorting out different scenarios. They went through the garden and into the kitchen, where he put her two bags down. Phoebe quickly surveyed the room to see if anything was amiss. A plate with the remnants of a peanut butter sandwich sat on the counter next to the sink. With an affectionate smile, she swept the crusts into the disposal and turned it on. Evidence of Nick's snack. Evidence of Nick, Emerson thought, then censured the thought. "I better get back," he said. "Sterling is about to show up."

"Stay just a little. Let's sit in the garden."

"I think you'll want to be with Nick tonight," Emerson said as he sat down on the porch step.

"Much as the little veal treats tempt me, I should be here. Thank you for understanding. You're a sweet man. You can freeze them. We'll have them later."

"Sure." A basketball began dribbling up the alley. She sat down next to him. "I saw some bee balm in a nursery last week that would be nice against your fence," he said.

"That would be lovely. What does it look like?"

"Has a comical blossom. As a kid, I used to think they looked like a clown's fright wig."

"More from East Liverpool," she said and linked her arm through his, pulling them closer together.

"It's a lot to put up with, I guess."

Phoebe said nothing. Redoing his past as he redid her garden may have become an intrusion, a tiresome repetition, or maybe her attention just then had fixed upon a task in her own present. She had returned not to him only. That was clear, he had to remind himself. So he was both saddened and cheered by the possibility that whatever had just slipped into her thoughts had nothing to do with him. He knew if he looked at her, the expression in her eyes would be sharply focused on a point straight ahead—a specific turn in her career probably already jotted down in the notebook in her purse. He guessed she might not even be aware they had strayed onto different paths—even as they sat side by side in her garden. He felt left behind. Phoebe pulled at stray blades of grass growing from between the bricks of the walk beneath their feet. "You should do this trip by yourself anyway, Sam," she said after a bit.

"I'm not without experience. I mean doing it by myself," he answered.

"Don't be peevish. Besides, you weren't by yourself. She did the best she could. And you had Aunt Rho, that remarkable woman. You're going next week?"

"Yes; while they're installing the new cooler. We're closing the restaurant down. Maybe when I get back, the thing in Seattle will be clear."

"Oh, I don't know—I don't know." Phoebe's voice had risen with exasperation. "Don't press me, I don't know, Sam." She had stood quickly as if remembering an errand, only to take several steps around the myrtle bed, then back. "I know what you want me to say, and part of me wants to say it. Most of me. Believe me. I'm almost sorry I did the interview."

"Don't be sorry," Emerson said. "Please, don't be sorry."

"I want to unpack and do something about supper before Nick comes back," she said briskly. Emerson stood, and she put her arms around him. "When you get back we'll have the *fagottini*. We'll celebrate. Edie Olson finally at rest."

The merry tone of her voice, tinted just a little by what Emerson read as her own genuine disappointment, lifted his optimism. "That rose bush looks like it could use some fertilizer. I'll put some on it before I go to France." About four blocks over from where they embraced ran the Allegheny River. Emerson considered the number of times in East Liverpool when he would sit on the banks of the Ohio, feeling included in that river's flow, its passing commerce, yet aware he was apart from it, and this current of memory swept through him even as he held Phoebe in his arms.

The news break on the radio in the restaurant's kitchen reported that the several men who had set off bombs in New York's World Trade Center last year were about to be sentenced. The Federal Reserve was considering raising interest rates, and a Manet painting had just been sold for millions of dollars. Then the jazz program resumed. Emerson had been watching Sterling Wicks prepare trays of Cornish hens for cooking. "Have you thought any more about making yogurt?" he asked his partner.

"You know, old sport, the subject hasn't been on my must-do list." The chef laid strips of bacon across the plump breasts of the small birds. They had been stuffed with sausage, orange zest, and thyme. "Tell me again?"

Again Emerson described the thick consistency of the yogurt melded with honey and studded with crushed walnuts, but as he spoke, the words dried up in his mouth, a tasteless fodder for conversation. Jimmy Overstreet's funeral had received respectful coverage in the local media, and the trial of the police officers had begun. "For a dessert," he added lamely. As he talked he had dipped his fingers into the ceramic bowl that held salt to distribute some over the hens.

With a dark look, Wicks noted his contribution. "I guess it's the presentation I haven't figured out. Yogurt lacks precision. Doesn't have that elegance that comes from the specific. It just lies there in the bowl. A blob."

"It's a pretty good taste," Emerson persisted.

"Amen to that, but let's give it more thought," Wicks said. He brushed a glaze of currant jelly over the birds and set the tray to one side. The line cooks were working side by side, and he looked quickly over their heads to observe their activity. Then he turned back to Emerson and leaned against the cool stove top, arms folded. "So, it's bon voyage. I hope you find him."

"Thanks. What are you doing while we're closed down?"

"Well, I'm going to make sure the auxiliary cooler is okay. We got a lot of stuff that has to be kept while they're installing the new job. Then this woman I've been seeing wants to go to Atlantic City." He made a face and shrugged. "I know—tacky, but she has other qualities that are rather distinctive." His eyes had become slits, shuttered against his own amusement.

Emerson suddenly felt light-headed; his stomach seemed to lift and fall as if the building had risen from its foundation then floated down again onto the cliff. His friend's *bon voyage* had jabbed his consciousness—he really was flying to France on this hunt with no idea where the hunt might end, no directions as to where this reunion would take place.

He had expected the customs agents in France to give him trouble about the brown box in his carry-on knapsack, but the neatly uniformed officials stamped his passport and waved him through, never inspecting his luggage. It had been years since that trip with Amanda and his mother, but he automatically made his way through the passageways and corridors of the airport and then the transfer into Paris as if he had followed this route only yesterday. He bought his ticket to Metz at the Gare de l'Est with no difficulty and walked to the men's room without even looking for the signs. He simply knew the way. He felt like a spy taking up his assignment in a foreign place, taking up residence temporarily in a setting that wasn't his but was familiar. An ersatz citizen.

In Metz, a facade of polished stone had transformed the hotel across from the station, and he considered for a moment staying there but decided not to intrude on the memory of himself and Amanda in one of the rooms above. Third floor, he remembered. He walked several blocks to a smallish place on a side street. In a back room, the space cramped by the large bed, the sounds of trains arriving and departing were muffled. He turned on the TV and located CNN; its continuous drone of current events—Jackie Kennedy Onassis had died—lulled him to sleep. He woke to have a late supper at a bistro. Steak and *frites*. He might put the dish on their late night menu for the after-theatre crowd. Completely satisfying. A simple red wine in a pitcher, probably a Rhône. Crusty bread and an apple tart that was on the old side. Not a bad meal.

The next morning Emerson rented a car and followed the Moselle River south from the city. Again, the road and fields beside the placid waterway were oddly familiar, and at midmorning, he stopped to contemplate the river as he ate an apple. He had paused in a small village and bought the fruit in a market. This waterway reminded him of the Ohio River where it passed East Liverpool, and a deep sigh surprised him as it welled up from within himself. He was self-contained within the small Renault; he had everything he needed right next to him in the passenger seat, and he could just keep driving and driving. But it was a melancholy contentment soured by the perception that Phoebe's presence was not necessary for his sufficiency.

It was a windy day, with gusts of turbulence spiraling from the fields to fall upon the little car so fiercely that he sometimes struggled to keep it on the road. He had to hold the wheel with both hands. But the day was sunny, very bright, and blackbirds sang in the roadsides. The industry of the farms continued undisturbed. All at once, he was in Pont-à-Mousson; the last time the drive had seemed longer.

The memorial to the American ambulance drivers still stood in the square, and the stone figures on the corner continued to look expectantly down the street. The young woman inside the tourist office was efficient and eager, prepared for almost any inquiry. Finding the old graves of American dead had become a feature of her office. But he was looking for *inconnu;* he had to try his pronunciation a couple of times for her to understand him. He was looking for the unknown. She didn't hesitate. Of course, she replied, with an efficient comprehension; each of these sites had such graves. She drew circles around a couple on the map on the counter between them.

The noon hour had struck, and from the steps of the Hotel de Ville, Emerson watched the town people disappear, a trick film reversal of what he had witnessed long ago. The large doors behind him closed tight. Several motorbikes circled the square, almost frantically it seemed to him, as if trying to find a parking space before some deadline in the midday lull occurred. From the city hall steps, his white Renault looked freshly made in this archaic setting, and a blue motorbike had just pulled in beside the car. The driver seemed to hesitate, to consider parking there. The biker took off his helmet, looked around, looked at the Renault, then slipped the shiny globe back on his head and roared away. He disappeared down a side street.

Emerson had considered calling Phoebe, but he bought a postcard at a *tabac* instead with the thought that his message on it, however banal the information, would be more permanent than words passed through the atmosphere. So he took this card out as he sat in a charming café in Pont-à-Mousson, put it down on the checkered tablecloth of his table, and considered his wording. It should be witty and without sentiment, which would grate on her, but he was unable to come up with the words. So he would compose a standard drawn from such messages. Weather. The flight. The food so far. He would probably be back in Pittsburgh before she received the card. As he looked at the blank card, pen in hand, he reviewed the subtle change that was happening to them. Whether she went to Seattle or not—the possibility of that move had sharpened his perception of their relationship and of the fault in it that had been there all along. In the final analysis, the difference between them wasn't to be calculated in miles nor even in the pace of Phoebe's ambition but in the uncontrollable flow of their history, advancing almost imperceptibly like the course of a glacier that would eventually carry her away from him no matter how much she loved him. The notion had never occurred to them—not to him anyway—but once imagined couldn't be ignored. The café's carafe wine, a Chablis that had some merit, produced a chemistry with the warm sun to lave his sentimental mood, and he had ordered the *truite almondine* from the café's chalk board. So Emerson slipped the card into his pocket and capped his pen. The gritty rasp of a motorbike further scattered his mood. It was the same one he had seen earlier, the blue one, but the helmeted driver had picked up a passenger. The girl riding behind him wore a longish skirt that she pulled up around herself as she slid off the rear seat. Her legs were long and elegant, and she wore sandals.

They were about seventeen, Emerson figured—the boy, even in his swagger, seemed less mature than she—and the two of them looked at the Renault and talked. They gestured and seemed to agree on the features of the car as she pulled up a cardigan around herself. The breeze was chilly, and she wore only a T-shirt underneath. She had a thin, childish neck. The café's waiter—a kid their age—came rushing forward, and they greeted with all the customary kissing and embracing that always made Emerson happy to witness, a display of intimacy whether it was spontaneous or a ritual. The young people talked and talked as if they hadn't seen each other in years. They took a table opposite him, the girl in a chair that faced Emerson. He could overhear and understand they ordered Cokes and *frites*. The waiter returned with Emerson's platter of grilled fish, and he dug in. The crusty bread and the crisp green salad were first-rate. His appetite had become demanding. As he ate, he became aware of the girl looking at him, studying him with an interested humor. The wind kept blowing her skirt up and around her legs, and she finally trapped it beneath her thighs. She smiled at him apologetically for this accidental glimpse of herself that may have diverted him from the pleasures of his plate. Or so her expression seemed to say. The waiter had brought the couple's fries, and she picked several up and greedily crammed them into her mouth, all the while chatting with her companion and darting looks over his shoulder toward Emerson. He was a little amused by her attention, a little flattered, too, though he also cautioned himself. He was a stranger in town, a tourist in advance of the tourist season and so a curiosity. She had pushed three or four of the potato strips into her mouth and doubled them over to wedge them into her cheek. Then she slowly licked the grease from her fingers, holding his eyes with her own. Emerson signaled the waiter for his check.

The cemetery rose gently from behind a low stone wall. Maybe no more than fifty graves, all neatly lined up in the parklike sward. The white crosses looked as if they had just been planted in the greenness, and small American flags fluttered in the strong, cool wind. A shower was on its way. Emerson had climbed to the top of the rise, reading the names on the white tablets in the ground. There were several unknowns. If this was the place, he looked over the immaculate farmland for an old house, a barn, or a line of trees still standing that could have taken his father's attention so long ago, that perhaps his father had framed in his viewfinder and focused and captured just as death had found him. If he had had time to press the shutter, that image might yet be lying around somewhere—a composition of light and shapes waiting in the dark chamber of the Contax or the Leica that still rested in the weeds by the side of the road, the image waiting—waiting all these years to be brought into the light. His father's last look at earth. Somewhere in the topography might be the only clue to his whereabouts. But three *inconnus*? If there had been only one, he could have convinced himself that his father lay nearby, where he sat on the grass. But three? Phoebe would have a sensible answer to this dilemma, and a sob escaped him with the thought of her patient explanation. What was he doing sitting alone in this foreign pasture, keeping company with the dead, some of whom were anonymous, and yet, as he had summoned the phantom of her practical wisdom, the image of her happy presence in his arms also appeared. His quick arousal was urged by the brilliance of the day, the wine of lunch, and probably the flash of that young woman's bare legs in the café. So, he would become a dirty old man, and he accepted the description with a sort of morose cheerfulness.

The breeze raised goose bumps on his arms; his sweater was in the car. He felt himself sag from the inside out, his body becoming heavier and folding in on itself. The jet lag must have been kicking in, but something else too. He could stretch out in the brilliance of this peaceful French meadow that had absorbed so many horrors of past conflicts, and maybe after a short nap he would wake to find the weight of his foolishness lifted, the board wiped clean as he figured the menu board of the café back in the village had also been erased by now so that the dinner specials could be chalked on its blank surface.

Movement below around his car disturbed his reverie. It was the couple on the motorbike. They had coasted into the parking area quietly so as not to disturb his thoughts, and Emerson was a little pleased to see them again. He would have the chance to meet them again, this time without looking at the girl's legs, but then the heavy certainty that he had been cased, dropped in his stomach; they had been following him maybe all afternoon. His naiveté was suddenly exposed in the peaceful meadow—a rube taken for a ride. His car door was open, and they were going through his knapsack.

"Hey!" he shouted. "Wait a minute. *Attendez!*"

The couple was well organized. The boy handed items from the knapsack to the girl, and she would evaluate them; keep or discard.

Emerson yelled again; they didn't seem to hear. The parking lot was about a hundred yards down the slope. He yelled again and started to run down the incline. They continued their routine. Cool. The girl had opened the brown box and pulled out the plastic bag. Emerson was now running full tilt. He yelled into the wind. She had opened the plastic bag and stuck her nose in it. The guy had jumped onto the bike and started its motor. She had a handful of the ashes and let them fall through her fingers. The guy shouted at her. Emerson was getting close. She hopped onto the back of the motorbike and gave Emerson a finger—the international sign. Then as they sped away, she threw the bag into the air and it split open. He heard her laughter over the bike's racket. She had such pretty knees, too, Emerson reminded himself and laughed. The ashes were caught on the wind, and they spiraled high into the air. Like a strange confetti. Some of them fell on Emerson, into his hair and over the cemetery. He snatched empty air around him, this way and that, endeavoring to seize some of the granules in his cupped hands. He jumped from one foot to another like a child leaping for a present, and he began to laugh at the fruitlessness of it and at the appearance of himself, of what he must look like—an ordinary man dancing in the sunlight in the middle of the road. The couple had taken his electric razor.

"So what's been happening?" Emerson asked Sterling Wicks.

"Well, Jackie Onassis died."

"Yes, I heard that on the news. I mean here—with the trial."

"Oh, the trial." Wicks adjusted the flame under a court boullion. "Well, it's become a nontrial. One of the assistants from the coroner's office spoke out of turn on the stand, and the judge closed the place down. Mistrial. So, there you have it. The cops get off." He patted his flat stomach and pursed his lips. So, nothing changed, Emerson thought. The same pattern lying dormant and then coming through like the design in wall paper appearing no matter how many times it had been painted over.

"They can still be prosecuted again," he said to the chef.

"Sure," Wicks replied. "Those guys will have to come back," Sterling Wicks continued. "The cooler door is not a good seal. Let me show you." He walked Emerson to the new unit. "See? It's okay for now, but it will wear wrong in time."

"Okay, I'll call them," Emerson said. The limo from the airport had only just dropped him off. His knapsack was on the floor of the foyer. His head was still spinning from the return flight. "What else?"

"Well, grab on to something—Cynthia's marrying that guy, which means we'll need a new front in a week. She's moving to his parents' house in Indiana." Wicks rolled his eyes. "But she brought in a girlfriend as a possible replacement. I talked with her. She might do. She's been maitering at Ciro's downtown."

"Oh, I remember her if it's the one I'm thinking of. She's black."

"That's the one you're thinking of," Wicks said flatly. "I told her to come back tomorrow to talk with you."

"Okay. I guess she'll be okay. Why is she no longer at Ciro's?"

"She quit to have a baby. She's a single mom." Wicks's regard stayed longer on him than Emerson thought was necessary.

"Ciro's doesn't have much of a wine list," he finally said.

"If I remember, Cynthia didn't know a Dubonnet from a Chablis when she started," the chef said.

"That's right," Emerson agreed with just a little pride.

Rita arrived and went into the dressing room to change into her whites. When she came out she gave Emerson a hug. "How'd it go?"

"Okay, thanks."

"Oh, yeah, sorry to be so insensitive," Wicks said soberly. "Mission accomplished?"

"Yes, everything went well. All taken care of." A vacuum sweeper droned in the dining room. "That reminds me, did you talk to the cleaning people about the bathrooms?"

"Yeah, they got the message." Wicks had finished scrubbing his hands in the deep sink used for cleaning pots and pans, dried them on a clean towel, and started to slice and cube meat on the butcher block.

"*Blanquette de veau*?" Emerson asked.

"Or something akin to it. Summer is a-comin' in, baby. Which reminds me, I need a whole mess of mushrooms." He eyed the clock on the wall. "Get down to the Strip, can you? There's a list on my desk."

Upstairs, the answering machine blinked; it was Phoebe. "It's only me," her voice said simply. "Welcome home. I want to hear everything. I've made a chocolate cake from scratch, so come over after the restaurant closes. A creamy pink flower has bloomed that you'll have to explain to me. I love you, which requires no explanation." He replayed the message several times, letting the sound of her wash over him as he took in the skyline. The buildings across the river looked machined, their surfaces cold and impervious. A jet following the Monongahela River turned slowly and headed for the airport. The afternoon light did not flatter the interior of the penthouse either. Upholstery looked worn, and the cushions around the black lacquer table were crushed and needed to be replaced. Maybe the whole arrangement should be replaced by a regular table and chairs. A couple of lampshades appeared ragged, one had a small dent in its fabric side—the place was beginning to look like an undergraduate's pad. Well, not that bad, but he'd have to do some redecorating. He rarely saw it this time of day, in this light. He would return Phoebe's call later; she was at work anyway.

Outside on the balcony, shifts of a breeze played on his face and lifted his hair. Not the same wind from France, not flavored with clover and trefoil, but a strong gutsy smell—a city smell, and he took a deep breath of it. The warm caress of it reminded him of Sterling's talk of summer—it was time to redo the menu. The tomatoes from Marietta would be showing up pretty soon, and he looked forward to a sandwich made from two slices of spongy white bread, mayonnaise, a slice of red onion and a thick slab of an Ohio tomato. Salt and pepper. He would enjoy the sandwich before Sterling's disdainful regard, as he did every year. It had become a seasonal ritual. And he'd do a wedding party for Cynthia, and he would cook it himself. He hoped she would find happiness in Indiana.

Far below, a small tugboat had just passed beneath the Fort Pitt Bridge, going downriver seemingly without a crew on board. Not a person visible. The tug, unencumbered by any barge, appeared to be on its own or maybe guided by remote control. It had entered the Ohio River, though no marker defined the new artery, then slipped under the West End Bridge, and continued downriver. Emerson imagined the resolute industry of its passage past all the river towns, large and small, as it made its way toward the Mississippi. From the boat, East Liverpool, too, would seem empty of inhabitants. No one in sight and no evidence that anyone had ever lived there—like a settlement that was deserted save for a memory waving from the shore like laundry left on a line.

The city lay before him, beautiful and incredible. All of its history, the endeavor of that history, and the generations themselves that had toiled on the banks of that history seemed to present themselves to him all at once. It would not be his last look at the skyline: it might look different in the morning. Overnight, it could be changed, but this view of it would always be part of his personal mural. To the left, across the Allegheny River and to the right of the stadium, a large airliner had banked over Phoebe's neighborhood, preparing to enter its landing pattern. It flashed in the afternoon light, radiant and astonishing in its flight. He could picture her house, the garden in back, the kitchen, and some of the downstairs rooms. He had never seen the upper floors. He could imagine her and Nick sitting down to dinner. Later, she would set up her briefcase at the table in the small library, fix her heavy glasses, and get down to work. Nick would be doing his own homework in his room. Later, Emerson might go over for some cake, if he wasn't too washed out by the jet lag. Whatever happened to him and Phoebe, he was prepared to be satisfied with this view of her from the balcony, not just a prospect to be tolerated, but his love for her clarified by every step of her deliberate stride.

But now, he had to get a move on. He had to get down to the Strip and do the shopping for the restaurant. Sterling would need to fold the mushrooms into the veal stew soon. A mix of cremini and button tops would do the trick. The jet lag had made him very thirsty, so Emerson went inside, picking up a vase with a withered flower off the black table. He dumped the flower in the garbage and opened the small fridge. He had heard the secret to lessen jet lag was to drink a lot of water, but there was no Pellegrino. He filled a glass from the tap and drank it down and then filled it again to drink more. Ordinary river water, but it tasted pretty damn good, and the women in the photograph seemed to be waiting for his order.

FINAL NOTES

The Women at the High Standard Café

There is Una Strickland and Viv Jackson and Rose Rutledge. There is Nancy Brower and Bea Leskovich. And there is Rhoda Olson. Nancy and Rose live in town, so they walk to work, most often together. Una and Bea are dropped off by their husbands on their way to work at the ceramic factory. The headlights of their cars sweep the darkened streets of East Liverpool, for it is before five in the morning. Rudy Leskovich always makes a wide U-turn in front of the restaurant and honks the horn when Bea gets out, as if they've been on a date, an all-night date—

the two of them always laughing and kissing like high school kids. Viv and Rho drive themselves. Elmore Jackson died of a heart attack a year ago, and Viv is still learning how to shift the gears on the Hudson. She can be heard coming blocks away in the still predawn.

One by one, they enter the High Standard, turn on the lights, and if it is winter, put away their coats and hats in the back closet next to the restrooms. They take turns in the restrooms, using both of them, changing into the peach-colored, crisp uniforms of rayon Bea chose from a Montgomery Ward catalog. They help each other fix the points of the orange handkerchiefs in the breast pockets of the blouses just so. The handkerchiefs did not come with the uniforms but had been run off by Rho on her Singer.

Every morning, Una collects the cartons of fresh eggs left earlier on the back stoop by Clarence Fisher, four dozen in all, and every one will be cooked in some fashion before the last meal is served that day. Then she goes back for the bottles of milk with their high collars of yellow cream at the top that Ed Wilkins's boy ran back from his father's truck as it idled at the front curb. Rho's grandnephew Sam Emerson would get that job in a few years when Ned Wilkins goes off to Carnegie Tech in Pittsburgh.

By a little after six, Nancy has turned out a dozen pies—eight fruit and four cream: banana, custard, coconut, and chocolate. Biscuits have been rolled and cut and put into the oven. Rho has stirred and smoothed the velvet consistency of sausage gravy—the first batch of it to be made, for she insists on making it up fresh throughout the day. Mounds of meatloaf wait under cheesecloth for their turn in the large oven, and the surplus of the mixture has been set aside for meatballs or stuffing for green peppers. Rounds of salmon patties are lined up to one side of the prep table and chicken parts soaked in buttermilk to be breaded and fried golden in one of several large iron skillets.

Viv has started coffee in the large urn at the end of the cafeteria rail and then turned to peeling potatoes, scraping carrots, and slicing onions. She has never been known to cry. Finally, she brings out large cans of green peas and string beans from the pantry, opens them, and pours them into their warming tins.

By now, George Wager, the owner, has shown up with the morning *Post* from Pittsburgh tucked under one arm. He sits at the front, by the large bronze cash register, and lights the first of his day's cigarettes. He'll go through nearly two packs of Camels. He reads every page, thoroughly and slowly, but has yet to relay to the women the facts of any news story, not even an obituary or a sports account. It is now just before seven, and Viv brings him a cup of black coffee, two sugars, and a butterscotch roll just out of the oven.

Say it is summer, so the early birds are the mayor of East Liverpool, Chuck Ingersol, and some of his unofficial cabinet, who leisurely take up the front booth that has a good view of downtown. Lately, the man he defeated, Roger Moore—he runs the coal yard down by the river— also comes in and good-naturedly gives himself over to some kidding. The women behind the counter carefully prepare him a large breakfast, making sure he has enough butter and jam, because there's been talk that his wife is not cooking much for him since he lost the election.

If it is winter, the boys from the town road crews will take up at least two booths. Some stay bundled in their outer clothing, hats on, as they drink coffee, eat flapjacks, or scoop up biscuits and gravy. But whatever the season, the figure of Rhoda Olson is at the center, a serene presence in the midst of the clatter and cooking aromas. She stands at the flat, black grill, turning pancakes, frying eggs, and cooking grits, bacon, and sausages. Later come hamburgers, hot roast beef sandwiches, salmon patties with cream sauce, and finally, the meatloaf with mashed potatoes and gravy, canned peas on the side. Liver and onions, fried chicken, and sometimes cubed steaks are readied to be cooked. Her authority in the place is evident. She handles the spatula and scrapes down the hot, glistening surface of the grill with a strength and dispatch that might be imitated but never reproduced. She is a tall woman, broad-shouldered. Her light hair is wound close on her head like a crown, so tight some believe the perpetual look of wonder on her broad face is the result. The peach-colored uniform doesn't look right on her, and her shoes are boxlike and black. A village wit once called them small barges, but they are comfortable and thick soled and ease the strain of standing at the grill fourteen hours a day.

But when she turns from the stove, when she brings around a plate of food—her arm raised and bending slightly forward from the waist just so—her whole image changes. What had seemed outsized and awkward about her suddenly harmonizes. Her blue eyes glow with a childlike pleasure, and her large-toothed smile reminds old-timers of the handsome girl Billy Brown left behind. Sure, some men have proposed marriage—she is one helluva cook after all—but a communal regret about what some consider her "widowhood" has kept her inviolate. She moves behind the counter of the High Standard Café like the drummer of a band, keeping the tempo for the cafeteria, her arms moving as if there were six of them and swaying to some rhythm inside her, bending and fetching and serving, and in the lulls, she scrapes down the griddle. "Pick up onto the ham, Una," she'll say delivering a plate precisely to the top of the steam table.

Young Sam Emerson loves to watch her as he eats his evening meal in one of the booths. Afterward he will do his homework there, keeping an eye on her, noting the graceful economy of her movements, her timing with the different parts of a dinner so they all come onto the plate at the same time. Face down in his history book, he is able to eye the sit-back look of pleasure on a regular's face when his dinner is placed before him, and young Sam secretly takes pride in that look. He wants to take some of the credit for that look himself. His own favorite dish is the fried chicken and biscuits, and then there are the pies—he's sampled them all and has decided that chocolate cream is the best in this best of all summers when all the people he loves are under the same roof.

"But we're putting her out," Sam hears his father say. This is the first night when they are all sitting in the humid dusk of the back yard, and the boy is catching fireflies to put in an old mayonnaise jar.

"You're just not used to being in a real house," his mother replies. "You'd prefer sleeping on the ground. There's one hotel in town, and it's a fleabag. Rho enjoys having us here. It's what she does. She'd be insulted if we didn't stay here." His mother is chewing gum as she talks, and it snaps and cracks in the darkness. A recent finding by dentists, she's told them, says that chewing gum keeps the teeth and gums healthy.

Young Sam has followed a firefly into the rear of the yard, so he hears no more of their conversation. He can barely make them out as they sit in the swing hung from the roof of the back porch. He wants to put the yard, the porch, the house—everything—in the jar with the fireflies to keep it just so. They are not together for the whole summer, maybe it is only for a week or two, but it seems like a whole summer to him—every day stretched out and every night like this one, never ending. He's even stopped wearing underwear, and no one has said anything. His mother goes around barefoot with one of Aunt Rho's big cotton dresses hanging on her, and his father wears no shirt, his suspenders pulled up over sleeveless, unbuttoned BVD's.

The collection of fireflies has been a performance to honor his father, a special ritual raised just to welcome him here in Ohio. A special Ohio mystery to reveal to him. Trying to make an accurate count of the insects as they flit and bounce against their glass prison only makes this homage more important. When he delivers the prize, his father has just said *yes* to something, as if it were the last word in a conclusion.

"Gee, they're swell, Sam." He accepts the jar. "A magic light show, eh?" He holds up the jar, and the natural gesture makes the gift even more important. "How brief they shine and why. That's the question."

"They're just lightning bugs," his mother says. "Spare us the sermon." Her gum cracks in the darkness.

Just then, the screen door slaps and Aunt Rho appears. "The bathroom is free now, if there's any takers." She is wonderfully fragrant in her large quilted bathrobe with peonies printed on it. Evening in Paris bath powder. Sam has studied the dark blue bottles lined up in the bathroom. She has plaited her hair into one long braid that falls over her right shoulder and across her bosom. A blue ribbon has been tied in a bow at the end, the same way some girls in his class do.

"Join us Rho," his father says. "We're taking the evening air."

"Well, all right, I will," she says, as if this were not her own back porch, her own back yard—as if she has just walked through the corn lot in her bathrobe to accept their hospitality. Sam thinks that's funny. She folds herself into a metal lawn chair on the opposite side of the porch. Sam sits on the steps between them, and all of them look into the yard without speaking, as if the deepening night has also drawn all of their speech out, making no comment possible. Or necessary. The square blackness of the small barn is barely distinct at the end of the yard. A chicken clucks and croons and settles back to sleep. Tree frogs wheeze. The Ohio River runs silently nearby.

No scale or yardstick can measure young Sam's happiness. No glass jar can contain it. The squeak of the porch swing's chain marks off the moment, gives it a dimension in the featureless night. The slow, creaky tempo makes Sam sleepy, but he fights to stay awake so as not to miss a moment of this night. Two weeks, he remembers them saying—maybe even three. Maybe every day could be stretched into a whole summer. Days in spring seem to get longer when the light is reluctant to leave, when the fields and woods are caught in a brightness that preserves them like the jars of peaches in the cellar, golden and round through the glass. Crows hang in the sky, printed on the air by the same mysterious force. The heavy fragrance of the petunia bed next to the porch steps lifts in the heavy air to drug him.

"I'd like to make some pictures of you," he hears his father say.

"Of me?" Aunt Rho speaks after a moment. She sounds surprised and without looking around, Sam knows she's pulled her robe tight at the throat.

"Well, you and the women you work with at the café."

"Oh my. Well, I don't know. We'd have to ask Mr. Wager."

"Please, Rho." His mother sounds excited. The swing has stopped. "It would be wonderful to have a picture of you."

"Why take our pictures?" She sounds interested but a little suspicious. "Nothing special about us. You think we're glamour queens?"

"Just for the record," his father says neatly. "I'm going over to this mess in Spain, and there won't be anything like you and your friends there. It will be a good image to take with me."

"Please, Rho." The flat-out want in his mother's voice startles Sam a little. That was a new sound. Then he slips back under the drowse the smells and sounds of the night have pulled up around him. He crawls up to lie across Aunt Rho's padded knees. The moist warmth of her flesh— the ample, clean aroma of her—permeates the material of the robe to suspend him further between sleep and waking. He hopes his mother's feeling are not hurt that he has gone to Aunt Rho.

"Somebody's sleepy," his mother says.

"No, no," Sam tries to disagree. "You promised me a story."

"I'll tell you one tomorrow, pal," his father says softly.

"I'll put him up," Aunt Rho says and hoists him onto her shoulder. "You two take in the evening." Then all of the woman's largeness rises smoothly and strongly, holding him to her. His cheek becomes sweaty pressed to her neck, where he feels the slow drumming of her pulse. The whole world of fireflies and tree frogs and crickets swirls dizzily as she turns and carries him safely through the kitchen and down the hallway and then up the stairs. He is safe in her arms, and the run of the river nearby is correct. Just right.

Sam has never seen his father look and act as he does taking the pictures at the High Standard Café. He's surprised that his father must have been studying the inside of the restaurant all along, taking measurements like a carpenter about to cut and fit a piece of wood. He knows exactly what he wants, where the women are to stand.

"Can we watch?" his mother asked the night before.

"It'll be about seven in the morning," his father said. "That's when the sun hits the front windows just right. Bounces off the steam table, the chrome on the cases. All the glass of the counter. The light should be okay if it's a clear morning."

Some of the High Standard's regulars also look on. George Wager stands to the side, smoking and looking perplexed and just a little pleased. Sam has seen his father take his mother's picture once or twice, but they joked around with it. This morning his father is all seriousness. The narrow lines of his face look like they come to a point between his eyes—just before his eyes. The small black camera—the Contax Sam has learned playing with it—hangs from his father's neck by a slender strap. Or he holds it in one hand as he moves from side to side, ducks and squats. Aunt Rho and her friends stand behind the counter, the black-board chalked with the day's specials behind them. Chicken croquettes today with peas and white sauce. Viv is laughing and has turned beet red in the face. Bea and Rose, arms around each other, strike poses like movie stars, batting their eyelashes and saying "re-ally" in a funny way. Some men in the front booth chuckle and cough. Una doesn't seem to care one way or the other, but Rho is all business. She keeps one eye on the grill where she's prefrying a pound of bacon and checks one of the ovens where a large pan of macaroni and cheese is becoming crispy brown on top. She also listens to Owen Emerson's directions.

"That's right, Rho, you stand in the middle."

"She's the tallest." Viv furnishes the reason.

"And you—Nancy is it? Yes, Nancy, come right up here and stand next to Rho."

"The champion of pie makers," Aunt Rho announces to everyone.

"Will says I'm liable to break the camera," Nancy says to Bea. She wears rimless glasses and has a small mouth.

"He always was a fool," Bea says out of the side of her mouth. Every-one laughs.

"That's good," his father tells the six women. They are now together in line behind the counter. Rho Olson leans her arms on the counter-top, and the other women gather naturally around her. Sam has noticed that the pie list for the day does not include chocolate cream, but butterscotch is included, and he might try some of that. Next to the pie list is a picture of President Roosevelt, and to the right of the hood over the grill is a hand-lettered sign. YES, WE HAVE ICED-TEA—*ASK FOR IT!*

Then, everything in the restaurant becomes silent—even the locals in the front booths have stopped their joshing. A kind of stillness wells up from Sam's father as he looks at the women, moves around in front if them, and the soundlessness of his concentration washes over all of them. He's crouching before the women, who lean on the counter, the camera held to his right eye, his left eye open and looking around the camera's black case. The shutter clicks.

"That's swell," he says. "What's for dessert?"

All six women take a breath together, seem about to answer, then laugh out loud. The camera shutter clicks again. Owen Emerson half stands, legs tense and bent as if he's leaning against a strong wind at his back. "You're gorgeous," he says softly. All of them look a little pleased, surprised to be pleased. Aunt Rho's smile is generous, and her teeth are prominent. It's an appreciative look, as if his father has just guessed a secret she's been keeping.

"Now." His voice is tender. "Can you do me one more? Can you give me just one more? Yes, I can see it about to happen. Come on girls. That's the way." The six women have not moved, yet they seem to press together, pliant and intimate. The light models the planes of their faces, and their eyes enlarge with some knowledge inside themselves and maybe about themselves—who they are and where they are—that has never occurred to them before. "That's the ticket," his father says. The shutter clicks.

Sam thinks the whole place has been holding its breath and suddenly lets go. He can't understand it, but it is like everyone in the restaurant has seen the picture even though it is in his father's camera, on film but not developed yet. Somebody coughs, and George Wager says something to make one of the townsmen laugh. His father stands up straight, hands at his sides. The women behind the counter slowly break apart, timidly glancing at each other; one or two blush as if they might have been strangers just before but now no longer. Una Strickland fingers a couple of strands of her hair and repins them—the picture taking had somehow mussed them. Rho Olson turns over the sizzling bacon and presses it flat on the grill with the large spatula she held during the picture taking.

Sam's mother pulls his father down into a booth. Owen Emerson drums the fingers and thumb of his right hand on the tabletop, and his whole person looks tight. He shivers a little like he's had a chill, though it's already warm in the place. Mr. Wager has turned on the large fan in the front corner. Edie Olson has put her arm around him. "Thank you for that," she says into his ear. Sam thinks they could be in one of those restaurants in New York—he's seen them like that there—and not just in the High Standard Café in East Liverpool, Ohio. "Thank you." His father has kept quiet but smiles at Sam. But the drumming on the table-top keeps up as if a motor within him is running and can't stop.

"Let me out," his mother says abruptly, and his father stands quickly to permit her to slide from the booth. She goes up to the counter and talks with Rho, who disappears and then returns with her keys. "C'mon, Scoop," Edie Olson says, jangling the keys. "Rho has loaned us her buggy. Let's take a spin. Let's go down to the river and watch the sub-marine races."

"I want to come," Sam says. He's on his feet. He's never seen subma-rine races.

"You can't go," his mother tells him right out. "This time, just your dad and me." His father has capped the camera lens and lifted the unit from around his neck. He holds the camera in his hand almost indiffer-ently now, and he seems more relaxed, too. He cups Sam's head in his other hand.

"We'll do something special this afternoon, Big Timer," he promises.

"What about a bear story?"

"You got it." And his parents leave the restaurant holding hands, his mother leading the way.

Sam sits back down in the booth. He hears the whack and turn of Aunt Rho's Plymouth just as Una brings him a bowl of oatmeal with brown sugar and thick cream. Sam decides it's probably the best oatmeal in the world. The best summer and the best oatmeal, and his father and mother together make it a special time, and he believes that his father tak-ing the picture of Aunt Rho and her friends is the reason it is the best.

Bear Story

Ralph lay halfway out or halfway in his cave when Bear walked up over the rise. He had come to ask Ralph something, but he couldn't remember what it was—on the walk up to Ralph's cave, he had forgotten the question. The pinewoods had been so fragrant and the birds in the trees so full of song that Bear had let the question loose, and it had slipped out of his mind.

So, he decided the polite thing to do would be to sit quietly near Ralph and wait. Maybe the question would come back into his head. Ralph lay on his back, paws held up and his mouth slightly open so the tongue lolled out one side of it. Ralph slept more than most bears, and that was why he was so smart. Just watching him sleep, you could almost see him getting smarter and smarter. Bear could see that Ralph was getting even smarter this day, so he decided to leave and come back tomorrow. He started to get up.

"I see that you have come by way of the small pine forest," Ralph said as he rolled over, one eye on Bear. "And that earlier you sampled some of the berries down by the pond, but you were a little too greedy."

Bear was always astounded how Ralph knew the things he did.

"It's very simple," Ralph explained. "Your right shoulder has some substance on it that looks and smells suspiciously like pine tar, so you must have rubbed against one of the trees on your way here. Your teeth are that purplish color that comes from eating berries, and I notice that you are slightly favoring your rear left foot, so I would suggest you may have bruised it on the large sharp rocks that lie just at the far edge of the berry patch, where the fruit hangs in thick clusters. Precisely why so many berries hang there, because most remember the sharp rocks underfoot at that spot and they don't go there."

"I forgot," says Bear.

"And because the berries were wrinkled and tasted a little sweeter, you have come to see me."

"That's right!" Bear says, amazed by Ralph's insight. He could almost remember his question now.

"And something about birds flying away and how the light on the old oak looks cleaner—something like that."

Bear was speechless.

"And because of these things happening you want to ask me a question, but it is always the same question."

"It is?" Bear asks hopefully. He felt they were now getting to the truth of the matter.

"Yes, because the same things happen over and over, which makes you ask the same question over and over. And I always give you the same answer over and over. Something to do with things changing so they can stay the same."

"But why do I always forget over and over?"

Ralph had to consider this question for a moment, since it was a new question, and it required a little thought. "Elementary," he finally says and yawns wide. His teeth are white as stones in the stream. "You forget something in order to remember it. You always want to remember, so you always forget. It's the same with the leaves on the trees coming and going—you used to ask me about that, too. You don't forget the leaves when they are gone. You remember them, and that keeps them in your head, where they stay the same. Always."

Bear waited for Ralph to say more, but he had slipped back to sleep. He knew that eventually Ralph would wake up again, and then he would give him the rest of the answer. But that would be a while, so Bear thought the respectful thing to do would be to sit quietly and wait for Ralph to wake up. Meanwhile, he told himself, he had some of the answer, and maybe that was enough.

Tell me another.

ABOUT THE AUTHOR

HILARY MASTERS is the author of eight other novels, two story collections, the acclaimed memoir *Last Stands*, a collection of essays, and a book-length essay, *Shadows on a Wall: Juan O'Gorman and the Mural in Pátzcuaro*. He's been a Fulbright lecturer and the recipient of an Award for Literature from the American Academy of Arts & Letters. His essays have been republished in *Best American Essays*, and his short fiction has been cited in *Best American Short Stories* and *Pushcart*. He is a professor of English and creative writing at Carnegie Mellon University in Pittsburgh, Pennsylvania.